THE WOODLAND WOLF PACKS: COMPLETE TRILOGY

AMELIA SHAW

THE PACK'S MATE

Dexter

My pack community grounds looked nothing like they did when I was a child. The once soft grass, still so fresh in my memory, was gone, worn down to dirt. The area, central to our town, was littered with beer bottles and cigarette butts, the playground equipment long since hauled off somewhere, probably to rot or rust in the woods. Out of our sight.

The sun was only just rising, but we were all up as usual, ready to start another long day's work. The heavy scent of testosterone filled in the air. My all-male pack, consisting of Taylor and Jay, bonded with the men with whom we grew up. Every one of them had been placed into small all-male families of their own now.

A sigh rippled through my throat as I glanced from the rock-strewn dirt at my feet, up to the pack. The group of men before me was a powerful, yet depressing sight. I loved these men. They were family, but I'd grown so tired of the same, familiar, *male* faces, day in, and day out. For a whole generation now, the Wood-lands pack had not borne a single female.

Not one.

For almost sixty years, the elders of my pack had questioned what happened to our breed, but they had not been forthcoming with any answers, so far. What would happen to our genetic lines if there were no female mates to carry our children for future generations? No one could answer that, either.

My mother and her sisters were some of the last pack-born women, and all of them had produced at least three sons each.

Which would have been great if there had been some other pack females around to mate with, when we all came of age. But there were none.

What went wrong? No one knew.

What we did know was that there would be no more children born to our purebred wolf-shifting women.

It would be impossible. The last of our fertile females matured past breeding age almost twenty years ago, so there was no longer any hope of a savior being born for our pack.

Something had to be done. If we didn't find women to breed with soon, our pack would likely become extinct.

There was an obvious option, and that was something we had been putting off as long as possible, because we didn't really know if it would work. We had decided to bring human women into the pack.

We needed to venture into the cities and acquire human females for breeding.

But no one knew if that would actually work, as it had never been attempted before. And that's why we had waited so long.

We had waited *too* long. It was time to take action, before there was no pack left at all.

We had something called a fated mate in our world. Wolf

shifters in my pack only bred with their true mate, the one chosen for them by Fate. We had no idea if a wolf shifter *could* mate with a human, in the sense of being a true fated mate pairing. It seemed unlikely, but with no wolf shifter females left, we had to try something to save our blood line.

I was told that if I ever met my fated mate, I would recognize her by her scent. There would be an instant attraction, an undeniable bond from the moment we laid eyes on each other. And when we touched... sparks would ignite. I didn't actually *know* if any of that was true or not, as I'd never experienced it before. No one my age had.

We had to rely on the stories our parents told us, which seemed to change with time, like fairy tales.

It was hard to know what to believe and what to discount; tough to discern between all the blurred lines between fact and fiction that had grown over the years. And if there were no more wolf-born women, did the fated mate concept still even exist? Would that magical, instant bond still exist outside of the pack community?

Probably not.

We were in uncharted territory and no one in the pack knew the answers, not even the elders. And everyone was afraid of what would become of us if the fated mate bond failed us all.

"Dex!" The greeting came out of nowhere, interrupting my maudlin thoughts. "Come quickly. It's your dad." Taylor, my Beta, came running at me at break-neck speed and grabbed my arm.

My dad?

"Where is he? What's happened?"

"Come on." Taylor tugged at my arm, then turned and ran in the direction of my parents' home. I followed behind, running to catch up and not thinking twice.

My father had been feeling unwell for months, and as one of the elders in our pack, that was a bad omen for everyone.

The elders are meant to be the strongest of us.

He can't die. Not yet. Not until we've secured the continuation of our bloodline.

Thoughts tumbled through my head, on a loop.

I'll be lost without him.

No. It's not his time to go. It can't be.

Taylor led me straight to my parents' house and into the lounge, where my father was laying on the couch and my mother was on the floor beside the couch, kneeling over him.

Dad's face was deathly pale and his breath wheezed in and out of his chest like it was consuming all of his energy just to stay alive for a few minutes longer.

He hadn't looked like that when I saw him last. "What happened?" I asked as I crouched down next to my mother. Fear scudded through my chest.

Mom turned and squeezed my hand. "Please, Dexter, please. Take him to the hospital in Little Creek."

Little Creek was the nearest human town. "Mom, no. You know that's not our way." Surely there was some other way to help him?

We had a healer in our pack, but he was rarely required for anything other than fighting injuries. Our paranormal genetics meant that we healed extremely fast and rarely fell ill, unless it was something very serious.

My mom grabbed my shoulders with surprising force. "Dexter, I am not ready to lose him. Not yet. He can't die. I am asking you to help your father. Take him to a doctor at the hospital. Please."

I looked at my father, who met my gaze with his own. He didn't nod, but he didn't shake his head no, either. Pain laced his expression and my heart jolted hard when, for the first time ever, I saw fear in my father's eyes. He didn't want to die.

The decision was made for me. I had to take him in.

"Right, let's do this. Taylor, grab Jay and the truck. Bring it 'round the front. I'll carry Dad out."

Taylor looked at me for a long moment, as though questioning my logic. But in the end, he saw that I was serious, and followed my instructions as any good Beta would.

"Thank you, Dexter! Thank you," my mother said, as she jumped to her feet and moved out of the way.

I leaned down and lifted my father up into my arms, grunting with the effort. He weighed more than me, and when he flopped against my chest I realized how weak he really was.

Up until yesterday, he'd been feeling unwell, but that was the extent of it. Mostly, he was still as strong as ever. Or so I'd thought.

Perhaps he'd been hiding this illness—or disease, or whatever was ravaging him—far better than I'd guessed.

I shifted him a little, arranging his arm over my shoulder and securing him properly in my hold so that I could safely carry him out to the truck.

"Let's go, Dad."

I didn't know if a human hospital could save him. I was suddenly concerned nothing could save him. I'd been blind to the seriousness of his condition, whatever it was. But if there was a chance to save him at the hospital, then we had to try.

I limped outside under the weight of my father's bulk, his ragged breathing echoing in my ear. His skin was clammy beneath my palms.

"Are you sure this is what you want, Dad?" I asked, as the vehicle pulled up.

If my father didn't want the humans to help him, then I wouldn't force him.

My father nodded, but just barely.

Okay. I was doing the right thing.

"Let's go then, old man."

That got the briefest of smiles from my dad as I hefted him as carefully as I could into the back seat of the full-sized truck.

Taylor helped me get him situated, then I climbed into the driver's seat.

I adjusted the rear vision mirror so I could see my father's ashen face during the drive.

"Little River is an hour away, so don't you dare die on us before I get you there, Dad."

I gave my words a threatening growl for good measure, and there was a weak laugh from the back seat. My dad couldn't muster any words, but he was still trying for humor.

Jay slid onto the floor behind my seat, at my father's feet, the perfect Omega. Lucky, we had good-sized trucks instead of small cars, or he would never have fit.

My pack was in, and my father wasn't getting any better just sitting here.

"Let's go."

I planted my foot on the accelerator and we took off toward the nearest town. I drove the roads as fast yet as safely as possible, my heart thundering in my chest the closer we got to Little River.

"Let's hope the human stories of hatred toward our kind have been exaggerated, huh?" Taylor joked, trying to ease some of the tension in the truck.

The silence had become overwhelming.

I managed to smile, though I suspected it might look more like a grimace. "Yeah, I think as long as none of us go shifting in the middle of the city, we'll be fine."

All of us of mating age had ventured into the cities for clandestine sexual encounters with random strangers on occasion, but we never went anywhere near the heart of the city, nor did we linger once our needs were sated.

We also steered clear of the hospitals and doctors when we were injured, in fear of the possibility of having our blood tested and finding a difference that they could not explain.

We'd been told since we were kids how much humans hated us. That they feared anything different and if they identified who —or in their eyes, *what*—we were, we'd be locked up in a zoo, or dissected on a scientist's table.

That was one of the reasons I didn't want to take Dad here to the hospital. Presumably they would need to take and test some of his blood. When it came back different to human blood...

I shook my head, figuring we would deal with that later. First priority was to get Dad well.

Taylor grinned and answered my earlier comment about shifting. "Yeah, I hope so."

We drove the rest of the hour in silence, broken only by the creepy rasp of my father's breathing.

Taylor pulled out his cell phone and directed me to the hospital using the maps feature.

"Turn left here. And it should be on our right."

The hair on my arms stood on end as we passed through the human city. So much light, so many people. A thousand shops and cars. Noise everywhere. Too much of everything. Chaos and cacophony that we weren't accustomed to.

My senses were already reeling when I pulled up outside the emergency department next to a hospital that stood a hundred feet tall.

"I'll take Dad in. Taylor, you park the truck and meet me inside. Jay, help me if you can."

Jay nodded and easily slid out the door, his agile, lithe body making every movement smooth and effortless.

I jumped out, opened the rear door and reached into the back seat for my father's form. His wheezing was getting worse. He was really struggling to breathe now, and his lips were turning blue.

His gaze on me was now full of fear, and I knew we couldn't waste any time.

I pulled my dad along the seat, hard. Adrenaline pumped through my bloodstream, making my muscles bulge and tingle with strength.

My instincts were telling me that Dad's time was almost up.

Jay got under my father's other arm and together we carried him toward the sliding doors.

They *whooshed* open and two men rushed out.

"Do you need help?" they asked, the foreign human scent rolling off their bodies making my hackles rise.

I grabbed for my father's huge bulk, a growl ripping through my throat as they attempted to take him from me.

Taylor pushed at me. "Dexter, they want to help. Let him go."

Fighting back the red shifting haze was harder than I thought.

I had to calm down, and fast.

Focus on Dad. Why you're here.

I gulped air into my lungs and forced my arms to unhook their death-like grip.

"This is my father. He can't breathe... I think it's his heart. Or his lungs. I don't know exactly, but his lips are blue."

"We need a gurney out here!" one of the men yelled and another man in uniform came running up pushing a white bed on wheels.

The man who'd called for the gurney touched my arm. "It's okay. We're going to take care of him."

"Thanks," I managed in a rough voice. They did seem like they were trying to do the right thing by my father.

Dexter

I helped them put Dad on the bed and they wheeled him away quickly. His skin was gray and sweaty, his eyes were closed, and he didn't seem to be moving. Just in the hour trip between home and here, he had deteriorated substantially.

"What the hell is wrong with him?" I muttered to Jay. "And what are they going to do to him?" Jay squeezed my arm, hard.

"Let's follow them and find out."

I walked into a human hospital for the first time ever. I'd spent my life in the woods, fighting bear shifters and protecting my pack, and this truly was the strangest scene I'd ever witnessed.

The fluorescent lights burnt my eyes and the stark, white walls stretched up before me like an enormous maze.

I skidded to a halt before an indoor cage. The sign said reception desk, but it was a cage nonetheless.

The smell of sickness was almost overwhelming. It permeated

my nostrils and I felt like I needed a long run in the forest to get the stench of illness out of my nose.

How did humans live and work in places like this?

A woman approached us and I searched my instincts. Despite the fact I hadn't seen a human woman in months, this one did nothing for me.

Her face was too coarse and pinched. Her aura was wrong and not attractive to me.

"Can I get you to fill in some forms for the man they just brought in? You're his son, right?"

I nodded, and she handed me a black clipboard and a pen. I managed to relax enough to sit on an uncomfortable plastic chair with Jay at my side.

Taylor came running in the door, spotted us and took the seat on my right.

The three of us against the world, as it had always been.

Pack mates. Alpha, Beta and Omega. Brothers, not by blood, but by a bond stronger than any other I'd shared.

"Whoa, I'd forgotten how hot these women are." Taylor whistled as more nurses moved about and patients staggered into the Emergency Room.

I shrugged my shoulders and focused on the human forms. "You're welcome to them, Taylor."

The pack took turns traveling to town, hitting up the bars. Finding women to bed for the night. I'd always struggled with fucking women I wasn't connected to. Slaking my lust and keeping my passions under control so I didn't hurt the fragile human women was not how I was designed.

The Alpha wolf inside me craved the constant contact of my true mate. A woman to love and protect. Someone to complete me and bear my children.

"What's wrong with you, Dex?" Taylor said.

I nearly answered, *my dad might be dying*, but that would have been churlish. I knew that wasn't what Taylor meant. I shrugged, looking at the various women in the room, before dismissing them.

Taylor frowned. "It's been months since we came to town. You must be horny as hell."

I was. But I'd been running miles every day to keep the horny demons at bay.

"I am," I admitted. "But I don't want any of those."

I gestured to the room as a whole and glanced up again as a young blonde woman stumbled over her feet as she stared at the three of us.

I didn't have any false modesty. I knew that we wolf shifters were appealing to human women. Our physical strength and good health were all out there for the world to see, and those I had hooked up with in the past had made it clear they would be happy for round two—or more—if I wanted it.

I'd just never wanted it that much.

I rolled my eyes and kept focusing on the paperwork. "When my mate shows up, let me know."

Jay sighed. "We may not have mates, Dex. A mate is a wolf shifter, pack-born. You know that's not our path."

I looked over at my Omega, battling to keep my sudden anger at bay, my gut burning at his words. "What is our path then? To die without a mate, lonely and childless? To watch the pack wither and die?"

Jay's mouth set in the grim line he always adopted when upset. "We're still a family, Dexter. Even without fated mates."

"I know that." I looked away, unable to properly express how I felt.

A lot of the men in our pack were content enough with their situation, but I wasn't. We'd grown up as one, huge pack, and at adulthood—twenty-one—we were ranked and chose who would share our own mini-pack of three.

I was ranked an Alpha, of course. All three of my brothers were Alphas, the same as my father.

As an Alpha, I was able to choose a Beta and an Omega to complete my family, my pack.

I was lucky. It was an easy choice.

Jay and Taylor had been my best friends from childhood and it was perfectly natural when we built a house and moved in together.

Our mini-pack, all ready for our mates.

But our mates didn't arrive, and despite how much I loved the guys, we weren't complete. There was a massive hole missing in my heart, and my life, and even if the other men didn't feel it as much as I did, it was still there, so prominent I couldn't deny it.

The receptionist returned to claim the clipboard full of information, and then we were left for what felt like hours.

"What's taking so long?" Taylor asked at one point, as he restlessly shifted on his chair, stood up, and began pacing back and forth around the seats.

We took turns wearing out the floor in the waiting area. There was nothing else to do.

I leaned forward on the chair and watched the white swinging doors that my father had disappeared behind. Over and over, they opened and closed.

And no one I knew walked through.

But eventually the doors did open, and a woman walked through. One I hadn't seen before.

I sat up straighter, my shifter instantly rising to the surface.

Who was she? And why did I suddenly want to take her in my arms and kiss the life out of her?

She was obviously a physician, dressed in blue scrubs and wearing running shoes that were well worn.

She spoke to the nurse, who pointed our way, and then the woman nodded and began to head toward us.

I jumped to my feet. My heart was pounding like I'd run a marathon, and my skin itched and vibrated like my wolf was about to spring forth.

"Dexter Monaghan?" she asked, meeting my gaze for the first time.

Sapphire blue eyes clashed with mine and a growl rolled through my chest. I only just managed to suppress the sound.

"Are you all right?" she asked, narrowing her eyes at my reaction.

Jay gasped and Taylor went rigid beside me. I could feel them reacting to her in the same way my shifter was, which should have been impossible.

We were meant to have our own mates. And she was *mine*.

I knew it with every fiber of my being.

I turned to my pack mates. "Go, wait in the car. I'll be out as soon as I can."

Jay's eyes narrowed, but he nodded and began to back away. Taylor set his jaw and shook his head. "No. I..."

I dropped my gaze away from my mate and turned to stare at Jay, willing him to do my bidding.

As the Alpha, my will was law, but I rarely exercised it with Jay or Taylor. I didn't want blind obedience from them. I believed that bred insolence and disrespect.

I wanted loyalty. Love. And trust. And those things were earned over time.

"Taylor. Go."

He turned and fled as the power reverberated in my

command, and then I turned my attention back to the woman before me.

"Doctor...?"

"I'm Doctor Claire Masterson. I'm the physician treating your father."

"Claire..." I managed to say her name, even though all I wanted to do was put her over my shoulder and throw her into the back of our truck.

She looked at me strangely again, before lifting a hand and rubbing her arm in an absent manner. Was I making her nervous? I obviously wasn't behaving normally, and I didn't want to scare her off. But how to behave normally, when all I wanted to do... I shut down thoughts of what I wanted to do with this woman, and cleared my throat.

"I'm sorry, Doctor. Please continue."

She straightened, her throat working up and down as she swallowed hard. The woman looked almost as uncomfortable as I was. Perhaps she felt this strange electric connection, too?

"Your father had a massive heart attack," she began, and my own heart began to thump hard. *A heart attack?* Even with our shifter healing abilities, damage to the heart was not something easily fixed.

I blinked a few times, trying to concentrate on her next words. "A cardiologist has been paged, and I believe the plan is to operate tonight, inserting stents into his abdominal aorta. I'm here to give you an update and to let you know that there is a good chance of him surviving both the initial attack, and the surgery."

Thank you, God.

Relief winged through me with such intensity, it robbed me of breath for a moment. It was all I could do not to collapse into the plastic chair behind me, but I somehow managed to remain standing.

I'd talked myself into thinking there was no way my father could die today, but from the look of this woman's face, it had been a very real possibility. Likely still was, if the stents didn't work.

My mother had said she couldn't live without my father, and hopefully she wouldn't have to face that situation. Not for another three or four decades at least.

"How long until he can come home?"

She cocked her head to the side. "Let's take this one day at a time."

I ignored her human pragmatism. She didn't understand what my father was, nor what his healing capacities were.

"We live an hour away. I need to get my mother in to see him. If you could give me a rough estimate, I can let her know."

Claire hugged the clip board to her chest. "Best case scenario, he may be home within two weeks. But he'll need to be managed by a local doctor after that."

She didn't know that my dad's shifter genes would heal him post-operation, if the doctors could repair the damage to his heart.

"Thank you, Doctor."

I extended my hand to shake hers, my arm trembling with anticipation of her touch. According to the old stories passed down by my parents and pack elders, I would know my mate fully, the moment I touched her.

Claire reached over and took my hand.

Her gasp was as loud as mine, the electricity pulsing between us like a thunderstorm on a dark night.

It would have taken out my knees if I wasn't so determined to stand.

Claire wasn't so lucky. Her eyes rolled back in her head and she began to crumple to the ground. I stepped forward and swept her up into my arms before she hit the floor.

Her eyes fluttered as she struggled to stay awake. She stared up at me with a confused expression, her eyelids dropping to half-mast. "What happened?"

"The mating call."

Her eyes closed and her body went limp in my arms.

I glanced around. No one was looking in our direction, and no one seemed to have noticed what had happened yet with Claire. There was plenty of activity, including some kind of medical emergency near those white swinging doors, and everyone's attention seemed focused over there. The medical professionals all seemed to be concentrating on the task at hand and not the room at large.

I turned slowly and began walking toward the hospital exit doors.

"Excuse me!" Right as I reached the exit, I heard a woman call out behind me but I kept walking, forcing my legs to keep moving, even though the scent of Claire made me want to kneel on the ground and thank the Fates for sending her to me.

I couldn't stop or they'd take her away from me. I couldn't have that. My shifter would not allow it.

When I got out into the fresh air it was easier to breathe and I took a huge lungful. My head cleared and I began to wonder what I was doing.

"Dexter!" Taylor called out from about ten feet away, having pulled the truck up near the entrance.

I didn't think about it again. I went straight for the truck with Claire still prone in my arms.

"Hey!" There were noises indicating a commotion behind me and I was pretty sure Claire's absence from the hospital had finally been noticed.

Taylor opened the back door without asking a question and I put her into the back seat.

"Let's go!" I jumped into the back with her and held her tightly against me.

Taylor slammed the door, jumped into the driver seat, turned on the engine and gunned it out of the parking lot.

I looked down at the sleeping doctor in my arms. A human, and my mate.

And I had just snatched her from her human workplace, where my father was about to have surgery to save his life.

What the hell had I just done?

Taylor

"What have you done, Dexter?" I yelled over the revs of the engine as we sped away from the hospital like the devil was on our tail.

I could see them in the rear vision mirror—a group of security guards and nurses staring after us and pointing, as we kidnapped one of their doctors.

"I don't know."

Jay gaped at him from the passenger seat beside me. "What do you mean you don't know? What are we meant to do now?"

"Just drive, Taylor," Dexter grunted at me.

My Alpha, the man I would follow anywhere, anytime.

"I am! But where to?"

"Home."

I turned the truck onto the highway and headed back in the direction of our pack.

Our *all-male* pack.

What were they going to do when we arrived home with a young, fertile female? There would likely be pandemonium.

"Why'd you grab her, Dex?" I had to ask. "I mean, I know she's hot and everything, but..."

"She's my mate," Dexter said, and I stared at him in the rear vision mirror.

That was how I'd felt when I saw her, but I hadn't believed my initial instincts. I'd put it down to hormones and my general level of horniness. It had been far too long for all of us, me in particular.

"How do you know?"

There had to be a way, other than animal lust.

"I knew it when I saw her. That smile, and her scent. But then I touched her, and the sheer force of the mating call knocked her out. Damn near knocked me off my feet, too."

I couldn't stop the laugh that bubbled up. "Are you serious? She passed out when you touched her?"

Was that really the way to know your mate? I couldn't imagine such a force.

"Yeah... I don't know why, though. The elders never said anything like that would happen. Nothing in the old tales about it. Maybe because she's human?"

While he spoke, Dexter was holding the doctor as he would a baby, stroking her face and looking at her like she was the most precious thing in the world.

Envy clawed through my heart like a wolf after its prey. I'd been to every major city within two hours' drive of our town. Slept with dozens of women, all in the fruitless search for a mate.

Then Dexter managed to waltz in and find her at the hospital where his father was being treated. What were the odds?

"Well, what are we going to do with her when we get back to the pack?"

"I have no idea, but I couldn't just leave her there, on the floor of the waiting area," Dexter said.

I agreed with him. If I'd found my mate, the last thing I'd do is drive away from her.

Jay piped up from the seat next to me. "But, she's human. How is it possible to have a human mate? I mean, we've talked about the possibility, but did any of you actually expect to find your fated mate in a human?"

The question hung in the air like a prayer, until Dex and I both shook our heads. "I hoped, kinda," I admitted. "But I never really thought…"

Jay cleared his throat again, his nervousness making my own skin tingle. "Ah… do you think it's possible that she could be all of our mates, Dex?"

The Alpha growled in a possessive way. Clearly, he did not like that idea one bit. "What do you mean?"

Jay looked at me and I glanced over to him for a moment. The kid had balls saying such a thing to Dexter, but I knew where he was coming from. There was something special about this woman, possibly for all three of us.

And it definitely wasn't my imagination.

I moved my focus back to the road, taking my cue from the Omega and gathering the courage to speak my mind.

"I think Jay means that we all felt a connection when she walked toward us. That call, the chemistry. Do you think it's possible that our pack may have just one mate?"

It was a hard thing for me to say, much less wrap my head around.

When Dexter didn't answer, instead looking confused, I continued. "Not that it's what we really want, Dex. We've always expected to each have our own mates, if we're lucky enough to find them, but the pack has changed. Maybe the legends have, too? I don't know why exactly... but I do know that I wanted her the moment I saw her as well. The only reason I left to get the truck was because you commanded it. And I almost ignored you, even though you are the Alpha."

Dexter looked from his mate to me, to Jay, then back again to the doctor laying in his lap.

For a moment he clutched her fiercely, bringing her close to his chest, anger pulsing over his face, but then he sighed, seeming to relax a little.

"I... can't answer that, Taylor," he admitted gruffly. "I suppose we'll find out when she wakes up."

I looked at my Alpha in the mirror again, guilt gnawing at my chest over the conflict I'd caused for our pack.

"Well, when she wakes, I want to shake her hand, too," I said, trying to alleviate some of the tension in the vehicle with a half-joke. "If she passes out again then we'll know that she's meant for all of us, I suppose."

No one laughed.

Dexter nodded slowly, though he didn't say anything.

Alphas didn't share their women.

Never. No one shared their mate.

Or, they certainly hadn't done so in the past.

I was experiencing anger and conflict myself. It burned in my skin, my heart, and right at my very core.

These two men were my pack mates, and jealousy was eating me up already.

I could only imagine how Dexter must be feeling. Whatever I had burning in my gut, as Alpha, he probably had it magnified ten-fold.

And all of this was contingent on her permitting us to share her. Or even agreeing to stay with us in the first place. Being human meant she would likely fight our ways, and our wolves.

I chuckled, stating the inevitable. "You know what she's going to do when she realizes we're wolf shifters? Run for the hills. No human will accept everything about us. We're paranormal creatures, and monsters to many humans. So why would Fate do this to us?"

Dexter shook his head. "Don't ask me."

We spent the rest of the trip in silence, though Jay tried to chatter and keep us occupied, as he always did. But the unease within all of us was obvious. Even my wolf was on edge.

What would this mean for our family?

Would she turn us away?

Reject us?

Would Dexter fight us for the right to have her to himself?

The unknown future was vast and quite possibly full of terrible things to come.

Once we reached our pack land borders without anyone catching us up, I began to breathe a little easier. I drove through the pack gates and along the long, winding driveway that led to the heart of our village.

What were the elders going to say when they found out what we'd done?

I parked the truck behind our home and turned off the engine. "I'll go unlock the house. You carry her inside. It'll be better if no one else sees her for now."

Dexter nodded and I snuck out of the truck, opening the back door and praying no one had caught sight of us yet.

I had the strangest need to protect and hide the woman Dexter had stolen. If she wasn't my mate as well as Dex's, I'd be shocked.

I opened the door and held it wide with my body.

Dexter got out of the truck and hurried into the house with the beauty in his arms and Jay close on his heels.

"Put her in Jay's room," I suggested, just as Dexter went to ascend the stairs, obviously about to take her to his bedroom.

We had a four-bedroom, double-story house that we'd built together when we'd first joined into our own pack ten years ago. Each of us had a bedroom, and the fourth was set up as a home office with the possibility of converting into a future nursery.

A dream we had feared would never come true.

"Why?" Dexter called out, his tone a touch aggressive.

"Because it's the least threatening," I answered as I brushed past him to open the door.

My point must have been valid because, after a moment, Dexter walked past me and placed her gently on Jay's queen-sized bed.

The colors in the room were blue and white, non-threatening and relaxing.

My room had a red and black theme, while Dexter had silver bedding and heavy wooden furniture. I could only imagine what Claire would think if she woke up in one of the latter two rooms.

Dexter backed away from the sleeping beauty and we all headed into the kitchen to talk about the next step in our non-existent plan.

I wasn't sure why she was still asleep. It wasn't normal to pass out for so long, surely? But what did I know about human anatomy and exposure to the fated mate pull?

Jay grabbed three beers from the fridge, popped the lids and handed them out.

I chugged half of mine down in a few gulps, my thirst stronger than I realized.

When I put down the drink, I glanced toward Jay's bedroom once again.

"Did we just kidnap someone?"

Dexter began to pace and growl in a strange way. "I need to

shift and run. I can't hold it together much longer. But someone needs to stay here with her."

Jay began to strip, shedding his clothes in record time. "I'll go with you. I've been itching to shift since I first saw her at the hospital."

Dexter stared at him. "Me, too... so that probably means that... maybe it is possible to actually share a mate..."

They looked at me and I raised my hands. "I wouldn't mind a run, but I'm more antsy to stay here with her. I'm happy to stand guard until you get back."

And it was true. Though my shifter circled within my mind, he was more settled than Jay or Dexter seemed to be. Which was interesting. Perhaps I hadn't bonded to her in the way I'd thought?

Only seeing her conscious and awake would answer that question.

Dexter pulled his tank over his head and pushed his black jeans to the ground.

"Thanks. We won't be long."

I watched as my human pack morphed into wolves and bounded out of the house and toward the woodlands that surrounded our home.

Dexter was silver, Jay was brown. I was black when in wolf form, and we all made the perfect triad of colors. One of the many reasons we knew we were a perfect, balanced pack. The fur never lied.

I crept over to Jay's bedroom door, unable to stay away. I watched our mate sleep for a moment, then shook my head at how she'd feel if she woke up and found a strange man standing over her. As I walked away the thought occurred to me.

What had I just said? *Our mate...*

I was getting ahead of myself here, and was still confused

about how it had all happened anyway. I hadn't known it was possible to have one woman complete a triad of wolves.

Maybe it wasn't possible. But honestly, it made perfect sense to me when I thought about it. Why wouldn't a pack be designed to protect one precious woman?

Though the sharing element of it all... a growl rolled through my chest that I couldn't control.

I wasn't too sure how that was going to work out.

Dexter would be the worst, the most jealous of us, of course. He was dominant and aggressive by nature—possessive, in fact. I wasn't much better.

Jay would go along with whatever we all wanted, as he always did. But it was nice to see him looking enthusiastic and uncharacteristically *wolf like* today. As an Omega, he tended to be the smallest and softest us of all, but not today.

Obviously, our mate brought out the best in us.

My keen hearing picked up a feminine gasp and shuffling movement from Jay's room. With my heart thumping in my chest as anticipation wound around me, I grabbed a bottle of water from the fridge and called out to her.

"Come out and have some water, Doc."

My heart pounded harder as I heard her moving about. I didn't even know her name, which was terrible. I should have asked Dexter more questions about her before he left.

She popped her head around the doorway, her eyes wide and the smell of fear catching sharp in my nose.

I stayed on my side of the kitchen bench, not wanting to frighten her by moving any closer.

But my wolf was rising, I could feel it in the heat of my skin and the way my arms trembled with both weakness and strength.

My Beta wolf recognised its mate, and human or not, my shifter didn't care.

She's mine.

I grabbed hold of the bench in front of me and forced a calm smile to my face. I was happy to see her, more than happy. That was the problem.

But I didn't want to scare her any more than I probably was going to anyway.

As she crept out of Jay's bedroom, all I could think about was stripping her clear of her hospital scrubs and taking her on the floor boards beneath my feet.

I'd been dreaming about my mate for as long as I could remember. And to finally be within reach of knowing the feeling of her wrapped around me, to feel her love and her heart beating against mine... it would be heaven.

"Where am I?" she asked, her hands clenching into fists at her sides as though she couldn't decide if she needed to fight her way out of here or not.

She was pale, and obviously still in shock.

I wasn't sure how to approach her. We wanted her to stay, not run from us. But how to do that?

"You're in the Woodlands. I'm Taylor."

She didn't seem to hear me, or respond, so I poured some cold water into a glass and pushed it across the bench.

"Here, have a drink. You fainted."

"I fainted?" she asked, coming forward and frowning as though she didn't believe me.

"Yes. At the hospital."

She put a hand to her forehead. "Oh, yes. I kind of remember that. I was talking to a man about his father and..."

"And you fainted."

"So why am I here?"

She looked at me expectantly and suddenly our reasons for bringing her back here didn't seem so straightforward.

And they certainly wouldn't make any sense to a human.

What was the best lie I could come up with, that was kind of close to the truth?

"Ah... you were talking to Dex at the time, about his dad, and when you dropped into his arms he kind of panicked and decided to bring you home to make sure you were okay."

Her eyes narrowed with what looked like anger this time, the bright blue irises flickering with fire.

Something inside of me cackled with delight. She was a feisty one. Good. She was going to need that heat if she was going to live out here with us.

"Why would he do that? I was at the hospital. They would have taken care of me."

I needed to cut off this conversation until Dexter returned. I was liable to stuff everything up and then where would we be? With a mate who didn't want us.

"Dex will explain everything when he gets back. He won't be long. But for the moment, I should introduce myself. I'm Taylor." I repeated my name, and this time I saw the words register. She was obviously coming more fully to her senses.

I held out my hand in a non-threatening manner and began to move around the island bench so that I could touch her for the first time. Would she faint on me as she had with Dexter? Or would she continue to stare at me with the fear I saw in her eyes when she first peered around the door frame?

"Taylor, this all sounds very dodgy," she said. "Are you sure I'm not dreaming? Because this isn't making any sense."

I kept my hand out and waited. "I still don't know your name, Doctor."

Her shoulders dropped a little as though she was letting down her guard for the first time. "It's Claire."

Claire. What a beautiful name. She reached out and shook my

hand, and electrical currents of sensation coursed through my arm.

Claire's eyes went wide and then her eyes shut. She began to fall to the floor and I dove forward with both arms out.

I caught her just before her head hit the coffee table and swung her up into my arms, loving the feeling of her weight against my body.

The front door slammed shut behind me and I turned toward Dexter and Jay, who were still naked and panting hard from their run.

"Well, that answers *that* question," Dexter said, his tone begrudging.

I looked up at him. "What do you mean?"

"That's what happened when I touched her, too. She's obviously your mate as well."

I smiled at my Alpha. "Our pack's mate, Dex. Told you."

Dexter nodded once and I carried Claire back into Jay's bedroom and laid her on the bed once again. I adjusted her limbs a little, to ensure she wouldn't be uncomfortable when she woke. Again.

When I walked back into the lounge, Jay and Dexter had their jeans on and I felt ten feet tall. I'd found my mate, and she was as beautiful as I'd always imagined she'd be.

"What are you smirking about?" Dexter asked as he cracked open a beer.

He was tense and I knew jealousy, like any other monster, was going to shred him if we didn't cut it off at the knees.

"I'm in shock. After all these years... I can't believe we finally found our mate. We're the first pack in the entire Woodlands area to find her, Dex. You have to see how amazing that is."

The Alpha's lips tweaked up at the edges. "Yeah, I can kinda see that."

"And if you think about all the reasons we're arranged into triad packs, it makes sense that the three of us are meant to make one woman perfectly happy."

Dexter took a swig of his beer and looked at me. "What do you mean?"

Jay sidled up next to me. "You're probably right, Taylor. I mean… I always wondered why the elders would do such a thing. To deliberately create every mini-pack to have an Alpha, Beta and Omega. What was the real reason other than to stop all the Alphas fighting amongst themselves? This means that our mate…"

He trailed off and I realized that, like me before she woke up, Jay didn't know her name.

"Claire."

Jay grinned. "Claire…" He said her name slowly, like he was savoring the taste of her. "She will have a perfect family unit. An Alpha to protect her, a Beta to build a home for her, and me, an Omega, to be her best friend and probably the one who looks after all the kids when they come, since she's a doctor. She'll probably want to keep working… and stuff."

Jay stopped talking as we stared at him in awe. Jay could be quiet, so I didn't always give him the appreciation he deserved. He was smart and had enough heart for the whole family.

"What? You know I've always wanted loads of kids around."

I moved my gaze over to Dexter's and our eyes met with an understanding. Sure, we'd always wanted kids, but we didn't want to hang around the house all day with them.

We wanted to work, provide for our family and the community. If our mate was an extremely intelligent, working woman, who would look after our house and the kids?

Jay.

Dexter cleared his throat. "Maybe you're right."

I nodded, trying not to let my happiness shine through my massive smile *too* much.

"So how are we going to convince her to stay, then? She's human, for one thing, and I can tell you, when she woke up, she wasn't too impressed that we brought her back here instead of leaving her at the hospital."

Dexter grinned. "It's simple. We seduce her into staying."

Jay stared at Dexter wide-eyed, but I was more sceptical.

"Seriously?"

Dexter nodded. "What woman wouldn't want the love and attention of three men?"

"At once?" I asked, trying to clarify the rules and intent.

I'd tried not to think about how we were going to share her sexually.

He shrugged. "Yeah, why not? If she's destined to be the mate to a full pack, then she'll have an appetite to match."

I grinned at my Alpha, lust heating up my blood.

"I like the sound of that."

FOUR

Claire

Oh. My. God.

Did those guys just say they were going to share me between all three of them? As in... sexually?

Like some footy slut on a team trip? All three of them at once?

No fucking way!

I managed to sit up and swing my legs over the side of the bed without alerting them. They were too busy discussing how they were going to keep me, to listen for my movement anyway.

Keep me!

Like I was a bloody stray puppy they found by the side of the road.

And what was with all the Alpha, pack... crap? They talked like they were a bunch of primitive animals—which they must be, if they were thinking of enslaving me.

Me! The girl no one *ever* wants!

I got to my feet and looked around the room for a weapon. Anything I could use to defend myself if necessary.

These guys sounded absolutely insane.

Who kidnaps a fainting woman straight out of a hospital and then takes her home to keep?

Psychopaths! That's who.

The room I'd been sleeping in was too bland for my taste, and other than a few books, there was nothing to throw. Not even a baseball bat to swing.

The window!

I tiptoed to the sash window and quietly opened the curtains. I could try to climb out and run away, but where the hell was I? All I could see outside was grass, and then woodlands surrounding the house.

I wasn't in the city any longer, that was for sure.

And if I did try and run anyway, would I be just jumping from the frying pan into the fire?

Because, although those men were talking about seducing me into staying with them, I had the strangest feeling that they wouldn't hurt me. Which was crazy. They had kidnapped me. They weren't normal men, so who knew what they'd do, if I tried to escape.

What did I know? I'd done only a brief stint in mental health during my residency and knew as much now as I did before the rotation.

"Oh, you're awake. Great."

I yelped and spun around as someone spoke to me from the doorway.

It was the one I hadn't met yet. I'd heard his voice out there, and wondered what he was like. He'd sounded... gentler than the others, somehow. He was much smaller than the other two, and had a radiant smile I hadn't expected.

"Who are you?" I asked, scanning this one for any signs of danger.

He was very pretty rather than handsome, and not much taller than me. But there was something very sexy about him as well. His smile said that he'd go to the ends of the earth to bring me my heart's desire.

I shook myself to dispel the romantic nonsense. I should be terrified right now but instead, I was entranced by the sight of this guy's amazing abs.

Why didn't he have a shirt on?

"I'm Jay. This is my bedroom. Do you need anything? Food? A beer? You must be feeling pretty strange at the moment."

His voice was calm, but strong. My whole body instantly relaxed. Maybe this one would give me a straight answer.

"Why am I here, Jay? And what keeps happening to me? At the hospital I fainted, and I think I fainted again just now."

Jay smiled and took a step back. "Come on out. I promise, no one here will ever hurt you. We can talk through what happened, and why."

I took a few steps toward the bedroom door, though my logical mind screamed at me to run.

Run hard, run fast, and don't look back.

But something deeper, more innate and instinctual wanted to trust this beautiful man before me.

So, despite my misgivings and the screaming of the modern woman in my head, I crept forward, until I was standing in the doorway once again.

There were two other men in the room, and I recognized both of them.

Dexter, the big brute from the hospital whose father was unwell. He was half-naked as well, and my gaze did an instant inspection of his massive chest and abs.

I almost groaned aloud.

Why does he have to be so damn attractive?

I looked away from the guys in front of me, heat coursing up my face, mostly due to embarrassment. I'd been perving on them in a most unprofessional way. Perving on the guys who had snatched me from the hospital. What was wrong with me?

Dexter was larger than a professional footballer, and so much more cut. There wasn't a scrap of fat on him.

"Don't you gentlemen own shirts?"

"Oh, sorry," Dexter said. "We forgot you humans care about that stuff."

My head came up at that one. "Humans? What do you mean?" I narrowed my eyes at him. "What are you guys, if not human?"

Okay, so I needed to revise my thoughts. These guys really were nutters.

I glanced from one to the other, then back to Jay. Dexter picked up a tank from the floor and pulled it on, then threw Jay one too.

Jay pulled on the top and came forward, holding out his hand with a grin. "Nice to meet you officially, Claire."

I looked at his hand suspiciously. If my foggy memory was correct, shaking the last two guys' hands was what instigated the fainting.

Which made no logical sense. So, what was I afraid of?

"Okay." I reached out and put my palm to his.

Pulses of pleasure coursed up my arm and my knees went weak.

Oh, no. Not again.

Jay surged forward and caught me before I hit the ground. But I didn't pass out this time. Instead, I was caught in his eyes.

Blue pools of magic and wonder.

I wanted to kiss him. I could feel it in my very bones.

My gaze dropped to his lips. His mouth was beautiful and so close to me.

And as he dropped his head and stole my breath, I floated up to the ceiling and watched myself kiss him back.

My rational brain couldn't believe I was doing it—letting a complete stranger kiss me like that. But then he slipped his tongue into my mouth and I was back in my body, feeling everything.

The heat of his thin, muscled body beneath my hands. His lips pressing passionately against mine. The taste of his tongue inside my mouth making me moan like a wanton slut.

It had been far too long since anyone had kissed me at all, let alone like *that*.

But then his strong hands moved to my ass, gripping my flesh and pulling me closer against his cock, which was hard beneath his jeans.

His flesh pressed against my belly, pulling me back to reality and the great big warning bell clanging in my head.

This was dangerous... and wrong. So wrong.

I broke away from his grip, breathing hard. I stood up and stepped back, holding my hand up so he didn't approach again.

I could feel the energy in the room, the heat. The atmosphere had changed, becoming charged.

I could actually smell their arousal. Their need for me. All three of them. And worse, I could feel my own arousal, slick between my legs.

They all made as if to step toward me and I pushed my hand out more firmly. "No. Please. Don't touch me!"

The three of them froze and Jay held up both hands. "No one will touch you, Claire. Not if you don't want it. You don't need to fear us."

Dexter growled, the sound both scary and strangely exciting. I could feel the wetness between my thighs, readying my body for their entrance.

No! I wasn't doing this.

I focused on Jay, reaching for my anger simmering just beneath the surface. "Oh, really? You kidnapped me! There's three of you and only one of me. You could rape me and kill me and no one would be the wiser! How can I not be afraid of you right now?"

Angry tears filled my eyes as I suddenly realized how vulnerable I was. Dexter took a step forward and I yelped.

"Not you! You're the scariest one of all."

Dexter fell back, his face a mask of hurt and distress.

Jay moved in front of Dexter to block him from my view, and my heart that had been racing like a steam train began to calm down.

"Claire, seriously. We would never hurt you. We couldn't. That would be like cutting off our own arm."

He seemed sincere, and I was a pretty adept at identifying a liar.

"Okay, well if that's true, you'll take me home. Now."

I put my hands on my hips to emphasise how serious I was and Jay's smile faded.

"Um... but we haven't even gotten to know you yet."

Pardon me?

"What do you mean? Why would you want to get to know me?"

Didn't he hear how insane he sounded?

"Um..." Jay didn't seem to have an answer for that.

Taylor stepped up next to Jay and got my attention, but didn't approach me, which was good.

"There's something special about you... for us. In our community we believe in love at first sight. Fated mates."

"Mates?" They made me sound like an animal. "Who are you guys? What are you?" I'm not sure why I added that last sentence, but it seemed appropriate, somehow.

Taylor looked at the other men, who both appeared reluctant to answer me honestly. I huffed out in frustration.

"You've gotta tell me, because you're starting to freak me out."

Taylor frowned. "You won't be able to handle the truth."

I glared at him. "Listen, mate, I'm a physician. I can handle anything you guys throw at me. Because all I want is the truth. That's very important to me."

After dealing for years with boyfriends who'd lied and cheated their way through our relationships, the last thing I wanted was more dishonest men.

Dexter moved to take a step forward and Taylor grabbed his arm.

Dexter frowned, that pained look on his face returning once again.

He looked at me and took a step back. "You don't need to fear me, Claire. All this…" He indicated to his body. "Is to protect you. That's what I'm built for—protection. I'd never hurt you. I'd do anything to keep you safe."

I held his gaze for a moment and eventually nodded. I could kind of understand that. But any men whom I'd met in the past who were as big as Dexter were real meat-heads. They cared only for looks and intimidation.

"Okay… well, then tell me what this is all about. And don't hold anything back."

The men shared a look again and finally Taylor stepped forward.

"Okay, but you may want to sit down."

Really?

I gave them a look that clearly said, "Are you serious right now?" but when they didn't move, I eventually threw up my hands and sat on the couch.

"Fine. But you guys need to sit down, too. It's like being surrounded by massive trees."

They all found a seat so fast I barely saw them move. Taylor on the couch, Jay on the edge of a chair and Dexter, who seemed to have taken my fear of him to heart, and moved all the way back to the stairs that I assumed led up to a second floor.

It was really strange, but seeing Dexter so sad and far away from the rest of us hurt me in the weirdest way. It was like a hand was being pressed to my sternum and applying extreme pressure.

I wanted him closer. But why would I, when he was by far the most intimidating of all the men? None of this made any sense.

I sat up straighter and steeled myself for a revelation.

"Okay, hit me with it. What is this about? And what have I got to do with it all?"

Taylor shifted forward on his seat and once again, I was struck with how beautiful these men were, each of them in their own way, but all incredibly sexy.

Taylor was hot, in the way men who graced the front of magazines were hot. His hair was shaggy, long and touchable. His eyelashes were far too long for a man, only on him they looked fantastic, and his shoulders were so wide, they left no doubt as to how strong he was.

Taylor grinned. "You feel that attraction between us?"

What could I do?

Lie?

When I'd just lectured them on how important honesty was to me, and when I was so obviously perving on them.

"Yeah... so what?"

That didn't actually *mean* anything.

He smirked at me. "Are you attracted to all three of us?"

I didn't even need to look at the other two men. "Yes," I admitted shortly. "But what's that got to do with anything?"

That couldn't be unusual. After all, they were seriously attractive men.

Taylor laughed. "Is that a normal reaction for you? To want to have sex with the only three men in the room?"

I gasped involuntarily. I didn't want to....

I sat back against the couch, crossed my legs and arms over my body and stared him down.

When he put it like that... "Well, no. But..." But what? I let my arms drop down, folding my hands in my lap. "Yeah, it is weird, actually. I haven't been attracted to anyone in... forever."

I shrugged, not wanting to get into the reasons for my lack of sex life.

Dexter got to his feet and began to pace at the back of the room. I could feel his aggression, his pent-up emotions. But they didn't seem to be directed at me.

"Keep going, Taylor," he said, not looking at me as he stalked up and down like a lion at the zoo.

I looked over at Taylor. "Tell me."

Taylor pressed his lips together and then spoke. "Okay. Well, the three of us are wolf shifters."

He couldn't be telling me they were some mythical being that belonged in the movies. "You mean... like werewolves or something?"

It was in *Twilight*, so why not? Right?

He smiled. "Not quite. We aren't a slave to the moon and we have complete control over our bodies, even in wolf form. Jay, Dex and I are a triad pack. We're part of a much larger pack as well. The Woodlands Pack."

These guys obviously needed their heads examined.

"So, let me get this right. You believe you're a wolf shifter... hmm... okay, then. Show me."

I knew, from a mental health perspective, I wasn't meant to shatter their illusions too quickly, but I was running out of time. Everyone at the hospital would be looking for me, and within a few days, my parents would start to worry, too.

I lived alone, so there wasn't a roommate or a husband to note my absence, which I wasn't going to admit to these guys. But I had to work out how I was going to get home from here and the easiest way was to get them to drive me back to the hospital and drop me there.

Taylor looked over at the other men in the room. "Um... I suppose Jay could show you. He's the smallest of us. Dex's wolf is pretty big."

Jay looked at me with big, wide eyes. "Are you sure you want me to do that, Claire?"

I wanted to laugh, but managed not to. These guys couldn't be serious right now. "Yeah. Go for it." I waved my hands in the air, giving him permission to do whatever he was about to do.

Although, if a real wolf materialized into this room, I might just end up shitting myself.

He began to undress and moved behind the couch. "Okay... but don't yell, okay?"

I nodded and Jay disappeared as though he'd never been there.

"Holy shit." I jumped to my feet. "Where'd he go?"

Around the couch stepped a small brown wolf.

"Oh my God!"

I jumped up onto the couch, shrieking a little as adrenaline thundered through my veins.

"Hey, stop. You said you wouldn't yell," Taylor said, as the brown wolf disappeared behind the couch once again.

"He's timid in his wolf form; you've gotta be quieter than that," Dexter said as well, his tone one that was protective of Jay and clearly a little annoyed at me.

For the first time I saw the link between the men. The family element. The brotherhood.

"Um... that's Jay?" I asked, pointing to the couch.

"We told you," Taylor said.

I swallowed hard. This was really happening. "Okay... what should I do, then?"

Should I apologize? Ask him to come back again?

"Well, maybe sit down and call him to you. If you want to be comfortable with us in both forms, I suppose you'll have to get used to it."

I was pretty sure I had no intention of being comfortable with them in any form. But what choice did I have at this point in time? "Um... okay. Jay, can you come around, please?"

The head of the wolf popped around the couch again and my stomach tightened.

Oh my God. It was a real wolf. I couldn't explain anything about this whole experience, but there was no doubting the animal that stared at me unblinkingly.

"Um... okay. Can I... pet him?" I asked Taylor, though the amount of sharp, pointed teeth in the wolf's mouth had me questioning my own sanity.

Taylor nodded. "Yeah. Absolutely. Go for it."

Taylor ran his hand over the back of the brown wolf, who was slowly walking toward me.

He had the biggest, most soulful eyes I'd ever seen on an animal and once again, I felt my anxiety drain away.

He stepped closer and I extended my hand to him, though my arm trembled and my chest burned from my inability to breathe.

He put his wet nose against my fingers and then licked my hand. I squealed with surprise this time and pulled my hand back.

Taylor laughed and the wolf backed away behind the couch.

I blinked and suddenly Jay was standing there again. Naked, and pulling on his clothes.

I stared, unable to speak.

What sort of world had I stumbled across here?

Jay

I pulled my top over my head and quickly buttoned my jeans. Adrenaline was pumping through my muscles so fast they trembled with strength and unease. I had the strongest urge to go outside, shift back into my wolf form and go running again.

But I didn't want to leave my mate, because that was certainly who she was. Sure, she may not have fainted at the touch of my skin on hers, but she'd kissed me. That was even better.

And as I glanced back toward my Alpha, I could see he knew Claire was mine as much as his and Taylor's. He was pissed that I'd gotten in first, but I shrugged. Could he really blame me for taking advantage when it was offered?

I walked back around the couch, presentable once more for the human.

"I… um…" Claire didn't seem to be able to speak, but at least she wasn't running from the house screaming, or passing out again.

"Are you okay?" I asked her as I settled down onto the couch arm.

I struggled not to stare at her. She was so beautiful. So clean and lush and just... amazing.

Her hair was the color of sunshine, with tips of gold. It had been all pulled back into a harsh style at the hospital, but was now tumbling down around her face.

"Ah... um. So, you can all do that?" she asked, her face pale.

I nodded. "Yes, everyone in the pack can."

Claire swallowed hard, her throat and face pulling and working with her stress.

"Um... everyone? Even the kids? The women?"

I glanced at Taylor. How were we going to answer that? Honesty was probably the best answer. She had said she wanted honesty, above all else.

"Um..."

Taylor stepped up. "Our mothers and aunts... yes, they can shift, though they don't much, anymore. They're getting a bit past it."

Claire glanced from me to Taylor. "What about your sisters? Girlfriends?"

I cleared my throat. We had to tell her the truth. "Our pack hasn't had a female shifter born in over fifty years."

Claire stared at me like I'd grown two heads. "Are you serious?"

"Yes."

She fell back against the couch and exhaled. "Whoa. That's crazy."

I nodded because I totally agreed with her. "So, we have a whole town full of three-man packs, and no women. No children."

Her eyes that had been glazed over and unfocused, snapped into place. "Hang on a second. Do you think that I... please tell me you didn't grab me so that I could fill the gap for you? I do not want some wolfie... woodsman. I don't want any man!"

I heard Taylor's chuckle and Dexter's growl and jumped to my feet.

"We understand, Claire. But in our community, we all have a true mate. Soul mates, in a way. Fate destined."

"Yeah, so?" Claire said, flicking her hair back out of her eyes. But she was nervous. More nervous than she had been, all of a sudden. Was it my mention of soul mates? Did she feel the connection, too? And if so, was she going to try and deny it, when the evidence was right there in front of us all?

I swallowed hard. Was I the one who should tell her?

Dexter got to his feet and walked over to the back of the couch, staring down at our beautiful woman. "So, you're *our* mate, Claire. Not mine, or Taylor's, or Jay's. All of ours. You're designed for us, and we're destined for you."

Claire jumped to her feet and pushed both her hands out in front of her like she could stop our words and everything she was hearing.

"Stop right there."

She took several breaths, her cheeks flushing with blood, making her look even more desirable.

And aroused.

"I am *not* a mate, to anyone. Let alone three men who can turn into wolves."

She was shaking her head, like she had no idea how this had all happened. And then she couldn't seem to stop shaking her head.

Taylor stepped forward, his heart on his sleeve. "Claire, you have no idea how lucky we are to have found you."

"No. *No!*" She was yelling now and a tiny part of me wished Dexter would make her pass out again.

Her hysteria was making my stomach tie itself up in knots.

"Stop, please. No one is going to hurt you," I tried, in a placating tone.

She fixed me with an angry stare. "Then you'll take me home. *Now*. Because if you don't... If you don't..."

Dexter chuckled and leaned against the couch, his arms crossed. "You'll what?"

Claire's face darkened and it made me proud to see that she wasn't scared of us. Quite the opposite actually.

I glanced over to where Dexter leaned with a deceptive casualness. He might look calm, but he was vibrating with energy, just like Taylor and me. We were all feeding off the tension emanating from Claire and her temper.

Dexter's arms were huge, his biceps the size of Claire's thighs. Did she seriously think she had any hope of fighting any of us off, if we were so inclined to hold her here against her will?

"I'll never forgive you for keeping me here. If I am some special soul mate person to you, do you really want me pissed off at you for the rest of my life? And that's if you can watch me twenty-four-seven. As soon as you're asleep, I'll run away. I can promise you that." She was practically hissing now.

I couldn't handle much more of this. The air was practically sparking, from all the overblown emotion in the room. From all of us.

I twisted around and stared at my Alpha and Beta, whose hackles were rising at the threat.

"Taylor, why don't you go see your parents? And Dex, catch up with your mom. Tell her about your dad's operation, and then maybe explain about Claire, and come back in an hour? I need to speak to her. Alone."

I didn't assert myself too often in our pack. I didn't need to. Dexter and Taylor did a great job of looking after us. But as I saw them register my words, I was glad I had chosen this battle to speak up. Because now they were listening to me.

"Ah..." Dexter began, then paused. "I do need to let Mom know, about Dad, and that he's going to be all right once the stents go in." His gaze was sheepish. In the shock of finding our fated mate, other priorities had dimmed.

I tilted my head toward the door.

Dex backed away without argument, and my respect for my Alpha grew. He was placing his trust in me, and I would make sure that trust was not misplaced.

Taylor followed, with only a long, hard look at me, and as they shut the door behind them and walked from the house, I turned back to our mate. Her shoulders were up almost to her ears and she looked far too stressed.

"Can we talk, Claire? I promise I won't hurt you."

She stared at me, as if debating something within herself.

"Do you want something to eat?" I prompted. "We don't have a lot of your city processed food, but we keep a good supply of meat and fruit and fresh things here."

I moved toward the kitchen, pulling out some berries from the fridge—berries that had been fresh picked from our fields.

"Ah... um..." She stumbled into the kitchen and pulled up a stool. "I suppose."

She noticed the variety of berries we had, their color and size not what normal supermarkets would carry.

"You grow everything here yourselves?"

I nodded and pushed the bowl toward her. "We're pretty self-sustainable. We have to go into nearby towns like Little Creek for some things, of course, but we try to stay off the grid as much as possible."

We had solar power for heating and electricity, farmed fields of crops, and we raised chickens and cows for meat, milk and eggs.

Our ancestors had done a good job of keeping our community safe and sustainable, and it was on my generation to keep that sustainability going.

Claire picked up a berry and bit into it. A soft moan surfacing from her lips made me groan in unison.

Her gaze caught mine and I shrugged. "Sorry. Your reactions are linked to mine. I can't control it. You get enjoyment from eating a berry, then I feel it, too."

She sighed, letting her shoulders fall. And when she looked at me, the sadness on her face broke my heart.

"Claire, please don't look at me like that. You're not defeated, you're not trapped. This is a blessing. I wish you could see it that way. We all need to work out the best way through the situation."

I hadn't realized how hard it would be for a human to understand us. I'd never had to think about it before today.

She looked at me with pleading eyes. "Please, Jay. You seem to be the most sensible of them all. Take me home. Please. Drop me off at the hospital and I swear I won't tell anyone what happened. Not about Dexter kidnapping me, or you guys turning into wolves. None of it."

I smiled at her, to hide my consternation. She still wanted to leave? Then her eyebrows flew up, a horror-filled expression crossing her face.

"Unless... oh, God. Do you have to kill me now that I know your secret?"

Kill her? I burst out laughing. I couldn't help it; the idea was too ludicrous to entertain.

"Claire, seriously. This isn't the movies. We're not the mob.

And even if you wanted to tell the world, who would believe you? That's not our concern."

Well, in a way it was. It was forbidden to tell the outside world about us, but did that apply to humans who found out about us? The whole area was gray, given this was my first experience of sharing anything about our life as shifters, with a human.

That was the last thing I was worried about at this point in time.

"What is your concern, then?" she asked quietly.

I sighed.

"Look, Claire, whether you believe us or not, you're the woman we're meant to be with. Me, Dexter, and Taylor. There is no one else for us, and there can't be anyone else for us. Not now that we've met you. Don't you understand? If you don't want us, then you can leave and we'll live here, just the three of us, forever. On our own."

And although yesterday I was relatively settled with the idea of the three of us being a family unit forever, today was different.

Today I didn't want to settle for less.

Today I knew the truth.

Humans were going to save our pack from extinction. New blood was necessary to keep us strong and help us survive.

Whether or not the elders had known that, when they broke us off into mini-packs of three men, was moot. *Something* had been guiding our pack in the right direction, and finding Claire had been a lightbulb moment in that regard.

Perhaps that had been the plan all along?

She gave me a strange smile. "That sounds... totally bonkers. You know that, Jay?"

I shrugged. "Maybe to you, but that's how we were brought up. One true mate for all of us. I mean, we did think we'd have one true mate each, but once we met you and felt the bond, we knew it wasn't going to be like that. You are our true mate, and we will need to learn how to live with that. So, yes... this is something different, even for us. For one, you're not a wolf shifter, and two, there's only one of you and three of us. Neither is the norm as far as our experience goes, but I'm sure you can handle us."

I gave her the sexiest grin I had in my arsenal and redness flooded her cheeks. She looked down as if embarrassed.

But she didn't say anything to negate what I'd said.

"You can feel it too, can't you?" I asked her. "You can feel the connection, the need, the desire?"

She still wouldn't look at me and I reached over and lifted her chin with one of my fingers.

Electricity sizzled through our connection, but in a muted, comfortable way.

When her gaze lifted to connect with mine, I smiled at her. "Don't be afraid of us. We will *never* hurt you."

She sighed heavily and jerked her chin out of my grasp. "It's not that I'm afraid, exactly. It's just that this is... well... crazy! I'm a logical woman. Cold and calculating if any of my ex-boyfriends are to be believed."

A growl rattled through me at the idea of her bedding other men. Men who failed to see the beautiful, sexy being they had in their grasp.

When she looked at me, I coughed to cover it up, but the possessive wolf in me raised his head.

CHAPTER
SIX

Jay

"Sorry... Anyway. You aren't crazy. I can guarantee you that. And if you're designed for us—all three of us—you really must be the most remarkable woman."

She stopped shaking her head and looked at me properly.

"What do you mean?"

I stared at Claire for a moment and realized that this was the key. The words, the compliments. She was beginning to open up like a flower ready to drink in the rain.

How deprived had she been of such words? Affection, too, perhaps? The men she had met before must have been imbeciles.

"Would you sit with me on the couch? I promise I won't do anything weird."

She smiled and wiped at a stray tear that fell down her cheek. "Okay."

I took her hand, loving the feel of the pulses of pleasure such a small touch brought, and took her to the couch.

I pushed my luck and sat first, then pulled her onto my lap.

She landed awkwardly and although she moved away a little, she stayed with her legs draped across my thighs. I was grateful for the contact, and for the fact that she seemed to be building toward a modicum of trust.

"Now look. I don't want to give you a thousand compliments, because you won't believe me yet. But what I will say, is that you are beyond beautiful. Your body is magic and your smile makes me want to drop to my knees and worship you."

She looked down at her hands, but I could see the small smile playing on her lips.

"But there's so much more to you than that, I know. You're a doctor, so I know you are also incredibly intelligent, hardworking and driven. Which will hold you in good stead with our pack, and the women at the Alpha's right hand. They are strong women."

She nodded and joined the conversation again. "I can imagine."

I squeezed her thigh, hiding my smile when I saw her suppress a shiver at my touch. "And if you're designed for three of us, then you'll be twice as strong, twice as courageous. I can see your fire, your temper, and your passion. You are an incredible woman, Claire, and I honestly cannot wait to see what the future brings for us."

She glanced down again and twirled her fingers together. "But I don't know anything about you. Any of you. How can I trust you? How can I possibly stay here and get to know you when I have a job... a life to get back to?"

Relief winged through my heart as she prepared to bargain with me. I could hear it in her tone, see it in the way she looked at me. She was listening to me... she *wanted* to believe me.

Time. We just needed time. To prove to her that we could love her in a way that would make her happy.

"Give us two days. We'll show you our pack, and you can meet the elders. Spend time with us. I promise you won't regret it, and then at the end of the allocated time, if you want to return to the city—we'll take you."

I held my breath against the pain such a statement brought. Take her back?

Never!

Dexter and Taylor would kill me for even offering her the option. But we couldn't force her to stay. That wasn't healthy for anyone. She'd hate us all.

"Ah... I do have the next few days off work. I was planning on catching up on some sleep and seeing my parents."

Yes! Thank you!

"Well, you can definitely sleep and relax here. You can take my bedroom—I'll sleep on the couch. Honestly, we'll do anything to make you happy. You need to see that to believe it, I know."

She looked at me with a sceptical expression. I knew that staying with us was the last thing she wanted to agree to.

"Please, Claire. Stay with us. Don't ignore this opportunity that Fate has presented."

She rolled her eyes at me. "Jay, I don't believe in Fate. No rational human does."

I smiled at her. "You've never seen a patient pull through, when all logic says he or she shouldn't have? Or, perhaps a perfectly healthy patient just passes away in his sleep? You've honestly never seen anything that couldn't be explained away with logic or reason?"

Her lips twisted up and she glanced down at her hands. "Well... yeah, I suppose so. There are always things that happen that can't be totally explained..."

She stopped.

I grinned at her, even though she wasn't looking at me yet.

"Trust me when I say that you need to throw everything you thought you knew, out the window. Two days, Claire. Please."

She stared at her hands for a minute longer then finally looked up at me, tears shimmering in her blue eyes and making them shine like sapphires.

I reached up and caressed her cheek, wiping away the moisture on her face.

"Why are you crying? Is your medical mind blown apart by everything you've seen and heard today?"

She nodded and hiccupped. "Yeah, pretty much. I suppose if people can turn into wolves at will, then anything's possible."

"Yes. It is."

I wanted to kiss her again, but did I dare?

She looked up and met my eyes, and suddenly I did dare. I reached over and grabbed her waist, pulling her back onto my lap and pressing my lips to hers.

She gasped against my mouth, but didn't move away.

I didn't rush her, but kept my hands on her waist, though I wanted to explore her body more than anything. I waited and waited, and then I felt it. A softening of her body on mine as she melted toward me.

I gripped her waist tighter and slanted my head so that I could open her lips. She moaned and opened to me. I tasted her tongue with mine once again.

Claire's hands crept up my arms until she was gripping my neck, dragging me into her. I couldn't stand it any longer. I had to get closer.

I pulled at her scrubs, wanting to feel her skin. Needing to remove the barrier between us.

The front door banged loudly and Claire jumped. She moved to slide off my lap but I held her for a moment as I looked toward the entrance.

Dexter and Taylor glowered at me, the rage in their faces clear for the world to see.

Claire began to struggle in earnest and I let her go. She jumped to her feet and I stood up next to her, smiling at my pack.

"Claire has agreed to stay for a few days and get to know us."

The black cloud hanging over Dex and Taylor's heads disappeared instantly.

Taylor stepped forward. "Really? You'll stay?"

I looked over at Claire, whose face was torn with indecision as she bit her lip and didn't speak for a moment. Then she cleared her throat. "You said two days."

I grinned at her and my pack mates. "Yes, I did."

"Claire, how about I show you around the house?" Taylor spoke up.

I didn't want to leave her side, so I added, "Then we can go out for a bit. Meet the pack maybe, if you guys think it'll be safe?"

I looked toward Dexter for guidance.

Our Alpha nodded. "Actually, Mom told me to bring her straight over, for a report on Dad more than anything, I think."

Claire's face changed, her professional persona slipping into place.

"Yes. I'd like to do that, if we can. I don't have any other clothes though, and I suppose you guys have nothing my size?"

The hint of a joke and a tentative smile from Claire made even Dexter grin.

"Ah no... although some of the older women may have some jeans and t-shirts or sweaters near your size," Dex said.

I assessed Claire's figure and guessed maybe a twelve or a fourteen. Perfect for pleasing all three of us.

"Yeah, I'm pretty sure my mom or even one of my aunties will have something for you," I said.

"Great. I'd like to speak to your mom, Dexter."

She walked forward without the fear she'd shown earlier, and I made a mental note that the healer in her was a fierce, protective personality. And that would suit our pack well. If she chose to stay.

"Let's go, then," Dexter said, shooting me another angry look as he ushered her out the door. I had to hide the smile that naturally spread across my face.

I was the only one she'd kissed today so far... but so what?

I was pretty sure that, by the end of the next two days, kisses were not the only things we'd all be sharing.

CHAPTER

SEVEN

Claire stepped up next to me and the scent of her brought my wolf right up to the surface of my consciousness. I pushed him down with all my might, unwilling to squander the little time we had with her by running through the woods as a wolf.

And that was if she didn't run from me screaming when she finally saw my wolf. It would be quite a different vision to that of Jay's wolf. The silver shifter animal I became could scare a full-sized bear.

We walked down the steps of our home and along the road toward my parents' place.

"Mom and Dad's home is ten houses down." I pointed to show her where we were headed, as we walked along the path.

Our small pack town was made up of four long streets surrounding a central set of shops, and the town center where we all convened for social events and meetings. The town was

60

surrounded by woodlands, hence our name, and the pack terri-tory extended well into the forest, giving us all plenty of room to run whenever we needed it.

Men started to appear from nowhere as we walked, as if drawn by the unusual scent of a young female. The Alpha in me grabbed Claire around the waist and hauled her into my side.

We hadn't had a woman under fifty in our town in years. No one brought the city women home. It was an unwritten rule.

Two young shifters from another mini-triad pack, Thomas and Grady, stood on their balcony, gaping at us as we walked past.

Grady called out. "Dexter, who you got there?"

Claire pushed at me, wriggling in my tight grip. "Can you ease up? You're going to break one of my ribs if you're not careful."

I immediately let her go and waved at Grady, unwilling to answer his question by shouting it out across the street.

"Yeah, sorry," I said instead to Claire.

She continued next to me, not moving too far away. "Why are they all looking at me as if I'm dinner? Oh God... you weren't exaggerating, were you? The town really is all men, isn't it?"

I laughed without humor. "Did you think we were lying about that?"

"Um... no. But you've got to admit, it's unusual. I've never seen anything like it."

Pack members were emerging from every direction, across the square and out of the shops. They must all have been able to smell her.

I knew I could. And it was making my balls ache and my skin tingle.

My mate was here! She was within touching distance, and I had to tamp down on my need and lust, and not take her in the street like my savage side demanded.

I wanted them all to know, to see that we'd found her. And I wanted to stamp my claim on her, in front of everyone.

She was *mine.*

Correction.

She was mine, Taylor's and Jay's. My pack.

Ours...

"There she is." I pointed to my mother, who stood on the steps outside her huge home, watching us make our way toward her.

She'd raised my three brothers and me in that house. It now seemed empty without us. Or so she said. To me it still felt like coming home, when I visited.

Claire walked ahead of me up the path and my mother welcomed her with open arms.

Claire embraced my mom and they walked inside with their arms wrapped around each other, as if they'd known one another their entire lives.

My heart thumped weirdly and a grin lifted my lips. I looked over at Taylor. "What's with that?"

He shrugged. "I don't know. Some sort of woman thing?"

I didn't know either, so I continued up the path and into the house. I could hear them talking from the kitchen. For the first time ever, I felt like an outsider in my own home.

Jay and Taylor quickly followed me inside, and the three of us piled into the kitchen and stood by the table, listening as Claire informed my mother of my father's condition.

"Will he be all right?" Mom asked, with a worried look etching her features.

Claire didn't answer straight away. But then she reached over and touched my mother's hand with hers.

"Honestly, I don't know. If he was just a normal man, I'd say his chances of surviving a year to be about fifty per cent."

My mother inhaled sharply. That was not the news she wanted to hear.

Claire continued. "But he isn't human, so I'm not sure I can give you a full answer. I'm assuming wolf shifters have increased healing, or some other abilities that I don't know about? Is that correct?"

She looked around the room and I nodded.

"Yeah, as shifters, we heal very rapidly. Damage to the heart is a bit different, but with the operation, I think my father should recover much faster than any other man his age."

Claire nodded and my mother fixed me with a stare. "Dexter, how about you go speak to Bill about what you've found out today? I'll keep Claire company."

The tone of my mother's voice was clear. She wanted me to leave.

But, why? And what if someone else came by and saw Claire? Could I trust the rest of the pack not to touch my mate?

"Mom, I don't think that's a good idea."

Claire turned in her chair and looked at me. For the first time I read understanding in her gaze. Did she know my protective streak was all for her? I couldn't help myself; I just wanted to ensure she was safe. And in time, happy.

"It's fine, Dexter," she said firmly. "I'm sure your mom can look after me as well as you men can."

I doubted that very much, but wasn't about to say that in front of my mother.

"I suppose Bill will be interested in what we've learnt about human mates," I managed. The elder was one of those who had split us younger men up into mini-packs of three. Bill would most definitely be interested in what we'd discovered about Claire being the mate of all three of us, but it was difficult at this early stage to consider leaving her in someone else's care, even for a short time.

I'd been brought up to be as selfless as possible. To believe the good of the pack was the most important thing, and to rise above selfish endeavors. And I stood by that ethos ninety-nine per cent of the time. This moment seemed to be the other one per cent.

"Come on Dexter. Let's go. The girls wanna talk." Jay tugged at my arm, and with a final huff, I let my Omega pull me away.

"Okay. Well, um..." I trailed off. Claire was already accepting a cup of tea from my mother and falling into conversation the way only women could do.

I turned away, fighting my wolf the whole time. He didn't want to leave his mate, and I felt the exact same way.

But once we trotted down the stairs and got back into the fresh air, the tortured feeling of being dragged away from her finally lifted a little.

And I could breathe again.

And then I remembered what Jay had been doing when Taylor and I walked into the lounge room.

I pushed him in the shoulder, hard, and he staggered sideways.

"Hey! What was that for?" he grumbled, shooting me a glare.

"For being the first one to kiss our mate... twice! And if we hadn't walked in when we did, you would have seduced her right out from under us."

Instead of denying anything, my Omega grinned. "What can I say? For the first time in my life, I'm actually enjoying being the smallest of our pack. She finds me the least intimidating."

I had to give him that. Jay had always hated that he couldn't hold his own the way Taylor and I could in a fight. He was the smallest, the slowest, and the most likely to get hurt if ever the bear shifters attacked.

No wonder Claire felt most comfortable with him first. He was the closest thing to a human we had.

"Yeah, well don't think you'll be the last, because I'm dying to taste her," I muttered.

Taylor grunted. "Me, too. So, what are we going to tell Bill and the other elders?"

I shrugged and kept walking, nodding to people as I went.

"I don't know. I suppose we have to be honest about imprinting on a human. After all, it may be the way to save the entire pack. If our triad did it, maybe some of the others will be able to, as well."

Jay nodded. "Yeah, I think it is a way to save our pack. New blood. New wolves when the children arrive. A way for the pack to grow and maybe even thrive in new and different ways. Ways we don't even know about, yet."

We made our way to Bill's house and regaled the astonished elder with our tale of finding Claire at the hospital, and her fainting spells when we touched her.

The old man's eyes lit up like the fourth of July. I'd thought he might be disappointed that humans were the answer to our problem, but clearly, he wasn't.

He shook our hands and thanked us. I think he even had the glint of a tear in his eye when he did so.

It seemed that, in finding Claire, we may very well have saved our whole pack from extinction.

Claire

"Mary, I just don't know what to think about all this," I said to Dexter's mother. "I'm sorry. I know you've grown up with it... I mean, you *are* one, I guess. But wolf shifters! Honestly... I feel like I'm stuck in some vampire movie on the T.V."

Mary Monaghan, Dexter's mother, laughed good naturedly. As soon as she had welcomed me in with a hug, I had felt calm and safe. As if I had found my way to the very place I needed to be.

"Well, sweetie, unfortunately I have to tell you that I think you're the strange one. Why wouldn't you turn into a powerful wolf at will, if you could?"

She grinned at me and I rolled my eyes and laughed with her.

She was right, of course. Everyone's version of normal was exactly that. *Their* version of what they saw and became used to every day in their own lives. Who was I to claim that I was the normal one in this situation?

I rubbed my eyes, still feeling a little like I had fallen down the proverbial rabbit hole.

"How do you feel about mating with all three of them?" Mary suddenly asked me, and I almost spat out my mouthful of tea.

I swallowed hard and then gasped for air, fanning my face to try and cool my suddenly hot cheeks. "How did you know about that? Oh, they told you."

Seriously, they were worse than gossiping women.

Mary laughed again. "It's nothing to be ashamed of. They're proud to have you as their mate—if you'll accept them, that is. But I do have to tell you that the threesome thing is new and different, even for us. Usually, or at least how it worked in the past, our mates and families are one-to-one. But then again, we've never had to make the boys group up into triads before. So maybe that's how it happened."

I cocked my head and concentrated on what she was saying. This could be important. "What do you mean?"

"Well, in the past, say when I was younger, most of us had mated by twenty-one. There were enough women for all the men. People rarely left the pack and we were a big enough lot to avoid too much cousin cross-breeding, or anything like that."

I couldn't stop the shudder that ran through my body. "Was that beginning to happen, though? Too much of the same bloodlines?"

Mary's face twisted up a little as though she was thinking hard. "I... suppose. You know, I've never really thought about it, but you're probably right. The actual true mate's legend was becoming less frequent and some people were pairing up with cousins only because there was no one left to mate with."

That often happened with small, isolated communities like this one.

It was unfortunate, but nature usually found a way around it.

"And the next generation—*your* generation—bore only males?" I asked, confirming what had been said by Jay.

"Yes. Not a single female has been born in almost fifty years. I bore my husband four sons, and the rest of the pack contributed thirty-five boys."

"And that's why you made them group up into threes?" I re-iterated. I wanted to get this right.

"Well, yes. There was going to be too much infighting, other-wise. Too many Alphas like Dexter, who couldn't mate. The hormones, the anger, the frustration. It could have led to the downfall of our pack."

I still had some questions. "So why three, then?"

I could see there were differences between Jay, Taylor and Dexter, but I really couldn't work out exactly what the balance was.

"An Alpha, a Beta and an Omega. The perfect triad of men," Mary told me, in a tone that indicated she assumed I knew what she was saying.

"Ah..." I didn't really want to ask her to explain again, but I had no real idea what those terms meant. I could figure out that an Alpha was a strong leader, and I could see those traits in Dexter. But the other terms... My confusion must have shown in my expression, because Mary sighed.

"An Alpha is a leader, the strongest and the biggest of the wolves. A Beta is close behind him. Slightly smaller in stature, he is an Alpha's right-hand man. An Omega is the smallest of our family, but the sweetest and most family-oriented of all."

"So..." This was easy. "Dexter's the Alpha, Taylor's the Beta and Jay's the Omega."

Mary nodded. "Yes, it's pretty easy to figure out once you see them all together."

"Okay, I'm understanding why you put them into families, but what does that have to do with me?"

Mary grinned. "You get the best of all worlds. I married an Alpha, see, and he is beautiful, but he is a little standoffish and can often put the needs of the pack above mine. More often than not, actually." She sighed and took a sip of tea. "But if you have all three men, you'll always be taken care of. You'll never be alone. All your physical and emotional needs will be taken care of. When one slacks off a little, one of the others will step up. You will get all the protection and strength and love and compassion you ever need. If I had my time over again, I'd jump at the chance to add a Beta and an Omega into the mix with my husband." She ducked her head, as if slightly embarrassed by her own words. "Even though he *is* my soul mate."

My mind went blank, in the strangest way. Like it had been blown apart and I could consider nothing other than the extreme amount of information that I didn't know, about this world.

Could it be possible?

"Do you, um, have a job, Mary? A career? How does that fit into this scenario?" I loved being a doctor. I didn't think I'd ever be able to give up healing. Not even for a soul mate—or three.

Mary shook her head. "I'm a homemaker, Claire, but honestly, that's by choice. All I ever wanted was to be married and raise my boys right. I never had a career like you, as a doctor. But I never wanted one."

"Do you think..." I couldn't believe where my thoughts were taking me. This was crazy. To even consider...

"If you're asking if you could still be a doctor, if you take on my son and his pack, I'd say you need to ask them that question. But with three of them there—including one Omega who loves looking after children..." She shrugged, and my mind reeled at the sudden possibilities.

"I hadn't thought of it like that."

I'd always been amazed by the flaws in a one-to-one ratio of women to men. I didn't know a single woman who was fully satisfied by her husband.

There was always something lacking. Sex, or friendship, or help around the house.

Every one of my married friends complained about their husbands in some way.

They didn't help with the kids.

They didn't make enough money.

There was no emotional support.

No sex.

Too much sex.

The lists were always endless, and for me, I always agreed with them. The few boyfriends I'd had were shallow creeps. No one even came close to fulfilling the emotional needs of my heart, let alone the physical needs of my body.

Was it really possible that this was what I needed? Three men? And wolf shifters, at that.

Because I knew that solitary human males had failed every task I'd ever set.

"Thanks for the chat, Mary. It looks like I have a lot of thinking to do."

Mary pushed a homemade cookie at me and smiled. "You do that. And no pressure or anything, but I would love to have you as a daughter-in-law. After four sons, I crave female company more than anything. As soon as I saw you, I felt a kinship connection."

Tears sprang to my eyes, though there was nothing to cry about. But Mary's words were so heartfelt I had to walk around the kitchen counter and hug her. How could I not?

She laughed as I held her. Then I remembered the other reason we'd come over.

"Oh, Mary. Is there any way I could borrow some clothes for a few days? Looks like I'm sticking around and I don't think the boys want to drive me home at the moment to grab some of my own things."

I had so many clothes at home it was embarrassing. The fact that I had to ask to borrow some felt ridiculous.

Mary laughed and dragged me into her bedroom. "Of course. Come this way."

We had a laugh and a chat as we found some jeans, tanks, shoes, and even a serviceable black dress for me to wear. Just until I went home, of course.

When we were done, Mary offered to walk me back to Dexter's house, and I accepted straight away. I didn't want to face the walk on my own, with all of those men looking at me again.

As we walked, I was glad the older woman was with me. The number of eyes on us was incredible. It was one of the most intimidating things I'd ever experienced, and I'd lectured at university before! But nothing in my past life came close to the feeling of dozens of male eyes on me. Assessing the way I looked, the way I walked. Quite possibly sizing me up as a possible mate.

But I wasn't their mate. Not at all. There was no pull toward any of them, like there had been with Dexter, Taylor and Jay.

Every one of the men was young and fit and had more muscles than I could count.

"Is everyone in this town a body builder?" I asked as we got closer to Dexter's house.

My heart was pounding in my chest and it took all of my self-control to keep walking at a slow pace, and not bolt for the front door. My arms and legs tingled with adrenaline. I wanted to run!

Mary smiled. "This is a shifter pack, hun. All the men are fit and strong. Some of the elders are getting a bit soft around the middle, but the wolf genes even keep them pretty fit."

I glanced over at Mary. She walked like a woman my age. With grace and strength and poise. She was slightly more fleshy than was currently fashionable, like me, but I could see the latent strength behind the curves.

"Thank you so much for helping me today, Mary. I really appreciate the insight."

She hugged me tightly and kissed my cheek, the sweet scent of her warmth washing over me.

"I know it must be hard for you, but try to be patient with them, okay?"

I nodded and watched her walk away. Two men stepped off their porch and began to walk toward me. I squealed as I ran inside, locking the front door behind me.

Fuck. That was intense.

I felt like *Alice in Wonderland*, because I had seriously fallen down a rabbit hole.

When was I going to wake up?

I wandered around the living area, the room much cleaner than I'd have expected with three men living in the house.

But where were the photos, the personal effects? I glanced toward the stairs. Their rooms, perhaps?

I shook my head and laughed at myself a little. I couldn't possibly... could I? I mean... would it be that bad if I had a little look around their rooms? I had to know something about these men. They seemed to know me.

My hand was on the rail and my feet were walking up the stairs to the bedrooms before I even finished making the decision to do so.

It was wrong to go snooping.

But so was kidnapping an unconscious woman from a hospital.

I giggled to myself. "This is merely touché."

The first room on the right was dark and, as I flipped on the light, my eyes bulged at the sexiness of the room. I was scared to move closer to the bed in case a sex swing dropped from the ceiling, or something.

I wasn't sure if it was Taylor's room, or Dexter's, but the details screamed *Alpha*.

Dexter's, I decided, studying the strong, confident space. The size of the massive wooden furniture. The silver sheets and mirrors that would match the colors of Dexter's wolf, or so they'd said.

There was something super sexy in the energy of this bedroom and the bed looked so comfortable, with massive pillows and a duvet just calling to my tired body.

I crept in and looked around the room, wanting details about these men. Dexter, in particular.

There was nothing too defining. No photos or memorabilia of any kind.

Did these wolves live minimalist lifestyles on purpose? Or was this the result of a lack of feminine touch?

"See anything you like?" Dexter purred from the doorway and I jumped and swiveled around.

"Oh, shit! You scared me." I put a hand to my chest, feeling my heart hammering away.

Heat flushed my face, mostly from being caught with my hand in the cookie jar.

But if I were honest, there was another reason my cheeks were hot—the intense desire that wove through my body whenever Dexter was present.

He leaned against the door with the casual confidence of a fifties movie star.

His jeans hung on his lean hips like they were ready to fall to the ground any moment and his shoulders barely fit through the door, he was so huge.

"Ah... I'm guessing this is your room? I wasn't sure, but it felt like it for some reason."

He began to stalk forward and I couldn't stop the way my throat tightened and my belly clenched.

Damn, he was so sexy.

I wanted him. More than I'd ever wanted anyone in my life. But dare I go after what my body so desperately craved?

He kept prowling forward and I backed up, until my legs buckled against the bed and I landed on my ass on the mattress.

He kept advancing over me and I shuffled up onto the bed.

He slid right over the top of me and I found myself staring up at the hottest man to ever rise above me.

NINE

Claire

He didn't kiss me though, as I had expected. Instead, he stared down at me, a muscle tightening and ticking in his jaw as though he fought our attraction with every breath he took.

That gave me the strangest sense of power, knowing he wanted me that much and yet would fight to give me the choice.

"Aren't you going to kiss me?" I managed to ask, though my chest was tight with expectation and I was literally squirming on the bed from the ache between my thighs.

He frowned a little, lines forming between his eyebrows. "You said I was the scariest of all."

I wanted to laugh. I wanted to run. But more than anything I wanted to grab him and pull him down on top of me, just to feel the sheer weight of his body on mine.

"You are," I admitted, and he began to move away, retreating from the bed, disappointment etched on his face.

I grabbed his arms and held him still. I didn't want him to go anywhere. "You didn't let me finish."

He slowly moved back above me, so he could look straight into my eyes once again.

"What else is there, Claire?"

I reached up and ran my hands slowly over his arms, the huge muscles bulging and flexing beneath my fingers.

I could feel the animal attraction between us as though it were a solid object. It burned and flickered like a flame, but not intense enough to knock me out again. *Thank God.* It was more muted now, but somehow stronger, because I was awake and could experience the full effect.

"You're scary because you're so strong. You could tear me apart with these muscles... couldn't you, Dexter?"

He clenched his jaw. "I'd never hurt you."

I arched my back, unable to stay away from him. I wanted to be naked, to feel him against my flesh.

God, I am such a wanton at the moment!

What have these men done to me?

"I know... but can't you see how scary that is for me? To know you could hurt me, yet needing to trust you to protect me instead."

Dexter groaned and dropped his weight down on top of mine.

My legs opened of their own accord and he settled between my thighs like it was the most natural thing in the world.

Then, suddenly, he flipped us and I was on top, looking down on the massive man.

"You have all the power, Claire. As my mate, a woman I've waited my whole life for, I'd die to keep you safe."

I sucked in a breath. The intensity of what he was saying was truly mind-blowing.

In my world, men didn't say such things, especially to women they'd just met.

I pushed the fear from my mind and slipped my hands beneath Dexter's tank top. His skin sizzled beneath my palms and I gasped at the way my core melted, arousal weaving through every cell of my body.

I stroked along his rock-hard abs, finding his erect nipples with my fingertips. Torturing both of us until all I could feel was an insatiable need to have him fill me.

And what was stopping me?

I hadn't been with anyone in months. More than months. It felt like forever. And I had three gorgeous men willing to fulfil every fantasy I'd ever had.

What was I doing... trying to run away from them?

I only had two days to decide whether to stay or go. What was I waiting for?

I lowered my body down on top of him and pressed my lips to Dexter's mouth.

He groaned against me and flipped us so he was once again on top.

I wanted to cry out with glee at how right it felt to have my arms and legs wrapped around Dexter's body, to have his mouth on mine.

My mind was whirling with pleasure, my body singing in rapture.

I pulled at his top, needing to get closer.

He rolled to the side and threw the shirt across the room.

I sat up and lifted my arms. My scrubs and old bra ended up on the floor beside me.

In the back of my mind, I knew I wanted Taylor and Jay here

too. I missed them in a strange way. But I was too desperate. Something innate was driving me to bond with Dexter first. Was it the Alpha thing they'd all talked about?

I didn't really know, and I didn't care at this point in time.

Dexter tugged at my shoes and my pants, then my underwear was gone too, in a flurry of moaning and laughing and kissing.

His jeans disappeared like they'd never been there, and suddenly he was back on top of me.

I would have liked to take my time exploring him, gazing at the wonder of his body. But my need was too great. I could read equal desire in his hungry gaze as he stared down at me, and I knew we wouldn't be taking our time.

I gripped his shoulders, unwilling to let him go for a moment.

I ground my pelvis against his and he leaned back a little, putting space between us so he could test my arousal with his fingers.

I gasped and he groaned as he rubbed around my swollen clit with his fingers, spreading my wetness and then sliding a single digit into my aching core.

I cried out and shuddered at the invasion.

I needed so much more than just one finger. I ached so badly for his solid hard flesh. I needed him properly seated inside me.

"You're very wet." His tone was full of wonder, and perhaps surprise.

"I am. Please..." I couldn't say anything else coherent, so I pulled at his arms to get him back on top of me again. Close, like I needed.

Dexter slid down, the head of his cock lining up at my entrance.

I could feel the rigid flesh butting against my entrance.

And then he was taking me, sliding in to the hilt. I cried out, gasping at his thickness. The length. The strange pain and possession I felt pulsing through me as we finally connected in this way.

I'd never felt anything like it. So perfect. So right. "Oh my God," I whispered, digging my nails into his arms and arching my back, trying to get comfortable enough to take all of him.

"Fuck... you're so tight." So was his voice. He sounded as if he were holding onto control by his fingertips.

I nodded. I knew I would be.

He waited and I panted, struggling to get comfortable around the invasion.

Then the throbbing began again, the need and the want building in me.

"Please," I repeated again, digging my teeth into the top of his shoulder and clenching hard with my internal muscles around him.

He groaned loudly, the animalistic noise vibrating right through to my core.

He pulled almost all the way out, then thrust back in. I cried out at the amazing sensation and wound my legs around his waist. Wanting more.

He did it again and again, torturing us both with the too-slow speed. But then he began to move faster and harder.

My cries became louder as he thrust into my needy body and I had no control over them. I heard them from a distance, like it wasn't even me making those crazy sounds.

I was a bundle of energy, of screaming nerve endings and lust.

The tension in my belly was building higher and tighter and as I began to climax, I called out to him, wanting to bring him with me over the edge.

"Oh... *Dex!*"

He slammed his cock into me again and again, the wooden

headboard banging against the wall until I cried out in the ulti-mate pleasure.

My orgasm swept me up and for several moments, I didn't exist. I was floating beyond the plane of existence... and then I was falling back into my body, which was screaming and shuddering and rippling around Dexter's thick cock.

He fell on me, grabbing my ass in both hands and burying himself deeply inside me one last time.

Then he began to come.

Torrents of heat pulsed into my body and I cried out as another, smaller orgasm hit me, squeezing in time with Dexter's squirting cock.

And then it was over and we both lay panting, gripping each other in the aftermath of what had to be the hottest session I'd ever experienced.

Dexter rolled us until he was on his back and I was laying on his chest, struggling to catch my breath and loving the sound of his racing heart beneath my ear.

I looked over my shoulder, half expecting to see Jay or Taylor there in the doorway, watching us. But there was no one except Dex and me in the room.

However, there was still a feeling of their absence. Dex was amazing, but I wanted Taylor and Jay there, too.

"You are incredible," Dexter groaned out, kissing the top of my head.

I laughed at the unfamiliar compliment. What else could I do? I'd been told previously I was boring in bed. I had never expected to hear any man say I was incredible, especially when it came to sex.

"Um... thanks. But you're the incredible one. Is that the mating thing you were talking about?"

He rubbed my back, his hand moving up and down my spine in a soothing rhythm I could get very used to.

"It's the start of it. Yes. But there's so much more to it than that. Sleep, beautiful."

"Oh... I'll just rest for a bit."

I didn't mean to fall asleep, and normally I never would.

Not after sex.

But the sense of peace and safety I felt when I was lying in Dexter's arms, was beautiful, and I didn't stop myself as my body relaxed against the pillows.

Taylor

The banging and screaming and noises of vigorous sex coming from Dexter's room had finally stopped, but the anger in my gut continued to stew.

"He's got her in his bed, upstairs. He's taken her, already, before us."

"Yeah, so?" Jay called from the kitchen. "He is the Alpha. It's how it should be."

Jay might have been right, in a sense, but I couldn't stay still. My feet shuffled and shifted, unable to stay still, and my heart raced like I'd been running through the woods.

"So... should we go up there? Should we join them?"

Jay and I looked at each other, considering my suggestion. Should we? Then it was too late. I heard a door open, then close, and Dexter's heavy tread on the stairs.

I turned and leaned against the kitchen counter, feigning

nonchalance. It wouldn't help anyone if Dex knew how jealous I was that he'd gotten to Claire first.

Dexter bounced down the bottom two stairs, his jeans hanging off his hips, the buttons haphazardly done up.

His smile was lazy, his other clothes were all missing, and I was pretty sure I could spy bite marks on his shoulder.

Bite marks!

I crossed my arms over my chest and struggled against the swirl of emotions whittling away at my gut. I could not be jealous of a member of my own pack. I couldn't. Especially not the Alpha. We'd never survive sharing a mate if this was how it felt every time Claire had sex with one of the other two.

Especially when I'd been the one to point out how many bene-fits this would bring for all of us, if we decided to embrace her as our mate for the whole mini-pack.

But it was a losing battle inside my own mind.

"How was she?" I bit out, unable to control myself. My tone was vile—even I could hear that—and Dexter gave me a reproving look.

"What's up with you?"

I uncrossed my arms and began to pace the kitchen. Back and forth. Vibrating with rage. How could he ask that? How could he *not* know... "I don't know. I feel... fuck... I don't know. Restless, angry. Like I want to punch something, or run."

I was full of testosterone. And I damn sure needed either a fight, or a good fuck.

Dexter laughed, and I nearly jumped over the countertop and launched myself at him. In that moment, I was prouder of my self-control than I've ever been in my life.

"That's just because you haven't mated with her yet," Dex said. "When she wakes up, go get her. She was looking for you and Jay during our session. I could sense it."

She was? His words calmed me, a tiny bit, at least.

"You felt like this earlier too?"

Dexter nodded as he moved across the kitchen and pulled out a plate of leftovers from the fridge.

"Oh, yeah. I was ready to rip Jay's head off for kissing her first, but now I feel... I don't know... happy. Settled. Whereas before, I thought my wolf might jump forth and shift without permission."

"That's exactly how I feel!"

He was telling me that relief was in sight? I glanced at the stairs. How long would it take until she woke up? And once she did, could I even guarantee that she'd still want me? Maybe Dexter had given her everything she needed, and the spark of attraction between her and me would be gone.

My teeth clenched at the thought. No. I wouldn't consider that option. I couldn't bear it, if that were the case.

"So, is this how we're gonna do things? Have her one at a time?" Jay asked, and we both turned to look at him.

"Ah... I suppose. Why?" I glanced at Dexter, considering what he'd said a minute or two earlier. *She was looking for you and Jay.* Then he shrugged. This was new to all of us.

Jay pulled more groceries from the refrigerator and began chopping fruit. "I don't know. I kinda thought that working on her together would be fun."

I caught Dexter's surprised expression and grinned at him. Our Omega wanted to work Claire's body *with* us?

I'd always thought Jay's testosterone was lacking. Clearly not. Obviously, he had simply needed the presence of his mate to bring out that aspect in him.

"Well, let's see what she says when she wakes up. Because no matter what, we need to get to know her individually, I think. We're still separate people."

One pack, yes.

But we were all very different, and Claire needed to know what she was getting herself into, one at a time, instead of as a package deal.

"I made a deal with Claire to get her to stay," Jay said suddenly, and we turned toward him.

"What did you offer her?" I asked, dread tingling on the ends of my nerves.

Jay bit his lip, a sure sign he'd done something wrong. "I told her that we'd drive her home again if she wanted us to."

"You what?" Dexter and I practically yelled at him.

Jay backed away, his hands held up in a sign of peace. "It was all I could think of. What else was I going to say when she was so afraid? And look what's happened already... Dexter mated with her."

I ran a hand through my hair, my arm vibrating with anger. "You told her she could *leave*?"

I wanted to wring his neck.

"I told her to stay for two days so that we had time to *convince* her to stay. She's giving us a chance, and that's thanks to me."

Jay glared at me and I glared back, and that's when I heard a soft sigh and tentative footsteps coming down the stairs.

"We'll deal with this later," I hissed at Jay, and turned around to see Claire gingerly stepping down the last few steps.

She'd put her scrubs back on but they were in pretty bad shape.

"Um... I was going to have a nap, but thought I'd ask if I can have a quick shower first?"

Her eyes were half asleep and there was a lack of tension in her body that I hadn't even realized was there initially.

"You look really relaxed," I couldn't help saying, even though the words came out of me begrudgingly, and the heat of a blush spread straight up her face.

"Oh... well..."

I could see by her expression she wanted to say more, but we didn't know each other well enough yet. And I needed to change that, but I wasn't sure how to start. Grabbing her and dragging her up to my bedroom so I could mate with her, too, didn't seem like the right way to woo her.

Maybe Jay was right, and we did need more time.

"Oh, sorry! I'll show you where the shower is and then if you're up for it, we can go for a walk or something, if you want. I can show you more of the town."

Claire nodded and grabbed the clothes off the couch before following me into the main downstairs bathroom.

"Here you go." I pointed to the stack of clean towels on a shelf in the bathroom, and then backed out to leave her alone.

She retreated quickly, shutting the door behind her.

I returned to the kitchen, feeling even more needy than I had before. Now all I could imagine was Claire's naked body under the cascading shower water. I felt like I was about to burst out of my skin.

Dexter laughed, as if sensing my frustration, and slapped me on the back. "Way to make her feel comfortable."

It was too much. I wanted to punch him in the face and he must have seen it, because he backed away quickly.

"Well, I'd better get over to work for a while, since I feel like I could seriously lift a building and... you look like you want to demolish one. Good luck, Taylor."

Dexter headed upstairs, presumably to grab some clothes, and I sat down with a plate of food in front of me and shoveled in as much as I could.

The feelings of anger and need inside me were building to epic proportions, and I wasn't sure how to settle them.

Claire emerged from the bathroom a few minutes later, her pretty face flushed pink from the hot water, dressed in some worn jeans and a white t-shirt.

"You look gorgeous," I managed, through my thick tongue. She looked good enough to eat. Literally.

"You hungry?" Jay asked her, and pushed a sandwich on a plate across the bench.

She pulled up a stool and sat. "Yeah, a bit. Thanks."

She tucked into the meal and Jay put everything else away, his movements sharp and jerky in a way they hadn't been before.

When he walked into his room and shut the door, I couldn't help but feel sorry for the guy. He needed to wait until I'd mated with her, and then it would be his turn. If I were him, I wouldn't want to wait, and he was obviously struggling as much as me.

"Do you want to check out the town?" I asked Claire. "Or is there anything else you'd like to do today?"

I could see her swaying on her feet. "Um... actually I'd love a proper nap, if there's somewhere I can sleep? I was at the end of a sixteen-hour shift this morning and I'm feeling lethargic."

A good orgasm will do that to you.

I looked toward Jay's room, where the door was firmly shut.

"Well... Jay is using his room, and I'm gonna assume Dexter's room is a mess, so you can sleep in my bed if you want, but I've gotta warn you, it's pretty male. Nothing too friendly and frilly."

She laughed. "Have you seen Dexter's room? It can't be worse than that."

I shrugged and pointed to the stairs.

In some ways it probably *was* worse than Dexter's room. Not warm or masculine, it was hot and modern.

She took to the stairs in front of me and I watched her ass swing as she walked.

Fuck.

Shouldn't have done that. I looked away, trying to control my lustful thoughts.

Now my cock was swelling and I wanted to knock her to the ground and mount her right there in the hallway.

I forced myself to slow my steps and watched her walk ahead. I gulped in deep breaths of the air around me, trying in vain to slow the beating of my heart. My hands clenched at my sides as I struggled with my own base instincts.

This was *insane*.

If I were a true animal, this had to be what it felt like to be around a female in heat.

When she turned back with a query on her face, I gulped and pointed ahead. "That's it, first door after the bathroom, on your left."

She turned into my bedroom and I could hear her gasp from where I stood.

It didn't scare me—instead that gasp made me ache for her even more. Ache to hear those sounds in my ear as she rode my cock.

"I told you," I said as I walked into my room behind her. "It's pretty different to Dexter's space."

My room was red and black. Harsh and dynamic colors, with steel furniture and hard edges.

"I love it. It's very... sexy." She moved over to the curtains and drew them shut.

Darkness enveloped us and she began to undress.

I could hear movement in the dark and my chest began to tighten and ache. I needed to get out of here, before I lost control completely.

"I'll let you sleep."

I turned to move away and heard her deep sigh.

It stopped me. I wasn't sure how I knew, but I could sense she wanted to say something.

"Is something wrong, Claire?" I asked, turning to face her slowly.

"I don't know how to do this. I'm so awkward."

Despite the desire raging through me, I laughed. "You are the opposite of awkward. You're sexy, sensual and beautiful. Not awkward at all. If anything, I'm the one feeling awkward right now."

I couldn't see the smile on her face in the darkness, but I hoped it was there. I wanted to make her happy.

"Okay..." She pulled back the covers and climbed in, but there was something else she wanted to say. I could feel it.

"Whatever it is, Claire, you can tell me."

Did she want to mate with Dexter alone, and not have anything to do with us? That would be my worst nightmare come true, but what else would make her hesitate like that? She must be able to sense how much I wanted her. And if she didn't want me in return...

"Would you stay with me for a while? Just, you know... to cuddle."

Hell, yes. "Of course, I will."

I was out of my clothes and under the covers in seconds.

I lay on my back on the pillows and Claire crawled over to me, laying her head on my shoulder and her hand over my racing heart.

My wolf was going crazy inside me.

I had no idea how I was going to lay here and let her sleep, but I had to. If she wanted to cuddle, then she'd get a cuddle.

I should be grateful she wanted me at all, even for a cuddle, after being with Dexter. The Alpha, after all, did have the best traits of a pack mate.

Her hand began to stroke my chest in a soothing, soft way.

"Are you naked?" she asked suddenly.

"Um... yeah. I sleep naked."

This was normal behavior for me. We didn't even bother with underwear. What was the point when you were shifting every other day?

"Oh... okay..."

She cuddled in closer and her heat began to envelop me. A scent I'd never before smelt caught my nose.

Was it Dexter's seed? No... she'd had a shower. Then what was it?

I inhaled again. My cock filled with blood. *Oh, damn.* That was desire I smelt. *Her* desire. She wanted me.

"Taylor?" Claire's voice was soft, but I knew she could feel the blanket shifting as my cock rose.

"I'm sorry. I have no control over that whatsoever."

"Oh... it's not a bad thing... I just wasn't sure... after Dexter... if you wanted me or not."

"Wanted you? Are you kidding me?"

I grabbed her hand and pushed it down my body, letting her feel my hard-on.

"This doesn't lie, sweetheart."

She gasped as her hand touched my flesh, then she wrapped her palm around the shaft and I let my hand drop away.

She wasn't moving and my cock throbbed with blood. It was getting thicker and harder by the minute.

"Um... Can I...?"

"Sweetheart, you can do anything you want." My voice was gruff with need.

She lowered her head and wet heat engulfed the head of my shaft as her mouth took me in.

"Holy shit." I bucked my hips up, unable to stop the reaction, shoving myself deep into Claire's mouth.

She moaned, but didn't stop, sucking and moving her sweet lips and tongue up and down my cock.

I clenched the sheets either side of me, not wanting to grab her head and force her down on me.

But, God did I want to.

She went up on her knees next to me, and in that position she could take more into her mouth, and the smell of her arousal hit me like a truck.

Fuck this.

I twisted and grabbed her, lifting her up and placing her over my face, her legs on either side of my head and her pussy over my mouth.

"What are you..." she began to ask.

I pushed her underwear to the side and delved my tongue straight into her pussy.

She gasped and moaned, throwing her head back and forcing her body back onto my face.

I held her thighs wide and tongue fucked her over and over again, licking her clit and tasting her juices as they ran into my mouth.

"Taylor... Taylor!" Her voice was breathless, the sound of my name on her tongue like heaven in my ears.

"Come here." I growled out, pushing back the blankets and twisting her around so she was straddling me properly this time. "Take me in, beautiful."

Claire moved her underwear to the side and I grabbed my shaft, holding it up so she could ride it like a pole.

She slid up, found the head of my cock and impaled herself in one, smooth motion.

"Oh... fuck!" I wanted to yell at the perfect feel of her around me, but swallowed the sound down and let out a choked groan instead.

I'd never felt anything like it, and my wolf howled inside my mind at the completion of finally mating with *the one*.

Claire groaned and gasped as she slid up and down on me, her pussy rippling and gripping me with each descent.

I grabbed her hips, planted my feet onto the mattress and thrust up, fucking her as hard as I dared.

She moaned louder and held tight to my arms, bucking like a wild cowgirl atop a bucking bronco.

The pressure was building in my balls, the tightness in my gut growing as my pleasure soared.

"Taylor... Taylor... I'm... I'm going to..." Claire gasped and arched her back.

Her pussy began to wring me tightly, her rigid body obviously on the brink of climax.

I gave her everything I had, screaming out her name as my own orgasm swept me up, and pumped my seed deep into her core.

Claire cried out to me, her nails digging into my arms as she squeezed my cock tight and came all over me.

I held her to me, loving every last tremor that ran through her body as we found perfect bliss together.

My wolf finally calmed, my appetite quieted, and for the first time since we'd met Claire, I could think clearly.

Damn.

This must be what Dexter was talking about.

Claire had collapsed on top of me and seemed to have fallen

asleep. Her breathing was slow and quiet and although I didn't want to wake her up, energy was leaping in my blood.

I couldn't lay down and stay still for the hours she might need to sleep.

I slowly rolled and shuffled her onto a pillow beside me. She half-woke a little but didn't speak, so I tucked her up in the duvet and slowly crept away.

I felt amazing!

As I stretched, I could feel new muscle growth, the sinew and tissues tighter and ready for anything coming our way.

Wow. Our parents had never said anything about this benefit when it came to mating.

I grabbed my clothes and crept out of the room, closing the door behind me so that Claire could sleep without being interrupted.

I didn't know much about the life of a physician, but she was obviously exhausted.

I pulled on my jeans as I walked down the hall and made my way down the stairs. Jay was sitting on the couch, determinedly looking at his phone and not me.

"Do I even want to know how it went?" he asked, not bothering to look up. "Wait, never mind. I heard it."

I grinned, happiness winging through my heart in a way I didn't understand.

"I'm heading out to work. See you for dinner."

I walked toward the front door and Jay called out. "What do you mean you're going to work? You seriously want to leave me here with her, after the two of you..."

I looked back at him, reading on his face the same discomfort that I'd been feeling earlier.

"Of course. You've gotta bond with her too, yeah? If I leave now, that'll give you some time alone to sort it out with her."

He nodded stiffly, and I wanted to tell him that relief was around the corner, if Claire was up for three in a day. That's probably why Dexter kept grinning at me earlier. He knew what was coming, and I had the feeling Jay would soon find out, too. But I didn't say anything further at this point. He wouldn't believe me, anyway.

Let him find out for himself.

I left the house whistling, the sun shining on my face. I closed my eyes for a few seconds and just breathed in the fresh air.

Life was sweet, and with our fated mate in our lives, it would only get sweeter.

Jay

What the hell was I going to do during the hours between now and dinner?

I glanced at the clock on the wall and relief swept through my body.

Okay... so that wasn't too bad. It was only three hours until Dexter and Taylor returned. Maybe Claire would sleep the whole time? And then what? I'd have to wait until tomorrow to hold her, kiss her. Love her the way Dexter and Taylor already had.

I tore at my hair on either side of my head, pulling hard to generate the pain I needed to push at the tension inside my body. I needed to shift and run. I needed... something.

The others now seemed so relaxed and carefree, while I wanted to pick up the fridge and throw it through the kitchen window. No prizes for guessing why.

My arms shook with the strain of holding in the need. And I couldn't even fully explain what it was, or why it was there.

I let loose a growl, my throat vibrating with the tension.

May as well get busy, and do something constructive with all this nervous energy and tension.

I put dinner on, cleaned the house and worked out in our home gym, pushing way past my normal barriers and lifting weights I'd never even contemplated before.

By the time the Dex and Taylor came home, I was covered in sweat and the whole house smelled like roasting lamb.

"Whoa, you went all out for Claire, huh?" Dexter said as he walked in the door, a big smile on his stupidly happy face.

I didn't know how to deal with all that happiness. "I need a shower," I said gruffly. "You guys dish up and I'll go check on her."

"Oh, she didn't wake up while we were gone?" Taylor asked, and shot a knowing look at Dex.

Great. Now the two of them would probably begin to pity me.

I shook my head and trotted up the stairs, deciding to check on Claire before the shower. As I left, I struggled to even look at my pack mates while they grinned at each other and then at me, like hyenas.

Obviously, mating with Claire had made them feel great. Sex would do that, I supposed. But this was different somehow. They seemed... really happy. More so than a simple act of sex would usually provide.

I trudged up the stairs and walked past Dexter's room.

The stench of sex was still there and I couldn't help but groan with frustration and longing as I walked toward Taylor's room.

This one would be even worse, I was sure. Fresher.

I knocked gently. "Claire?"

"Jay?"

I sighed. Yeah, I was going in. I cracked the door open a little and stuck my head in, the scent of sex pungent and hot as flames in my nostrils. It was like a slap in the face, to know what had just gone on in here, and without any involvement by me.

I sucked in a shallow breath and tried to speak while not breathing any deeper. "Dinner's ready whenever you are. I made roast lamb, if you like it?"

"Oh... great. I love roast, thank you. I won't be long."

I began to pull away. "Take your time. I'm gonna go have a shower. Meet you downstairs, okay?"

"Okay."

Her voice was quiet and as I shut the door, my heart ached.

Did she feel this? The need that actually hurt when it wasn't returned.

Probably not. She'd had Dexter and Taylor already today. Why would she feel the same needs I did?

It would be impossible.

I walked past the upstairs bathroom and paused in the hallway.

Maybe it was better to wash up here?

My shower, the one downstairs, would smell of Claire. She'd probably used my soap, one of my clean towels... I shuddered to think of the sensual torment such a thing would be like, to have a shower and be surrounded by her scent.

I stomped into the upstairs bathroom and shut the door. I needed a good, cold dunking more than anything else. I also stunk to high heaven, so a bloody good scrub was in order.

I flicked on the shower, stripped out of my clothes and jumped beneath the icy needles.

I yelped a bit when the water first hit my steaming skin, but sucked it up and dove beneath the fray. The cold water pummeled down on my head and I closed my eyes, splaying both hands onto the cold tiles and letting the water run down my back.

My heated skin began to shiver, and the frantic need within my muscles started to abate. A little.

Thank God for that.

I stood up straighter and turned the hot on, balancing out the temperature.

Slowly, the heat seeped into my bones and my muscles relaxed more fully. The steam began to rise around me and I took some deep, calming breaths.

That's better.

I turned my back on the head and grabbed the shampoo, pouring some of the liquid into my hands and scrubbing my hair with it.

My good stuff was downstairs, but this would have to do.

Taylor and Dexter would wash in the creek if I didn't insist on having soap and shampoo and showers in the house.

I was probably better suited to the human world than they were—and speaking of which...

The door to the bathroom slid open and a pair of dainty feet poked out beneath the steam.

Damn. I hadn't turned on the fan.

"Jay?" Claire's voice echoed in the small, tiled room.

My heart jumped and I couldn't stop the grin that spread across my face. Just hearing her speak made happiness pound through my body.

"Hey, beautiful. Do you need something?"

Please say me.

Maybe the other guys hadn't bothered to get her anything to eat? What was she doing in here?

"Um..."

She wasn't moving and she wasn't talking other than that first mumbled 'um'. I really didn't read women's minds, especially those I wasn't related to. I wanted desperately for her to want *me*, but for all I knew, she was about to ask for a ride home.

"If you give me a couple of minutes, I'll get out and help you."

With whatever it is you need.

"No! I actually.... um... could I join you, do you think?"

Could she join me? Hell, yes! "Of course, you can, but, ah..." How did I tell her that unless she wanted to get fucked again, she better stay away from me?

I didn't really get a chance to tell her anything of the sort.

She walked through the cloud of heat and moved toward me, joining me in the huge shower before I could even open my mouth and get out the words.

Naked. She was naked.

When had she gotten undressed? And why?

"Ah..." I didn't know where to look, without causing offence, but at the same time, I couldn't keep my greedy eyes off her beautiful curves.

Claire naked was even more delicious than I'd imagined.

She stood facing me and leaned back beneath the spray, wetting her hair and tipping her head back.

She lifted her arms to run her hands through her hair, her perfect breasts jutting up at me, the pink nipples erect and begging to be kissed.

I had about two seconds before I lost control, so I'd better get consent before my wolf took over.

"Claire, I don't know how to say this nicely, so I'm just gonna say it. I'm dying to mate with you and I'm afraid that if you don't leave this shower cubicle right now, I'm not going to have any chance of controlling myself with you."

Normally, this would be the furthest thing from the truth. I'd stopped myself at every level of sex with a woman, even after she'd come on me and I was balls deep inside of her. She'd asked me to stop, and I had.

That level of control was beyond me when it came to Claire, especially today, when I could scent my pack mates on her and her heat was causing a chemical reaction inside me.

"I don't want you to... fight that," she said. Her voice was husky in the steam. "I want you, too."

That was all she had to say and I was charging forward, picking her up and pushing her against the cool tiles.

"Oh my God. I need you, Jay. As much as the other two."

She bit into my shoulder and wrapped her legs around my waist.

I growled, deep in my chest, and supported her beneath the buttocks with my hands.

She needed me? Thank the gods for that!

I grabbed her ass more firmly, and lined her pussy up with my cock. I was so primed I had no hope of going slow today.

"Are you ready?" I managed, and she nodded quickly, clinging to my shoulders.

I tilted her pelvis with my hands and thrust up into her in one long, smooth movement.

"Oh my," she groaned out as her pussy swallowed me up and gripped me hard.

She was so wet, so aroused, and yet so tight. The perfect combination, and I growled as my shifter and human sides both recognized the rightness of our connection.

I had to squeeze my eyes shut and think of anything else but Claire, in order to gain some control.

I was going to blow right in that moment if I didn't.

What could I focus on? The cold floor beneath my feet... the tiles in the bathroom...

"Jay..." she whispered, and I was lost.

Nope. There was going to be no finesse today. No slow build.

This was going to be a hard, fast race to completion and possession.

I hoisted her further up the wall and her face lifted to look at me. I fastened my mouth to her lips, tasting her kiss as I began to ride her body.

I pumped into her hard and fast, slamming her into the wall and swallowing her moans as we kissed.

The water beat down on us and Claire broke off from our kiss to scream and cry out into the air.

"Yes. Yes. Yes, Jay! Harder!" she yelled, and I gave her all I could.

She began to come on me, her pussy rippling around my cock, tightening like a wound-up spring.

I was going to join her soon enough.

As she began to arch and stiffen, I thrust into her as deeply as I could, my balls hard against her ass as she started to orgasm.

Her pussy sucked on me like the perfect mouth, milking my cock and calling for my sperm.

I let all control go.

The heat that had tingled at the back of my legs erupted into a brush fire up my back and I allowed it to spread. My cock pulsed inside her, spouting my seed and giving her everything I had to give.

She shuddered in my arms, laying kisses on my neck and face.

I turned to her and kissed her deeply, slipping my tongue inside her mouth until the last of the tremors had stopped.

Then she pulled back and smiled up at me. "I can't believe how good that was."

I let her untangle her legs and slide to the floor.

She stumbled and I wrapped an arm around her, pulling her beneath the water and turning up the heat once again.

"Well, that was unexpected," I managed, and searched my body for any remnants of the raging testosterone that had been pumping in me all day.

She laughed and washed herself again and I couldn't stop a huge smile from spreading across my face.

It was gone.

The anger. The unsettled feeling I'd had driving my actions and busy activity around the house all day had disappeared. My shifter was happily curled up in a quiet corner deep inside me, sleeping the sleep of the satisfied.

This woman was indeed our mate, and it seemed that she had a magic pussy.

TWELVE

Claire

I turned away from Jay to hide my hot cheeks and let the shower water course down over my shoulders and back.

What had I become?

I'd had sex with three different men in one day, when it had taken me a decade to sleep with three different men in the past.

What was happening to me?

I grabbed the soap and washed my body for the third time today, my breasts and the area between my legs tender, and my thighs trembling and sore.

"Thank you, beautiful." Jay turned me back to face him, and pressed another kiss to my lips. Then he stepped out of the shower, drying his magnificent body with a huge gray towel.

"Can I ask you a question? It'll probably sound strange," I queried, though a laugh trembled on my lips, a post-orgasm high making my head spin.

At this rate, I wouldn't be able to think after a day or two.

Perhaps that was their plan? To make me so weak with sexual satisfaction, I'd never be able to leave, because my brain would be mush and all I'd want would be more of this. More of them. All three of them.

I shook my head, filing the idea away to think about later, because at the moment, my body was telling me it might even be worth it to throw away my career.

I frowned, annoyed at where my thoughts were taking me. To throw away my career for the sake of sex, after twelve years of schooling that had led me into a profession that I loved, seemed ludicrous. And yet, hundred-hour work weeks and no sleep, versus being loved and cherished by three strong men... I almost let out one of those growls the guys threw around so easily. Why was I even thinking along those lines?

"Yeah, of course, ask me anything," Jay responded, wrapping the towel around his lean waist and looking at me expectantly.

Seriously, if I'd had a camera in my hand, I'd be click-clicking. Jay's eyes were dark and intense, his hair was wet and falling perfectly over his face.

And his body... *oh my God.* "How come you all have perfect bodies? Is that a wolf thing, or something else?"

Jay laughed and ran a hand through his hair, the movement making his abs ripple and his shoulder muscles flex. "Ah, yeah, kinda. We have extremely fast metabolisms, and we run a lot, of course. Not to mention the fact we're all tradies of some sort. Plumbers, electricians and builders. Physical jobs that keep us fit. We can pretty much do everything."

I stared at him and couldn't believe my eyes. Jay was the smallest of the three men, by far, and yet the strength behind his build was impressive.

After all, he'd just given me the hottest shower sex of my life, holding me up against the wall with ease.

No guy had ever been able to hold my weight for a few seconds, let alone for a vigorous session like that.

"Well, you're distracting me." I waved my hands at him. "I'll be down in a few minutes."

"Okay. I'll give you some time alone. But don't forget, dinner is downstairs when you're ready." Jay left with a soft smile on his face and I could finally breathe and think.

There was something pretty magical about these men, and it wasn't just the fact that they could turn into wolves. It was how I felt when I was around them.

Hornier than I'd ever been in my life, that was for damn sure.

Each time I went to bed with one of them today, I'd felt completely satisfied for several minutes afterwards, and then the ravenous hunger was back.

I searched my feelings and ran a hand between my thighs.

"Oh, thank God."

The insatiable need had subsided—finally.

It had grown all day, from the moment I woke up here in this strange house, and with each sexual encounter the pull had gotten stronger, to the point that I really had no idea how to satisfy the hunger in my body.

But now, it had settled. Calmed. I felt like I might actually be able to think now.

But why? Was it because I'd finally had sex with all three of them?

Was it possible that the strange mating connection thing they talked about might actually be true? Because I knew one thing. I wanted all of them. More than I'd ever wanted any one man before, I wanted all three of these guys, with a desire so strong I had never felt anything like it.

They were so different, so individually beautiful. And sexy... damn, were they sexy!

I'd convinced myself after my last failed relationship that the traditional path was *not* for me. There would be no doting husband, or multitude of babies for me. I'd have my work... my patients... my...

"Holy shit!"

I turned the water off and began scrubbing myself with a nearby towel.

Babies!

I hadn't even thought about contraception throughout the day. How crazy was that?

What sort of woman let three men come inside of her without a second thought?

A nymphomaniac for one, and a slut for another, said the shaming voice in my head.

"Oh, shut up."

I tried not to let the voice win and increase the panic that was already fluttering in my mind.

I counted on my fingers. My period had been two weeks ago, which meant I was probably on day sixteen of my cycle.

I should be fine. There was never a perfect science to conception, nor a completely safe time, but it *should* be okay.

I'd been on and off the pill for almost fifteen years now, though I wasn't on it at the moment. And the chance of ovulating at all after so many years of artificial hormones, let alone getting pregnant in one month at thirty-two, was... slim.

Not nil. Slim.

My medical brain was screaming at me about the repercussions of such rash actions, while my modern female brain chided me for being so reckless.

"Oh, fuck, off!" I practically yelled at myself in the mirror.

I'd never done a reckless thing in my life. Not once. I'd never taken drugs, never had a one-night stand, never taken a chance on anyone, or anything.

This was different.

I'd met werewolves, for goodness sakes! And then I'd bedded all three of them, in the very same day!

Surely some of the rules could be bent in this situation. Damn it, surely this one time I could even break the bloody rules.

I made my way back to Taylor's room and pulled on the jeans and tank I'd borrowed from Mary.

I was throwing all my pre-conceived ideas out the window. *Screw it.*

I had one more day with them, and I wasn't going to waste it worrying about whether I was doing the right thing or not by following my feelings.

Twenty-four hours until I had to go back to the city and start another fourteen-hour shift in an under-staffed hospital with a supervisor who hated me.

My heart ached at the idea of leaving, and with that strange thought came the realization of how much I was going to miss the three guys when I returned to my old life.

Which was crazy. I barely knew them.

But there was something there, between me and them.

They certainly believed I was meant to be here for them and I owed it to myself, and them, to see where this led. If for nothing more than scientific curiosity, although I knew this was so much more than anything scientific or logic-based.

I made my way down the stairs, noticing for the first time the wooden staircase and the carved details I'd missed when I passed this way last time.

Had they built this house?

All of it? How brilliant was that if they had.

There was general chatter going on in the kitchen, and as I

made my way down and entered the room to find three smiling faces turning my way, my heart sang in recognition of a home I hadn't even known I needed.

"Ah, hi," I managed, my face flaming with heat.

Dexter got up off his stool and came toward me, sweeping me off my feet and twirling me around as though I weighed less than a child.

Which I could guarantee, I didn't.

I was a comfort eater, and it showed in my physique. Or so I'd thought, until I met these three men and they made me feel beautiful and valued, regardless of my weight.

"You hungry, gorgeous? You've barely eaten all day."

"Um..."

"Come, eat."

I had no idea how I felt... other than high on life. But I couldn't really answer that particular question without sounding a bit nuts.

I was ushered to the table to sit down to a plate of roasted lamb, crunchy salted potatoes, salad and fruit. My stomach began to gurgle at the sight of the delicious-looking food.

Maybe I was hungrier than I'd thought.

I began to eat and the men around me, who had already eaten, it seemed, fell into a natural conversation about work and the various people and activities going on in their lives.

I listened absently and looked around the kitchen, the space clean and well used.

Much nicer than my own apartment really, I thought, despite the feminine touches I'd added for color and warmth. After all, I was never home, so why bother keeping it nice all the time?

"So, what do you guys usually do after dinner?"

They all looked at me with sudden heat, the suggestive expression in Dexter's eyes in particular making me glance away.

Okay. It was clear what they wanted to happen, after dinner. And by the curl of anticipation deep down in my belly, I suspected they might get their way. Again.

But that wasn't what I'd meant. "No," I clarified. "I mean, on a normal night."

"Depends," Taylor said, leaning over the table and grabbing a handful of berries. "Sometimes we just watch some TV, other times we go out for a run through the woods. We're up before dawn most days, so we go to bed pretty early compared to humans, I suspect."

I grinned at him. "And you know a lot about humans?"

He shrugged. "Not personally. But I guess just what we see on TV, or when we go into one of the cities, which is pretty rare."

Dexter moved across to me and ran a hand over my back. I looked up at him in query. "What would you like to do, beautiful? There's a pub of sorts nearby, where a lot of the guys hang out, play pool and drink. Would you like to meet more of the pack? Or..."

I shook my head. "Not at the moment. Maybe tomorrow."

The last thing I wanted to do was be around more of those intense stares, especially when there was alcohol involved, and my men would be outnumbered.

My men... what a concept.

"I'd love to see you all shift, if that's what you mean by going for a run."

I wondered if it would blow my mind, actually. Some part of me still didn't believe I was in a paranormal world, even though I'd had plenty of evidence of that, already.

I wanted to see it again. To verify that I hadn't been dreaming the first time.

Because if all of this were true, then the part of me that didn't believe in fated love or sex with multiple people might just be silenced forever.

The men looked at each other and I could see the fear in their eyes. Why were they afraid? Did they think they might accidently hurt me? I couldn't imagine such a scenario, not now that I'd connected with each of them physically, but then, I hadn't seen all of them in their wolf form. Maybe it changed something innate inside them?

"What's wrong?" I glanced between all three of them, waiting. Taylor was the one who eventually spoke up.

"Oh... ah..." He glanced at Jay and Dexter with an uncomfortable look on his face. "We're a bit concerned about how you're going to respond when you see us. We don't want to scare you off."

Oh. They weren't afraid of hurting me. They were afraid I wouldn't like them anymore. I wasn't sure how I was going to feel about it, either, but I could guarantee I wouldn't like them any less.

"Well, if you have a bottle of vodka, a couple of shots couldn't hurt."

"Ah..." That look again.

"Don't tell me you don't drink. Because I've seen beer in your fridge."

"Oh, we do." Taylor said. "Just not much hard liquor. With a pack full of unfulfilled, testosterone-fueled men, having an abundance of hard alcohol on hand isn't a smart move."

"I see." I winced at the thought. Yes, they were probably right.

"Well," I offered, "how about if Mary comes with me, or some of the other older women? Surely, they'll keep me calm, and make sure none of the guys drag me off." I laughed to show I was joking, but no one joined me.

I knew they were worried about the full male pack and, if I

were honest, so was I. These young men had no women with whom to let off steam. It was a rather disconcerting concept, to say the least, and was one of the main reasons I had for not staying here, and wanting to return back home.

Eventually, Dexter nodded. "Mom may be the best plan," he said. "She's pretty relaxed with everything, and you two seemed to hit it off."

He sounded like he was talking to me in words, but I could see he was mostly speaking to himself, trying to reason out the best way to manage this.

Taylor nodded. "My mom wanted to meet Claire too, so how about I go pick her up and meet you guys back here?"

"Sounds like a plan." I clapped my hands and grinned at the guys.

I was high on life and sex and... sperm.

Ew.

God, it was good, though.

I'd never been able to orgasm during penetration, but with these men it seemed almost guaranteed. Their sperm alone seemed magical. I'd had a simultaneous orgasm with them every time.

Maybe that was also a sign that we were meant to be together?

"Hey..." I opened my mouth to ask something about the topic, and realized what I was about to do to myself. If I asked the question that hovered on the tip of my tongue, I was likely going to open a can of worms that I wasn't prepared for, and might lead to the green-eyed monster spewing forth.

Did I really want to know if they made all their lovers come during ejaculation?

I slammed my mouth shut.

No.

No, I did not want to know that.

"What, beautiful?" Jay asked as Dexter and Taylor headed out the front door to fetch their moms.

I thought quickly, trying to come up with an alternative. I couldn't ask the question I had planned to. Honestly, I just couldn't.

"Nothing. Just thinking about the wolf thing. You said you'll be in complete control, yeah?"

He nodded solemnly. "Yeah, always."

"Okay, then let me grab that sweater Mary loaned me and I'll be ready to go."

I stuffed a few more of the delicious berries into my mouth before I left the table.

Mary had let me borrow the softest black wool sweater, and as I pulled it on over my head and arms, I snuggled my face into it.

There was the sweetest smell attached to the wool. Whether it was the washing powder, or Mary herself, there was something that reminded me of Dexter in the scent. And that meant I wasn't taking off this sweater anytime soon. I loved the idea of being surrounded by my big, protective man.

Jay and I moved to the window together and he opened the front door for me, a sweet smile on his face.

"You look happy," I said to him.

He laughed and grabbed me around the waist, squeezing me tightly for a minute before letting me go.

"Of course, I am. I've got you. Life is perfect."

Claire

For the first time since I'd had sex with them all, a tremor of unease ran through me.

I understood what Jay meant, of course. There was a huge part of me that felt the same way. I was happy here with them and knew I could continue to be, if I decided to take up their offer and stay.

If I never went back to my old life, things would be so simple.

But that wasn't me. I wasn't simple. I wasn't easily content. And a part of me knew I'd be fighting all three of them *when and if* I needed to go home tomorrow. The flicker of unease grew larger, but I managed to tamp it down, mostly. I would deal with that tomorrow. Tonight, I was going to witness magic. I was going to see all three of my men shift into another form.

"Looks like Dex is bringing the whole party here," Jay said, his tone dark.

What did that mean?

He grabbed my hand and we went through the front door, down the stairs and walked out onto the road in front of the house.

There was a large group of men and two older women walking toward us. Dexter and Taylor were with them, but they both had grim looks on their faces.

I stepped closer to Jay and he slid his arm around me, holding me tight against his body.

"It's all right, Claire." Then he addressed Dexter. "What are you doing, Dex?" My men stepped out of the group to come closer to Jay and me. I counted six other men, besides my three.

Dexter was shaking his head. "Don't worry, I don't like it any more than you do."

Taylor and Dexter moved around to stand behind me and I relaxed again, feeling safe and warm now that my three men were surrounding me.

God, I could get used to this feeling. It was almost drug-like in its intensity.

Mary stepped closer too, smiling warmly. "Claire, some of the neighboring mini-packs wanted to meet you. I hope you don't mind."

Did I mind meeting six hunks with more muscles than I'd ever seen in my life?

Ah, no. Not really.

"Considering the lack of women in town, I can understand the interest," I murmured to Jay, and then I turned and addressed the strangers. "Hello, I'm Claire."

They all stared at me, but with none of the heat and lust I'd gotten used to seeing in my men's eyes. My tension reduced a notch.

One large man stepped forward, an Alpha I presumed by his bearing.

"I'm Grayson."

He didn't seem to want to come much closer, but I extended my hand anyway.

"An Alpha, I presume?"

He reached out with a sudden grin and I heard my men inhale sharply. Surely, I wasn't going to keel over if I touched this one, too?

"How'd you know?" he asked, and shook my hand in the same way that had occurred a hundred times a day since becoming a doctor.

Nothing happened and I felt the pack at my back breathe a collective sigh of relief. My shoulders relaxed. I was still on my feet. No dizziness whatsoever.

"You're big," I said.

He glanced down in a sort of shy manner that surprised me. A gentle giant, perhaps? "It's nice to meet you, Claire. May I ask you a question?"

"Of course."

Damn, he had beautiful eyes, a nice manner and huge shoulders. And I could appreciate all that, yes, but there was no attraction. No want, need, or craving.

Perhaps I was fully satisfied? I turned to glance at Taylor over my shoulder, and my belly tightened. A smile lifted my lips. Nope. Still there.

I turned back to Grayson, who seemed to be weighing his words.

"Go on," I prompted. "Ask me whatever you want."

I was feeling relaxed and part drunk on sex. I'd tell them anything they wanted at this point in time.

"Can you give us a hint about what to look for with our mate, since it appears we all need to be on the hunt for a human now."

Ah. They wanted their own mates. Of course, they did. I was nothing to them beyond a source of information.

Some more of my internal fears relaxed. These men didn't want me, I just represented what they were looking for.

"Well, for one thing, I wouldn't use the word hunt when you're talking to a potential human mate." I grinned at him to let him know I was half-joking, and he smiled back. "But to be honest, I'm not sure what to tell you. Did Dexter mention the fainting thing?"

Grayson nodded. "Yes. But I was wondering if you had an idea before that. When you first saw them. Something I can look for in my mate, because I've met human women before and no one has ever fainted at my touch."

I assessed the big hunk and made some conclusions—fair or not, I wasn't sure. But I was about to find out.

"Maybe that's because your mate has a brain, like me, and you've been picking up tiny blondes with more boobs than anything else?"

A surprised grin stretched across Grayson's face, a cheeky light entering his eyes.

"They weren't all blonde."

Some of his pack mates laughed and then tension in the whole group began to ease.

"Look, I honestly don't know what to tell you. I'm a doctor who has barely dated in a decade. Maybe your mates are the same? Women who work too much and never get out, not to the places you'd usually go to find a date, anyway."

"Then how am I meant to find her?"

I couldn't believe I was going to say it, but there was no other answer.

"Fate. You have to trust that you'll stumble across her when the time is right. But I wouldn't be avoiding going to town during the day. If you guys can start going in more often, you'll have much a better chance of meeting the right one."

The men looked amongst themselves and nodded in agreement.

"That makes sense. Any other tips?" One of the other guys spoke up, and by his lesser size I'd guess he was one of the Omegas.

"Well, I will tell you that I knew there was something special about Dexter the moment I saw him," I said truthfully. "My heart was pounding and I could barely breathe. I've never had a response like that to any man before and I'm sure your mates will feel the same when they meet you."

They seemed happy enough with my answers, thanking me and heading off. Dexter pulled me into the circle of his arms and kissed the top of my head.

"Thanks for that, Claire."

"Oh, no problem. Happy to help." And I was. Why I was, I had no idea. I didn't belong here, and I certainly didn't know if I was going to stay.

But at the moment, I was going with the flow, and it had felt good to give those other guys hope.

"Let's go to the woods to watch them shift and run," Mary said, holding her hand out to me.

I pushed out of Dexter's embrace and linked arms with his mother, a small amount of fear suddenly weaving through my blood.

"Okay. Sure."

We walked around the back of their house toward what I assumed must be their shifting area. The whole town was cut into the woods in a natural way. Very little clearing had been done for the houses, and if these people were wolves who liked to run, I couldn't imagine a better location for their territory.

Another older woman walked up to us on my other side. She had long brown hair pulled into a ponytail, with streaks of gray lightening her temples.

"Hello Claire. I'm Sue, Taylor's mom." She introduced herself as we walked, shooting me a bright smile. I could see traces of Taylor's features in her face. I smiled back.

"Hi. It's nice to meet you."

We continued walking and my mind balked at the weirdness of the situation. If this was a traditional type of relationship, I'd have three mothers-in-law. How strange would that be?

"Have you seen any of them shift yet?" Sue asked as we settled to sit on a large wooden bench.

"Ah, yes. Jay sh...shifted." If that was the word for it. "He turned into a brown wolf right in the lounge room, which was pretty extraordinary... to put it simply."

Sue laughed. "Well, you're about to get a treat, because an Omega wolf is rather small and timid compared to mine and Mary's sons."

She indicated to the woods, where my three lovers stood about twenty feet away.

They stripped out of their shirts and began unbuttoning their jeans. Were they seriously going to get naked right in front of their moms?

Before I could look away, or voice my discomfort, the men were no more.

"Oh my God."

Instead, there were three huge wolves standing on the men's clothes, in varying sizes and colors.

I stood up, unable to sit. Unable to run away.

I took a few steps closer. I wanted to touch them. Something compelled me forward, as if I couldn't help myself. I stopped before I got too close, but I found that I wasn't afraid at all. I was enchanted by the sight before me.

"Dexter's the big silver one, isn't he?"

"Yes," said Sue from behind me. "And the black one is my Taylor."

They were magnificent as they began to jump and run and play around the trees of the forest.

"They're really beautiful."

And they were. Gone was my fear. In its place was awe and gratitude, and a burst of love.

Yes, *love*. Love for these amazing creatures and the world I'd been introduced into.

I watched my men—no, I corrected myself, my wolves—run for several minutes. There was a freedom in their movement that I couldn't take my eyes away from. I found myself grinning from ear to ear as I watched.

Then, out of the blue, there was a deep and unexpected growl that reverberated from the shadows in the woods, and all play among my wolves stopped. Instantly, they began racing toward me.

I staggered back and the mothers grabbed me.

"You need to get back inside the house. Now, Claire!" Mary's voice was urgent.

My wolves had run to me, only to turn and face the woods, ready to fend off whatever was coming.

Another growl sounded. What the hell was it? Another wolf? Something worse?

My heart began to pound with genuine fright. "Why? What's going on?" I asked breathlessly as Mary and Sue practically dragged me back to the house, up the stairs and in through the back door. My men were still out there. What were they facing?

Mary stared at me, her eyes wide with shock. "The bears are here."

Four words I never thought would accompany the terrifying sound of the ground shaking as what seemed like a dark and furious army charged toward the house.

FOURTEEN

Dexter

The ground shook with the bears' approach. I'd never seen so many in my life, and they were all charging toward us as one.

A wall of fur and fury. But I would not let them through. Not while my mate was in the house behind us.

Was that why they were here? To take my mate from me?

Never!

I bared my teeth and let out a vicious growl, then threw my head back and howled to the sky, calling for support.

We'd need help, and Grayson's crew shouldn't be far.

The bears broke through the woods line on all fours, running at full tilt.

I started toward them, growling and snapping as I assessed the best way to attack. The bears had more weight, but wolves were more agile. I leapt through the air and tore my teeth along the side of the Alpha bear's ribs and flank as I passed him.

He stumbled and fell, and I jumped onto his back, tearing at his throat as I attempted to roll him over.

He lifted a massive paw and swiped, pushing me down, hard. I swiveled, getting out from under his grip, and then jumped back onto all fours, snarling.

More bears ran past us and I wanted to scream in frustration. They were headed straight for my house!

I left the injured Alpha and raced after the bears that had broken away from us.

I reached the slowest one and sunk my teeth into its leg, trying to bring it down. As I did so, a pack of six wolves joined in the fray.

Grayson's pack, and Axel's too. Good. We were going to need them.

I tasted blood as I tore at the bear's flesh and it swiped at my face with a massive paw, tearing at my cheek.

I took a second to glance around, calculating. There had to be a dozen bears.

They'd never attacked us with such numbers before. Why now?

I could see Taylor and Jay out of the corner of my eye, working in unison to attack one of the bears.

It wasn't enough. We needed more reinforcements.

My mother's silver wolf bounded down the back steps of my house, growling and snapping at any bear that came close.

Fear whistled through me. They were trying to get into the house. They were here for Claire.

Should I get her out of the house, shift back to human and drive her to safety, drawing the bears away?

Or should we kill them all?

There were more wolves coming now, piling through the trees. We were outnumbering them two to one.

I raced over to my mother and stood in front of her, baring my teeth at any bears who made it to the stairs of our house.

This was my *home*. My *mate* was in there, and she needed to be protected, at all costs.

Why were they attacking? I needed to understand, but to do that, I needed to shift back to human. Did I dare? I would be vulnerable if I did, but it seemed to be the only way to get them to explain this attack.

The bears and the wolves had been rivals for years, however nothing had ever come out of these useless fights.

I let go of my Alpha wolf, the shifter howling in anger as I released my strongest self.

I ran up the back steps and stood on my porch, naked and angry.

Some of the bears had begun to retreat but there were three still fighting, including the Alpha I'd taken down initially.

"What the fuck are you doing here?" I bellowed out, though my voice was strained and garbled from shifting. "Explain yourselves!"

The wolves fell back to line up with my house, guarding the town.

My pack stayed in wolf form, and rightly so. No one would be stupid enough to shift back, except me.

The Alpha bear began to transform. In his place stood a massive man, with a shaggy black beard and tattoos covering his upper body.

I walked down the two steps to the ground and glared at him across the grass. "What are you doing here?"

"We came to see your mate."

Taylor and Jay growled loudly from the line of wolves, their teeth glistening in the dusk light.

"Who the hell told you we'd found our mate?"

The man's eyebrows rose high. "*Our* mate? She's the mate to your whole pack... well isn't that interesting?"

His tone was nasty and I didn't like the way his eyes shone with malice when he spoke.

"You didn't answer my question," I spoke in a loud, commanding tone, so that everyone could hear our conversation.

"No. And I won't." He was equally commanding. Likely the leader of the whole bear pack. "You wolves should be extinct in a few more years and that's what Fate has decided. You cannot bring humans in for breeding. That is not our way."

"Our way?" I repeated. "We are nothing like you."

"You're more like us than you know, wolf."

The man shifted back, and the wolves of my pack crouched down, ready to fight again if necessary.

But the bears turned and left, moving like big, wounded elephants, through the woods and beyond, until they disappeared back into the shadows.

A couple of wolves followed, making sure the enemy really did leave our territory. I knew they would call us all in howls if they ran into difficulty.

Taylor and Jay began to shift back but I couldn't wait for them. I rushed inside to check on Claire.

Sue was with her in Jay's room, her arms around Claire's shaking form.

"Oh, sweetheart..." My heart broke to see her so scared.

"Dexter!" She leapt up and ran at me, throwing her arms around my neck, holding me like she'd never let me go. "Were they real bears? Or were they shifters too?"

"You didn't see the Alpha shift?" I drew her into the lounge and pulled her into my lap.

"No. I was with Sue."

Sue walked over to the door and my mother joined her, tugging her clothes back on.

"Dex, we're going to speak to the elders. Someone has to do something about this. It was a completely unprovoked attack."

I nodded and was glad when the women left.

"Do you know what they wanted, Dex?" Claire asked me, and I couldn't lie.

"They said they wanted you."

She had stopped shivering, and stood up to stare down at me. "But why?"

Taylor and Jay came in through the back door, dressed again, and threw me my jeans.

I quickly pulled them on.

"They didn't say why, exactly, just something about our pack being extinct in a few decades and that we're not meant to have mates, especially not human mates."

"You need to tell the elders," Taylor said, already heading toward the front door. He stopped when Claire began to speak.

"I need to get back to my apartment. Now. It isn't safe here," she said.

My poor love. The worry in her expression was very readable.

"Claire, you're okay. You're safe here, I promise," I said.

She looked at me with hurt in her eyes. "How can you say that, Dexter, after what just happened? They want *me*. What if they come back when you're not here?"

"We'll always be here. I'll make sure of it."

But I couldn't guarantee that, not really. Not the way the house was set up. We were the closest to the forest's edge.

And if I left Jay at home with Claire, how would he fend off a bear attack single handed? Even if we could get back here to help him, from wherever we were working at the time, it might be too late.

Impossible.

I turned to my pack. "I want to know how the hell the bears found out about Claire. She's only been here for a day."

"They have spies, obviously," Taylor said.

"Or surveillance cameras," Jay added.

I shrugged, and then shook my head. What were we going to do?

Claire was trembling again, and her face was red. She was obviously full of emotion, and looked ready to burst into tears.

I walked over to her and put my arms around her. "Claire. Everything is all right. You're safe."

She was shaking her head. "No. I want to go home. Now. Jay said you'd take me home if I asked, and I want to go home. Now."

What were my choices? I needed to attend to the threat to our pack, but my mate needed me, too.

Taylor stepped up next to me and laid a hand on my arm. My Beta. My best friend.

"I'll go to the council for you, Dex, although I'm sure the elders'll want to speak to you tomorrow. You look after Claire."

And there was the answer, in the strength and numbers of a pack. We all stepped up for one another, when we needed it.

"Thanks, Taylor." I shot him a warm look, letting him know without words how much I appreciated him. "Let them know I'll come over to discuss strategies in the morning. For now, I'll take Claire to bed."

Taylor left as Claire began to mumble. "No, I don't want to go to bed. I..."

I took both of her hands in mine. "Look at me, beautiful."

She wouldn't initially, but eventually she pulled her gaze up to meet mine.

"I know you're probably in shock, and want to run away, but right now it's dark, and it's dangerous to drive these roads when you're not in the right head space to do so. The bears won't come back tonight, and if they do, we have three packs next door who will jump at the chance to protect us."

Claire was nodding but I wasn't sure how much she was hearing.

"So, let's get you into bed and get some sleep, and tomorrow, if you still want to go home, I'll drive you back there myself."

It hurt to say it, but what other choice did I have?

"Do you promise?" Her voice was a whisper.

"Yes, darlin', I promise."

I'd never keep Claire here against her free will, and if she was the one the bears were after to stop us from breeding and continuing our pack, then perhaps she was safer in the city.

They'd never find her among the constant crowds at the hospital.

"Okay," she said quietly.

I picked her up into my arms. "I'm going to put you in my bed and we'll all join you to keep you warm and safe tonight, okay?"

I looked over at Jay, who nodded with a relieved look. We'd slept together on camping trips and when we were in our wolf form.

And considering we were about to spend the rest of our lives sharing a mate, if Claire agreed to stay, we might have to look at a redesign of the house. We could knock through one of the walls upstairs and create a huge bedroom with one massive bed, so Claire could be surrounded by all of us.

Or she might want us separately, but for some reason, I didn't see that happening.

Only time would tell, of course.

"Let's go, beautiful."

I carried her to my room.

The smell of our earlier sex still lingered, but it was the darkness and warmth I knew she craved now.

We stripped off our clothes and climbed into the king bed. Claire lay in the middle, and Jay joined us. He and I cocooned Claire, one on either side of her.

I lay awake for hours, listening to the sound of Claire's breathing, feeling her soft skin against mine, and hearing the regular breaths of Jay nearby. It was remarkably comforting to lie like this.

Taylor came home sometime around midnight and, when he poked his head in, I gestured for him to join us. He quickly undressed and settled into the other side of the bed next to Jay, his fear and worry a tangible presence in the room.

Eventually I heard Taylor's breathing change too, as he fell asleep.

We didn't speak until the morning, but for me, my whole world changed that night.

My life no longer revolved only around my pack.

My world had expanded to include Claire. Her safety, her love, and the health of my individual pack mates were all now my priority.

If we needed to move, to live somewhere else, become new people with new identities, I'd do it.

I'd do anything for the woman whom Fate had deemed the perfect person for me, for Taylor, and for Jay.

She'd carry our babies and love us forever, I was sure of it.

She was the only constant, the only thing I could count on now. Maybe she didn't know it yet, and maybe we'd have to beg her to stay after the fear the bears had instilled in her, but we'd work it out.

We all would.

Because no one was getting between my pack and our fated mate.

Claire

I was wrapped in warmth and love and protection, like a pillow and dreams and chocolate.

My stomach grumbled. Hmmm... chocolate... damn I was hungry.

I was also sweating.

I opened my eyes slowly, my body enjoying the feeling of being in the bed with Dexter, and... I opened my eyes. Jay lay beside me.

I lifted my head and looked over his shoulder. Taylor had joined us as well.

All three of them were fast asleep in bed with me, and I felt... complete, for the first time ever.

Happy.

Whole.

God!

I rolled my eyes at my own stupidity. My own feminine fairy

tale gone wrong.

I'd never wanted to be a woman who defined herself by the man in her life, or in this case, the *men*.

But here I was, for the first time in my whole life, feeling truly happy. My mind began to clear, allowing through the feelings of love that had been complicated by the fear of last night.

In the light of day, my fear of the bears had lifted, though not entirely disappeared.

In its wake was more confusion and questions than anything else. And a need to make sure the wolves were not simply a smaller version of the bears.

I had to go home, where I could have the time and space to think clearly and make some important decisions about what I wanted in life.

And if they let me go, then that would prove to me they cared.

If they didn't... then I wasn't sure what I was going to do. I couldn't be with three men who held me against my will, and yet, I couldn't imagine not being with them.

I almost groaned aloud, and shifted impatiently at my own recalcitrant thoughts.

"Good morning, beautiful." Dexter's voice rolled over my head and I looked up to see him smiling down at me. He must have felt my movement, and it woke him.

"Good morning."

My stomach gurgled again, and I was suddenly very aware of being naked and surrounded by three naked men. Three very sexy, naked men.

"Ah... breakfast time?" Jay smiled sleepily at me, too, and I nodded.

Taylor stood up first, his tight body drawing my gaze, as did his semi-erect cock.

Morning glory... three of them.

My cheeks heated, and my belly fluttered. If I had time... boy, would that would keep me busy!

"What are you in the mood for?" Taylor asked. "Pancakes? Bacon and eggs? More sex, perhaps?"

I giggled as I slid off the bed and away from the temptation that was my triad.

They could so easily drag me into another full day of sex. One-on-one, or three-on-one, I wouldn't care.

When there were no set limits, the list of things that I could do was astronomical.

"Maybe later." I smiled at Taylor. "Some pancakes first would be amazing."

Jay stood up, his body just as beautiful and aroused as Taylor's. God, these men were gorgeous. "They're my specialty. I'll start mixing up some batter."

I watched him leave, enjoying his tight ass flexing as he walked. I sighed.

I lived alone. No one had cooked me breakfast in years, if I didn't count the Starbucks down the street. The barista who worked there often made me coffee and handed me a fresh muffin.

But to have a man who cooked? Completely independent men who could do everything for themselves? What a dream. Every married friend of mine would be jealous once they found out.

Found out what? That I had three boyfriends, all of a sudden? How was I going to explain that?

A cold shudder flowed over my skin at the thought of the disgust, the fear, and the misunderstanding that would surround me for the rest of my life if I accepted this way of life for myself.

"Um. Thanks, I'd love that. I might throw some clothes on. They're downstairs, I think."

I fled the room before I sank to my knees for the men. I

could feel the need growing in my belly, the heat between my thighs flaring. But I had to be smart about this. I needed a clear head.

I raced down the stairs, my breasts bobbing up and down and still tender from yesterday's attention.

I held them with both hands and snuck over to where I'd left clothes last night on the couch.

Mary had loaned me a dress, so I pulled that on, not bothering with underwear. I wasn't going to wear what I'd had on yesterday, and I wasn't borrowing any.

Wearing one of your lover's mother's clothes was a little strange as it was.

"Pancakes coming right up!" Jay announced, as he bounced down the stairs wearing only a pair of faded jeans. At least one erection was neatly tucked away. For now.

I bit my lip to stifle the moan as one after another, the guys came down the stairs and stepped into the kitchen.

They were like a well-oiled machine, getting out ingredients, plates, drinks and fruit.

I hung back and watched, my mind instantly thinking about how well they'd work on me if given half a chance.

I barely stifled the giggle that rose at the thought and Dexter turned to stare at me with his sexy eyes.

"What shall we do today, beautiful?"

Ah. This was where it was about to get tricky.

"Don't you guys have work today?"

Dexter grinned. "Yeah, tons. But that can wait."

"Um..." I had to say it. I took a deep breath and blurted it out. "I'd like to go home after breakfast, please."

All three men stopped stirring, pouring and generally moving, to turn around and face me. Three matching sets of shocked eyes stared at me.

Dexter cleared his throat. "Claire... I know the bears scared you last night, but you don't need to leave straight away."

"Yes. I do. I need to get home. Make sure they haven't put out a missing persons' report on me. Little River is only an hour away. You said you'd take me home today, if I asked."

And that was the cruncher for me. They'd promised.

I had to know I had a choice to be here with these men. We'd started this bizarre relationship with them pretty much kidnapping me. It couldn't continue to be so one-sided.

"True... I just didn't think you'd want to go home so soon. We could spend the day together..."

Dexter's tone was suggestive and despite my stomach quivering at the idea of what would happen if I stayed, I put up both my hands and metaphorically pulled my big-girl panties on.

So to speak.

"No. I have a job and a life to get back to, not to mention your father, who I'd like to check up on. So please, after breakfast I'd like you all to take me back. Come see my apartment, my life. If we're going to make a go of this... relationship, you have to accept parts of my life, too."

It couldn't all be one way. They couldn't just move me into their home and forget the rest of my life existed.

It wasn't fair, and I deserved choices.

The three men all looked at each other, confusion plain on their faces.

Eventually Jay spoke. "Okay, Claire. We'll come back with you. Let's just finish eating breakfast, and then we'll leave."

They were letting me go? Something deep inside me let go and I began to relax. I'd won this round, and I could put some distance between us so I could think.

Which was impossible when I was around these guys.

They were too sexy, too sweet, too intoxicating.

So, we ate pancakes and then bundled into the truck and headed back to the city. Back to my life.

The drive was awkward, and despite Jay chattering away, trying to break the tension, no one seemed to know what to talk about.

When we hit the city outskirts, I began directing them to my apartment.

"Left here, and then you can park in front of the apartment block. It's the tall one just over there."

I'd bought a place only a few streets over from the hospital a few years ago, since my whole world revolved around work.

"Just here. Great. Do you want to come up and see my place?" I asked them, and they all looked at me like I'd asked them to cut off my hand.

"Is there an elevator, or stairs?" Taylor asked.

I had to laugh a little at his expression of concern, equally obvious on all their faces. "There are stairs, but we'd take the elevator to mine. You don't have to. I can just go change and come back, and we can go to the hospital, if you'd prefer."

"I'll come," Jay said, popping out of the back seat and opening the door for me.

Taylor and Dexter stayed firmly in the car. "We'll wait for you. No problem."

I turned away to hide my smile. These men had taken on bears set on ripping them apart, and not shown any fear. The idea of climbing into an elevator and entering a human apartment? I could see how much the idea alarmed them.

"Let's go, Jay."

The smallest, the Omega, and he was the one willing to brave the terrifying elevator ride? I grinned at Jay as he walked next to me, not so close as to touch me, but like my shadow, moving as I did.

We went into the building, up the elevator and along the corridor to my sixth-floor apartment.

"You okay?" I asked him.

Jay nodded, swallowing hard. "Yeah. I'm not used to being this far off the ground. Feels weird."

I shrugged. "I don't even think about it, really. It was the best I could afford when I was a resident. I paid it off and haven't really looked for anything better since. I'm barely at home anyway, to be honest."

I kept a spare key in a lock box at the end of the hall and as I grabbed it, my stomach tightened with unease.

What was I doing back here? At my old apartment that I never really liked anyway?

Oh, stop it. Now you're just being silly.

I palmed the key and walked over to my apartment. *Number three.*

The irony of that made me smile as I opened the door.

Jay walked in behind me and whistled as he looked around. "Nice."

I tried to see my sterile living space the way he did. As a flashy new piece of technology with all the mod cons.

"Yeah, thanks. Let me change and we can go."

I went straight to my bedroom and pulled out a pair of black slacks and a long, gray sweater.

Comfortable, covered and professional. Always, unless I couldn't help it.

I reached for my old, comfortable cotton knickers and hesitated. If the guys came back to my place tonight... no.

My hand hovered over the lace.

Yes. I grabbed my nicest bra and panties—the only matching set I owned.

They'd love it, I was sure. If they got the chance to see it, that is.

I rushed back out and found Jay in the same spot I'd left him.

"Wow, you look great," he said.

I smiled in thanks. I didn't feel that great. Nor that comfortable back here, actually. I thought I'd be relieved to be back home, with all my familiar things. But the trip back here was more disappointing than I'd expected.

Then again, considering I did little more than sleep in my apartment, I shouldn't be that surprised.

It was the hospital that was my true home.

"Let's go see Dexter's dad."

Jay nodded and down we went once again, not seeing a single soul I knew. Jay seemed relieved to be back on ground level once again, and I patted his arm to show him I appreciated his effort to accompany me upstairs.

I was anxious to see Jack Monaghan, not only from a doctor's perspective, but also from a personal one. What would Dexter's dad be like?

"They should have operated last night, so we should be able to see him in recovery today," I said, as we drove the few blocks to the hospital.

"Park in the underground car park. I've got a staff card."

Dexter pulled in and I swiped my card so we wouldn't have to pay for parking.

The light went green and we went into the familiar concrete cage.

When we got out, all three men were stiff and uncomfortable.

"What's up?" I asked, leading the way to the elevators.

"This place is terrible," Dexter said, looking around at the concrete walls and dark spaces.

"Yeah, I suppose it is." I'd never really thought about it, except from a safety aspect, which was typical for women.

It was daylight, so for me it was much less scary than at any other time. Walking into the carpark alone at three a.m. wasn't fun.

"Let's go see your dad."

We made our way up to the surgical ward and I located Gerry, the surgeon who'd worked on Jack last night.

"Where'd you go yesterday, Claire? No one saw you leave and some of the nurses said they saw a big guy carry you out of Emergency."

"Um... yeah. I wasn't feeling well yesterday, Gerry. Tummy bug." I waved vaguely in my stomach region. "Sorry I didn't stick around to do hand-over properly."

He shrugged, although I could tell he wasn't impressed by my lack of professionalism in running off mid-shift.

I opened my mouth to apologize again, but decided against it and shut up. I strived to be an exemplary employee. I was never late, often did doubles, accepted extras, and was always on call.

Unlike Gerry, I didn't have a wife, or kids, or golf. So, for the one time I didn't do everything right, which was not even my choice, I wasn't apologizing again.

"Tell me what happened with Jack Monaghan."

Gerry launched into a post-op round of information and I took the chart from him to study the entries while he spoke.

"He handled the operation better than any surgery I've ever done. He's bouncing back like he never had a problem in the first place."

I smiled gently and tried not to roll my eyes. So, they hadn't picked up the fact that Jack was a werewolf.... Correction—wolf shifter.

Good.

His bloodwork looked normal, too, which surprised me. Obviously, if there was a marker for the paranormal side of these shifters, it didn't show up on routine checks. Or perhaps, humans just didn't know what to look for. Relief filled me. For some reason, I felt protective of the life the pack had built for themselves, alongside the human world but not quite of it.

"Great. I'll pop in before my shift to check on him. Thanks, Gerry."

I turned and left the surgeon, who was giving me looks like I had no right to speak to his patient.

I did. And I would.

I made my way around to Jack's room in the surgical ward without telling the guys, who were waiting for me out front. I wanted to meet Jack by myself, for some strange reason.

With butterflies fluttering in my gut, I knocked on the glass window and made my way into the room.

"Hello, Jack, I'm Doctor Claire. I was here when you were admitted yesterday."

Jack's gaze came up and my breath tightened in my chest. They were Dexter's eyes. Same cool blue. Same calm, steady confidence.

"Hello, Claire. When can I go home? And where is my family?"

I laughed, pulled up a chair next to him and sat down.

"You certainly get straight to the point, don't you, Jack?"

"I know what's important, and that's getting out of here and going home."

I smiled and picked up his wrist, counting his steady heartbeats with my fingers. His color was good, with no blue in the fingertips.

I stood up and checked his hour-by-hour chart. "This all looks great. When you came in yesterday, I wasn't even sure you'd survive the surgery, let alone be practically ready to go home the next day."

His eyes lit up and a smile curved his full lips. "I can go home today?"

"Soon."

I walked back around the table, wanting to stay close to him for some reason. The pull of an Alpha male, perhaps?

"Hey, Claire..."

"Yes, Jack?"

"Why do you smell like my son?"

I glanced toward the other bed in the ward. The other patient was asleep, and intubated. Probably not capable of hearing or understanding what I was about to say.

"Um... because yesterday after he dropped you off, your son kidnapped me and took me home with him."

I tried to say it with the same calm and professional manner that I reserved for my patients, but I lost the battle when heat flushed up my face.

Jack's eyes went wide and he studied me with more interest. "He took you back to the pack?"

I nodded. "Yes, and I met Mary and Sue, and Grayson, and Jay and Taylor, of course."

"But why would he..." Jack was looking confused, until his gaze snapped together sharply and he stared hard at me. "You're his mate, aren't you?"

He looked me up and down like he was assessing my size, weight and strength.

I grinned at him and nodded. "Not just Dexter, but Taylor and Jay's, too," I said softly.

His mouth dropped open. "But... you're human," he said. "And... three of them? A whole mini-pack?"

I laughed out loud at his shock. "Ah, yeah... on both fronts. Human, and all three of them."

"But that would mean..."

"That we humans are going to save your pack, Jack."

He sat up straighter in bed, his naked chest catching my attention. The strength and size of him at sixty years old would rival his son. And the huge scar now bisecting his ribcage only added to the image of toughness.

"You've mated with him? With *them*? You're going to stay?"

"Oh... ah..."

Shit! Why had I said I was going to save them?

Did I want to stay with the pack? I had no idea at this point, but surely we could work something out.

After all, the hospital was only an hour away from where they lived.

"We're working on a compromise. But for now, I'll go get them if you'd like? They're here in the hospital."

"Mary, too?"

For the first time I saw a softness in the Alpha's eyes and it touched my heart to know the depth of love he still felt for his mate after all these years.

"No, just Dexter and the boys. But I'm sure we can get your wife in soon."

A nurse bustled in, checking vitals and being a general annoyance, if the look on Jack's face was to be believed.

"I'll bring your son in to see you in a few minutes, Mr. Monaghan."

I winked at him as he rolled his eyes.

And I went and found my wolf triad.

CHAPTER

SIXTEEN

Dexter

I looked up from the uncomfortable hospital chair. Claire was waving at us to come over to her.

"Let's go," I said to Taylor and Jay.

We stood up and followed our mate through the sterile hospital, until I finally saw my father, alive and well. He was sitting up in bed with a smile on his face like I'd never seen before.

"Dex!"

I leaned down and put my arms awkwardly around my dad, holding him tight. I hadn't realized how much I'd missed him until now. I didn't want to let him go.

"Good to see you, Dad."

I pulled back and the nurse excused herself from the room.

Claire pulled the curtains around us and we all squashed into the small space.

My father looked at me with an expression I couldn't read. "You've found your mate."

Surprise pushed through me and I looked from Claire to my father.

"Claire told you?"

"I could smell you on her... and not just you." Dad's gaze went from Jay to Taylor and back to me.

He suddenly looked slightly less impressed.

"Yes. Claire is our mate—my pack's mate. She's bonded to all three of us."

"So I understand. But, how is that possible?"

Claire giggled and shook her head, putting her hand on her forehead. "You tell me, Jack. I think we'd all love to know the answer to that question."

Dad looked around the circle and we all began to smile. He'd missed so much and he'd been gone only a day.

"When I met Claire yesterday, I knew she was my mate as soon as I saw her, and then she fainted the moment I touched her."

Claire rolled her eyes and my father's mouth dropped open. "Really? Well, that's a new one."

"It happened again when I shook her hand," Taylor piped up.

"And sort of with me, but she didn't quite pass out," Jay said, his smile showing how proud he was to have Claire as his mate, too.

My dad fell back against the pillows, his eyes wide with wonder. "Well, I'll be damned. It's actually true."

I laughed. "Yeah, it looks like we do have mates, Dad, but they're not from our pack."

"And we all thought it was the end," my father said, almost to himself.

Claire stood up and began opening the curtain. "I have to check in before my shift tonight, but you guys stay for a bit, if you want. I left my phone and everything in my locker yesterday, so my parents probably think I'm dead."

She headed off with a smile and I sat down into the chair she'd vacated.

"It's been a pretty full on twenty-four hours, Dad."

"I can imagine."

Taylor leaned against the wall with a beeping machine mounted upon it. "Yeah, and with the bears attacking last night, we're not sure what to do with Claire now."

"What?" My dad sat bolt upright, then winced and put a hand to his scarred chest.

"Relax, Dad. No one was hurt, except a couple of the bears."

But they'd heal like we had, and wouldn't be feeling it by next week.

"Why would they attack?"

I shrugged and leaned back in the chair. "They said it was to get Claire, though I don't know what they were going to do with her if we'd have let them in the house. Kidnap her? Kill her?"

I shuddered as prickles of unease worked their way up my spine.

"But how did they even know about her?" Dad asked.

Taylor grunted. "We either have a spy in our mix, or they're watching us and put two and two together. Claire is only the start. Once the other packs begin finding their mates, we'll have a proper town again. Children. Full of life and laughter and love. We'll be stronger than ever and the bears aren't going to like that."

We talked for a while, but eventually I could see that my father was getting tired.

"We'll come back later, Dad. I'll bring Mom in, if you want?"

"Yes. I'd like that."

The nurse returned and started making annoyed noises and looking at us as though we weren't meant to be there.

"We're going. Don't worry."

"He needs to rest," she said, checking his suture wounds and tapping at the IV attached to his arm.

"Thanks for looking after him," I said, giving her a smile.

She softened and gave me half a smile back.

And then we left to find Claire.

"What are we going to do about our mate, boys?"

I could tell Claire was unclear about her path and the last thing I wanted to do was force her into a decision that would ripple poison through our future.

Taylor stared at me. "I want to take her home again. But, I guess we can't do that, unless she wants it."

I laughed. "Life would be simple if we could just lock her in the bedroom so she can never leave. But no. We can't."

Because, boy did I want to do that as much as I could sense Taylor wanted it. My wolf was in total agreement with that plan. But we had to be smarter than that.

"But... we can't," Jay said quietly.

"No," Taylor said, and I nodded my agreement. It had to be Claire's choice, now, as to how our future would play out. We had to trust that the connection she felt with us was as strong as what the three of us felt, for her.

We made our way out of the hospital and into the sunshine. I breathed in and gratefully inhaled the fresh air. Damn, it was stuffy in there.

"We need to give her a choice, whether we live here in the city or go back to the pack. But I won't let her go, not for anything," I said gruffly.

Taylor nodded and Jay grinned. "Agreed."

So now we just had to tell our gorgeous doctor that.

"Let's go find her."

We went back into the hospital with our heads held high, gave the nurse in charge a message for Claire, and sat back to wait.

I'd do anything for my mate. Even get a job in this filthy city to stay close to her, if it came to that. It probably wouldn't be too bad... but I had one condition.

I wasn't living in that massive building with those dog-box apartments.

I'd build her a house, as close to the hospital as possible. A ground-level house, with all the mod-cons she wished for.

And my mate could have everything. Her job *and* us.

If she still wanted it all.

Claire

"Doctor Masterson, there's a patient in the E.R. wanting to speak to you." The nurse had been passing my desk and stopped.

"Me? Oh, who is it?"

I'd just finished answering the hundreds of texts, emails, Facebook notifications and messages on my phone.

Now, back to my men.

"He wouldn't tell me, but he's very agitated and asked for you by name and description. I can tell him you've left for the day, if you want?"

I wanted to go back to Dexter, Taylor and Jay, but what if this was a shifter who needed my help? Grayson, or one of his pack? Had one of them been injured in the fight last night?

"That's okay. Which bed is he in?"

I couldn't text Dexter or Taylor, which was going to be a problem long-term. Cell phones for all three of them were going to be a necessity, especially if I kept working the hours I already did.

The nurse told me where to find the patient. I walked into the E.R. and grabbed a clipboard. But when I pulled back the cubicle curtain, a shriek caught in my throat.

This man was a shifter, I was sure of it. But he wasn't a wolf. From the shaggy hair and beard, and the heavy build, I could tell he was more likely a bear.

"You!" he growled as soon as he saw me, lunging for me with both hands out.

I ducked his attack and ran straight to the wall that held the emergency alarm. I pulled on the red lever as hard as I could and a siren shrieked through the main floor.

He grabbed my arm and threw me across the room. Pain splintered through my elbow as I knocked into a metal trolley and rolled across the floor.

People started screaming and running through the E.R.

A security guard attempted to stop the bear, and the big, bearded man threw the guard into a glass cabinet as if he were a small toy.

Oh, fuck.

I hugged my elbow, pain radiating everywhere. There was a surgical tray above me and I used it to stagger to my feet. I grabbed a scalpel from the tray, the only weapon I could see that might be of use.

"Come at me again and find out why I got top marks in all my anatomy classes," I managed to growl at him, baring my teeth for emphasis.

I may not win this fight, but I knew where all the main arteries were, and I could make him bleed.

He charged at me, ignoring my threat,and I ducked beneath

his outstretched arms and hit the floor, slicing out with my knife and cutting across his big gut.

He had jeans on, which made his legs harder to get to, but if I was quick, I might get him next time.

The bear howled and grabbed for his stomach.

Now my ankle was killing me in addition to my elbow, but I focused on the man, searching for weak points.

The wrists, the jugular, the femoral artery.

I had to get him before he got me, and as my heart pounded with the ferocity of a steam engine, I knew I was in trouble. I was too small for this.

He put his arms wide out and began thundering toward me once again.

I heard a deep growl in the background but didn't turn to look as I gripped the scalpel and prepared myself for the impact to come.

Dexter rushed past me and knocked into the bear like one truck against another.

The impact was enough to shatter bone.

Taylor and Jay were on him too, punching and wrestling and thumping him until the bear stumbled toward the exit. My men rushed out after him.

I dropped the scalpel, and trembled like a leaf. "Holy hell," I muttered, unable to believe what had just happened.

More security guards ran by and followed the man outside. But they'd be too late, I was sure. The bear would run. He'd have to.

My legs weren't going to hold me much longer, so I staggered to a nearby seat and managed to land on the plastic rather than the floor.

One of the nurses rushed over. "Are you okay, Doctor?"

"Ah, yeah. I think so."

My ankle was throbbing and my left arm was hanging by my side at a weird angle. But the arm had mostly stopped hurting.

Hmmm... adrenaline's a wonderful thing.

"Let's get you admitted."

I stood up as Taylor came barreling back into the E.R.

"Claire! Claire." He came straight over and grabbed me. Pain screamed through my body and I yelled out.

"Oh, fuck. Are you okay?"

"I... yeah. But I think I broke something."

Taylor backed up a step, his face a mess of concern. "Oh, God, I'm sorry." He stepped forward again, and gingerly cupped my cheek for a moment. The warmth gave me a tiny burst of strength. I smiled at him, and then a wheelchair was pushed at me and I fell into it. "I need an x-ray, and some pain meds, I think."

I let the nurse wheel me away and left Taylor in the E.R. to wait for Dex and Jay.

I tapped the nurse with my good hand. "Can you make sure the guys find me later on? They'll be pestering you, I'm sure."

"Who are the guys?" she asked.

I couldn't help my smile. "*My* guys. Dexter, Taylor and Jay. You'll know them when you see them, trust me."

I'D BEEN MORE accurate than I realized. My men made the nurses' lives hell for the next few days as I was patched up, medicated and told to rest. My ankle was merely sprained, but the arm had indeed been broken, in two places. It would heal, eventually, but for now was a damn nuisance.

They wanted to visit constantly, and between Jack and myself, one of them was on the hospital grounds at all times.

"And don't worry, we have Grayson's pack guarding the

hospital too, in shifts," Dexter told me a few days later as I packed my bag to go home.

"That's a bit of overkill, don't you think?"

My Alpha had been wracked with guilt for days over my injuries and I'd barely been able to calm him.

All three of them had been nothing but doting since the incident, and it was beginning to wear on me.

"Not at all," he said as he puffed out his chest.

"Hey, Claire, I have your final blood test results, and you might want to check this out."

Toma, one of the interns, handed me the sheet with a smile, her eyes flicking over to the massive Alpha standing by the window.

And then she left.

"What does she mean by that? Is something wrong?"

"No... I don't think.... *Oh...*"

I stared down at the results in my hand.

I was pregnant.

Already? How is that possible?

I folded the piece of paper and tucked it into the back pocket of my jeans. That was a conversation for later.

I wasn't even ready to think about it myself yet.

"What's wrong?" Dex asked.

"Nothing," I lied. "My iron's low, so I'll grab some supplements on the way out."

That wasn't entirely a lie. I did need iron supplements now. And folate too. And maybe a whole range of amino acids if I was growing one—or more—babies, inside of me.

What did wolf shifters have anyway? One at a time? I had no idea.

Dexter grabbed my bag and we walked to Jack's room, where he, too, was being packed up to go home.

"I cannot wait to get out of here!" he declared.

Mary smiled and kissed her big man, who was on his feet and looking strong.

"We can't wait to have you home," she said. Then Mary turned to me with that calm expression that never faltered. "Are you coming home with us, Claire, or staying in town tonight?"

My options were laid out in front of me, and the guys had made that crystal clear too. I could live anywhere, as long as they were allowed to go along for the ride.

And despite the stress and danger of the bears, I wouldn't have it any other way.

"I've been put on sick leave for four weeks with my arm, so I may as well come home with you for a bit."

I caught Dexter's eye and he grinned, but no one said anything more. It was like they were afraid to break the spell in case I changed my mind.

Jack and I signed all the release forms, and when we walked out the front of the hospital, I got a nice surprise.

"What are you guys doing here?"

Jay and Taylor leaned against a new four-by-four, with a bull bar, roll cage and more. "And what's with the new ride?"

Taylor threw Dexter the keys and he held them out to me. "We got it for you."

"You bought me a car?" Well, a truck was more like it.

I blinked at them, unable to believe they were really handing over such an expensive gift.

My own parents made me buy my own dinner on my birthday, and my men were just handing over a brand-new, monster-sized truck?

"Of course! We want you to be safe when you're driving. This thing'll run over a bear if you happen to come across one," Taylor said with a wink.

Jack and Mary walked up. "Nice truck! We'll see you at home."

I moved closer to my new truck, awestruck by the sheer size and shiny paint. "Um... I don't know what to say."

Jay opened the passenger side door. "Say thank you and jump in."

I grinned and resisted the urge to kiss his beautiful lips. "Thank you, guys. It's great. *Really* great."

I got in, with a little help from Jay, given my one-armed effort didn't quite work, and we headed back to the pack. I left the window open and took lots of breaths of clean air as we followed Mary's car.

My men and I hadn't had much time alone in the past few days, and I could feel the need for them growing in my belly.

"It'll be great to get home. I've missed a proper bed."

Among other things.

"We think you'll like what we've done. We've rearranged Dexter's bedroom so we can fit two king size beds in there now, side by side," Taylor said from the back seat.

I swiveled around to grin at him.

"You guys moving in to one bedroom, huh?"

Jay rolled his eyes. "Only if you're there. I'm not sleeping with them on the nights you're at the hospital."

I laughed, the happy sound filling me up and making me settle into the huge bucket seat and fully relax. "Well... I look forward to seeing it when we get home."

Home. That word meant something, when I considered where we were headed. A smile lifted my lips.

There was nothing but comfortable silence in the truck for a while, then Dexter cleared his throat.

"Um, we were wondering if you'd prefer to live closer to town, Claire? We've got money, and skills that are hireable. We could get a plot of land, and build a huge house for you."

I glanced across at him.

They loved their pack, and their home. "Why would you do that?"

I looked back at Jay and Taylor, who were glancing at each other nervously.

"Because we love you," Jay said, quietly, as though scared to voice such a thing.

Warmth filtered through my chest and made stupid tears spring to my eyes.

"But why would you leave the pack? It's your home."

Taylor sat forward on his seat. "Because you're our future. Our family. We'll do anything to make you happy. Go wherever you want to go. Well, anything but live in that tiny apartment of yours. That's where we draw the line," he said with a gorgeous grin.

Once again, I didn't know what to say.

"I love that you want to make life easy for us, and I love that you're willing to compromise, but so am I. I can drop some shifts at the hospital, and only stay in the apartment when necessary," I said.

I saw Taylor's brows come down and smiled at him. "Or we can buy a house on the outskirts of town and all be there most of the time, together. I don't care. An hour's drive is really nothing."

My proclamation was met with broad grins and Dexter's hand slid across my thigh in a possessive move.

"There's been no sign of the bear shifters since the hospital. In fact, when Grayson's pack went to investigate their known dens, they seem to have moved on," Dexter said.

"That's great."

I was relieved to know that the men who seemed to want me killed were gone for now.

Some people... seriously. They just didn't want anyone else to be happy.

"How are you feeling today?"

A shiver raced straight through my tummy at Dexter's question.

"Why? You wanting to show me the new bed?"

Dexter shot me a grin. "Yep."

I turned back around to face the road and settled into my seat.

"Sounds like a plan."

We were home before I knew it, and the sun sparkled bright, happy light all over our house.

Talk about a homecoming.

The guys all jumped out, and Taylor opened my door and scooped me up like I weighed nothing at all, although he was very cautious of my injured arm.

I didn't bother complaining, I just clung to his neck and hoped he didn't drop me.

He went straight inside and up the stairs, into what used to be Dexter's room.

All furniture had been removed except for one massive bed filling half the room, wall to wall.

"Whoa." They hadn't been joking. We could fit a whole football team on this bed. Or four big, strong shifter men, and their woman. My tummy wobbled in anticipation.

Taylor put me down gently and I flexed my fingers inside my cast. I had to be a little careful of the arm, but everything else was working just fine.

"Looks good, doesn't it?" Dexter asked as he walked up behind me, his massive chest vibrating with his words.

I leaned back against him, loving the feel of him. His strength, his size, his warmth.

"I have no idea how I'm going to explain you guys to my family or my friends."

Dexter chuckled and wrapped his arms around my waist. "Tell them Taylor's your boyfriend and we're his cousins, friends, whatever."

I twisted around in Dexter's arms and looked up into his heated gaze.

"Why Taylor?"

"Yeah, why me?" Taylor asked, as he stepped up to the bed.

"Because he's the most socially acceptable. I'm too big, Jay's too nice. Go with Taylor."

I laughed and lifted my head up for a kiss. "I doubt they'll believe me, when they see how we all are with each other. But we'll work it out."

And we would. I knew we would. I was home with my men, and I certainly wasn't worrying about semantics now.

Dexter ducked his head and kissed me, his lips tasting of need and pure male.

Salty and sweet and so delicious I bit into his bottom lip with my teeth.

Yum.

I tugged at his shirt, wanting to feel his skin, but struggling with one hand.

"Can you strip? I can't with this stupid arm."

There was a deep chuckle that sounded from all three men simultaneously and within a few moments, I had all of them naked before me.

Three men, three hearts, three cocks.

And they were all *mine.*

Happiness pulsed through me as I pushed at my clothes and Jay stepped forward to help me, getting me out of my dress and underwear like a pro.

And then they were on me, kissing me, touching me, lighting my body on fire.

All three of them.

Just as I had imagined, over and over, ever since the day I mated with them all.

Dexter lay me down on the bed and knelt on the floor between my legs, while the other two lay beside me.

He grinned at me with that devilish smile, kissed my thighs and stroked my belly with his hands.

Jay, my sweet one, licked my breasts, sucking at the sensitive tips and making my nipples ache.

I moaned and gasped and searched for Taylor, who met my lips with his, stifling my groans and making me drink kisses from his mouth.

Dexter lifted my legs so that my feet rested on his shoulders, opened me right up, and ate my pussy. Licking my core's juices and suckling my clit until I was screaming.

He didn't stop, pushing me higher and higher while Jay's teeth tugged at my nipples. My pussy exploded in an orgasm so sweet it brought tears to my eyes.

I shuddered and shook, my belly convulsing with the pleasure they'd brought me.

Dexter stood up and grinned down at me, his cock thick and hard in front of him.

I had to taste it.

I sat up and bobbed my head down, sucking the tip into my mouth and groaning at the exquisite taste of him.

Then Jay and Taylor knelt on either side of me and I was turning my head to suck one and then the other in turn.

None of them needed the foreplay—they were all hard and ready for me, but I loved the teasing. Pleasuring them. Drawing out the moment until they took me.

When my arm was better, we could take our time—one day, when the need wasn't so great.

For the moment though, I was aching, my belly tight and desperate for them.

I sucked Dexter one more time and then looked up at him.

"How are we going to do this?"

The men moved into position, as though they'd been planning this.

"You're going to take all of us," Taylor told me as Dexter lay on his back on the bed.

"At once?" I asked, swallowing nervously.

Jay nodded.

I needed to go with it. Fate had gotten me this far, so there was no point being afraid now.

"Okay."

"Come here, beautiful," Dexter called, and I climbed on top of him, loving the feel of his huge, hot body between my thighs.

"Take me inside you," he demanded, and I lifted up. The feeling of Dexter holding his cock against my entrance made a squeal of excitement rise in my throat.

I can't wait.

I slid down on his shaft slowly, loving every inch of him stretching me, filling me up.

"Oh, God... that's so good."

Taylor's hand pushed at my back and I leaned forward, resting my good hand on the bed.

Taylor's fingers ran something cold and wet over my ass and Dexter began to thrust up into me, distracting me from what was about to happen.

"I'm not sure..." I hadn't done that before.

"Trust us," Dexter said, playing with my nipples while his cock pumped gently inside me.

Taylor slid a single finger inside my ass and I gasped out against the burning pain.

"Relax, if you can," Taylor urged, and I concentrated on all the other sensations in my body. The pulse of my pussy tightening around Dexter, the pleasure in my nipples.

Then the burn began to fade, replaced by a strange emptiness, a hunger. He stretched me until I was moaning from the pressure.

Taylor withdrew his finger and I gasped out, pushing back toward the pressure again. Needing it.

But then his cock was sliding into me and I had to force myself to breathe, the pain overcoming the pleasure. He was so big!

And then there were vibrations. A small clit vibe was being held to me by Jay, who grinned at me.

"Let go, Claire. We've got you."

I closed my eyes and let the feelings consume me.

Neither man was moving, and I needed them to do something.

"Move. Please."

Taylor slid out and slid back in, and Dexter grabbed the vibe and began pumping up and down with his hips.

"Oh. My." The pleasure in my core amplified to the extreme.

I couldn't think, couldn't breathe. Could only feel.

And then Jay pressed his cock to my lips and I opened for him.

The moment his taste slid across my tongue, I came.

I cried out as my whole body tightened and spasmed around them, rejoicing in the joining of all three parts of me.

Dexter groaned and began thrusting faster. Taylor did too, jerkily moving in and out.

"Oh, fuck, I'm gonna blow!" Taylor yelled out.

I sucked hard on Jay's cock, not wanting him to miss out.

Jay thrust his hips in time with my other mates, all three of my holes full and aching for release.

Taylor was first, filling me with his seed and pushing heat into my body.

"Oh, fuck!" Dexter cried out and Taylor pulled out, leaving Dexter to pound into me, faster and faster.

My pussy was tightening again and I let go of Jay's cock. "Please, fuck my ass, Jay."

I couldn't believe the words were coming from my lips, but I was empty and wanting him back there.

Jay jumped down the bed and stood behind me, sliding straight into my body and crying out with me as we were once again joined.

Jay stayed still, pulsing inside of me as Dexter thrust so hard he moved all three of us.

"I'm gonna come," Dexter groaned, grabbing my hips with rough hands.

Jay grabbed my waist and began thrusting fast and hard.

The waves of pleasure picked me up and tightened me, cutting off my air, my thoughts, everything but the feelings between my thighs.

I heard Dexter cry out first, and his seed began to pulse inside of me. Then Jay followed him.

I couldn't hold on anymore.

I screamed, digging my nails into the mattress as I came so hard I saw stars.

Jay filled me from behind and my body shuddered and shook until I collapsed onto my mate's chest.

I was finally connected wholly to my entire pack.

Jay slid out of me, but I stayed on top of Dexter, wanting one of them inside of me. I'd feel far too empty without him.

Jay and Taylor fell onto the bed beside us, their gasps and groans of satisfaction filling the room.

"I cannot believe how hot that was. I can't even explain it." Dexter was stroking my back and chuckling with happiness.

"Best day of my life, by far," Jay was saying, and I looked up with a dopey smile, almost incoherent.

But I had to say it.

They had to know.

"I think I can make this day even better."

Dexter pulled a pillow down for himself and tucked it beneath his head. He ran a hand over my cheek.

"Oh, really? How?"

I smiled up at them all, their full attention on me.

"I'm pregnant."

EPILOGUE

One year later.
Dexter

It had just gone sunrise and the packs were gathering in the meeting area.

The area was so much cleaner now, thanks to the mates who had completed our families.

I didn't stare at broken beer bottles and dirt any longer, with the scent of testosterone choking me.

The packs were settled, happy, and flourishing.

"Claire's still sleeping, so I thought I'd let her rest." Taylor handed me one of our twins, a boy, born three months ago.

Another wolf for the pack.

"Hello, my son, did you give your mother hell all night again?"

My babe gave me a sleepy smile and nestled into my arm, where I held him tight.

"They both did, didn't you hear them?" Taylor scowled at me and I shrugged. I usually slept through most of their crying.

162

"You're the most demanding, aren't you, beautiful girl?" Taylor held our daughter up in the air, and a sigh of true contentment stole my breath.

The first daughter born to our pack in over fifty years.

A true miracle—just like her mother.

I looked back over the yard. The grass was tended, the tables and chairs arranged in an orderly manner.

The women had brought so much with them when they moved in. Not just happiness, love and sex for three frustrated men.

But they had also brought with them the need to prosper and grow. To protect and nurture, as we were designed to do. Our mates had truly made us whole.

"She's perfect," I declared.

Jay groaned as he walked out of the house rubbing his eyes. "That's because you don't spend half the night walking her up and down the hallways."

I grinned and took my daughter in my other arm, loving the feel of our children nestled against me.

"You wanna go back to the way it was last year?" I asked them both, already knowing the answer.

That despite all their belly-aching, they loved our new family.

"What, with no Claire? No kids? No, thank you," Taylor declared.

Jay shook his head. "Hell no."

I laughed and watched as the other packs began to rise and my mother walked toward me with her arms stretched out for her grandchildren.

I handed my daughter over to her and kept my son tight against me.

All of these changes were thanks to my mate.

Her strength, her kindness, and Fate.

Fate had shown me the way to our mate, and in the process, we had healed our whole pack.

THE END

CLAIMING
THEIR MATE

PROLOGUE

I could smell the fear rising from the woman in front of me. The scent made me want to back away, to save her from the discomfort.

But this wasn't about me, this was about my pack. My family.

I *needed* to speak to this human mate that Dexter's pack had found. *Claire*.

Dex had said I could ask some questions of Claire if I kept my distance. It was an odd request but I was willing to honor it, if it meant I might get some answers.

What was Dex worried about? I wasn't going to hurt her. He knew me better than that.

Or I thought he did.

Because if he was worried about me trying to steal Claire away from him, that was laughable. The last thing I'd do was try to take something that didn't belong to me. That wasn't my style at all.

Not that Claire the doctor wasn't pretty. She was. But I

couldn't sense the animal magnetism that Dex and his pack mates, Taylor and Jay, boasted about.

To me, she didn't smell sexy. Instead, she smelled like... *theirs*. And my Alpha wolf didn't stir for any taken woman. Especially not one already mated to another. Or in Claire's case, with three fated mates.

Claire stepped closer to Dex's Omega, Jay, who grabbed Claire and hauled her against his body in an uncharacteristically alpha-like gesture.

I turned my face away, to try and avoid them seeing my disbelief. It was all I could do not to laugh out loud. What did Jay think I was going to do? Grab their mate, strip her down and take her in full view of everyone here?

"What are you doing, Dex?" Jay demanded, and Dexter stepped away from our group to stand by his mate once again. Dex's Beta, Taylor, quickly joined him. Claire was flanked by her three pack mates, all of them vibrating with tension.

Dexter shook his head. "Don't worry, I don't like this any more than you do."

Seriously? What was wrong with these guys? Their human mate *could not possibly* be that precious.

Taylor and Dexter flagged Claire, with Jay moving slightly behind, and she relaxed into them, a soft smile lighting up her face.

That smile, and the comfortable familiarity between them all, was the first sign I'd seen of a true connection between her and her mates, and it was reassuring to see. I hadn't really been sure it was real, until now. Their connection was what I wanted... what I craved. A mate. A true love. Someone who would feel like the missing part of me. Someone I would die for, if I had to.

Mary, Dexter's mom, stepped up to speak to Claire for us. She'd brokered the discussion with Dexter, raising the issue we wanted answers to, and it was due to Mary's influence that Dex had agreed—albeit reluctantly—to let us meet his mate.

"Claire, some of the neighboring packs wanted to meet you," Mary said. "I hope you don't mind?"

Claire looked us up and down from the safety of her mens' arms, and said, "Considering the lack of women in this town, I can understand the interest." She looked straight at me this time. "Hi, I'm Claire."

I was the one who needed to step up and talk on behalf of the others, obviously. "I'm Grayson."

Claire extended her hand. "An Alpha, I presume?" she asked with a raise of one delicately arched eyebrow.

I grinned in acknowledgment and heard Dex inhale sharply. What was he worried about?

"How'd you know?" I reached out and shook her hand.

After a couple of seconds of what felt like tense silence, there was a collective sigh of relief from Dex, then Taylor and Jay.

Claire shrugged and withdrew her hand. "You're big."

I fought the heat that flashed up my face and glanced down at the huge body my Alpha genes guaranteed. "Ah... you're learning our ways, I see. It's nice to meet you, Claire. May I ask you a question?"

"Of course."

I opened my mouth, and then shut it again, hesitating instead of plunging forward. How did I ask her what we needed to know? She represented a solution to our problem, but it was a solution none of us had considered, until now.

For fifty years, not a single female had been born to our pack. The elders had believed that it meant our fated mates were non-existent for our generation. A romantic myth that had ended with our parents' matings. And in that assumption, the inevitable decline of our pack had been at the forefront of everyone's minds.

But Dexter had found his mate in the human population. And even more unusual, he'd found one female for his whole pack of three wolves. Claire had turned out to be the fated mate of Dex, Taylor *and* Jay, and she was one hundred percent human.

Was that really the future for the other mini-packs of three men, including mine? To share a woman in such a way?

"Go on, ask me whatever you want," Claire repeated.

I sighed and just went with what was in my head. "Can you give us a hint about what to look for with our mate? Since it appears we all need to be on the hunt for a human now."

Claire tilted her head. "Well, for one thing, I wouldn't use the word *hunt* when you're talking to her." She grinned at me and I couldn't help grinning back.

This one had a cheeky streak. Dex and his pack would need to stay on their toes.

Claire continued. "To be honest, though, I'm not sure what to say. Did Dexter tell you about the fainting thing?"

He had... and I suddenly realized why they'd been so hesitant to have me touch her. They'd been waiting to see if Claire keeled over when we shook hands.

But we hadn't. Interesting. That meant she really was fated for Dex's triad of wolves.

"Yes," I said, after a moment. "But I was wondering if you had an idea before that? When you first saw them, maybe? I need something that I can look for in my mate, because I've met human women before and no one has ever fainted at my touch..."

Claire looked me up and down like I was a piece of meat in a butcher's case, assessing me in two seconds and somehow coming up trumps. "Maybe that's because your mate has a brain, like me, and you've been picking up tiny blondes with more boobs than anything else?"

A grin stretched across my face. I couldn't help it. So, what if I liked them easy? We only had one night each visit in town to get them into bed, and then we had to kick them straight back out again.

There was no point trying to pick up any of the decent chicks. We literally didn't have the time, nor the desire before now, to connect with humans in a long-term manner.

I was unable to resist rising to her bait. "They weren't all blonde."

My Beta, Aaron, laughed beside me, and the tension in the whole group began to relax.

Claire shrugged. "Look, I honestly don't know what to tell you. I'm a doctor who's barely dated in a decade. Maybe your mates are the same? Women who work too much and never get out—not to the places you'd usually go to find a date, anyway."

Why didn't she just ask me to find a needle in a haystack?

"Then how am I meant to find her?"

Claire bit her lip and glanced away. Then she looked back at me with a reluctant smile.

"Fate," she said. "You have to trust that you'll stumble across her when the time is right. But I wouldn't be avoiding trips to town during the day. If you guys can start going in more often, you'll have a much better chance of meeting the right one."

I looked over at my Beta and he nodded.

"Any other tips?" Brad, my Omega, asked.

Claire looked to Brad. "Well, I will tell you that I knew there was something special about Dexter the moment I saw him. My heart was pounding and I could barely breathe. I've never had a response like that to any man before and I'm sure your mates will feel the same way when they meet you."

A sense of relief filled me at her words. There was hope. I had to focus on that element. Hope that there was a mate for me. For *us*.

I just had to ignore the surprisingly massive mountain of doubt and worry that threatened to bury the hope.

I leaned forward and got her attention, my mind spinning with the implications of what she was saying. I needed to get a job in town. At the very least, it would bring in more money for my pack, and best-case scenario... I'd actually find our fated mate.

"Thank you, Claire."

Dex pulled her into his arms and I took that as the signal to move off.

"Thanks Mary." I nodded at Dexter's mom and gestured to my mini-pack—my Omega and Beta. "Let's go."

Fifteen years ago, the elders of our pack passed a new law. Due to the lack of females and over-abundance of male shifters in our pack, we were told to arrange ourselves in triads. We had to form our own mini-packs, with an Alpha, a Beta and an Omega to each family.

I hadn't known Aaron or Brad very well when they'd approached me to become their Alpha in a pack, but it had worked out better than we'd expected.

I'd die to save them, every day of the week. They were my family. But I also wanted my mate, and if that meant sharing her with Brad and Aaron, as Dexter had done with his pack, then I would.

Anything to have a true family, and maybe even children one day.

I hoped our mate—if she existed—would one day fulfil the aching need inside my chest that I'd had for more than a decade.

I loved the larger pack, the elders and my blood-related family. But there was a place inside my heart that was gaping wide open. Empty. Ready and waiting for a woman to love and cherish.

"So, what do you want to do?" Aaron asked me as we walked to our front door and stepped inside our too-large home.

"We need to go into town and cover as much ground as possible. I'll apply for a job and see what happens. Our mate has to be out there."

"A job? Where? On a building site full of men?" Aaron rolled his eyes and I stopped to consider his words.

He was right. We were tradies. How were we going to meet women that way?

"There're women at employment agencies. You could apply for jobs everywhere and not necessarily take any," Brad piped up, and I turned to smile at him.

My Omega was quiet, but smart as a whip.

"That's an idea. Somewhere to start, at least." I glanced at my watch. It was only one p.m. There was still plenty of daylight left, to begin the process of looking.

"I'll go and ask some of the elders if they need anything from town. Might hunt around a little now."

"I'll go with you," Aaron said, his mouth setting with determination.

Brad shrugged. "I've got work to do here. Let me know how you go."

Aaron and I headed to the elders, but it seemed they needed nothing today. Then we jumped in the car and drove to town, a strange vibration of excitement rattling through me. I could tell from the way Aaron held himself, that he was feeling the same kind of strung-out anticipation, too.

When we arrived in Little River, I looked around with fresh eyes.

The air was cleaner, crisper and better than it had been the last time I'd been there. The colors were brighter and the sounds around me happier.

I knew it must be all in my imagination, but how could I not be feeling more positive after the chat with Claire? There was a chance that we could meet our mate, and soon.

"Should we split up and try different places?" Aaron asked, clearly struggling to hide his own smile.

Women walked by us, their gazes skimming over our bodies and some of them sending subtle invitations with their eyes.

I knew that humans were attracted to us. They liked muscles, of which we had an abundance.

It didn't mean much in the pack. Everyone was strong, hard-working and super-fit.

But in this world, where people worked while sitting in a chair all day, the men were not as strong, healthy, or trim.

"Yeah, why not," I said in answer to Aaron's query. "We could walk around, and see if anyone faints at our feet." I grinned at Aaron and he laughed.

The hunt was on.

I glanced around at a pair of women walking up the street, their long, straight hair billowing around their faces, their too-skinny legs wrapped in thin skirts.

I inhaled deeply, hoping to smell something new, sweet, and distinct.

But there was nothing except the normal scents of the city. The people around us offered up a range of scents, but none grabbed my attention and held it.

I went to turn away, but Aaron grabbed my arm. "Do you think we'll have a different mate each? Or one to share like Dex's pack?"

I shrugged. "No idea. Doesn't really matter, either way, does it?"

"Guess not." He sounded a little uncertain. Then he added, "You don't care?"

I stared at him, surprised by his question. "Of course, not. After spending a decade coming to terms with our shitty, one-night-stand existence, I'll do anything to find my true mate. To have a woman to come home to, and children. If she's meant for you and Brad too, then so be it."

I didn't have jealousy issues like a lot of the other Alphas.

I lived for my pack.

And if Fate had decided one human was enough for us, then I would ride that wave and be grateful for it.

"Oh, good." Aaron seemed happier now, more relaxed. "I feel the same way."

We grinned at each other, and I could read the hope in Aaron's eyes, now.

"Let's go," I said. "See you back here in two hours."

He grunted and we turned in opposite directions.

I walked along the streets and ducked into a pharmacy, a green grocer and a liquor store, making small talk with the locals, telling them I was looking for some work in housing construction.

None of the women smelled any different to me, and I shook so many hands. Everyone's hands.

They must have thought I was the politest person around.

And yet, no one fainted at my touch. Not even an offer to go out for dinner or a drink.

Not that I should have expected to find my mate on the first day. That would have been ridiculous. But as the time dragged on, my heart grew heavy. And when the designated time came and went, I forced myself back to the car, to discover Aaron's sad face.

"No luck?" I asked him, though the question was barely necessary. His slumped shoulders and the defeated set to his jaw made the answer too apparent.

"No. Although I inquired at a job recruitment agency and they said they'd call in regards to an interview... or something like that. I wasn't really listening, to be honest."

We got in the car and I turned the key. I was surprised by the amount of disappointment running through my blood. It felt like a cancer, insidious and potent.

I forced out a laugh, trying to lighten the mood. "After a decade of thinking we had no fated mate, we shouldn't expect her to just turn up on our doorstep in the first hour, right?"

Aaron nodded, then stared out the window and didn't say anything else.

Mopey bastard.

I sighed and turned the car back toward the pack.

Despite my conscious efforts to stay positive and grateful, Aaron's shitty attitude pretty much summed up how I felt, too.

We'd waited long enough.

I didn't want to wait any longer.

It was our time to find our mate. To begin our life. To finally be a true family. Because, without a woman or children, we were nothing.

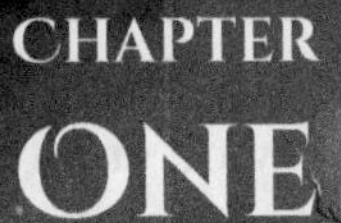

A month later
Nevaeh

"Seriously, Claire. Why on earth would you choose to move *all* the way out here?"

My old car bumbled along the dirt road that led into some sort of secret compound that no-one knew about.

Not even Google could find the address when I plugged it in. If Claire hadn't left me hand-written instructions at the hospital, I would never have found the place.

That should have been my first hint that something dodgy was going on.

"Oh... There they are."

Houses began to appear out of nowhere, on properties cut into the hill side. Well-made, large homes sitting on big plots of land.

I glanced at the sheet of paper from Claire for the thousandth time.

First house on the left.

Number seven.

Double story with my new black truck parked around the back.

I looked up at the house to my left.

Yep. Looks like the right one.

I pulled up into the area at the front of the house—I couldn't really call it a driveway—and got out of the car.

The roads weren't that wide and the lack of driveways made no sense. Did everyone park around the back? Or did most people from this town walk everywhere?

"She's lured me out here to la-la land."

I admired Claire more than any woman I'd ever known. She was easily the most driven, accomplished female physician I'd ever met, but she'd changed somehow in the past month or so. People at work thought it was due to her breaking her arm during the attack at the hospital, but I had another theory.

I had a feeling it had everything to do with the man she'd moved out here for. And I was here to find out if I was right.

They said men made women soft... or was it the other way around? I couldn't remember. I spent too much of my time working and staying away from those of the other gender, so I wasn't sure what they were or weren't.

Didn't matter. I wasn't hooking up with anyone of any gender, anytime soon.

I clutched my bag to my side and kept my keys in my hand, just in case. In case of what, I wasn't sure. But that was my instinctive reaction as a small female in an unknown town.

Movement caught my eye and I turned to see three men step onto the front porch of the property next door.

Three large, exceptionally well-built, gorgeous men.

The effect on my body was embarrassing.

I couldn't breathe and my heart began to gallop, pounding against my rib cage in an unending way.

What was wrong with me?

I locked eyes with the largest one of the three and heat poured through my belly and worse, lower still.

The other two turned to stare at me. My knees buckled under what felt like the weight of the three combined gazes, and I stumbled forward.

No. No. This wasn't happening.

I ran for the front door of what I prayed was actually Claire's house, and banged on the wooden panels.

Somehow, I could still feel the men next door staring at me, the sensation making the hairs on my neck stand up.

I couldn't stop myself from looking across to them once again. They stood in their jeans and tank tops, their muscles bulging out of their arms and shoulders.

None of them were my sort of men... not at all.

Fear skittled along my spine at my own inexplicable reaction, and I called out.

"Claire!"

The front door swung open and there was Claire in the doorway, her arm still in a full cast past her elbow.

"Nevaeh! You made it."

I launched myself at my friend and shut the door behind me.

My heart was still pounding and I couldn't quite catch my breath, but I was finally safe inside Claire's home.

"Nevaeh, are you okay?"

"Yes, yes. Just ran here from the car."

To get away from the sexy trio next door.

I looked at my friend and was blinded by the glow of good health surrounding the woman who had once worked a hundred hours a week.

Whatever Claire was doing out here certainly agreed with her.

"Doctor Claire Monaghan," I addressed her in a mock-stern tone. "What are you doing this far out of town?"

She grinned. "Enjoying the fresh air."

I glanced around the well-made house, noting the carved staircase and a hand-made table that drew my eye. I could see Claire's touch everywhere, too. From the colorful pillows on the sofa, to the lemons arranged in a glass bowl on the kitchen counter.

"Wow. This is a really beautiful house, Claire. Elegant but still homely at the same time. It must be nice to have so much space."

Like most shift workers who lived in town, I shared a two-bedroom apartment. In my case, my room-mate was another hospital nurse. Our space was cramped and old, but it was home. A place to rest my head at the end of a shift.

My apartment had nothing on this place.

"Oh, yeah, thanks. The boys built the whole house together. I've just added a few touches to make it more homey. I want to get a huge sofa so we can all sit together, but that hasn't happened yet."

She pointed to her arm, as though that was the reason she hadn't been shopping.

But my head was stuck on her phrasing. *The boys?*

"Um... what do you mean by that, exactly? I thought you moved out here to live with your boyfriend? Does he have house-mates, or something?"

I looked around as though the house would give me a clue as to what she'd meant, but there were no signs of anyone. And no photos, either.

"Ah, yeah. Sort of."

Claire's face was doing something I hadn't seen before. It was turning red, and if I used my nursing intuition, she looked like she was lying or hiding something. That was a look I'd seen on many patients' faces, but had never seen on *this* doctor's face before.

"Claire." I frowned my confusion. "What's going on?"

She clapped her good hand to her face as if aware how heavily she had blushed, and laughed softly. "I've gotta get better at lying."

Now she had my interest.

"What are you lying about? Why you're here? Or about your guy?"

Claire's gaze slid sideways and she bit her lip. "Kind of both."

My stomach tightened with foreboding. An instinct I didn't ignore. Did it have something to do with the guys next door? I hoped not... but I couldn't discount anything at the moment.

"What's happened, Claire? What is this place? Are you in danger?"

I had a nose for bad guys now. Maybe this had something to do with the men I'd seen outside. Especially the really big one. In my experience, they were always cruel.

Claire's laugh shattered my tight stomach. "Oh, God, no. These men would die to protect me. It's not that... it's just... I'm not dating one of them... Seriously, I can't believe I'm saying this aloud finally." She paused and a small, strange giggle emerged before she said, "I'm dating all three of the men who live here."

Shock rippled through me. I felt it first in my face, which stiffened into what I know must have been a horrified expression. Then the shock traveled through the rest of me, like a cold lake, freezing each of my muscles, one at a time.

I slumped against the back of my chair and let my gaze drop to the ground. Three boyfriends? And they all lived here together? How was that even possible?

This woman was my idol. Now she was some sort of... what? I was afraid to even *think* anything critical in relation to Claire.

"Nevaeh, look at me."

I pulled my gaze up, to where Claire was sitting forward on her chair. Her eyes, and her tone were beseeching.

"Don't look at me like that, please. You have to understand, it just kind of happened."

Seriously? That echoed in my head like the excuse every pregnant teenage girl ever said.

"How does something like that just happen, Claire?"

I could hear my tone and it was angry, and I couldn't work out why. This was Claire's life, not mine, and I had no right to judge her decision-making.

There was a tingle of something akin to adrenaline in my veins, so I stood up and began to pace the room so that I didn't start to twitch.

"It... that doesn't make any sense, Claire."

Her eyebrows snapped up. "Hey! It's not you that needs to sleep with three men at once. I do, and I love it, not that you asked how I feel it about the situation. So, what's gotten into you? I thought you'd be happy for me!"

I whirled at Claire's angry voice. "I am!"

It was an automatic response and not at all true, and both of us knew it.

Claire's gaze narrowed. "You're lying, and I think you need to work out what's going on with you, because this is not about me."

I threw myself back down onto the couch, embarrassed by my hissy fit, tears in my eyes. I could barely even explain it to myself, let alone Claire. "I thought you were like me," I began. "You know..."

"No, I don't know what you mean. In what way?"

"Married to your job. Single. You know... not into men."

Claire's eyes opened wide. "Oh, I'm not gay... is that what this is about? Because I'm sorry if you thought..."

That snapped me out of my doldrums, double time. "Oh, no. No! I'm not a lesbian or anything, it's just..."

Claire *was* the job, as I was. Or she had been, until now. There was nothing else in my life that I relied on *except* my work.

I heaved a sigh. I didn't know why I was being so rude. I dashed away the tears on my face and took a deep breath.

"Let's start this again. Hi, Claire. You look amazing. Obviously living in the woods and not working agrees with you. Your skin is glowing!"

Words I never thought I'd say, but there they were. Out in the open. And these words, I meant.

Claire smiled and her eyes went suspiciously glossy. "I'm pregnant."

To who?

"That's brilliant... are you happy about it?" I didn't know how else to ask.

Claire coughed over her laughter and tears slid down her face.

I rushed over to her couch and took her hand in mine. "I'm so sorry for being such a wreck. You know me and my issues. I didn't mean to push them all on you."

Claire laughed properly this time, and wiped at her tears. "Oh, I'm not sad. Don't worry, just emotional. Bloody hormones."

Well, at least it wasn't my fault. I couldn't stand the idea of causing Claire harm. "So, you're... happy about the pregnancy, then?"

Claire turned to me and squeezed the hand she held. "Yes, definitely. Look, as far as the world is concerned, I'm dating Taylor. Dexter and Jay are just our housemates. But as my friend, I wanted to be honest with you. I love them all, and they love me, which... you will see soon enough, because I think I hear them coming."

I jumped up and ran across the room to my previous seat as

the door banged open and a flurry of testosterone and muscles came in the door.

I looked for the men I'd seen this morning, but they were nowhere to be seen, and amazingly I recognized a twinge of disappointment inside of me.

"Hey, baby, what's wrong? You okay?" one of them asked, his concern obvious as he moved toward Claire.

There were three of them, just as Claire had said. Small, medium and large.

The small one went straight to Claire's side and cupped her face to look at her tears.

She nodded. "Yeah, I'm okay. You know what I'm like at the moment."

The small one smiled and dropped a tender kiss on her lips. "I do."

Then he looked up and saw me. "Oh! You said you had a friend dropping in. Hey, I'm Jay."

The guy, who had a big happy smile and spiky hair, made me instantly comfortable and at home in this house.

How he did that, I had no idea, but I was grateful for his warmth.

"Hi, I'm Nevaeh. I'm a nurse at the hospital."

The other two men approached and their strength pushed through the room as though they'd reached out and touched me.

I pulled my legs up and hugged my knees into my chest.

Medium and large kissed Claire too, their touches on her face and neck both possessive and caring. Despite my earlier reservations, I was transfixed watching them all.

I didn't dare blink in case I missed something, and yet my belly tightened. And it wasn't with fear. These men were kind of... hot. The whole situation was kind of sexy, in a hugely taboo way.

I began to think about some of the advantages to Claire's

system. She'd get three times the kisses, the affection, the time and the effort.

Though in my case, it could just as likely be three times the vicious attacks and stalker-type behavior.

I shuddered as my thoughts turned dark.

"I'm Taylor," the medium one introduced as he sat beside Claire and casually pulled her onto his lap.

"Dexter," the big one said, crossing his arms over his chest. My throat thickened and I swallowed awkwardly.

He was as big as a wrestler.

Claire reached up and patted Dexter's big, beefy arms. "I know he's huge, but he's a massive teddy bear. Don't be stressed by him. He works his ass off building houses every day. Don't you, hun?"

Dexter looked down at Claire and I saw the hardness around his features fade to warmth.

Yep, in this case it was clearly the woman who made these men soft.

"Oh, I'm not scared... it's okay."

Taylor rolled his eyes from where he sat on the couch. "Really? 'Cause you smell like a rabbit about to bolt. But in this case, you probably want to run like your ass is on fire."

"I *smell* like it? What do you mean?"

Was I farting or something? Because it was literally impossible for humans to smell fear. Animals yes... humans, no.

Claire cleared her throat. "Ah... what he means is..."

"Would you like a hot drink or something, Nevaeh? Did I say that right?" Jay asked, getting up and moving to the open plan kitchen area.

"Ah, yeah, you did, and a coffee would be great."

"You working tonight?" Claire asked.

"Yeah. Caffeine needed. You know what it's like."

"Yeah... if you can get it by IV, then even better."

I shared a smile with my friend, my colleague. I finally began to relax.

The men must have felt it too, because the two bigger guys got up to leave.

"We gotta get back to work, but we'll see you for dinner, okay?"

They both kissed Claire, waved to me and left.

I could breathe again, and Jay brought me a strong coffee in a massive mug.

"Oh, perfect. Thank you."

He smiled. "We don't do caffeine much, but Claire loves her coffee and we made sure we bought a good machine so she could have coffee whenever she wanted."

He sat down next to her with easy confidence and wrapped an arm around her shoulders.

It made me uncomfortable, the easy affection between them.

Happy couples often had that effect on me, and I wasn't sure why.

"Hey, Jay, you okay if Nevaeh and I have an hour or so to chat?"

"Oh, yeah, cool. I've got some computer work to do. I'll just be in my room if you need me."

Jay walked away to a room off the lounge and shut the door.

"They all have their own rooms?" I asked, now far too curious for my own good.

"Sort of. They've kept their own bedrooms from before I came into the picture, but we've made the master suite our main room and we mostly sleep there together. But the men still like having their own space, and when I go back to working nights, they'll probably sleep alone then. There's a fourth bedroom for the nursery too, which is nice."

"That does sound nice, so much space."

Claire glanced around. "Yeah, I kind of forget what it was like at my tiny apartment. I need to put it on the market soon."

She was selling up? Already? That wasn't very smart. She barely knew these guys.

"You're planning on living here... forever?"

"Yeah, definitely. If I do sell the apartment, it'll be to buy a bigger place in town, though. I like the idea of having somewhere to sleep after long shifts, and I'd love to have the guys with me, too, but the apartment freaks them out, and I agree with them that a house would be better for all of us."

That was better. I didn't like the idea of Claire having nowhere to go if they broke up.

"Wow, sounds like you've got it all worked out."

Claire nodded slowly. "Yeah, we kind of do."

"What about work? Are you going to reduce your shifts, or...?"

How could she want to give up working? After so many years of study, and struggling to become the best she could be, Claire was going to give it all up, for... men?

"I'll have to come back slowly after my arm heals, and by then I may need to reduce hours because of my pregnancy, but you know... work isn't everything."

Work *was* everything, for both of us. Or... it had been.

I wanted to laugh, or cry—or both.

Instead, I crossed my arms over my chest and glared at the woman opposite me.

"Maybe not for you, but it still is for me, Claire."

She'd sold us out. And by us, I meant all the other single, work-minded women out there.

Claire cocked her head to the side, and I could almost see the bevy of questions whirling around in her mind.

"What's up with you, Nevaeh? Why do I get the feeling that you want to tell me something?"

"I don't know what you mean. I only came out here to visit and see how you were getting along after being away from work for so long. I kind of figured that you'd be going out of your mind with boredom."

Claire cackled with laughter. "Oh, yeah, those were the days. When my whole world revolved around work, double shifts, and patients."

She was talking about it like it was the past.

"Are you seriously going to give up your whole life for these guys?"

She pinned me with a glare this time. "I'll give up whatever I want to for love, sex and the babies I've always wanted, Nevaeh. In fact, I'm *gaining* a whole life, not giving one up. What is it to you?"

My face flamed with the heat of shame. Yeah, I deserved that.

"I'm sorry, Claire. I just always saw you as a woman who was kind of married to her job. Like me."

I managed to pull my gaze up and meet her eyes. I could see the anger fading, replaced by a kindness that made me want to cry again.

"What really happened to you, Nevaeh? Is it childhood stuff? Or have you been burned too many times?"

This was so not where I wanted this conversation to go.

"I think it may be time I head home."

I moved to stand up and Claire commanded, "Sit your butt back down. You're acting like a spoiled little brat, and I want to know what's going on. And if you won't tell me, I'll get Dex to sit on you until you talk, and believe me, that is two hundred and seventy pounds you don't want squishing you."

A shiver crawled up my spine and I bounced my legs up and down.

"I don't like to talk about it."

"No one does."

She waited and so did I.

Finally, the words crept out of me. "My childhood was okay. We were poor, but my parents did the best they could."

"Okay... so it's a guy, then. Is he still around?"

I shook my head. "No, I... have a restraining order on him. He was one of my first boyfriends. You know, bad boy, wrong side of the tracks, all the normal cliché things..." I laughed to cover the tension I felt talking about Trevor.

There was a tight fist in my gut that never really went away. A bone-deep fear that I'd never really be free of him.

"But he, uh... got weird, possessive, after a while. And I don't really know why, to be honest, because it's not like he loved me, or even seemed to like me, actually. But he couldn't stand me being at work."

I sniffed and grabbed for a tissue from my handbag, blowing my nose in an attempt to tell my story without crying. I hated admitting to anyone that I'd been such a bad judge of character. That in my need for love and acceptance, I'd ended up with several black eyes and a stalker instead.

"Anyway... it ended badly. I've reported him to the police, but he still stalks me. I get messages on my phone, and no matter how many times I change my cell number, or move jobs or apartments, he always finds me. I even moved interstate for a while, but he just followed me. So, I ended up coming back home in the end."

Claire's mouth dropped open. "So... let me get this straight. You don't like men, and understandably so, because your first, and probably only boyfriend was an abusive creep who still stalks you?"

I choked on my own forced laugh. "Yeah, pretty much."

"And how long ago did all this happen?"

"Um… I was nineteen. I'm twenty-three now, so about four years ago."

"And you haven't been with anyone since?"

I shook my head. There was no way I was going anywhere near another man. Unless he proved without a shadow of a doubt, that he was perfectly trustworthy.

And I didn't know how that would be possible, because trust had been destroyed in me.

"Nope… So, I'm pretty sure I'll be alone forever, because I can't imagine any guy taking on all the baggage I come with."

Claire laughed suddenly. "Oh, sweetheart, you're too young to give up on love."

I stared at her, not sure what else to say. If my story wasn't enough to convince her that I was cursed in the game of love, I didn't know what was.

And the biggest problem was, I kind of agreed with her. I had my whole life ahead of me, and yearned to find someone to love, yet the idea of going back to that place of vulnerability gave me nightmares that haunted me right through all my waking moments.

I didn't trust myself to choose well this time.

"Maybe you're right, Claire. But for the moment, I think I'll concentrate on work, and try not to envision you with three men at once."

I shot Claire a sidelong look and waggled my eyebrows.

She giggled, actually giggled! "It's hotter than you can even imagine, my friend. Oh, speaking of which, what's happening with Dr. Ferrari and that patient who had the hots for him?"

"Oh, it's gotten so much worse since last time you were there!"

We slid into a comfortable conversation about hospital gossip and the afternoon fell away under our friendship.

CHAPTER

TWO

Aaron

After seeing that gorgeous woman a few hours ago, my world tipped on its axis. I couldn't seem to settle my racing mind, nor the racing of my heart.

Which didn't make any sense. It was just one human woman.

A friend of Claire's, probably.

We'd managed to go to work, but all three of us had been desperate to come home for lunch, unable to stay away for some reason.

Her beautiful face... it had haunted me all day.

And the way she'd run away from us had worried me. Were we really that scary to a human woman? How would we ever find a mate if that was how normal women responded to us in our natural environment?

As I stepped onto the porch and turned my head toward Claire's house, sweetness tickled my nostrils with a scent that hadn't been there before. "What's that smell?"

I put my nose in the air and took a deep inhalation of crisp, fall air—something I didn't normally do because, well, I wasn't in shifter form and it could have looked like strange behavior.

Especially if the human woman was watching.

But I did, because I couldn't help myself. There was the most incredible scent on the air. Like honey and apple cookies, comforting and yet arousing somehow.

My Alpha, Grayson, appeared beside me on the porch. "What..."

He immediately did the same thing as me—inhaling deeply until a rumble rolled through his chest. "That's our mate," he said. "Fucking hell... It's the woman we saw this morning, isn't it?"

Grayson began moving, looking around, sniffing the air. Walking toward Dex's house.

He seemed a little stunned. No doubt I sported the same expression as I followed my Alpha.

"How is that possible?" I said. "We've been looking for a month with no success, and she just suddenly turns up out of the blue? Next door. What are the odds?"

I'd been to a dozen interviews, as had Grayson. We'd scoured the streets of Little Creek, even going into town like the rest of the larger pack, frequenting bars and restaurants most nights.

I hadn't been able to find her and neither had my Alpha.

"Come here, quick!" Grayson called from the front of Dex's house.

I ran over to the small black car parked out the front.

"Smell the air here. It's her."

Grayson garbled some more words and I realized that his ability to talk had disappeared. His teeth had shifted partially and some of his fangs had descended over his bottom lip.

He was holding onto his wolf, but barely. Which was danger-ous, especially for Claire and our mate.

"Do you need to shift and run? Because if our mate is human, the last thing you want to do is scare her off."

Grayson shook his head, breathing deeply through his nose, trying to contain himself.

I wanted to go inside Dexter's house and meet our mate—the woman for whom we'd waited our whole lives. But I needed to ask Grayson a question first.

"Does she smell like your mate? Because she certainly smells like mine."

I grinned at my Alpha and he tried to do the same. Since Dexter's triad had learned that our destined mates were no longer born to the pack, but instead were humans we had to seek out, the whole pack had transformed. Mostly for the positive, except for some petty jealousies that had arisen in small pockets here and there. Some of the men were determined not to share, the Alphas in particular. They wanted their own mates.

Not our triad, though.

Brad and I had been best friends since childhood. He was an Omega, and I was a Beta, and when we learnt of the new laws that meant we had to create our own mini-pack with a male Alpha, Beta and Omega in every triad, we did our research.

Grayson was a gentle giant who put the needs of the pack first. He was the perfect Alpha for the two of us. Strong, but not an asshole.

And that's what we wanted.

Someone we'd be proud to call our family.

So, when Grayson told me that he didn't mind sharing a mate, I'd been relieved, but not surprised. It spoke to the fact that he was as magnanimous as always.

"She does smell like my mate," he confirmed. "Let's go see her then."

We stalked toward Dexter's front door. My heart was beating like a bongo drum in my chest. I could hear the roar of my blood, the thump of my racing pulse inside my ears.

Grayson stepped up to the door and knocked, hard.

I looked back at our house. Maybe we should have waited for Brad before we approached her.

The door opened and our neighbor Claire's familiar face smiled up at us.

"Hey, guys. What's up?"

I arched my neck, looking around Claire and my gaze connected with the woman sitting on the couch.

She had long brown hair and a beautifully delicate face and I had to fight not to push Claire out of the way and rush over to the visitor.

"Ah..." Grayson coughed to clear his throat and I realized he was still struggling to contain his wolf.

I jumped in. "Would you introduce us to your guest, Claire? Please?"

She studied the two of us, and I could see understanding dawning on her face. Her mouth opened and her eyebrows flew up and then lowered slowly.

"Ah, yes... are you sure?" she whispered.

I met her intense stare and nodded slowly.

"Okay, but you need to be cautious. Nevaeh is... gun shy."

I had no idea what that meant but nodded regardless.

We moved inside their house slowly, the scent of Nevaeh rising up into my nostrils and saturating them with pleasure.

God, she's beautiful.

The arch of her cheek, the blue of her eyes... she was perfection.

And she was clearly *not* happy we were here.

She stood up and extended to her full height, her gaze hard as flint as she stared at us.

"Hello."

Grayson glanced at me, as surprised as I was about the harsh tone of her voice and the defensiveness in her body language.

Claire jumped between us. "Nevaeh is a nurse from work, and one of my best friends. Nevaeh, this is Grayson and Aaron. They live next door."

I didn't know what that tone or her facial expressions were trying to say. All I could feel was the electricity in the air. The hairs on my neck standing on end and my cock thick, pressing against the fly of my jeans.

I hoped to God she couldn't see it. I had black jeans on today, and hopefully the dark, thick fabric hid my arousal.

"I'm Aaron. It's nice to meet a friend of Claire's."

Grayson wasn't moving, but I was itching to touch her. To feel her skin against mine and to see if Dex had been right about our mate's response to our touch.

And if Grayson wasn't going to step up...

"We didn't mean to barge in like this and shock you." I walked forward and held out my hand.

I heard Claire's sharp intake of breath but kept my eyes focused on Nevaeh.

She didn't smile. "It's fine. I was just leaving, anyway."

She wasn't taking my hand and I shot her a smile of encouragement. "You gonna leave me hanging?"

A ghost of a smile shivered across her lips. "Sorry, I'm being rude. It's nice to meet you, too."

She took my hand and a loud gasp filled the room. Mine or hers, I wasn't sure.

The pleasure was almost painful as it filled my veins and my lungs. I couldn't escape it. I couldn't breathe.

Then she was falling and Grayson scooped her up into his arms.

She shuddered violently as soon as he touched her, moaning loudly.

"What's happening to her?" I asked Claire.

The doctor shrugged. "No idea. I was the one fainting, so I don't remember much else. She's probably just responding to touching you and then her Alpha on top of that."

Nevaeh arched her back and cried out, then she passed out again, limp in Grayson's arms.

The Alpha's muscles bulged as he trembled with her.

"You want me to take her?" I asked him.

He growled a low warning at me and clung to her. It was a noise I'd never heard in my life.

I backed away, my hands up in a placating gesture, and let him hold her.

Pain and confusion rippled through my skin and Claire walked over and put a hand on me.

"Calm down. This is new and strange, and you need to find a way to work through this together."

I nodded and began to pace the large living room. She was right, but now that it had happened, the idea of sharing Nevaeh wasn't as easy as I'd thought.

Growls were surfacing in my chest as well, and an unaccustomed anger toward my Alpha rose.

The door opened and Dexter walked in, stopping short at seeing us in his living room.

Dexter and his pack were very protective of Claire, and we approached her with caution everywhere she went. On the street, in the restaurants, and in town.

We certainly never entered their home when the boys weren't here.

"What's going on, guys?" Dexter asked, his tone strangely calm.

Claire bounced over to him and grabbed him in a huge hug. "Nevaeh is their mate! Look!"

She pulled Dex a little closer to Grayson, who growled and bared his teeth.

I fell back, expecting Dexter to lash out. Two Alphas in any pack could be dangerous, which was the main reason we were forced into our own triad families. To stop as much in-fighting as possible, in a world where there was no release for the testosterone, except running, or fighting.

Until now, that is.

Instead of arcing up, Dexter's shoulders relaxed and he began to laugh. "And you thought I was crazy for wanting to protect Claire! Karma's a bitch, Grayson."

Dexter kept chuckling, moving to the kitchen and opening the refrigerator door.

I was stunned.

He was suddenly all calm?

What about us? How would Grayson and I reach calm again?

"What do we do, Dex? When will she come around?" I asked.

Dexter grabbed some food from the fridge and began making a platter. Fruit, sliced meats and chocolate.

"Claire was knocked out for over an hour when I touched her, about ten minutes with Taylor and just kinda fell against Jay. So, get comfortable, guys. She's not coming around any time soon."

He brought over the platter and kissed his mate. "Eat up, beautiful. You need it."

I looked at Claire again. Her glowing cheeks, the food her mate was shoving at her...that could only mean one thing.

"You're pregnant?"

Claire grinned at me and Dexter scooped her up and put her in his lap, sitting on the couch with her.

"Yes," she confirmed.

Grayson began to move closer and slowly sat down on the other end of the couch with Nevaeh, who hadn't stirred and whose head still lay on Grayson's chest.

"Congratulations," he managed to get out, and I could see the calm Alpha in him coming back slowly.

"It will probably help if you put her down, Gray." Dexter turned his head and called out. "Jay, you here?"

A door opened and Jay came out, rubbing his eyes like he'd been working too hard at a computer screen.

"You called? Oh, hey, guys. Didn't know you were here. Sorry." Then he did a double-take at the sight of Nevaeh in Grayson's arms.

"It looks like Claire's nurse friend is their mate. Can Gray put her down on your bed?"

Jay's gaze bounced around the room at everyone, finally coming to rest again on Nevaeh. "Wow. What are the odds?"

Grayson growled a little again, and this time I wanted to roll my eyes. He had to know that of all the guys in the larger pack, Claire's three were not the ones who would ever want our mate. They had their own.

"Probably a good idea, Grayson," I chimed in, not sure how this was going to play out. "Or we could take her home now?"

"I think maybe you should keep her here," Claire said, standing up and walking over to Grayson. "She's pretty scared of men, and if she wakes up in your house without me, she's going to freak out. Come on, Grayson, I'll show you where to put her. You'll probably calm down once you stop touching her."

Grayson did as asked, though it was obvious from the set of his jaw that he didn't want to.

They disappeared into the room Jay had emerged from, then returned without her.

My stomach hurt, so I grabbed for some of the food in front of us.

"So, um... congratulations," I said. "That's great news. A baby for the pack will be considered a true miracle."

"Yeah, if it's only one," Claire said, eating the fruit on the platter by the handful. "I'm going to organize an ultrasound in a few weeks, but considering our relationship, I wouldn't be surprised if it's a multiple pregnancy."

"Which would be even more of a miracle," I said.

Grayson shook himself and walked to the kitchen where he grabbed a bottle of water. "I'm sorry about the... wolf crap. I don't know what came over me."

Dexter didn't even flinch. "Grab a beer, Gray. Not water. You're gonna need the extra kick."

Grayson, who didn't drink, turned back around and grabbed a beer from the fridge. "Anyone else?"

"Yeah, me." I was still shaking and my nerves were stretched tight, ready to pounce on an enemy that didn't exist.

"Not for me," Dexter said, and Jay shook his head.

Grayson handed me a beer and sat next to me, the tension between us shaky, but finally settling.

"Well, that was more intense than I expected," I said.

Jay laughed at us. "I remember it too well. It's not something that ever leaves you, really."

That didn't sound pleasant.

I looked at Claire. "What do you mean about Nevaeh not liking men?"

Fate would surely not have sent us a woman who wouldn't accept us?

Claire bit her lip. "I'm not sure I should be the one to explain that to you."

I groaned. "Oh, please, help us out a little. You know we're going to struggle as it is. We have to explain to a human that there's three of us to love and that we're wolf shifters in a world where there are no shifter women left."

My head was spinning with all we had to accomplish and I suddenly realized how ridiculous it might sound to someone not of our world.

I began to laugh and wasn't sure why. There may have been a slight note of hysteria in it, because Claire smiled gently. "Okay, I'll help you. But only because I know how hard it was for me to accept my mates, and I didn't have half the baggage that Nevaeh does."

Grayson and I shared a concerned look, then sat down again on the couch, opposite Claire, and waited.

My heart pounded and my stomach tightened. I grabbed my beer and chugged some down, the cold beverage soothing some of the dryness in my throat.

"Okay... well, let me preface this with the fact that I only found out about her history today. I knew Nevaeh was a bit... gun shy. She never dates, and works any shift anyone asks her to. She's really careful with her money and never goes out."

I glanced at Grayson but couldn't gauge his expression.

"And today I found out why. It's because her last boyfriend, who sounds like he was her first and only boyfriend, stalked her after they broke up."

I glanced at Grayson, not really understanding the human reference. But it sounded bad. Like she'd been treated as prey.

"Sorry, Claire, you're going to have to explain that to us. What is stalking, in the human world?"

"Oh... um. You guys probably don't do that with women. Well, if a man is obsessed with you and you break up, he may try to stay in touch, even though you don't want to. He might follow you, call you, watch you—all against your will. It's scary and makes you afraid all the time."

As a male, and as someone who'd grown up in a small town where nothing bad really ever happened, this was a foreign concept.

"Ah... okay."

I wasn't much clearer now, unfortunately.

"So, what do we do?" Grayson asked from beside me. At least he'd gotten his voice properly back again.

"You need to be patient, and take it slow with her. She's not going to jump into bed with you guys the moment you put the moves on her. If anything, she'll run—as quickly as possible."

Claire bit her lip and I waited.

"What's wrong?" Grayson prompted.

"Just remembering what happened here with Dex and the guys, with me. They asked me to stay for two days to get to know them. That really helped me accept them as my mates. You could try to do that as well, but I don't think Nevaeh will be able to. She'll fight the natural attraction she feels, because of her fear, and you won't be able to stop her from going to work. She's far too driven for that."

"Then what do we do?" I asked.

Claire was making the situation sound impossible to fix, which it wasn't. It couldn't be.

I believed in the power of Fate, and the old stories of fated mates and perfect women. I always had. Even when I'd been told that path in life wouldn't be for me, I somehow knew that somewhere, there'd be someone waiting for me.

And now I knew I'd been right.

It was Nevaeh, and she wasn't just waiting for me, she'd been waiting for *us*.

"Well isn't she lucky that there are three of us to look after her?"

Claire laughed, and then put a dainty hand over her mouth. "Ah, no. That's gonna work against you, I'm afraid. She was horrified when I explained about my triad."

"Shit," Grayson grunted.

"I'll second that," I said.

This was getting worse by the minute. What could we do?

I looked around the room, then stood up so I could pace. I always thought better when I was on my feet.

We needed someone to talk to her, to explain. Someone she trusted...

"Claire! You can help us. You can talk to her, explain about our ways. Vouch for us. You know we'd never hurt her."

I'd spoken to Claire practically every day since she'd moved in with Dex's pack.

Sure, I didn't come too close, nor did I venture inside her house, but she knew us. Surely, she'd help.

She looked from me to Grayson, to Dexter, and back again. "Ah... I suppose I could. I know her better than anyone, and I know how hard it is to accept this world when you've been raised as a human."

"So, you'll help us?"

Claire nodded, her eyes wide with what looked like trepidation. "Yes. I will."

"Thank you."

Nevaeh

What the hell were they talking about? *Me?*

I didn't know if anyone was in the room with me, and tried to stay still in case someone was close by. Prickling unease and fear made me hold my breath so they wouldn't know I was awake, but the pain in my chest became too great, and my breath whooshed out in a fast stream.

My eyes flickered open and I glanced around the room. I was alone.

Why was I on a bed, in a strange room?

My heart beat so loudly I could barely hear the people talking over the thumping in my ears.

I rolled onto my side and sat up slowly.

The bed creaked under my weight and I froze. Not breathing, but instead listening and waiting for someone to come.

No one did.

They'd left the door partially open and as I got to my feet and moved over to the door, the voices became more distinct.

It was Claire.

So, I was still at her house.

Thank God for that.

Had I fainted? Or fallen over, or something? I didn't remember.

But that was definitely Claire and she was talking to a whole group of men from the sounds of all the deep throaty voices I could hear.

"So, we'll wait for her to wake up, and then I'll explain what's going on here." Claire laughed awkwardly. "It's gonna shock the pants off her, though."

I grimaced. I was keeping my pants on. No matter what they put in the water out here, I was not becoming a version of Claire. Shacked up with three men, pregnant, and letting my career slip through my fingers.

I'd worked too hard to make it through college and get away from my trailer-park parents to let go of my job now.

It gave me purpose, happiness, not to mention the money to pay my rent and save for the house I'd one day buy myself.

A house of my own. My greatest dream.

One day.

I took a deep breath, and put my hand on the bedroom door. I had to go to work, so I needed to leave this room and face the music, so to speak. But the idea of walking out into that lounge area with all those men made my heart pound and my throat thicken with stress.

Time to pull myself together. I'd handled much worse.

I grabbed the handle and opened the door.

The room went suddenly, deathly quiet as I stuck out my head.

My breath caught in my throat and my ribs tightened around my chest.

Damn...

"Oh my God."

There were four of them! When had that happened?

"Nevaeh!" Claire rushed to my side and grabbed my hand with her good arm, resting her fingers on my ulnar artery and looking into my face. "Are you okay?"

"Yeah, what happened?"

"Ah, well, you fainted."

"I fainted? Seriously?" I'd never fainted. Not a single time. Not during college, or my thousands of hours in the E.R. and the horrific surgeries I'd witnessed. Why would I faint now? "My iron is probably down. I've been pretty exhausted lately."

There had to be a good explanation for this.

I tried to focus on Claire, but most of my attention was on two of the men in the room. They were the ones I'd seen this morning. The next door neighbors. And they were staring at me like a hungry man would look at a juicy steak.

Like they wanted to devour me.

Like they'd never seen a woman before.

And unfortunately, my love-starved body was experiencing the same thing.

Arousal curled in my belly, creating heat in my loins. And over perfect strangers. How utterly insane was that?

"Nevaeh, I think you should stay here for the night. We have heaps of room, and I don't think you should be driving."

I raised an eyebrow at my boss. "You know I don't call in sick —ever. Three years running and never had a sick day."

Claire frowned. "You've been unconscious for over half an hour. That's not normal, hun. And if you have to go back to the hospital, I insist on giving you an escort. Grayson and Aaron can drive you."

She indicated to the two hot men across from us and a shiver of excitement coursed down my spine.

There were both gorgeous. Sex on legs. And judging by my reaction, clearly lethal for a weak woman like me.

"No. I'll be fine."

Claire gave me *the look*, the one she reserved for errant patients. "You have two choices. You can call in sick, stay here overnight and drive yourself home in the morning, or Grayson can drive you back now. You know me, Nevaeh... and I don't back down easily."

Dex laughed from the couch. "Easily? How 'bout never?"

I shivered. From what, I wasn't sure. I wasn't cold, and funnily enough, I wasn't scared.

But the way those two men, Grayson and Aaron, were looking at me, was causing major issues with my internal thermostat.

"Ah... you're not giving me much choice, Claire."

She grinned at me and I relaxed even more. This was a woman I trusted, and if she said I should stay, then I'd stay.

I wasn't letting two strange men drive me an hour back to the hospital.

"I'll stay here if you have the room. A good night's sleep would probably do me the world of good, actually." I'd been pushing hard lately. Fifty, sixty-hour weeks most of the time. "But only if it's no trouble."

"No. No, not at all. You can sleep down here in Jay's room if you want, or Taylor's room upstairs. We all sleep in Dexter's room when I'm home."

My mind flashed with images of how they'd sleep together. Coiled and sensual and naked. Pressed up against one another, having fallen where they may after a hot session of sex.

Or maybe they lay like puppies. On top of each other and in a pile.

A giggle escaped my lips at the idea and Claire cocked her head at me. "What's funny?"

"Ah... nothing, I'll ask you later."

My face heated with a blush, and I was mortified to think I was so obviously being inappropriate in front of all these people.

Grayson, the huge, hot one, was backing towards the front door, "Ah, Claire, Brad will be getting home from work soon. Do you mind if we come back after dinner?"

Although he was talking to Claire, his gaze kept darting toward me.

I smiled at him, though I wasn't sure why I wanted to reassure him that everything was okay.

Everything was not okay. I'd fainted, a first for me, and was being told I wasn't allowed to go to work, or go home.

My two safe places.

Well, as safe as a place can be when you have a stalker that tracks your every move.

"I'm going to put on some dinner," Jay said and headed off to the kitchen.

Dex kissed Claire and moved to the front door. "I've gotta talk to Dad about a few pack matters but will be back with Taylor soon."

Grayson was still standing by the door with Aaron, and my heart lurched to see them leaving.

They were so much better looking than Dex. How could Claire go for her guys, when the ones next door were so much hotter?

Grayson's skin was so clear and healthy I wanted to rub my own face against his.

Dexter grabbed Grayson and they kind of fell through the doorway.

Clair turned away to seize her phone and my brain clicked into gear.

"Hang on a minute. Did he just say pack?"

What sort of person referred his family as a pack? A pack of what?

"Oh, yeah. It's just a nickname. There's a high percentage of men in the town. Not many females have been born in the last few generations, which is why the guys live together in triads."

That sounded like something out of a dystopian movie.

"That's a bit strange. How many is 'not many'?"

In most communities there was generally an even amount of males and females born, as long as there were no rules about how many children one family could have.

That tended to outweigh the odds.

"Ah... none, actually."

"What? How is that possible?"

I stared at her, watching her face for signs of deceit or misunderstanding.

Claire shrugged. "They don't know. Dexter's and Taylor's moms were some of the last-born females in this town. From then, only males have been born. Which is why I'm hoping I have a girl in here." Claire stopped to pat her still-flat stomach. "Because that would be a miracle."

I looked away, toward the front door, a chill coursing down my spine.

"So, you're telling me that out there is an entire town filled with sex-starved men, who haven't seen a woman in, what... days, weeks? Months?"

My stomach tightened until I wanted to be sick. Was this why Claire had lured me out here? To be some triad's woman?

"I think I should go home, Claire. You can't keep me here. Not with this many men... I..."

I couldn't breathe. My skin was on fire.

"Claire! I... I..."

My breath was wheezing in and out, and my lungs hurt too much.

My mind raced with escape plans. *The front door.*

I ran for it. Tripped on the rug and fell straight into the wooden door. My shoulder screamed with pain.

But I didn't stop. I couldn't.

I grabbed for the door handle with sweaty hands, "No... no... no!"

I could feel them coming up behind me. I screamed out as I pulled open the door and raced down the stairs toward my car.

My keys were in my pocket. I grabbed for them and pulled them out. My hands shook and my heart pounded in my chest like I was running away from a bear.

"Hey, are you okay?" a man to my left called out to me, and as I beeped open the door I was grateful to see that he was smaller than all the others. Just a little taller than me, thin, and he had a kind face.

He jogged over, his eyes going wide as he took in my trembling form.

"I'm Brad. Are you okay? You're as white as a ghost."

"I need to go home. Now. I can't stay here. You don't understand..."

"I probably don't, but I'm sure I can help you. Okay?"

He put his hand out and touched my arm, and I didn't stop him.

The feeling of his fingers on my skin soothed all of my anxiety. Instantly. Like he'd switched off a tap.

The blood drained away from my arms and legs and the sky began to spin.

The man gasped and gripped my arm harder as I began to fall.

He swept me up into his arms, and after the day I'd had, following the year I'd endured, I let the darkness pull me under.

CHAPTER
FOUR

Brad

She was heaven and angels, and perfection, all in one beautifully scented package.

I took a deep breath through my nose, the heat of arousal racing through my blood like a driver speeding on the last lap of a five-hundred-mile race.

"Whoa."

If this woman wasn't our mate, I'd bite my own ass.

People came running from everywhere, it seemed, and although on one level I recognized all of them, I pulled my mate into my chest and backed away from everyone.

"What on earth is going on here?"

"Give her to me, Brad." Grayson came toward me with his arms outstretched.

I didn't want to hand her over.

Indeed, my teeth descended and my wolf rose to the surface to fight the Alpha for the woman in my arms.

"It's okay, Brad. I know how you're feeling. She's our mate. I won't harm her." Grayson said soothing things, and I focused on his words to calm the animal in me.

"Okay."

Finally, I let him take her and she began to stir in his arms.

"Why did she faint like that? Is she unwell?"

"No, don't you remember what Dex said about Claire?"

The memory hit me all at once. "Oh, yeah, that's right. The mating thing."

We began to walk to our house and Claire called out, "Bring her back to our place. I told her she could sleep in Jay's room."

I frowned at her and shared a concerned look with Aaron, who had appeared at the same time as Grayson.

Claire crossed her arms over her chest. "Grayson. Bring my friend back to my house."

Grayson did, and we followed.

My head was spinning.

Aaron was grinning.

"How long have you known about this?" I asked him, angry accusation in my tone.

"Like... two hours. We got home from town, caught wind of her scent and found her in Claire's house. We would have told you sooner if we knew where you were."

I nodded, unable to deal with the emotions coursing through my blood.

My arms and legs tingled, as though ready for battle. To run, to shift. I wanted to get rid of all this excess energy, but didn't want to leave our mate.

"What's her name?"

Aaron smiled. "Nevaeh."

It was pretty, but what did it mean?

Then it hit me, my brain rearranging the letters and coming up with the answer.

I laughed, loudly, the tension in my body dissipating.

"What's so funny?" Aaron asked me and I waved at him to indicate not to worry about it.

Obviously, no one else had figured it out, and I'd explain later.

Grayson was putting Nevaeh down on the couch and she was sitting as stiff as a board, uncomfortable and embarrassed by the look of her red cheeks.

"I fainted again, didn't I?"

Claire nodded. "Yes. Told you. You need to stay put. I'm going to call the hospital right now, and you're going to take a few days off."

Claire walked into the kitchen with her cell phone and began talking to someone.

I walked past my Alpha and Dexter and moved to sit on the couch near my mate. Not close enough to touch her as I ached to do, but near enough to drink in the beauty and the scent of our 'Heaven'.

"Are you okay?" I couldn't help but ask.

"Yeah... I met you just now outside. Thank you for helping me calm down. I was... not coping."

"You looked like you were having a panic attack. Do you suffer from anxiety?"

I'd read a lot about depression and anxiety in the human population. It wasn't something we wolves suffered from, fortunately.

"Yes, I do. Though it's usually under better control than that. Why, do you?"

"Ah... not exactly. But I do empathize with the idea that your life is spinning out of control and you don't know how to change it."

I'd felt like that for years, and it was only in the last month when the hope of a mate had come into our lives that I'd started to feel a little better.

A tear slipped down her face and she huffed out a laugh.

I moved over to her and sat right next to her.

I couldn't help myself and she didn't seem to be afraid of me the way she was of the larger men in the room.

I reached up to cup her face and wipe the tear from her cheek.

"Don't cry, beautiful."

I wiped her tear with the pad of my thumb and little shocks of awareness passed over my skin.

She shivered and pulled away a little, but didn't move to another seat.

"What is that? Why do I feel so strange when you guys touch me?"

"Because you're our mate. We're meant to be."

"What?" Nevaeh lowered her eyebrows, glared at me with a stormy expression, then got to her feet so she could glower down at me from a height.

I hadn't expected such an intense response.

"What the hell is that supposed to mean?"

Claire came around the couch and stood beside Nevaeh. "What's happened? What's going on?"

"He just told me we're meant to be, and I'm his mate. Claire, what the hell is this bullshit? What are you guys smoking out here? And why the *hell* are these men so big? I've seen professional football players who were smaller."

Claire suddenly took charge of the room.

"I need everyone but the Omegas out while I talk to Nevaeh."

"But, Claire..." The men began to complain.

She waved her hands at them. "No! You don't understand how

confusing this is for us. Go to Grayson's house. Have some dinner and a beer. We'll call you back soon."

The Alphas and the Betas left with their metaphorical tails between their legs and as soon as the front door shut, I laughed. I couldn't contain it a moment longer. Jay joined in, and Claire gave me a stern stare. "This is no laughing matter, Brad."

I grinned at her, the lightness and happiness in my heart making my head feel woozy.

"I understand that, but you need to know that I have never, in all my life, seen anyone boss around the Alphas the way you do. It's awesome. Truly."

Jay chuckled from beside me. "It's true, Claire. And we love you for that."

Claire huffed at us, but her bright smile was returning. "Well, I'm not scared of them. Those muscles of theirs are for protection, not to cause us harm."

"So true." I nodded at her and gave her my best smile. "Still doesn't change the fact that watching you go up against them is awesome." I looked straight at Nevaeh. "Take note, seriously. Grayson and Aaron are big teddy bears, and you'll soon be bossing them around the way Claire does with Dexter and Taylor."

Nevaeh gave me a glare that was quite ugly, and it twisted my gut.

"Why are you looking at me like I've done something terrible?"

Nevaeh's face crumpled and although she didn't smile, the glare lost its strength. "You haven't. I'm sorry. I just don't know what I'm doing here."

Claire and Jay got up and moved around the kitchen, preparing food. Maybe.

I turned my attention back to my mate.

"Tell me about yourself, Heaven spelled backwards."

Her face screwed up and she looked skyward. "I *hate* my name so much. Bloody hippie parents."

I couldn't stop myself from reaching out to her. But she slid away before I could feel her skin beneath my palm.

That hurt. And it shouldn't have. The poor girl didn't know me, even though it felt like I'd known her my entire life.

I cleared my throat and pushed away the feeling of rejection that had no place in this situation. Not yet, anyway.

"Why do you hate it so much? It's beautiful."

She rolled her eyes and groaned. "Because it has been the bane of my existence since high school. At home it wasn't too bad. My mum called me her angel sent from heaven because she'd been told she couldn't have children, so to her, I was a miracle."

"That's really nice."

And it was. I'd feel the same way about any children I had.

"Yeah... I suppose, but it's given every guy, or bitchy girl who's not liked me, the perfect way to tease me."

"What would the guys say?"

She looked at the floor and began imitating a man's voice. "Oh, you sure look like heaven. Heaven on a stick, sex on a stick. You must have been sent from Heaven. You feel like Heaven. Blah, blah, blah. They made me feel so dirty all the time."

The words were just spilling out of her now.

"Not that I'm complaining, but how come you're suddenly talking? You were practically rendered mute before."

Nevaeh's gaze met mine. "I don't know. I just... don't like being around too many people. Or really big guys. This is nice. I feel less... threatened with just you."

She glanced back toward the kitchen, where Claire and Jay were working together.

So, she didn't like being intimidated or outnumbered. That was going to be a problem in our family.

"I can understand that. You were an only child?"

She nodded, though her posture became guarded. "Yeah, why?"

"Because it makes more sense why you want to be around less people, so to speak. I grew up with three older brothers, so I feel lonely if there aren't at least three people in the room."

She rubbed her hands together, appearing to think about my observation.

"Three brothers? That would have been nice. I always wanted siblings."

"Maybe you still can, you know... have a big family when you're ready."

She shook her head. "No. I don't think so. I'd have to find a man I could trust enough to marry and have children with, and that's not going to happen any time soon."

That didn't sound normal, so I continued to ask questions.

"How come?"

She cocked her head. "Why do you make me feel safe when the others make me want to run to my car and drive away?"

I laughed; I couldn't help it. "I always thought it was the curse of the Omega, but you're making me feel special, rather than inadequate."

"What are you talking about, Brad?"

I sighed as Jay and Claire sat down, placing platters of cold chicken and cut up vegetables before us. Perfect for chatting around the table while we ate.

Jay was looking at me with understanding, and I realised now was the time to explain our world to my mate.

"I'll explain what I mean, but please be patient while I do, okay? It'll sound strange to you."

She grabbed a piece of chicken and nodded. "Okay."

"All right... well, in our town, there hasn't been a single female born in over fifty years, did you know that?"

"Yeah, Claire told me."

"Good. Well, the way the elders handled that had never been done before, but in retrospect, was kind of a brilliant move. They asked us guys, when we reached twenty-one, to make groups of triads. But we had to choose one Alpha, one Beta and one Omega for each family."

"And, other than ancient Greek letters, they are?" She smiled as if to soften her query, as she picked up a carrot and crunched on it.

"They're a..." I wasn't sure exactly how to explain it, especially to a human.

I looked to Claire for help and she smiled. "They're a classification, so to speak. For size, job and personality traits."

"Okay, so you're an Omega?" Nevaeh looked over at me, but Claire sat forward in her chair and took over the conversation.

"After you see it once or twice, you'll recognize it each time. An Alpha is the leader, and the largest of the three. He'll be the most possessive and physically huge, like Dex and Grayson. But they're teddy bears. Gray even more so, actually. A Beta is next. They're the Alpha's right-hand man. Slightly smaller but still fast and strong, and also extremely protective."

"And an Omega is the smallest and the nicest?" Nevaeh asked, shooting a tiny smile my way. "Is that why you thought being an Omega was a curse?"

I shrugged, but I liked her description. "Yeah, what can I say? I hated being the smallest of my family, both as a kid, and now. I can't run, hunt or lift the way Gray and Aaron do. I could train every day for the rest of my life, and I'll never be as naturally strong as Gray."

Nevaeh smiled more widely this time. "But if that makes you the nicest one, why would you care about all their puffy muscles?"

I laughed.

"I wouldn't describe them as puffy muscles, beautiful. But I appreciate the sentiment."

Nevaeh looked away and I realized my error. "Oh, sorry. That just slipped out."

When she looked up, her gaze was harder. "Can I ask you a question?"

"Anything."

"What am I doing here, really? I mean... I came to visit Claire, but there's something else, isn't there? And you know. Can you tell me?"

The heat of her awareness and focus bore down on me.

I didn't really want to tell her, and risk having her be mad at me. I wanted to remain in this moment where she was looking at me, with a clear, open face, wanting my help.

But it wasn't meant to be.

I had to tell her the truth.

"I can. But you have to promise you won't... freak out."

Claire laughed, but there was an edge to the sound. "Oh, she's gonna freak out, Brad. If you can't handle that, you can leave and I'll tell her."

I straightened and tried not to snarl at the doctor.

"I'm not going anywhere."

"Then tell her." Claire flicked her hand and indicated to Nevaeh, who waited patiently for me to spill the beans.

"Okay." I slid over and took both of her hands in mine. Amazingly, she didn't move away, but instead waited for me to speak, with wide eyes. "Nevaeh, you're our mate. Grayson, Aaron and mine."

"Your... mate. What do you mean?"

God, her eyes were beautiful. Aqua, flecked with silver and a rainbow of sky blues.

"It means you're meant to be ours. Our... wife. Our partner—whatever you want to call it."

Nevaeh withdrew her hands and stared at me with a strange smile on her face. It didn't look like a happy smile.

"You seriously think I'm going to believe that you and I are meant to be together? You're really nice, and very hot... but I don't know you."

Pride blossomed throughout my body at her compliment.

No one had ever said I was hot. *Ever.*

"But you will. And you'll learn to love me and Grayson and Aaron. Just like Claire has done with her pack."

That's when I lost her.

Her eyebrows flew up and her jaw snapped together like the clapping of hands.

"You've got to be fucking kidding me, right?"

The sarcastic tone wasn't subtle.

"Ah... nope. Personally, I'd love to keep you all to myself, but you fainted at Grayson's touch, and Aaron's too, from what they said. So, you have to be everyone's mate in our triad. That's what the fainting thing means. It's how it works."

"I fainted... What? Hang on... What are you saying?"

Nevaeh abandoned her food and stood up to throw her hands around and yell.

"Because this better be a joke, Brad! Seriously. I am not getting sucked into your weird cult where there's some sort of upside-down polygamy thing going on. I don't even want one husband, let alone three! What the hell would I *do* with you all?"

Histrionics was how they used to describe it, and for the first time in my life I thought how blessed I was, *not* to have grown up with a sister.

"Nevaeh, calm down."

"Calm down? *Calm down? You* fucking calm down. I'm out of here, and if any of you— Claire, this goes for you too—tries to stop me leaving, I swear to God, you will be sorry."

She found her keys and, despite her threat, I ran to the door to block her exit. I had to convince her we were meant to be, and I had no idea how to do that.

"Nevaeh, can't you feel the connection between us? The attraction? You have to feel something. We do. And Claire said she knew straight away when she met her triad that they were meant for her."

Nevaeh stormed up to me. "Get out of my way, Brad. Now. Or I will call the cops and have you guys arrested! I already have one restraining order up on my ex. I'll happily put one on you, too."

I fell away from the door and Nevaeh yanked it open.

While my heart was breaking, I heard a feminine chuckle from Claire behind me.

"Fight it all you want, Nevaeh. But you're never winning this battle. You're meant to be theirs, and you will be."

Nevaeh let out a feral growl as she stomped to her car, slammed shut the door, and drove away. A cloud of dust billowed up around the spot where her car had once been.

Claire and Jay walked up to me and Claire patted my arm as I stood there gaping at the empty space. "That actually went better than I expected."

She laughed as she walked away, but my heart fell.

Had I driven our mate away for good?

"What did I do wrong, Jay?"

Claire's Omega stood with me as I stared after the retreating car. "Nothing, Brad. You forget how weird this must be to a human, especially one who's been abused by a man like Nevaeh.

Wait until you have to tell her you guys are wolf shifters. That one will likely go down like a lead balloon."

Jay walked off and the other men came running at me.

"What happened?" the Alphas demanded.

"I just..." I swallowed hard around the lump in my throat. "I told her about the three of us and she lost it. Screamed at me and drove away. I didn't even get to tell her about... anything, really."

Grayson grimaced. "Unfortunately, it sounds like Nevaeh's background will dictate her actions."

He sniffed the air and frowned. "Do you smell that?"

Aaron and I turned our heads in the direction Gray was looking, and there it was, faint, but definitely noticeable.

"Bears," I said.

"At least one. Dex!"

Dexter came to the door and Grayson called out, "There's a bear shifter around. We're going after our mate. You keep yours safe."

Grayson began to strip and we joined him in dropping our clothes.

"Okay, but be careful," Dex said. "The closer you get to town, the more dangerous it is for you with hunters around."

We nodded, before the shift ripped through the three of us at the same time.

My eyes transitioned to ones with great night vision, my hearing and sense of smell intensified, and the thrill of the hunt curled up my back as I dropped to my paws and shook my coat.

Grayson put back his head and howled to the sky. Then we took off after the woman meant to complete us.

FIVE

Nevaeh

Can you bloody believe it? They expect me to...

I couldn't even finish the thought! They expected me to....

I burst out laughing, in a strangely hysterical way.

How was it possible that today had gone so incredibly wrong? Claire... dating not one, but three men at once.

And her next-door neighbors expecting me to do the same thing with them.

"Over my dead body!"

I was too hot in the car and rolled down the window to let in some fresh, night air.

The strangest sounds met my ears.

Deep growling.

I tried to keep my eyes on the dark road ahead, but my gaze kept darting to the side to see if I could catch a glimpse of whatever was making that noise.

A bear?

Wolves, maybe?

I pushed myself to concentrate on the road before me. I didn't recognize any of the landmarks and the road was winding in a way that required my attention.

My heart began to thump harder in my chest.

My stomach twisted until I tasted acid in my throat.

This was bad.

I shouldn't have left Claire's house.

They weren't going to hurt me. I would have been safe.

Sure, Brad was saying crazy, stupid things about me being his mate… or something like that. But they wouldn't have hurt me. Claire wouldn't have let them.

And now I was driving in the dark, *in bum-fuck nowhere*, surrounded by weird animal growling noises. And I was scared.

Despite the curves in the road, I pushed my foot down harder on the accelerator and turned on the radio to drown out the external noises.

Some stupid guy singing a dumb, stupid, love song came on the radio, and even though I'd usually switch it off with an angry flick of my wrist, I didn't care. I needed the distraction.

My heart thudded against my rib cage.

Maybe I should turn back? I was still closer to Claire's house than home, and I could always head home in the morning.

I took my foot off the accelerator, slowing down in preparation to turn back. That's when I heard it.

The roaring of an enraged beast.

And then a huge bear charged out of the darkness, straight at my car.

"No!" I screamed and jumped on the accelerator again. The car burst forward at the same time the bear plowed into the back-seat door on the driver side, buckling the metal.

The car spun out of control and I braced myself for the impact. I kept screaming as I was flung around and around.

My breathing came in spurts and pants, and I could hear the continued growling.

My car came to a rest, and thank the heavens, didn't roll.

My neck was killing me and my shoulders were rigid as I gripped the steering wheel, but there was no blood. No broken bones.

An enormous black bear shuffled into view, visible in the headlights. Its terrifying gaze met mine through the windshield, and fear flashed through my body as I grappled for the keys. Would the car re-start?

I needed to get out of here.

Now!

Then a wolf appeared. A big, silver wolf, and I think I must have passed out from sheer terror then, because I only remember flashes of what happened after that.

The vicious noises of an animal fight.

The sinking feeling of knowing I was about to die.

And realizing how stupid I'd been, to race off into the darkness in an unknown area of wilderness.

My pride had gotten the better of me again... No, not pride. My temper.

Someone was carrying me. I should have been scared. Who had me? Where were they taking me?

I half-emerged from the fog around my brain, but then the blackness took me again and the next time I woke up I was warm, in a bed, with a woman hovering over me.

"Claire..."

I quickly closed my eyes again. The pain in my head was like a hammer pounding on my skull.

"Take these," she said. "It'll help with the pain."

I put up my hand and took the pills Claire handed me.

"Thanks."

She held a glass of water for me, and I washed the pills down my tight throat. I struggled to open my eyes, but eventually forced myself.

Claire was not the only one in the room.

I let my gaze roam around. There were the three next door neighbors, all hovering like expectant parents.

And they were all shirtless.

They wore jeans, but nothing else.

The most embarrassing part of it all was, despite my confusion and soreness, my attraction to them flared, flooding my belly and between my legs with the certainty that I desired them. All three of them. I winced at my traitorous body.

"Um... why are they not dressed?"

Claire crossed her arms over her chest. "If I tell you the truth, do you promise not to stomp off like a toddler and get into another car accident?"

I nodded quickly, dragging my eyelids up to focus on Claire's face.

"Tell me."

Claire gave me one of her stern looks, one she usually kept for her wayward patients.

"Okay. I'm going to spill this out all at once, because I've been through it myself, and I can tell you, it's fucking... unbelievable. And amazing. And perfect. But I know you, and you're going to fight it with everything in you."

I wet my lips with my tongue, my focus returning as the pain receded into the back of my mind. What on earth was she about to say?

"Tell me, Claire."

"This is a town full of wolf shifters. All the men, and the

women, can change into a wolf at will. Yes, it sounds crazy, but it's true, and the guys can show you when you want them to... But it'll freak you out, I guarantee it."

If only Claire knew. I'd been introduced to the paranormal world already, several years ago now, when something horrific had happened. Something so bad, that I had managed to block it out of my mind. Until now.

So, hearing about shifters was surprising, but it didn't completely freak me out like it would if I hadn't had that earlier experience. "Wolves... I heard wolves in the woods tonight."

"Yes. Grayson, Aaron and Brad shifted, and followed your car when they smelled bear shifters in the area. They fought one of them, a large black bear, and Brad was injured."

I turned my head to look at Brad. Claire walked across and turned him around.

His back was slashed, blood still dripping down his beautiful skin.

I sat up straight, pain ripping through my head, but I fought back the wave of nausea.

"Oh my God. Brad, I'm so sorry."

Brad turned back to face me, his eyes focused on mine. "You're worth any amount of pain."

I looked down and shuffled back so that I was resting against the bed head.

"Is that everything, Claire?" I swallowed hard as my voice shook, but I forced myself to keep going. "I mean not that... that isn't enough. But I feel like there could be more?"

Claire nodded, "There is. The truth is, these three are your mates. Fate, as it was, has chosen you to be with them. Love them. Marry them—however you want to put it. As Fate chose me for my three."

Shock ricocheted through me like machine gun fire, one bullet after another, puncturing everything I knew about myself.

I'd believed I was meant to be alone. Apparently not.

I wasn't good enough for anyone to love. Or so my ex-boyfriend said.

But what was Claire saying now, right in front of me?

"Let me get this right. You think that these three, men, if I can call them that..." They did, after all, allegedly turn into wolves if they wanted to, so I wasn't sure on the exact terminology. "Are my... husbands?"

"Well, mates is a better term for it. Grayson is your protector, Aaron would die for you, and Brad will be your best friend and companion forever. They are everything you've ever wanted in a man, and so much more. I'm telling you this to save you some time, but it probably won't help. You're even more stubborn than me."

I'd give her that, she was probably right.

"Ah... okay. What do you want me to say, Claire?"

"I want you to say that you'll stay here for a few days. We need to identify the bear shifter who was following you, and I think you owe it to your triad, and yourself, to see if you can make this work."

I knew who the bear shifter was.

Or at least, part of me did, even though I didn't want to believe it.

One night, I'd seen a man turn into a bear, but I'd spent years convincing myself it was a nightmare. A bad memory that needed to be blocked.

And it had been.

Mostly.

"I... ah, can do that."

What choice did I have?

Claire looked at me strangely once again. "You're taking this too well."

I took another sip of water.

"Well, to be honest, I don't have much energy left to fight, and after what just happened, I doubt my car is drivable."

I glanced across to Grayson, meeting his gaze for the first time since I'd woken.

He was a wolf shifter? And so intense.

His eyes dug into my soul, deep, where I kept only the darkest of my desires and secrets.

My stomach fluttered and my heart squeezed.

And I knew...

I *knew*.... They were right.

There was something mythical and magical about this place. About these people.

These shifters.

And I knew they were telling the truth about these men, and the fact that all three of them were my mates.

But how was I ever going to let them into the walled-up fortress my heart had become?

And when they found out what sort of person I was... they'd never stick by me. No one would. I was one-hundred percent sure of that.

CHAPTER

SIX

Grayson

Looking at my mate and staring deep into her eyes for the first time ever, made me want to drop to my knees and thank the heavens for their gift.

It also made me want to run. To shift. To rip apart the man responsible for her car accident.

My fingers curled into fists and I tightened them, fighting the inner demon that threatened to overtake me.

"Thank you for saving me, for bringing me back to Claire tonight," Nevaeh said, staring first at me, and then at Aaron and Brad in turn.

I nodded once, feeling my teeth descend.

She stared at them, then jerked her gaze to Brad, who chuckled. "Grayson is having trouble controlling his wolf. I don't think he can talk."

Nevaeh pulled up her blankets in a move that indicated fear.

I couldn't have that.

I forced my wolf down and my anger back inside.

"It's... not you. I am... angry that the bear shifter got away." I took some breaths, calming the racing of my heart. "I'm sorry you were in that accident at all."

Claire began to back toward the door. "I'm going to go put the kettle on so I can make Nevaeh a hot cup of cocoa, then she's going to sleep. You three have five minutes before I kick you all out."

I smiled at the diminutive female. The very fact she could joke about such a thing lightened the mood in the whole room.

She left us, though the door remained wide open, and we moved slowly toward the bed.

"Is there anything we can get you before we go?" I asked Nevaeh, stepping close and reaching out to touch her leg.

She pulled back, shrinking into the pillows.

"What's wrong?"

"I know you guys are probably, like, naturalists or something. But could you cover up a bit? You're intimidating me."

Brad grabbed one of Jay's shirts and pulled it on, then sat on the bed with her.

Aaron and I had to walk out to the lounge room to pull on the shirts we'd left on Claire's doorstep.

Claire was laughing from the kitchen.

"What's so funny, Doc?" I asked her.

"I knew she'd have an issue with you guys being half naked. I didn't want to say anything because everyone was so tense in there, but just so you know... humans aren't used to massive muscle-bound guys walking around, looking like that."

I glanced down at my now-covered body.

"Okay. Thanks for the tip."

So, we would stay clothed.

At least until she got used to us.

We crept back into the room, where Brad was sitting next to her.

"You're okay with Brad more than us?"

Dex had explained that Claire had been the same, less intimidated by the Omega's size.

Unfortunately, it hurt me to know I was her least preferred.

Why didn't she see that I was here to love her, to protect her?

I was the one who had driven that bear away.

"Well... he's not as big as you guys. My ex was really tall, and muscly, like you."

I shuddered against the jealousy that crawled up my skin.

"And this ex-boyfriend... He hurt you?"

Her gaze dropped instantly and I knew we'd come to the root of the problem.

I walked closer and dropped to my knees before her.

I was now looking up at her from the most submissive position I could manage. I wasn't sure if she knew how difficult this was for an Alpha, but I didn't care. I would do this, for Nevaeh. Her shoulders relaxed as the power of the situation was released and given to her.

She gave me a tentative smile.

"Nevaeh, I'd never hurt you. Quite the opposite. I'd die to protect you. So would Aaron, or Brad, for that matter. You need to know that, because anything less would shame us all."

Her gaze met mine and love wove through me, binding me to her.

She gasped and put a hand to her chest.

"What is that?"

I smiled. "The magic of the bonding. It will get stronger with time and you will learn to trust it. But please, we only have another minute or so."

"One minute exactly," Claire called loudly from the kitchen.

I rolled my eyes and Nevaeh's lips kicked up into a smile—this one more sure.

"Tell me what he did to you, so that we can go about repairing the damage."

"I'm not broken," Nevaeh declared, straightening her spine, her voice taking on a tone of indignation.

I laughed. "I know you're not. You're perfect. But I need to prove to you that I'm not like this last... man. So, I need to know what he did."

Claire walked in with a hot drink and placed the mug next to Nevaeh on the bed.

She didn't try to make us leave, she only waited for Nevaeh's answer.

"He, um... Well, he hit me, for one thing."

Our gasps could be heard around the room, then Aaron's low, dangerous growl.

I put a hand out and touched Nevaeh's knee gently. "Please continue."

"Um... it's hard to explain. It seemed he didn't even like me, but forced himself to be with me. But it wasn't always that way. He was nice at the start, but that soon changed. Telling me how stupid I was. How, when he hit me, I caused him to do it. He told me I was a curse to him, a poison to everyone around me. I broke up with him, but he would follow me. Send me threatening messages. I've tried to get away from him, even moved three times, left the city and came back here. But he... he's obsessed with me, or something."

She trailed off and I got the hint that she wasn't telling me everything.

"Is there anything else?"

She shook her head, her long, brown hair falling over her face.

There was. She was hiding something, but only time would allow her to trust me enough to tell me. I was sure.

"Okay. Well, Claire's sending us back to our house for the night. But if you need us, we are literally one house away."

I stood up and she looked at me, her eyes wide and frightened as she took in my size.

I couldn't stand it.

I bobbed down and rested on my haunches.

"Give me your hands, beautiful girl."

She didn't, so I unbuttoned my shirt slowly. When she didn't move, I picked up her hands and put them against my skin.

"I'm huge because I'm the Alpha of my pack. It comes with my genetics, it's not a choice. It's not for intimidation. It's not to hurt you. I'm strong so that when a bear comes for you, I can literally beat him to death, if need be."

She flattened her palms against my skin, "Did you kill him tonight?"

She sounded... strangely expectant.

"Ah, no. It was more important to get you back here. Why? Do you know who the bear shifter is?"

Nevaeh withdrew her hands, and the cold that flew in to replace her warm palms was like ice on my skin.

"No. I just... You said..."

"I said I could protect you. That is the reason I am so big and strong."

I stood up again and walked to the door.

She was lying to me. And I wanted to find out why.

But perhaps tonight was too soon.

"Claire, we're right next door if anything happens. You have our numbers."

"Yes. Thank you, Grayson."

Aaron and Brad came to the door also and bid our mate good-bye, and we all left, retreating to our home.

It hurt to do so. I can't deny it. But we were playing a long game in this moment, and I needed to remember that the only important thing at this time was Nevaeh feeling safe.

Thus, our mate would sleep beneath Dex's roof tonight, though it rankled me extraordinarily.

"What's going on with her?" Aaron asked, as we stomped inside our house and began to pull food from the fridge.

None of us had eaten properly and it was time to take stock of what was happening.

"What do you think she's hiding?" Aaron asked.

I grabbed some leftover pasta and began forking it into my mouth.

"I think she knows who the bear shifter is. And I bet you it's that douche bag of an ex-boyfriend of hers."

"Really? Well wouldn't that be an odd bit of luck?"

I shook my head, shoveling more food into my starving body.

"It's not luck. There's something else going on here. I just need to figure it out."

"What do you mean?" Brad asked, eating himself through half a leftover pizza.

"It's too much of a coincidence. That the bears have always been our enemies... that they came for Claire when they found out she was a mate of ours. Now to know that *our* mate dated a man who was abusive, and now keeps constant tabs on her... it's too much to be coincidence."

"He's big like you, too, and the bear we ran into in the forest was aiming to take her car out specifically. He was a black— they're Alphas, I believe," Brad finished off for me.

Aaron groaned after he downed his beer. "So, we need to find out more about this ex of hers, and if all of this is some sort of crazy coincidence, or if the bears are finding our mates and keeping them from us."

"Oh my God. Imagine if that were true." I stared at my pack, my friends, my family.

The very idea that was possible completely floored me.

There could be so many women out there under the same threat.

"This could be so much bigger than we know," Aaron said with a massive sigh.

I nodded, my gut tightening and gripping with fear for my mate.

Sure, I'd felt anxious, tired, hurt, even depressed over the fact that I may never have a mate.

But now that we'd met her, and I knew she was next door—well, my wolf was pacing and circling inside of me like a restless animal.

"We sort out our mate first. We need to get Nevaeh to trust us, love us. Then we can find out if this is part of a bigger plan to keep our mates away. The whole pack may need to know."

We went to bed early, and I tossed and turned all night.

I needed my mate beside me. In my arms, in my house, in my life.

And tomorrow, I would find a way to have it all.

Nevaeh

Claire gave me a sleeping tablet, and I still had a bad night's sleep.

I kept seeing that massive bear coming for me.

And my guilty conscience weighed on me like a fridge laying across my chest.

I'd lied to them.

I did know who that bear was who attacked my car last night. Or, I think I did.

It was Trevor, my ex. Or one of his biker friends.

They all turned into bears, or so Trevor said. Deadly, vicious bears.

And he'd said that if I told anyone, he'd kill me. One of his many, many threats.

I'd tried to block out so much of that part of my life. Away. Hidden in the depths of my subconscious.

But here it all was. Spilling out for the world to see.

"Good morning," Claire said as she opened the door to my bedroom—Jay's bedroom.

"Oh, hey." I sat up, wearing some of Claire's spare joggers and a tank.

They were too big for me, and perfect for sleeping in.

"How'd you sleep?" she asked, and I shrugged.

She laughed knowingly. "You slept like shit because your mates are next door and you aren't with them. I know the feeling."

I looked at her, my head spinning with all the information they were all throwing at me.

"You know how surreal this feels, Claire? Yesterday I was single, happy, and focused on my career. And today you expect me to believe I'm 'meant to be' with three complete strangers? Men who aren't whom I'd choose for my husband anyway."

Claire gave me the eye. "You mean because they're hot, horny and too dominant?"

I looked away.

"Don't ignore me, Nevaeh. I know you want a guy you can control, who's totally harmless. Short, chubby and less intelligent than you."

Tears sprang to my eyes as she vocalized the exact thoughts I'd had. I wanted someone who wouldn't hurt me.

And a chubby computer programmer sounded about right.

"Look at me, Nevaeh."

I dragged my gaze back to Claire, now sitting on the edge of the bed.

"But that isn't what you need, and you know it."

"Oh, really? You're gonna tell me what I need?"

Even as I said it, I knew Claire had an answer for me.

"Of course, I will. You need a guy who's strong and passionate and smart and amazing. Just like you are. The best part of having a triad is that you're never lonely, and if one of them doesn't have what you need in any given moment, one of the others will."

"What do you mean?"

Claire grinned. "Well, for example, Dex hates cooking and so do I. So, Jay and Taylor do most of that. Jay's super-affectionate and smart, and Taylor can build anything you could think of. No matter what I need, one of them will always fit the bill."

I hadn't thought of it like that. "Look, Claire, it sounds great in theory, but I couldn't imagine letting a guy like Grayson, who looks just like Trevor, anywhere near me. I know you said he's a sweetheart but..."

Claire groaned and stood up. "Look, hun. Give them a chance, okay? This Trevor guy sounds like a narcissistic asshole, and Grayson may be many things, but he is not that."

"How do you know?"

"Well, for one thing, the bear shifters attacked a month ago. They came for me."

Shock rolled through me. They came for Claire? Why?

"What happened?"

She shrugged. "They didn't even get into the house. My mates and yours stopped them. Grayson, Aaron and Brad all risked their lives for me that day, and they've been perfect gentlemen ever since."

I couldn't even imagine men being that selfless.

"I don't know what to say."

"Say you'll give them a chance to prove to you that they are who they say they are. Because I will vouch for them, Nevaeh. I will. They're hard-working, extremely sweet and you have to admit... pretty bloody hot."

A smile kinked up my lips, though I tried not to let Claire see it. "Yeah... they are good looking. But that's part of the problem—my attraction for hot guys in the past has gotten me in trouble."

Claire literally threw her hands up in the air, or her non-broken arm, anyway.

"Fine! You know what? Go! Go back to your old, lonely life, and I'll see you at work."

Claire stomped off toward the door and I jumped to my feet.

"Wait! Claire, that's not fair. You don't know what it's like to have a guy hurt you the way Trevor hurt me."

Claire turned back to stare at me. "Yeah, maybe I don't. But you know what I know? That asshole men are always bad lovers, even when they're being nice and trying to suck you in. Do you agree?"

I shuddered and nodded. Sex had always been terrible with Trevor. I'd tried to believe that his speed in coming and lack of caring was because he wanted me so much.

But the lack of intimacy, touching and caring afterwards never made sense.

"Yeah, I agree. Men are always selfish lovers, though. All the girls at work say it. Even the good husbands are bad in bed."

It was a biological problem. The continuation of the species was not contingent on whether we had an orgasm or not. It was all about them.

Claire gave me a smug smile and crossed her arms over her large breasts.

"Well, I can tell you that they're wrong. My men are amazing in bed. Give me non-stop attention and don't come until I'm fully satisfied."

I just stared at her. That wasn't possible.

"And I guarantee that if you go to bed with your triad, you'll find out the same."

Heat surged up my face, and into the lower half of my body.

"Why would I do that?"

"Because you want to know if they're different than your ex?

242

That's the perfect test. No man can hide his selfishness in bed. It all comes out when the pleasure is there for the taking."

"But I... wouldn't even know how to... Even if I wanted to..."

Which I didn't.

My body screamed out in pain at my lie. I wanted to. God, how I wanted to.

It had been years for me.

I was practically re-virginized, or so Google said.

Claire chuckled. "Go over to the house and see them. Let your guard down, and I guarantee you'll end up in bed with them. The mating attraction is too strong for them to resist, and in the end, you'll fall for it, too."

I indicated my clothes. "I don't have anything to wear. Wait, actually, I think I packed a change of clothes for after night shift."

I hadn't even thought about it until now.

"Good. Have a shower and some breakfast, get changed, and go spend some time with your triad. If you're not convinced that they're different from any other man you've ever known by the end of the day, I'll drive you back to Little River myself. Tonight."

She left the room and began puttering around the kitchen.

I sat back down on the bed, more confused than ever.

If I were completely honest with myself, I was very attracted to the three men who saved me last night. Grayson, most of all. Which I hated myself for.

Why did I have to want the guy with the biggest muscles?

I sighed and got to my feet once again and walked through the lounge room toward the front door.

"Oh, shit... my car. My clothes... How do I get to them?"

"Eat this, and Grayson will probably take you to your car this morning, if you want." Claire shoved a plate of toast and fruit at me.

"Okay."

What else could I do?

I shuddered at the idea of going back to the scene of the accident.

"Actually, it might be better for me just to stay here. Do they have any shops for women's clothes?"

"They do, but they're pretty plain. Jeans, sweaters. Not much call for them, at least for younger women, here."

"Works for me."

I was most at home in a tank and jeans anyway. No bra if I could help it. My breasts were small enough to get away with that most of the time.

I ate the food in front of me and finished the glass of water Claire gave me.

There was a single knock on the door, then the front door opened and Grayson walked in. His huge presence and smile made me jump to my feet, my heart pounding against my ribs.

What was it about him that I was so attracted to?

I couldn't put it down to just one thing.

He was gorgeous, sure. The symmetry of his features, the strength of his jaw and the fact that his body could grace the cover of any sports magazine in the country certainly helped.

But I'd never felt anything like this before.

Not for any man, and definitely not for Trevor.

Grayson made me want to walk over to him and kneel in front of him.

My mind went far further than my conscious thoughts dared and it made my cheeks flame with heat.

What was this?!

Surely it had something to do with the fact that he had saved my life yesterday? Or the fact that I hadn't had sex in years, literally.

But after Claire's suggestion of testing out the men on their giving natures in bed, I couldn't get the thought out of my head.

Because, despite my initial horror at her suggestion, it now made perfect sense.

I just had to work out a way to "seduce" them into it.

Though, from the heated look I was getting from Grayson, it may not be a problem.

"Good morning, Nevaeh."

"Good morning," I said, pulling the tank down at the front, conscious of how fat this top made me look.

I was naturally quite thin, though Trevor had always pointed out how big my ass was in comparison to my boobs.

Not that I had a choice about that one.

Plastic surgery wasn't in my scope, not this early in my life.

"Nevaeh needs to buy some clothes that fit her. Would you guys mind taking her to Sharon's shop?" Claire asked, with the casual calm of someone who was always in charge.

"Of course." Grayson said, quietly. Strongly. Without taking his eyes off me.

My lower belly tightened and clenched.

"Now?" I asked, my voice hopping in my throat.

I needed a shower, but there was no point until I had clean clothes to put on.

"Sure. Aaron and Brad need to head off to work for the morning, but they'll be back for lunch."

I dragged my eyes across to the other two men, who both looked at me with the same hunger as Grayson.

But for some reason, the need to be close to the biggest man of the group was tugging at me.

"Great. I'll come now and walk with you guys, if you like?"

Their eyebrows flew up in identical signs of surprise.

I almost laughed.

Had I been that bitchy toward them yesterday?

Probably.

I'd been told more times than I could count that I was an ice queen, and a frosty bitch.

I grabbed my shoes from yesterday and pulled them on. I didn't know where my other clothes were. Knowing Claire, they were being washed or burned.

I rushed to the front door and stepped outside into the bracing cold.

I inhaled sharply, wrapping my arms around my body as my skin prickled into goose bumps.

Then, I was being surrounded by warmth and the smell of a man. A far too sexy man.

A scent that was designed to drive me insane.

I looked up at Grayson, who'd taken off his jacket and wrapped it around me.

"Thank you."

It was like being a kid wrapped in your parents' clothes. Too big, but so comforting.

He shrugged. "I thought you may need it."

I looked over to see that neither Brad nor Aaron wore jackets. Only tank tops.

He brought the jacket just to give it to me if I needed it? How thoughtful.

"You guys don't get cold?"

Aaron shook his head. "Not really. If it's snowing, we need our jackets, but our wolf genes keep our metabolism burning pretty fast."

"Oh, I wish."

Brad looked at me strangely. "But you're very skinny. Why would you want to be more so?"

I wasn't sure how to even approach that. "Um... because I

don't eat much. I'm sure you guys eat whatever you want and can stay as you are."

Brad took my hand and lifted it to his lips, kissing my fingers in a strangely intimate way.

"I hope you learn to be happy here. In your own skin. Because you have to know that we will adore you no matter what you look like. It's one of the conditions of us being your mate."

I pulled my hand back gently. "What do you mean?"

We began walking along the road and I started to notice all of the other men.

There wasn't a single woman my age, though I saw a few older ones.

I stepped closer to Grayson, who squeezed my waist once then let go, though he stayed close. "Don't worry, beautiful. None of them will come anywhere near you."

And somehow, I believed him. "Tell me more about this mating thing."

"Well, for one thing, none of the other pack members will want you the way we do. Dex was extremely possessive over Claire when they first met, but she just doesn't do it for us. She's nice, of course. But we aren't attracted to her."

"Don't like big boobs?" I joked and the men looked confused.

"Oh, it's not a literal attraction thing. We wouldn't care if you were even skinnier, or if you were twice as big as Claire. The attraction is a chemical one we can't control. You're our mate, and we'll never want another woman again. You're it for us."

I stopped in the street and they all turned to look at me. "Are you kidding me?"

They couldn't possibly be telling the truth. Three men this hot couldn't be telling me that they would be faithful to me for the rest of their lives. It was impossible.

"No. What's wrong?" Grayson asked.

"We better go, Gray. You got this?" Brad asked and Grayson nodded.

Brad stepped forward and pressed a kiss to my forehead.

Aaron stood still, shaking in a strange way. Like he couldn't decide what to do.

"Bye," I said, waving at him and giving him as much of a smile as I could manage.

"Ah..." Aaron leaned forward, then turned and walked away.

When they were out of earshot, I asked Grayson, "What's wrong with Aaron?"

"He... um... It's hard to explain. Brad's bonded with you already, and I get my chance this morning. I think Aaron's jealous, or something. He hasn't really explained."

That made sense. How would three men share me anyway?

"I kind of get it."

"Yes, I do too. But hopefully we'll have a lot of time together, so there's no need to hurry."

My body disagreed with him. The further I walked, the longer I spent with Grayson, the more my body ached.

Quite literally.

My pussy throbbed and my nipples tingled.

"Um... you were going to tell me more about the mate thing. You weren't serious about being faithful to me, were you? Not all of you."

It was impossible. Totally impossible.

Male animals were seed spreaders. Not settle-down-and-commit types.

Grayson grinned. "Of course, we were serious. That's part of the mateship. We won't desire another woman for as long as we live. None of us. We've found you now and we know what it feels like to have you close by. Anything else would be wrong."

"So, if I decide to return to town and stay single?" Which was the most likely thing at this point.

"Then we'll wait for you to come back."

He said it like there was no other choice.

"But what if I didn't want to be with you? If I wanted to stay single for the rest of my life?"

Grayson shrugged and opened the door to a shop. "Then we would wait. And if you decided you never wanted us, then we'd stay single, too. However, you have to understand that we're not going to go down without a fight."

His smile made my stomach quiver.

"What do you mean?"

He leaned forward and whispered in my ear, his hot breath causing a shiver to course down my spine. "I mean... I'd use all my seduction techniques to convince you otherwise. But after that, if you decide not to have us... Then again, I would wait."

When he stepped back, my knees trembled and buckled and I fell forward.

Grayson caught me against his hard body and held me tight.

I moaned and his hands slid lower, gripping my ass.

My pussy tightened.

I had to get away from him. I couldn't think straight.

"Ah, well... I'm glad you aren't one to give up easily or quickly."

I managed to get up again and walk into the store, though I could feel how hot my face was.

An older woman was standing behind the counter, her shock at seeing me a palpable thing.

"Hello. I'm Sharon."

I walked forward and stuck out my hand. "I'm Nevaeh. I know I look ridiculous, but I had to borrow some of Claire's clothes."

She looked me up and down. "Size four?"

"I prefer a six," I said from pure habit.

She **tsked** at me, as older women were wont to do. "Why? Because you still feel like you're not skinny enough?"

She pulled clothes from her racks.

Jumpers, jeans, tank tops.

"Well... um..."

She walked up to me and gave me a straight look in the eye. "You're perfect, and compared to all the women in this town, a good fifty pounds too light, so go try on some clothes that fit you."

I stared at her for a minute, then looked back at Grayson.

"Um..."

"Do what she says. Everyone else does."

I took the jeans and moved into the change room. I wasn't sure what world I'd fallen into, but for the first time in a very long time, I felt truly safe.

EIGHT

Grayson

I smiled at my mom and watched her frown right back.

"You didn't tell me, Grayson."

I fought to stop myself from bowing my head in shame. "We only found out yesterday. She was at Claire's house."

"We? You mean she's your pack's mate? Like with Dexter's pack?"

My mother sounded surprised.

"What's wrong, Mom?"

She crossed her arms over her rather large chest. "Oh, nothing. I just... Some of elders thought this may be a pattern, one mate per triad. I wasn't sure. But now..."

The curtain to the dressing room moved aside and a woman stepped out.

One with long, flowing brown hair, thin legs and perky breasts that lifted her tank top.

Whoa.

"Everything's too tight," Nevaeh said as she tugged at her tank and the jeans that hugged her ass.

"No," my mother said, her tone one of someone who is not to be trifled with. "They fit your thin, perfect body. Not strong yet, but you will be if you stay here with us. Now, go home, stay warm. There's a storm coming and everyone needs to get indoors."

Mom packed the few extra clothes in a bag and handed it to me. "Take these. And, Nevaeh, put this on. The temperature's dropping."

My mom handed Nevaeh a thick wool sweater.

"How do I pay for all of this, Sharon?"

My mom stepped over to where Nevaeh was staring up at her like she was some mythical creature to behold.

Mom cupped Nevaeh's face and spoke softly. "You look after yourself and my son. Now, go."

"Your son?" Nevaeh looked at my mom, probably assessing her face and seeing the same blue eyes that ran in all of my mother's sons.

She looked over at me with the softest expression. "This is your mom?"

"Yeah." I sighed heavily as Mom shoved us toward the door and flung the "open" side over to "closed".

"I wasn't joking about those storms, Gray. Get going."

I nodded and pulled Nevaeh into the street. My mother was never wrong about these sorts of things. The wind had turned, the air now biting into my skin with the sting of coming snow.

"Let's hurry."

We jogged across the street and in the direction of our house. I held Nevaeh's hand. The smallest, warmest hand I'd ever been able to touch.

"Almost there," I yelled over the wind.

People were running everywhere. I pulled Nevaeh closer as we pushed toward my house.

She cried out as she fell, tripping over something on the ground.

I turned and swept her up into my arms and walked on.

When we got home, I ripped open the door and had to walk in and push my back against the heavy wooden panel to get it to close.

When I set Nevaeh down, she was shivering. "Oh my God. How did that happen?"

"I don't know."

We didn't have heating in the house. All of the homes in the pack were very well-made, and well-insulated, but without women, we hadn't bothered to put in fireplaces, or central heating.

"We're going to have to keep you warm."

I looked around the room. We didn't have blankets hanging over the couches. Everything was either in a linen closet or in our bedrooms.

"Your house is really beautiful. Different than Claire's."

Nevaeh didn't seem to be as worried as I was about the heating issue. She was staring at the walls, the kitchen, the intricately curved cornices with a look of fascination on her face.

"Ah, yeah. Brad's a plasterer and Aaron's a carver, so our house has details that some of the others don't."

"Cool," Nevaeh said as she wrapped her arms around her body and walked around the room, studying it in more detail.

I needed to get her wrapped in a blanket, and there were a few ways of doing that. "Would you like a tour?"

She nodded and I pointed to the study.

"Down here is pretty much like Claire's house. Kitchen, living space, laundry and a spare room we have set up through there.

Upstairs are our three bedrooms and another lounge room and library."

"Library?" she asked, her eyebrows rising high as she took a few steps up the staircase.

"Yes, we all like to read. Learn. Especially Aaron. He's kind of the brains of this triad."

She nodded and walked up to the top of the stairs.

"Is this your bedroom?" she asked as she walked into my room. A place no woman had ever been.

"How'd you know?"

She smiled. "It's at the front of the house, so I suppose any offender would have to get through you, wouldn't they?"

"Yes."

I prowled forward, watching as she took off her sweater and placed it on the bed.

She was looking around my room, seemingly innocent, but I could sense that something had changed in her chemistry. Her scent had morphed into something sweeter, hotter, somehow.

It appeared the choice now for me was to push forward, or wait for Aaron and Brad to join us.

She sat on the bed. "It's so warm in here."

I walked forward and knelt before her, put my hands on her thighs and opened them, sliding between them with my body so I could look into her eyes.

"Will you stay with us, just until we know if you feel what we do? That you're our mate and we're meant to be together."

In her eyes I saw so much vulnerability and fear, yet she didn't run.

She cupped my face in her small, warm hands, and nodded. That was all the sign I needed.

I leaned forward and kissed her.

She moaned as our lips met, and pleasure shook me to my very core.

I slid my hands around her skull, through her thick hair and held her face to mine, sipping from her lips, tasting the inside of her mouth.

I kissed her until we were both breathless and the air around us was filled with the sounds of our sighs.

I stood up and threw back the blankets, then pulled her to her feet.

"You look amazingly hot in those jeans, but I'm afraid I'm going to have to get you to take them off."

I reached for her jeans and she helped me undo them, pushing them over her lean hips and to the floor.

Next was her tank. Nevaeh lifted her hands so that I could pull the top over her head and then suddenly she was before me, standing in only her underwear.

Heaven.

"God, you're beautiful."

I kissed her again, wrapping my arms around her small body and loving the moans she expressed in her throat as we continued to kiss.

"Lie back."

She slid onto the bed and lay on her back, quivering.

"Are you cold?" I asked her, reaching for the blanket.

She shook her head emphatically. "No."

Her ribs were rising and falling at a rapid rate and I caught the scent of fear in the air.

"Don't be scared. I promise, I will never hurt you."

I slid onto the bed and moved over the top of her.

She reached up and encircled my neck, pulling me down.

I kissed her nose, her cheek, her forehead. Every inch of her had me dying to pleasure her.

Would she welcome me into her body at this point? I was pretty sure I could seduce her into just about anything.

But something told me to stop. A strong instinct told me to wait until my fellow pack mates were home to fully satisfy her.

That didn't mean I couldn't have a little taste to whet both of our appetites.

I slid down the bed.

She arched her back for me, and I moved my hand around to unclip her bra. With one flick of my hand, I discarded it.

She laughed. "That takes a lot of practice."

I shook my head as I moved down her body, kissing her breasts, suckling on the sensitive nipples that might one day feed my young.

"Practice for you, my mate."

She moaned loudly as I drew her nipple deep into my mouth.

She dug her nails into my head and I moved lower.

Until I finally found Heaven.

I knelt up on the bed and pulled her underwear down her long, thin legs.

"Open up for me, beautiful."

She was holding her legs together, but on my command, she spread her thighs wide and showed me her pussy.

She was so clean.

So beautiful.

So perfect.

"Is it okay... I mean I know it's ugly anyway, but I try to keep it as tidy as possible."

I looked away from her center, to her beautiful face.

"Ugly? A man would kill to have this pussy in his bed. Who told you it was ugly?"

"Ah..."

Suddenly I wished I hadn't asked that question.

"Nevaeh. This is the prettiest..." I leant and kissed her clit and she gasped. "Most beautiful..." I ran my tongue down her center. "Most perfect pussy I have ever seen."

And as she was coming down from her third moan, I put both hands under her hips, grabbed her perfectly tight ass and got down to eating her properly.

She screamed as I set my mouth to her already swollen clit and thrust my tongue from side to side. Her moans vibrated in my ear as I worked my way down her slit, tasting her juices, then back up again, spreading her moisture and moaning myself as my cock swelled inside my jeans.

Keeping my clothes on had been the right thing to do. If I hadn't, this would be the perfect time to slide up her body, kiss her lips, and thrust my cock into her.

"Fuck! Grayson."

I groaned. Yep, that would have been the moment.

But that was for another day.

I moved one of my hands back out and slid my middle finger into her tight core.

She screamed again and arched her back, her pussy clenching onto my finger with a death grip.

Damn she's tight.

We'd have to be careful here.

I thrust my finger up and curled my digit, reaching for those hidden spots that would give her the most pleasure.

She began to pant and tighten and cry out.

I licked around her clit in large circles, then closed my lips around the swollen nub and moaned as her taste changed.

Her gasps grew louder and she grabbed for my head, tugging at my hair.

She keened and arched as her body began to ripple around me.

I groaned as she screamed, her pelvis bucking beneath my mouth as she tried to both get closer and crawl away at the same time.

I withdrew my finger and slid up the bed, holding her in my arms while she shivered and shook. Her eyes rolled forward and back, her body gloriously naked.

Her nipples were tight and peaking.

That's when I heard the front door open and close.

My instincts told me to pull up the blanket and cover Nevaeh's perfect body.

But that wouldn't be fair to her, nor them. Because I was pretty sure my pack mates were going to want to pleasure our mate just like me.

Suddenly my door opened, and Brad and Aaron stood in the doorway.

"Come in, you guys have perfect timing," I said. "We were just getting started."

CHAPTER

NINE

Nevaeh

The spasms in my belly spread through my whole body like ripples in a pond. I couldn't control them. The shudders and shakes rolled through me, and it was truly the most magnificent moment of my life.

I never knew it could feel like this.

Heat seared my eyes and slid down my face, completing this moment as a true first for me. Love and sex and orgasms. Just like all the romance novels said were possible.

Amazing.

"I... Um..." I swallowed, trying to get my bearings. Return to a sense of normality, whatever that may be.

No one had ever given me an orgasm before. Ever. Especially like that. I hadn't thought it was possible.

"We have company, beautiful girl. Are you ready for all of your mates to adore you?"

My stomach tightened and my eyelids popped open.

I lifted my head and forced my unfocused eyes to see the other two men standing in the room.

"Aaron... Brad..."

My insecurities once again swam to the surface of my mind and I could just imagine all the horrible things they were thinking after seeing my flawed body.

I reached for the blanket to cover myself.

Aaron and Brad stepped back, away from me, which wasn't what I wanted.

"If you want us to go, Nevaeh, we can go. We didn't mean to interrupt." Aaron's tone was hurt and I sat up, forcing myself out of my incredible bliss and looking at the men before me.

Surely, they weren't the ones feeling rejected, were they?

"I don't want you to go. I just... feel strange, being the only naked one in the room."

Brad laughed. "Oh, we can change that."

He dropped his jeans and stripped himself of his tank in mere seconds. Then suddenly, he was naked.

Gloriously, beautifully naked.

Brad's cock was already hard, pointing toward me, red and swollen.

I swallowed and dragged my eyes away from Brad's hypnotic shaft to Aaron, who still hadn't moved.

"You don't want to?" I asked him, a heavy weight pushing against my heart.

I didn't know how to take this man. He was darker, more intellectual in his approach, and from what I could tell, more hesitant than the other two.

Grayson had moved from his place beside me, and I kept my gaze averted. I wasn't sure I could look his way if he was naked, too.

All that strength....

I shivered and focused on Aaron.

He cleared his throat with a strangled cough. "Of course, I do, Nevaeh. You're my mate too, but I don't want to force you, or the situation. If you'd rather not…"

He glanced down and stuck his hands in his pockets, looking like an insecure adolescent in the principal's office.

It filled me with an empathy for his struggle, a need to reassure him.

"Aaron, would you…" I swallowed. I'd never asked a man this question before. "Would you make love to me?"

Would it be love for them? Is that how this mating thing worked?

I was certainly going to find out.

Aaron's head came up and his gaze caught with mine. His intense, dark eyes burned into me. I held his gaze, my body trembling with the hunger Grayson had woken in me.

Aaron didn't speak but he began to undress.

His tank came off first and my breath caught in my throat. He was huge, like a wrestler.

His waist was so lean it made his shoulders look even bigger. Every inch of his body was covered in rock-hard muscles.

He hesitated as he began to unbutton his jeans.

"I'm bigger than Brad…"

It sounded like a warning.

I was pretty sure he would be. In every way.

I nodded. "Show me."

The smile that kicked up Aaron's generous lips made my heart melt and tears linger once again in my eyes.

Was this what it felt like to fall in love? With kind, generous souls?

His black jeans fell away to reveal huge thighs and a cock that bobbed up and down as though bowing in introduction.

I threw back the blanket that covered me and jumped off the bed to stand in the warm room. My throat thickened with embarrassment, but I pushed the feeling away. Instead, I walked the few feet separating Aaron and me and looked up into his face.

His beautiful, intense, strong face.

He didn't reach for me, though I could sense that he wanted to.

The control he was exerting over his own desire inflamed mine.

And the best part of it all was that by handing over the power to me, Aaron made me feel truly powerful. As though I could either stop this or go on if I wanted to. That was a heady aphrodisiac.

He wasn't moving, so it was my turn to go out on a limb. "Kiss me."

Then Aaron reached for me, one hand going around my waist and pulling me flush against his body, the other sliding into my hair.

I groaned at the first moment of skin-on-skin contact, heat and desire weaving through my blood.

My knees gave way.

Aaron grabbed me against him and held me firm.

I lifted my thighs and wrapped my legs around his waist, holding on to his strong body. The move came naturally to me, as easy as breathing.

Aaron's groan filled the room before he whispered a word I'd always hated. "Heaven."

On his lips, pulled from his very soul, this moment we were sharing was exactly that, however. *Heaven.*

I wrapped my arms around his neck and pulled him into me for a kiss.

Our lips met and sparks tingled on my skin.

His tongue slid through my parted lips and he tasted me.

I parried back, letting my eyes slide shut, and put all my pent-up passion into the kiss.

He moved us around the room and I held on until he was sitting down.

I opened my eyes to see that he'd brought us across to the bed. He was lying on the mattress and I was now straddling him, his cock lying on his belly in front of me.

Thick and hard, and so temptingly beautiful.

Aaron was breathing hard, but not moving us to the next level. As I stared at him, I realized I needed to push all my doubts away and follow my instincts.

And my instincts told me to ride him.

I arranged my legs around him so I could lift up, and Aaron grabbed his shaft, holding himself upright for me.

I leaned forward, my already aroused and juicy body sliding over the massive head and welcoming him in.

I slid down a few inches, gasping with the intensity of it all.

"Fuck. You're so tight," Aaron groaned, reaching for my hands and shaking with the strain of staying still beneath me.

I raised my hands and linked our fingers, connecting on a level I'd never experienced with anyone.

My soul tugged at me, connecting and weaving together with Aaron's.

But there was so much more to be had, I could feel it.

I rocked my pelvis, swallowing as much of him as I could, over and over again, moving up and down.

"It's been... a very long time," I managed to say.

I was tight, and tender. But the soft pain made way for plea-sure, and I needed more.

Aaron groaned again, louder this time, his fingers pressing

into my hands. I pushed all the way down until I was sitting on his hips, his huge cock filling me right up.

My eyes flew open and I found Aaron's gaze on me. Not lost in the moment, not trying to take his pleasure from my body and depriving me of mine. He was focused, waiting. Sharing this with me.

"Tell me when you're ready to take me properly, beautiful."

I exhaled deeply, my belly finally relaxing around the intrusion.

I nodded. "Okay. I'm ready."

He moved his hands to my hips and I unlinked his fingers so that I could hold onto his arms.

"Let me know if you need me to stop, but I need you so damn much. This is going to be difficult to control."

I nodded, though fear shivered through me.

What was the worst thing that could happen? A bit of pain? I'd had a lot of that before.

Aaron grinned and planted his feet on the bed, then he began to move, thrusting up into me and moving me up and down on his cock in time with his own rhythm.

I gasped as pleasure shot through me.

I leaned forward to make the position more comfortable and even more pleasure raced through me.

I rode the wave with him, thrusting down as he thrust up, his moans and mine filling the room.

"Damn… you are so fucking perfect!" Aaron panted, and my pussy began to tighten. To ripple. The pleasure of my first orgasm made it so much easier to recognize the signs in my body, and reach out for my next one.

I held myself up and still as Aaron pumped into me, over and over again.

I threw back my head and let the waves of pleasure come. I

screamed out as his cock pushed me over the edge, and his own orgasm was triggered.

Heat shot through me and caused an even greater orgasm to take over my body.

I shuddered and shook, falling forward to hear Aaron's groan as he filled me with his seed.

The pulse of heat like I'd never experienced made me moan with wonder.

It was perfect.

Aaron put his arms around me and rolled us, so I was on my back and he was softly kissing my lips, my face, and my neck.

I couldn't open my eyes at first, but as Aaron withdrew and the weight of another person tipped the mattress, my need renewed. An ache in my core woke me out of my daze.

I lifted my eyelids to see my sweet Brad, sliding over me and on top of me with a smile.

"You ready for more, beautiful?" he asked, as he settled between my thighs.

He couldn't possibly be ready for me already?

"Don't you need—" I gasped as he lined up and thrust inside me.

I groaned and lifted my legs to accommodate him. "Obviously not."

He kissed me, his lips sipping on mine. Feeding me while taking what he needed.

His pace was gentler and slower than Aaron's to start with, as he rolled his hips and took his time.

But need was clawing at me, making me frustrated with the care he was taking. It was stupid to feel that way, but true. I wanted—needed— more. So, I put my arms around his back and dug my nails into his flesh.

He cried out and thrust into me. Hard.

"Yes..."

I groaned and bit into his shoulder, wrapping my legs around his waist.

"Please," I begged him. I wanted more.

I needed him to want me, to need me as I needed him. To fill the emptiness that was somehow still present.

He slid up inside of me, thrusting over and over again. I rejoiced in his body on top of mine. The weight and pressure, the feel of him against me.

I kissed his neck, his face, and he groaned. "I won't last if you keep doing that."

I didn't want him to last. I could feel Grayson in the room, hovering, waiting his turn. He would be my biggest challenge.

"Don't wait. Come inside me."

I'd never said such erotic things in my life, and I don't know if it was the primal dance or the energy in the room, but I wanted something I'd never wanted in my life.

A man's true mark on me. And I wanted to mark my men in return.

I kissed Brad's neck and sunk my teeth into his skin.

He shivered violently and began to cry out.

I squeezed his cock with my internal muscles and an orgasm rippled through me as his seed pulsed into me.

My body soaked up his orgasm, milked his shaft, and settled as if part of my raging need had been met. Part, but not yet all.

He groaned loudly and fell on top of me.

The weight on my chest was too great and I began to pant.

"Brad, you're squishing her."

It was Grayson.

His deep tone rolled over me like a warm blanket.

The man who'd given me my first orgasm.

Brad pushed up with his arms and I could breathe again. *Phew.*

"I'm so sorry, beautiful." He rolled to the side, and there he was.

The *Alpha.*

Stroking his long cock slowly, mesmerizing me with his action.

"Come here, beautiful."

I jumped straight up and fell to my knees before him, the submissive part of me that had always wanted a man I could truly trust coming to the forefront.

I opened my mouth and he walked forward and slid his huge cock between my lips.

I moaned as he took my head and gently fucked my face.

He didn't force himself down my throat.

I barely had the head in my mouth, but as he thrust between my lips, my whole body relaxed. I was strangely... happy.

But not sated. Quite the opposite of sated.

He gently tugged at my hair and I pulled back to look up at him.

There was no rush in Grayson's movements, no urgency. This dance was going to be a slow burn to satisfaction for both of us.

He'd waited this long, and he was going to make me wait a little longer.

"Are you too sore for me, beautiful? I can wait."

I stared up at him.

He was serious.

He would walk away now, even if he was hard and needing me. Having watched his two friends already have me to their end.

He'd wait.

What sort of man was this?

The answer whispered itself into my mind. *He's an Alpha... and a decent, kind man who protects those he cares about.*

"No. Please don't make me wait."

A strange laugh chortled out of him. "Make you wait?"

He offered me his hand and lifted me to my feet.

He stared down at me with all the passion and intensity I'd ever dreamed of seeing from my lover.

"Are you sure? Because you know...."

"I do."

I didn't care how he was going to finish that sentence. My answer was yes.

I knew he was big. I knew his passion for me would be enormous, too. And I didn't care.

"I just want you."

He grinned and pressed his lips to mine in a super-sweet kiss.

"You're sure?"

I nodded again and he smiled, took a breath, then stood up straighter and said,

"Get on your knees, on the bed. Present your cunt to me."

Oh. My. God.

My pussy pulsed with expectation as I turned and dove back onto the bed.

On my hands and knees, like he said. Waiting for him. Waiting for possession.

He didn't immediately move over to me.

I flicked my hair out of the way and looked over my shoulder at him.

"What's wrong?"

"I said *present*. Reach back and open your cheeks for me. Show me where you want me to put my cock."

Oh. My. God.

Was I really going to do that?

I dropped my head to the mattress and reached back my hands and did what he ordered me to do.

I opened myself up for his perusal.

Never in my life had I been so mortified by my own behavior, yet so turned on.

But I was rewarded for my bravery because Grayson set his hands on my ass cheeks, opening me up further for his cock, and set the head at my entrance.

I let go of my flesh and put my hands on the mattress once again.

He slid into me slowly, and kept going, and going. Forging inside already tender tissue until I was so full, I could barely breathe.

And yet my wanton body pushed back against him, wanting all of him.

Grayson called to his pack. "Aaron. Brad. Come and touch her."

Then I was surrounded, Brad's lips on my face, against my ear, and Aaron's hands on my back, caressing my breasts, tweaking my nipples.

All while Grayson slid his cock in and out of me, very slowly, for which I was grateful.

He was much bigger than either of the other two.

The feelings were overwhelming, in the best possible way. There were hands and lips and cocks everywhere.

My whole body was being pleasured, adored. Loved.

And that's when the first orgasm suddenly hit.

I screamed out as it rippled through my belly and squeezed Grayson's cock.

He cried out and grabbed my hips, thrusting deeper, harder inside of me.

"Damn it, you almost dragged the cum right out of me."

Grayson's erotic words didn't stem the tide of orgasms as they began to roll over me, one after another. They wouldn't stop.

Just when I thought I could catch my breath and relax, my belly would tighten and another would roll straight through me.

And I didn't try to stop them.

Nor was I silent, or quiet or lady-like. I groaned, and moaned, and screamed like a wild animal.

How could I not?

"Fu...uck." Grayson began to pound into me, his fingers digging into my hips as he rode my body straight through every belly-tightening scream.

I pushed down on my hands to give Brad and Aaron full access to me and pressed back against Grayson, welcoming the heavy thumping in my belly.

They squeezed my nipples and flicked my clit, making everything so much more intense.

"Grayson! Please!"

I cried out as another orgasm rolled through me and I squeezed his shaft as hard as I could.

"Oh, God! Yes, okay.... You got me. I can't hold on any longer. You better come with me, little one."

I wasn't sure I could, not again. But as the Alpha growled out his pleasure and shivering and shaking took over my whole body, I had no choice but to surrender to the power that was Grayson. Our Alpha.

I fell forward onto the bed, my body wracked with heaving spasms. Three men's bodies were around me, beside me, behind me.

And as bliss descended and exhaustion flowed through me, sleep pulled me down into blessed release.

Grayson

I stared down at my sleeping mate and admired every little bit of her. The shape of her spine, the curve of her ass, the sweetness of her face... Everything about her told me that I'd finally found my home.

I stretched my back, sweat covering my skin. "Whoa," I said. "That was intense."

Brad and Aaron nodded in agreement, though they didn't answer verbally. They were well on their way to falling asleep too.

I, however, was nowhere near it. I still buzzed with adrenaline and the intense pleasure that had come from mating with my woman.

"You guys climb into bed and stay with her. I'm gonna have a shower."

Aaron and Brad nodded as they lifted Nevaeh up onto the pillows and pulled the covers up.

I stood frozen for several minutes, watching them, unable to move, although I itched from the sweat that stuck to my skin.

My heart was breaking. In the very best possible way. I'd never seen anything as beautiful as the sight before me. My mate, nestled between my Beta and Omega. All of them sleeping soundly from the mating that would bond us all together for the rest of our lives.

I had a life. I had a real family. I had a mate.

I was complete.

I struggled with the strength of the emotions swelling in my chest.

I glanced to the door, a part of my soul wanting to shift and run. To expel all of this extra energy and race through the forest with the dirt beneath my paws and my Alpha wolf in his natural element.

But a hot shower called me, and I gave into my human side. I walked into the ensuite and turned on the hot water.

I was tense, but full of bliss. Itchy, yet settled. I was everything all at once, and it totally blew my mind that this was where my life was at now.

I stepped beneath the spray, scrubbed my skin and washed my hair.

What a world this was.

Just... wow.

When I was dry and dressed again, my family finally woke.

Aaron and Brad were first to stand up and move around the room, then finally our Queen stirred.

I slipped into the warm spot on the bed Aaron had left and took her, still naked, into my arms.

"How are you feeling, beautiful girl?"

She buried her head into my shoulder, her lips caressing my skin.

"Good."

I chuckled. "Just good, huh? We need to try harder next time to make you feel even better, do we?"

She looked up at me, her eyes wide and scared. "I didn't mean..."

I laughed loudly. "Oh, sweetheart, I was joking."

Her smile was full of relief. "It was amazing. All of it. I've never known anything like it."

"Good! Then I hope you're going to stay here with us."

She nodded. "Yeah, I can. For a day or two, but I have to get back to work. My car needs to be fixed... I have to get back to my life."

I bit the inside of my cheek to stop from growling out loud.

She wanted to get back to her life? To what? A job and an empty apartment?

"Ah... all right. I suppose we can sort something out. Little River isn't far."

She sat up suddenly and slid out of bed, her gorgeously rounded ass catching my gaze while she ducked down and grabbed her clothes up off the ground.

I sat up too but stayed seated so I didn't loom over her.

"We kind of skipped lunch. Shall we go down and have something to eat?"

She smiled when she was finally clothed. "That's a good idea. I think we all worked up a bit of an appetite."

She was smiling and saying all the right things, but the stone in my gut was heavy.

Something was wrong.

We hadn't done enough to get her to trust us yet, that was obvious.

"Have we upset you somehow, Nevaeh?"

She walked to the bedroom door and pulled it open.

"No, not at all. But I'm not quite ready to throw my whole life into chaos. Not yet, anyway. I know Claire jumped at the first chance to move in with her men, but I'm different. I'm sorry. I can't throw my life away like her."

Disbelief shot through my veins, followed quickly by anger.

Surely not...

"Is that how Claire phrases it? That she threw away her life for her mates?"

I couldn't believe it. That didn't sound like the woman next door I'd grown to know and like.

"Oh, no.... No. She's totally blissful in her ignorance."

What a horrible way to put it. Being in love was blissful ignorance?

"What's that supposed to mean?"

This conversation was getting worse by the minute. Was it possible our mate had more than a bit of shrew in her?

Nevaeh heaved a sigh and her face closed up, that cold aloofness that I'd hated seeing on her from the moment we met, returning. I couldn't believe it. Despite everything we'd shared, she was planning to leave anyway.

"Grayson, this conversation is getting out of hand. I mean... All I meant was..."

I continued to wait, staring at her intently.

She didn't finish the sentence.

Brad and Aaron came along the hallway from their bedrooms, where they'd gone to grab clean clothes, and Brad asked if we wanted lunch.

Nevaeh agreed and they took off down the stairs, followed closely by Aaron, all of them laughing and chatting happily.

My head was in turmoil. What was in her mind? Should I wait and let her figure it out on her own, or push her to admit what her fears were so we could try and allay them?

. . .

I JOGGED down the stairs without having decided which path to take, which was never a great idea.

My mom always said I was too emotional to be an Alpha. Controlling what came out of my mouth, and being patient, were not strengths of mine.

I stepped onto the landing and turned, finding our kitchen a bevy of happiness.

Food preparation was underway and drinks were being poured.

At the heart of it all was Nevaeh, smiling at Brad and letting Aaron drop kisses on her cheeks.

How could she possibly want to leave us?

I pushed down the need to explore that gaping hole of sadness and leaned against the couch.

Brad glanced over to me. "You gonna help?"

I laughed. "How? There's three of you in the kitchen already and with my bulk, I won't fit."

I'd get in the way, and I wasn't sure I could trust myself not to ravage her again.

Aaron grinned. "Yeah, with Nevaeh here permanently now, we should look at expanding. I know humans do extensions on their houses all the time. What do you think, beautiful?"

Nevaeh froze, but I was the only one to see it.

The others continued to smile and move around the kitchen, preparing food, oblivious to her reaction to Aaron's words.

I felt bad for everyone.

Nevaeh was obviously overwhelmed and probably feeling a little trapped, and my pack mates were about to get their balls handed to them.

I waited, my chest aching. It was like watching a car on the road, slipping and sliding amongst the elements. Knowing an accident was imminent but there was no way of stopping it.

Nevaeh moved further away, around to the side of the room. "Ah... I'm heading home later today. I have some things I need to do."

I crossed my arms and stared at her.

"Didn't Claire ask you to stay for a few days, so that we could get to know each other better? Plus, I think she also made sure you had the time off work."

She glanced over to me, then back to Aaron and Brad.

"Yeah, she did. But I'm not comfortable staying here tonight. Little River's only an hour away. I can come back tomorrow."

She was lying.

She wouldn't come back tomorrow.

Brad and Aaron's faces both took on dark expressions, and the atmosphere in the room changed dramatically. The temperature dropped from comfortable to sub-arctic.

Everything in me calmed down and stilled.

"What do you mean, Nevaeh?" Aaron asked.

"What did we do wrong?" Brad queried.

Her gaze bounced between the three of us.

"You didn't do anything wrong. I just need to go home. You must know what that's like. There's no place like home."

Aaron moved toward her, the pain on his face obvious. "What do you mean? You're our mate. We want *this* to be your home."

Nevaeh groaned and rolled her eyes, her temper catching up with her now.

"Listen... I met you guys yesterday. *Yesterday*! And I know you believe in this mythical fate thing, but I don't. I control what happens in my life, and you can't tell me that great sex is enough reason to rearrange your entire life."

Aaron fell away like she'd struck him and I stepped forward. Enough was enough.

I had to protect my pack from the person hurting them, and at this moment, it was our mate.

"That's quite enough."

She whirled on me and I was happy to take her wrath. Aaron and Brad couldn't handle Nevaeh at full tilt, I could already tell.

"What did you just say to me?"

Her shock was obvious. She may have had an abusive male in the past, but she wasn't used to being spoken to like she was a child, which was what she deserved at the moment.

"I said, that's enough. You were just given the best possible gifts that all three of us could give you in bed. All the love, attention and time we have. Do *not* tell us that you want to go home because we're just 'great sex'. You're obviously more inexperienced than I realized, otherwise you'd know that great sex only comes with pure intent, and love. So, if you need to go back to your life and your 'home', Nevaeh, go. But don't insult us in the process."

I held her gaze with mine and saw the spark of anger flare.

"You can't control me, Grayson. Not with sex, not with this supposed fated mate thing. You're lucky I'm still here. Because the last thing in the world that I wanted was three boyfriends with more muscles than brains."

A growl rolled through my chest and my wolf jumped to the surface.

"Be careful, Nevaeh. You're crying out for a damn good spanking, so I suggest you don't push me any harder, or you'll see how dominant I can be."

Nevaeh's eyes opened like saucers. "You wouldn't."

I laughed, though there was no humor in the situation.

"You've already proven that you have absolutely no taste in men and can't pick a protector from a prick. So, I suggest you stop pushing to find out which one I am."

She narrowed her eyes as she shuffled like a crab, sideways around the room, toward the front door.

"No. Nevaeh. Don't go." That was Aaron, though I didn't look his way.

I kept my gaze on the woman aiming to tear our hearts from our chests.

Her eyes spat fire and I knew I was about to get another dose.

"I knew it! I knew you were as bad as my ex. Thinking you can control me, own me. I'm not a fucking possession, Grayson."

This time my laugh sounded mean. Even I could hear it.

"Oh, sweetheart, you have no idea what you are, or what you want. So, stop spitting and hissing at me like some sort of feral cat, and go home."

She ran to the door and threw it open, her hair flying around her in a beautiful arc.

Brad rushed forward and I grabbed his arm to stop him.

He struggled with me. "No, Grayson! You can't let her leave. We'll never find her again. We'll be alone. Forever."

I looked over to where Nevaeh was freezing up on me.

"Tell him he's wrong, Nevaeh. After all, Little River is only an hour away."

I gripped my Omega harder as he struggled against me.

"No... Grayson. You can't..."

"I'm not doing anything, Brad. This is all on the mate who Fate sent for us. Look at her. Isn't she magnificent as she runs off and leaves us?"

My sarcastic tone reverberated through the room. Brad sighed as Nevaeh slammed the door hard enough to shake the foundations of our house.

"She's Heaven," Brad whispered.

I echoed his sigh and let him go.

"Yeah, that's the twist with Heaven. You've gotta earn your way there. And the road is often fraught with pain."

ELEVEN

Nevaeh

I grabbed my car keys from Claire's house, fuming with rage at Grayson and my stomach churning with emotions. Luckily, Claire was nowhere to be seen. Then I ran outside, before remembering that my car was still in the woods, broken down and bear-trampled.

"Shit!"

I could scream.

Literally.

"*Argh*!"

Those fucking... stupid... men! What the hell did they think I was? A possession?

I looked toward the road that led out of town. Some exercise wouldn't hurt me.

I picked up my cell and called the local cab service.

"Hello. Yes, my car's broken down and I'm on the river road

about fifty miles out. Can you send someone? I'll be walking, and you can call me on this number. Yes. Thank you."

I started off, pounding the pavement and pumping my arms to push the blood through my body to keep me warm.

I needed to cool my temper as much as keep my body heated. Hopefully, walking in the fresh air until the cab arrived, would help with both.

A calmer part of my brain reminded me that the last time I'd tried to leave this town I'd ended up in a car accident and was almost attacked by a crazed bear.

"Well, you don't have a car and it's the middle of the day still, so..." I tried to give myself a pep talk as I walked, but in fact, it wasn't exactly the middle of the day anymore. Darkness was heading over the horizon.

I walked harder. Faster. A part of me wanted to turn around and return to the safety and the warmth of Grayson's house.

No. Not again!

I was never going back to a situation where someone else could control me, belittle me, and alter my life to suit him.

But the biggest problem, if I were honest, was that I didn't trust my own judgment when it came to men.

Claire had said that the sex would show me what sort of people they were.

Oh, God, it had.

Super dominant and... I couldn't even think about it...

I wanted to believe they were cruel, or selfish, but that didn't fit. They had been thoughtful, and sweet, and willing to offer me the world.

But it was still hard to know what to believe. Trevor had been nice too, at the beginning. Said he loved me, gave me attention, gifts. Then the abuse started.

How could I trust Grayson not to take me down the same path? After all, he'd just shown his true colors, hadn't he? Calling me a venomous cat. Letting me leave when the others wanted me to stay.

Rejecting me.

The hot sting of tears made my eyes burn and I blinked rapidly to stem the flow. A few slipped free and made me shiver.

In walking away, I knew on a rational level that I was the one rejecting them, but it hurt that Grayson hadn't seemed to care whether I stayed or not.

I pushed the tears away and kept walking, the occasional car now driving past as I got closer to town.

I focused on my feet, the feel of the road beneath my toes. The tingle of cold on my hands. And I tried not to think about the fact that the weight of their rejection was the underlying cause of my tears.

Claire had said she'd vouch for these guys but how was that possible, when at the first sign of me asserting myself, wanting to go home, as I had every right to do, they just tossed me away?

A taxi cab drew closer, so I waved my hand and the driver pulled over beside me and rolled down his window. "You the one who called the cab?"

I nodded my head and jumped in.

"Yes. I need to get to work, please. St John's Hospital."

"Alrighty."

He did a U-turn and we drove back to town. I tried to push aside the pain that surrounded any thoughts of the pack, and the men who'd said I was their everything.

That sure hadn't lasted long.

~

THEY DIDN'T COME for me. Not the day after I left, nor the day after that.

Which shouldn't have surprised me. After all, men were inconsistent, fickle creatures. Weren't they? Or was that women?

I couldn't tell anymore.

But every day I was away from them, my heart hurt.

My throat ached.

And I wasn't battling a cold. I was sure of it. My head thumped with a headache and I had chills while I slept.

"Good night, Nevaeh," my supervisor called out as I headed for the exit after my shift. I was back at work, doing what I loved. So why wasn't I happier about it?

"Night, Trish."

It was cold and dark, and I couldn't wait to get home.

Home.

What a strange concept now.

I'd busted my butt, and Grayson's, to come home to an apartment I shared with a girl I barely knew. It was old, and untidy, and not at all what I wanted for my home.

But I was making do, as I always did. Until I reached my goal.

Enough money to own a house for myself.

I called an uber and walked up the stairs to the apartment, my heart heavy and tears on the tips of my lashes.

Damn it. Pull yourself together.

"Sophie?" I called out as I pushed open the door. She should be home at this time of night.

When Sophie didn't respond, I locked the door, flicked on the lights and moved into the kitchen.

She could be asleep. We kept odd hours with our shifts at the hospital, but it would have been nice to have someone to talk to when I got home.

Maybe I should call Claire and ask how she was going; how *they* were doing.

No, that would be stupid. And probably unwelcome. I could only imagine what Grayson and the others had told her about me.

"Hello, Angel."

I froze.

That voice was at the center of my nightmares.

There was a man in my dining room. He was not welcome within a hundred feet of me. He was not wanted, and least of all, was he permitted in my home.

I turned slowly, my eyes flicking toward the knife block in the kitchen.

I had to be careful not to make any sudden moves because Trevor, despite his massive size, was as fast as a whip.

"Trevor... what are you doing here?"

He'd changed in the months I hadn't seen him.

His hair was long and bedraggled.

He looked like he hadn't showered in weeks.

"I've come to see my girl. I don't know why you keep avoiding me."

I shivered, the cold dread of disgust curling in my belly.

I forced myself to stay calm, though my heart hammered my lungs like a blacksmith working an anvil.

"Avoiding you? Trevor, we broke up years ago. I've been getting on with my life."

"Oh, really? And what life is that, Heaven?"

His tone made me shudder and brought back so many terrible memories of times he'd called me that. Times we'd had sex... times he'd hit me. Every memory related to him was disgusting to me.

Where was my phone? If I could get away from him, I could

call the police. That wasn't going to be easy inside our small apartment.

Damn it... What could I do?

I went about unpacking my bag on the counter as casually as I could, considering my heart was pounding in my chest.

I pulled out my water bottle, my lunch box. I washed them both out in the kitchen sink, moving slowly and steadily.

I injected as much humor as possible into my tone. "You know what I'm like. Work, work, work."

He laughed, too, but the sound was ugly and cruel. "Oh, I do know you, and you're a little slut is what you are. Going for three men at once. Tut tut tut." He tsked at me and I knew my time had come.

He was about to increase the pressure.

I took my cell phone from my backpack and slid it into my back pocket.

"I didn't..."

"Oh, yes you did."

He stood up and I began to panic. Adrenaline raced along my veins, making my arms shake.

He grunted and raised his voice. "I can smell them on you! You should have listened to me! I tried to warn you the other night, in the forest."

I walked toward the door, but kept my gaze on Trevor so he didn't know I was about to bolt.

"That was you? In the woods? The bear?"

I'd assumed it was him, of course. But to *know* it was him, now that was a different story.

Trevor puffed up like an arrogant peacock.

"Of course, it was me. You know I have bear shifter genes."

"You could have killed me."

He growled, low and menacing. "No... I didn't want that. But you do need protecting. I can't have you mating with those wolves. That pack's destiny is to die out."

I stilled. "What do you mean? What destiny?"

He laughed and moved closer, so I walked away from my potential exit to keep him talking. I circled the island bench.

"Tell me, Trevor. They all said I was their... mate. But I didn't believe them."

He grinned. "That's my girl."

He didn't give me any more information and a part of me *ached* to know more.

To ferret out the truth.

"Is that why you chose me, Trevor?"

I'd always wondered why a guy who seemed to hate me, professed to love me.

"I could smell it on you... you know? That wolfy, magical shit. Smells disgusting."

He spat on the ground, on my tiled floor, and kept following me in the circle around the bench.

A dangerous dance.

"Then why date me, Trevor?"

"To keep the wolves off you. To make you smell like me. They'd never go for you if they could smell bear on your pussy."

He grinned, that terrible expression of humor that I'd always hated.

"So... let me get this straight. You could tell that I was meant to be a wolf shifter's mate, so you... what? Deliberately sabotaged their plans?"

He growled again and I jumped.

"I didn't want to," he said. "My father, our Alpha, demanded it. Those wolves are meant to die out. Their bloodlines aren't meant to continue on. There have been no female shifters born in generations. Fate has chosen it for them. You humans aren't allowed to step in and contradict Fate."

I held up my hand and he actually stopped moving closer. "Hang on a second. You think Fate's trying to wipe them out? Then why create a human fated mate at all? And what do you care about me now, anyway? They've got Claire, so their line will continue, no matter what. And they'll find more of us. Why try and stop me from going to them?"

This wasn't making any sense to anyone except this idiot before me.

That was when his malicious grin skittered across his face.

The one that told me to run.

"Because you're mine. And if I can't have you, no one can."

I ran. Straight to the only room in the house with a lock.

The bathroom.

I bolted inside, the pounding of his footsteps behind me on the tiles echoing everywhere.

I slammed the door and locked it, but that wouldn't hold him for long. So, I sat on the ground, with my back against the door and pushed my legs against the bathtub to leverage my weight.

It was all I could do. There was nothing else to move, or put in front of the door.

"Open the door! Now!" Trevor bellowed.

I grabbed my phone out of my back pocket and that was when I saw a very recent message from an unknown cell number.

Are you okay?

Tears sprung to my eyes as I hit dial on the number.

Only three people in the world could feel my panic, and that had to be my soul mate shifters.

The phone rang once and then Grayson answered. "Nevaeh. Are you all right?"

"*No!* Trevor's here—at my apartment. He's trying to hurt me!"

"We're on our way."

"Ninety-nine Shalloway Street, Apartment Three. You'll hear the.... *screaming. Fuck!*"

Trevor slammed his weight against the door and pain shot down my spine.

"Call the police," Grayson yelled. "We'll be there soon."

He hung up and I called nine-one-one.

"Oh, please... please hurry," I begged, when I got through.

Trevor must have run at the door with all his strength, because the next thing I knew, my ankle gave way, pain shot through my skull, and the whole world went black.

Grayson

The night air flew past my face as we ran through the forest at break-neck speed.

Aaron was at my right. Brad had gone to Dex for extra help, so hopefully the other pack was close behind us.

My thoughts were jumbled, angry screams as we ran as fast as we could, straight toward town.

We could sense that Nevaeh was hurt, but how badly?

If he'd hit her again, that ex- boyfriend was going to die. And if he'd done worse... well then, he'd die slowly.

My paws hit the dirt and propelled me through the forest until we reached the outskirts of town. Aaron had matched my break-neck pace and was still at my side.

It was past midnight, so luckily there weren't many people out and about to freak out about two wolves running through the town. We turned the corner and kept going. I used my connection to Nevaeh to guide us in the right direction to her apartment. I could scent that it was close, but I couldn't sense Nevaeh's presence nearby.

Where was our mate?

We took the next left and saw her street name.

Thank God, we were almost there.

We found the apartment and pushed into the open door.

I shifted back into human form and so did Aaron, sweat dripping down our burning hot skin.

"Where. Is. She?" Aaron panted, our bodies close to exhaustion already.

"I don't know. Nevaeh! Nevaeh!"

We ran through the apartment, the smell of fear and bear permeating my senses. "Fuck. He's a bear. The ex. It must have been him. The one who knocked over her car that night."

That made sense, of course, but I'd hoped the logical conclusion wasn't the correct one.

"Where did he take her, then?" Aaron asked, looking around the tiny apartment but not seeing any clue. I couldn't sense her at all, now.

"I don't know. But we need to find them."

A car screeched to a halt at the front of the apartment and I raced to the window.

"It's Dex and Brad," I called over my shoulder to Aaron. "Let's go."

There were two trucks out the front.

They were barely minutes behind us and they weren't exhausted.

We jogged down the stairs, naked and cooling down.

"Maybe we should have brought the car?" Aaron said, his tone full of sarcasm and wry humor.

I glanced at him. "Did you think about that when you found out Nevaeh was in trouble?"

Aaron shook his head. "Nope. My wolf took over and I was running beside you before I'd even decided to shift."

That's exactly what had happened to me.

"Yeah. I know the feeling. Let's go."

We jogged outside and Brad tossed a pair of jeans at each of us.

"Get in, guys. From the smell of this place, we have a bear to hunt." Dexter gestured to the second car.

We jumped into the vehicle Brad was driving and Dexter jumped out, stripping to his birthday suit.

"I'm gonna shift and follow the scent. You guys drive behind me. Save your strength. There's going to be a fight at the end of this. I can feel it already."

Dexter shifted into his massive, silver, Alpha wolf and I drank the bottle of water Brad put in front of me.

He was right. Aaron and I were tired from the frantic dash here, and if we were going up against a den of bears, then we were going to need all our strength, or at least, as much as we could recoup in the time it took to find our mate.

Dexter took off and we drove after him, through the town. He stopped at different spots, sniffing the air, different vehicles. Doors.

I could smell the bear too... and then something else.

Someone else.

Someone sweet.

"That's Nevaeh," Aaron said through growling teeth.

I nodded, unable to speak.

My wolf rose to the surface, wanting to run, fight, protect my mate.

Even though she'd left us, run away from her destiny, I wanted her.

The cars pulled over and we jumped out, heading over to Dex, as he shifted and stood in his human form.

"The scent of the bear ends here. Maybe one of you guys can pick up Nevaeh's scent instead?"

Brad stripped off his jacket and threw it at me. He peeled off the rest of his clothing in record time. "My turn."

Brad's human form disappeared and his brown wolf stepped up to us, lifted his head and sniffed the air.

Then he turned and started running.

I hesitated for a moment. My wolf wanted to run with my Omega, lead my pack as an Alpha should. But it was time to work together and use our brains as well as our raw instincts.

I jumped back into the car with Aaron and we took off, through the other side of the city and into the woods once again. Heading in the opposite direction of our pack.

We were on our own if things went pear-shaped out this way.

We drove deeper into the forest, no longer on actual roads, feeling our way along dirt paths. Following Brad.

Then a shotgun sounded in the quiet of the night and Aaron slammed on the brakes.

Brad dropped to the ground.

"Brad! No!"

I jumped up and shifted, racing straight to Brad, grabbing him by the scruff of the neck and pulling him behind the cars.

The gun boomed again somewhere over my head but I kept dragging. I had to get my pack mate to safety.

I shifted back once we were safe, and Dexter came over to check him out.

Brad was still breathing, but only just.

"He needs the hospital. Now."

He wasn't shifting back, which was a bad sign. He had a

gunshot wound in his hindquarters and I knew he'd likely require surgery.

Jay, Dexter's Omega, stepped up. "I'll take him and will call Claire on the way. Get him into the car."

Dexter nodded. "Yes. Perfect plan. We'll stay and help you guys."

We lifted my Omega into one of the cars and Jay took off.

"God, I hope he's okay," Aaron said.

I nodded, too worried to answer out loud.

Another gunshot blasted next to the remaining car and we jumped behind it.

Dexter groaned. "He'll be fine, I'm sure. But we've gotta stay alive long enough to visit him in the hospital. So, what's the plan?"

I crouched down with the other Alpha and our Betas.

"We go in, save my mate, and kill anyone who gets in our way."

The other three wolf shifters nodded, and we turned to assess the best way to take the cottage.

Because somewhere inside that small house was my mate, and I wasn't going home without her.

THIRTEEN

Nevaeh

Blood dripped down my nose, making my lips taste of metallic salt.

Yuck.

My right eye was swollen shut, and I was tied to a chair in the middle of some backwoods cabin, but there was nothing wrong with my hearing.

For the past God knows how long, Trevor had been fighting with an older man who sounded very similar to Trevor.

His father, probably.

And they were arguing over what to do with me.

Trevor didn't want his dad to hurt me, but he didn't want to keep me, either. The guy really didn't know what he wanted. Not at all.

And although I should be terrified, and a part of me was, somehow I knew my mates would come for me.

I could hear the two men moving around. All I could think was, what was going to happen when my mates arrived?

Would they get hurt?

What if it was Brad who arrived? Would he be strong enough to take on two bear shifters?

My heart just about tore apart thinking about it, until I couldn't breathe for the pain it caused me.

My men...

The people I'd run away from, rejected and decided I couldn't possibly live with.

They'd come for me. They'd save me.

I knew they would.

Because they thought I belonged with them. And at this point in time, as my head throbbed with pain and my hands were bound behind my back, I called myself ten kinds of fool for running away.

Why was I so scared??

Because it was too perfect?

Because I'd had too many orgasms?

Because I was too chicken-shit scared to actually love someone?

Yes, it was the latter, for sure. Because loving someone meant really trusting them.

And I had trust issues.

Obviously.

"Fuck! There they are! Get your shotgun and give it to me." The older man stomped around the room and I tried not to move and draw his attention, though I was so uncomfortable I could barely refrain from wriggling around to find a position that hurt less.

Slowly, I lifted my head and opened the eye that was not swollen shut.

The older man was definitely Trevor's dad, if his physique and receding hairline were to be believed.

He lifted the weapon that Trevor handed him, and said the best thing I'd heard all day.

"Fucking wolf shifters."

Then the gun went off and I cried out, my heart pummelling into my ribs as adrenaline raced through my veins.

Trevor ran over to me. "They're not going to rescue you, you stupid little bitch. You were mine first."

He yanked at my arms and it felt like he was untying me. Then I was on my feet and being hauled to the front door.

"What's happening? I can't see," I whispered, leaning against Trevor as though I didn't even have the strength to stand on my own.

I did, though.

And I could run if the need rose.

"They're leaving. Ha! Your wolves are cowards. Look at them run."

"What's happening, Trevor? Tell me," I whispered.

He chuckled and I relaxed into him even more.

I didn't care what he did to me today, as long as I was alive at the end of it and could tell all three of my mates I was sorry for running.

"We shot the little brown wolf."

My heart skipped a beat. Little brown wolf? Was that Brad? Was he alive?

"They're taking him away... hang on. Shit. The other four are still here. That's two Alphas and their Betas. Dad, we can't take on all four of them."

"Oh, yes we can. You shift and attack the Alpha and I'll be right behind you with the shotgun. It's time we got rid of this whole pack."

I held my breath, waiting for them to decide what to do with me.

Trevor seemed to think me inconsequential, because he tossed me aside and strode out the front door. Pain shot through my elbow and my leg as I landed on the floor.

The older man chuckled. "I wish he hadn't hit you quite so hard, girly. This is something you'll want to see."

I didn't want to see anything happen to my wolfe shifter men. But I couldn't help myself from looking anyway. I dragged myself slowly across the floor to the window and managed to pull up to a stand.

My whole body ached, but as my one eye that worked focused on my men stalking toward the cottage, my pain disappeared, and fear consumed me.

My throat closed up and an invisible band pressed against my ribs.

They had come to save me.

They hadn't rejected me, nor abandoned me. They were here for me, when I most needed them.

When had anyone else in my entire life been able to be counted on like that?

Tears blinded me and I sniffed loudly, wiping at my face with my sleeve.

A growl rolled through the clearing as Trevor pulled off his shirt and his soft, but very large body transformed into an eight-foot-tall, ferocious-looking black bear.

The old man in the cabin with me said, "Okay, Alpha. You're going down."

I had to save them.

I screamed out as loudly as I could, "Grayson! Watch out!"

The shotgun blasted beside me and I fell sideways, away from the sound and the man who shoved me. Trevor's father growled and began to tug at his own clothes.

He was going to shift, it seemed, and that wasn't something I was hanging around for.

When he opened the front door and ran outside, beginning to transform, I realized that was the only chance I'd get to escape.

I staggered to my feet, scrabbling over the dirt littering the floor, and my own painful injuries, and ran the other way through the house, wrenching open the back door and stumbling out into the forest.

I started to run, then heard the sound of a howl.

A wolf. Hurt.

I stopped running and turned back.

I couldn't abandon them now. Not that they'd see it that way, I was sure. But I had to help, somehow. Only, how?

The gun!

I raced back inside the cabin and grabbed the shotgun from where it had fallen to the floor.

My parents were classic trailer trash, and they loved their guns.

I hadn't fired one since I was a teenager. But I knew how to load one, and God help me, I knew how to shoot straight.

I hit the barrel breach lever, checking for shells.

Empty.

I stared around the room for the box, forcing my one eye to focus despite the stress.

I felt for them, checking the shelves, the drawers in the table.

"Yes!"

There was a red box in the bottom drawer, full of shotgun shells.

There was a flurry of noise outside. I looked through the window.

The fight was vicious and from my vantage point it looked like the bears were winning, somehow. My men needed me.

I loaded the gun quickly and slid extra shells into my back pocket.

I walked out onto the front step and leveled the gun at one of the black bears—the one who had his jaw clamped around the black wolf beneath him.

I lifted the gun and set it right in my shoulder, sighted with my one working eye, and squeezed the trigger.

Bulls eye.

Or in this case, *bear's* eye. Sort of. I'd hit him, but not anywhere that would kill him.

The bear released the wolf and staggered sideways.

Then he turned on me.

His slobbering, saliva-covered mouth opened to reveal a mass of sharp teeth.

He charged at me.

I raised the gun again and fired directly into his face. Then I closed my eyes and waited for the impact.

None came.

I opened my good eye and looked down.

He was sprawled at my feet, a dead four-hundred-pound animal.

In death, the bear remained a bear... which surprised me.

Why wouldn't he turn back into a human?

Then I heard the blood-curdling screams of his son, still in bear form. Larger than his father. And completely and utterly enraged.

Trevor dropped to all fours and charged me.

I found the lever on the break action, quickly expelled the shells and reached into my back pocket for two more rounds. If I didn't reload quickly, it would be too late for me.

"Shit!"

I pulled them out, then dropped one. My hands were shaking too hard.

And then he was nearly on me.

As I opened my mouth to scream, a massive silver wolf jumped in front of me, his growl making the hairs on my neck stand up.

He launched himself at the bear, tearing at his throat.

Then another silver wolf attacked too, jumping in to support the first wolf, taking out the bear's legs and sending him to the ground.

I grabbed again for the shells, my hands trembling so much I could barely re-load. But finally, I managed it.

I held up the shotgun.

The bear suddenly began to shift back to human form—back to Trevor—his bleeding body heaving with exertion.

The wolves shifted back too, obviously assuming the threat was over.

I wasn't so sure, and kept the gun relaxed, but in my hands, ready to lift and fire if he so much as threatened any of my mates.

My mates... Damn, how the tables had turned.

"What's wrong, Trevor? Lost the fight and want to surrender?" I asked, my tone goading as I stood there with my battered body.

But I was still standing.

"No. I wanted to see the look on these guys' faces when they saw my marks on you. Isn't she beautiful like that, boys?" he asked, gesturing to my face.

"Why, you..." Aaron dove for him, and Trevor, fast as lightning, got Aaron in a headlock and began backing away.

Aaron tapped at his arms, struggling in Trevor's grip, but he was gasping for air.

"Drop the gun or I'm going to break his neck."

Grayson danced on his toes like a boxer about to go into the ring.

"Let him go, you coward," Grayson said. "You know I'm the one you want. Come on. Alpha on Alpha."

Trevor laughed and tightened his grip on Aaron's throat.

I didn't want this.

I didn't want any of my men hurt, and Aaron was turning blue.

I yelled out to the man I hated. "Take the car and go. Get out of here. Grayson, throw Trevor your keys."

"Drop the gun," he demanded again, and this time I placed it on the ground.

"There. Now let Aaron go."

"Keys," he grunted.

Grayson hesitated. "They're in the car."

Aaron was drooping, his eyelids fluttering as he began to lose consciousness.

"Trevor! You won, let him go! Now!"

Trevor dragged Aaron the few more feet to the car, then threw him to the ground. He lay there unmoving, as Trevor jumped into the car and revved the engine. He yelled out, "Thanks for the final fuck, baby. It was awesome!"

I would have rolled my eyes at the ridiculous statement if I wasn't so worried about Aaron. I hurried over to him while Trevor sped away.

I moved Aaron onto his side and made sure his airway was clear.

He was breathing on his own, thank God, and would likely come back to us in a few moments, though his throat looked bruised and he'd be sore when he woke up.

"I should chase him down and kill him for what he did to

you," Grayson said, though I could see he was torn whether to leave us.

I played on that indecision.

"I know. But we need you here, Grayson. What if other bear shifters come and attack?"

Grayson nodded, and for the first time I noticed his nakedness.

And Dexter's... oh, and Taylor's, too. Damn. Naked men everywhere.

"Ah..." My cheeks were hot with embarrassment. I looked down again at Aaron. "How are we going to get out of here now?"

Aaron woke up slowly and groaned. "Nevaeh... God, what did he do to your face?"

I sat down on the ground, wincing as I did, pulling Aaron's head into my lap.

"Nothing he hasn't done before."

Dexter and Taylor stepped close in human form and even though their nude bodies didn't make me react inside the way Grayson and Aaron's did, I couldn't help noticing that Claire was as lucky as I was in that department.

"We'll go," Dex said. "Find a car and come back to you. If you're lucky, though, Jay may get back here first. He'll likely return from the hospital to check on us once he's dropped Brad off."

Grayson shook hands with the other Alpha. "Thanks, Dex. We'll be here waiting for you."

Dexter and Taylor shifted into incredibly beautiful silver and black wolves and took off.

"Whoa, that's incredible."

Grayson squatted down beside me. "Why aren't you more freaked out with us shifting? Dexter said Claire practically had a heart attack the first time she saw them do it."

I swallowed hard. "Well, I'd seen Trevor shift once before.

Years ago. But he threatened me, and told me he'd kill me if I ever told anyone."

"Uh huh." Grayson sounded as though he didn't believe me.

"It's true, Grayson. I promise."

He looked me straight in the eyes. "Well, sweetheart, I think we have a lot to talk about, don't you?"

I nodded, a sinking feeling hitting my stomach.

Aaron's eyes closed from fatigue and I stroked his thick hair and tried to relax, until a car pulled up to take us to the hospital and find out if Brad was all right.

FOURTEEN

Brad

I opened my eyes to the sounds and bright lights of hospital. Why was I in a hospital?

"He's awake."

Nevaeh was beside the bed, holding my hand and staring at me like she'd never seen me before. One of her eyes was swollen shut and I could see she was in a lot of pain.

"Hey, beautiful... what happened?"

I couldn't pull my mind together long enough to put the pieces together.

"You got shot."

I glanced down to my white sheet-covered body and although I couldn't see the injury, I could feel it.

The ache in my leg.

"Oh... great. How long have I been out?"

"Only a few hours," Grayson said from the other side of the bed.

"What happened?" I grabbed Nevaeh's hand and squeezed, hard. "I don't like to see you hurt."

She gave me a small smile. "I'm okay, now you're awake. Trevor's dad shot you. There were shell fragments lodged inside your quadriceps muscle, but one of the surgeons managed to extract them." She lowered her voice. "We told them it was a hunting accident."

I wanted to laugh, but instead my heart ached at how loving our mate was.

"No, beautiful. I meant you. What happened to you?"

"Oh..." She drew back her hand and pulled her fingers through her hair, glancing down as though she were embarrassed. "Ah..."

"He beat her up," Grayson growled out. "And for that, we're going to kill him."

"No, please, don't," Nevaeh said. "I don't want anything bad to happen to you. None of this matters, as long as the three of you are okay."

Grayson stared at her. "You care about us now, do you?"

"Of course. You know I do."

Aaron laughed. "How would we know that?"

Nevaeh sighed. "I... I... can we do this later? When Brad and I are better?"

Aaron and Grayson nodded.

I sighed. They knew we all belonged together.

"How long do I have to stay here?" I asked her, grabbing Nevaeh's hand again.

"Well, usually it would be a few days to a week. But Grayson said you guys heal very quickly, so I don't know."

I flexed my foot and bent my knee. It hurt, but nothing I hadn't dealt with before.

"I can probably go home today, sweetheart. Another few

hours and I'll be strong enough. Can you go tell the doctors? I need to talk to Grayson and Aaron."

She nodded and left the small cubicle. I pinned my Alpha with a stare.

"What the fuck happened out there? One minute we're pulling up, ready to save our mate, then I get shot and wake up here. What did I miss? You said we're *going* to kill him. That means you didn't kill that asshole yet?"

"No. We couldn't." Grayson's gaze slid to Aaron. "He had Aaron round the throat, and if we didn't let the bastard leave, he was going to kill him."

Aaron's face reddened and he looked away, then crossed his arms over his chest.

"Not sure you made the right choice there."

"Of course, I did," Grayson said, his tone deep and growly. "I'm just angry the bear got away."

"And what happened with Nevaeh? Why is there so much tension? I could slice it off with a knife."

"I don't think that's the expression," Aaron said.

I raised my eyebrows and stared at him. "Oh, seriously?"

He must be really embarrassed by what had happened out there if he was trying to make jokes like that.

Grayson took a step toward the door. "Now that we know you're all right, we'll go home for a bit. I need a shower and some sleep. But we'll come back to pick you up when they say we can take you home."

"Hang on, you didn't tell me what happened with Nevaeh."

The woman in question stepped into the room.

"We'll let *her* tell you," Grayson said, before disappearing from sight.

Aaron nodded once and left too.

Nevaeh was left swaying like a leaf in the wind, looking lost and confused.

I grabbed her hand and tugged her back into the chair next to my hospital bed.

"Hey, beautiful. Seems like I've missed a few things. What's going on?"

Nevaeh clung to my hand. "I don't really know. I mean... I know I left your place in a huff the other day, which was wrong and stupid, but when you three turned up to save me, I assumed you'd be happy to see me. But Aaron and Grayson are standoffish and angry. I mean... I know I stuffed up, but I..."

She stopped.

"You what, sweetheart?"

"I was hoping we could sort everything out, but it looks like they're not going to forgive me for my stupidity."

Silvery tears slipped down her cheeks and she wiped at her nose with a Kleenex from the table by my bed.

"Oh, sweetheart. Why are you upset? You haven't even asked a question of anyone. We came for you. We fought for you."

Well, Aaron and Grayson had. I'd have fought for her too, if I hadn't been shot.

Nevaeh stood up and moved away, swiping at the tears. "Oh... I'm not... I..."

I stared at her.

Did she assume we'd rejected her?

Chasing our mate was part of our very DNA. Did she not know that? But at the same time, we also needed to know that she wanted us, too. That she hadn't permanently rejected *us*.

"I need to go, Brad. But I'll be back later."

"Sweetheart, let me say one more thing before you run away. I know that we are a lot to take. Three of us claiming you're our mate, the whole wolf thing... but we want you. All of you. We want to love you. But we won't force you to be with us. So, if you want to try again, or at least give us another chance to see if this relationship will work... assuming you do...?"

She nodded quickly and relief winged through my heart.

Thank the heavens for that.

"Then perhaps you should say something—or do something, to let us all know. Aaron and Grayson just threw themselves in front of guns and crazed bears for you."

"So did you," she whispered.

"Of course, I did. You're my mate."

She nodded and practically ran out the door.

"Oh... shit."

I scrubbed my face with my hands.

What a mess.

DURING MY DINNER, Grayson and Aaron turned up in my hospital room once again.

I was forcing down the food with a fork made of plastic.

Disgusting.

But I was hungry.

"Let's go, Brad. It's getting dark and we want to be home at a decent hour."

I threw back the sheet and swung my legs over the edge of the bed. I was moving a lot better now. The difference of a few hours.

"Great. Let's go."

The nurse wheeled in a wheelchair, a grim look on her face.

"We don't advise this, Mr. Thompson. It's too soon after surgery to be leaving the hospital."

I smiled at her. For a human it probably was too early, but I was ready.

"Thanks for all the help today, but I'm pretty right. We heal fast in my family."

I stood up, grimacing as pain shot through my thigh and made a liar of me.

Okay, so I was *on* the mend, but not quite there yet.

"I'll be right to walk."

She rolled her eyes at me. "Absolutely not. It's hospital policy. Get in."

She pointed to the wheelchair.

I looked at Grayson, the big powerful Alpha, who was grinning his head off.

"Shut up," I warned him, before turning to sit my ass in the bloody wheelchair.

Aaron laughed, loudly.

"Asshole," I muttered.

I was wheeled out of the tiny room, into the stark hallway and out big, double doors.

The clean air on my face was one of the best moments I'd had today.

I pushed up out of the chair and stood up.

"Thank you, Nurse Melanie."

She huffed and puffed and pushed the chair back into the hospital.

Grayson dangled his car keys and opened the door to his black car.

"Get in, you poor sick dude."

I did get in, somehow.

I sat in the back seat and put my leg over the other two seats.

The others got in and we started driving back to Woodlands territory.

I sighed, my heart aching for my mate. "I can't believe we're going home without Nevaeh."

Silence.

Were they going to ignore me?

"Seriously guys, what the hell happened after I got shot? Did Nevaeh shout to the world that she'd never love us, or something?"

Grayson stayed silent. Stoic. His normal strong, stubborn self.

I turned my attention to Aaron.

"Come on, Aaron. Tell me. What happened with the bears?"

Aaron huffed and sighed for a bit. But I had time. It was an hour's drive home.

They wouldn't make the distance if I kept poking and prodding at them.

After a few more minutes, Aaron broke. "Okay, fine. Basically, we fought the bears, we killed the older one... or Nevaeh did, actually. She shot it dead. Then the younger one... Nevaeh's ex, shifted back. We..." He sighed. "Got sucked into shifting back too. Idiot that I am. And he grabbed me."

Everything started to fall into place.

Their pride had been hurt.

They were angry and upset.

"So, he used you to get away. What happened after that? Why is Nevaeh's face all smashed up like that?"

Aaron looked out the window. "He did it before we got there. And we don't know what else he did, because she wouldn't talk to us. Or look at us. Or..."

I waited, and no one continued to talk.

"So, hang on. We had, like, the fight of our lives, which I missed—and our mate walked away—beaten up, but still alive. And you just... what? Let her go?"

Grayson finally grunted and spoke.

"Look, we didn't let her go. She ran... literally ran away from us. Even after she'd been attacked in the woods that first time, in her car, she.... she decided she'd rather *walk* all the way home, than be with us. What does that say about her? About us! About our mating and our lovemaking ability. Fuck, Brad, I give up. Okay? I can't...."

Grayson broke off, and for the first time in the ten years since we'd become a family, I knew he was broken.

She'd broken him.

And she was the only one who could re-build him into the Alpha he was meant to become.

I stayed silent for the rest of the drive, secure in the idea that our mate was ours. That we'd touched her heart as deeply as she'd touched ours.

She was as broken without us, as we were without her.

She'd come for us.

If it wasn't today, it would be tomorrow.

And if it wasn't tomorrow... I'd bite my own ass.

Nevaeh

My hands shook as I pushed open the front door and watched the boys' car pull up.

I'd been at their place for over two hours already, timed by Claire to give me maximum time in the house without them.

After my talk with Brad, I'd realized he was right and that I needed to do something to show them how sorry I was for walking away. I'd called Claire and we formulated a plan for me to show them how much I wanted to be with them.

I'd brought my clothes, my knick-knacks, my tampons and my food. They were about to get me hard, fast, and perfume-clouded.

All of me, Brad had said. The three of them wanted all of me.

Well, I was about to find out if they were telling the truth.

This had to be the biggest, scariest moment of my life.

I waved from the door as the men got out of the car. They

stopped when they saw me, looking stunned, then started forward.

I'd iced my injuries and was dosed up on anti-inflammatories and pain meds. No way I looked too pretty at the moment, but I wasn't feeling any pain.

I smiled, though my heart beat so fast I was terrified I was going to throw up in front of them all and ruin my classy reunion.

I didn't cook, but I had organized take-out. Lots of it. And the house smelled like hot apple pie, Thai noodles and pizza.

"Hey. Welcome home."

Grayson walked up to the door first, his lips ticking up at the sides in a smile, so we were off to a good start.

He wasn't kicking me out, which I had worried was a real possibility after the way he spoken to me today at the hospital.

He shoved his hands into his pockets and rolled his shoulders forward like an awkward teenager. God, he was beautiful. So strong, and yet so shy.

Aaron walked up next. His chin stuck out and his eyes looked guarded. He wasn't smiling, but at least he didn't scowl at me.

Brad limped up last, a big grin on his face.

At least one of them was happy to see me.

They lined up, all three of them. Staring at me.

And although my belly quivered with nerves and fear that they might reject me, my heart sung with happiness to see them all here and in one piece.

I'd never known these feelings existed until a few days ago. This clawing need to be close to them was almost overwhelming.

"Hey, beautiful." Brad said, then grimaced.

What? Oh, shit. His leg! "Come in, so sorry! You should be sitting down, Brad."

I rushed forward and moved right in beside him, letting him lean on me.

"I'm okay." He laughed "You go in and fluff the pillows."

He pushed me forward and I did as he directed. Ran inside and moved the pillows around, and got a chair from the kitchen so that Brad could elevate his leg easily.

"What's that smell?" he asked with another big grin as he hobbled inside and set himself up on the couch where I'd arranged everything for him.

Grayson and Aaron followed, but they didn't speak and I began to worry.

"It's, ah... I brought some dinner. I wasn't sure what you guys like, so I got a little of everything."

Brad took my hand and pulled me down next to him. "I'm starved after a day on that hospital food. Grab me some pizza, would ya?"

I did. I grabbed one of the three boxes and brought it over to the couch.

Aaron and Grayson continued to stand near the door.

I swallowed hard and turned to study them.

They were looking around the room, probably noticing the little things I'd brought with me.

"Are you guys hungry too? Can I get you something?"

Grayson sighed. "What's this about, Nevaeh?"

"I told you. I wanted to bring you dinner, but... you should know, I don't cook."

Aaron glared at me. "We don't need you to cook. We're not looking for a housekeeper. We've gotten along very well without you for all these years."

Nerves hit me and I swallowed hard.

I should have known this wasn't going to be easy, but I hadn't thought my courage would desert me so quickly.

"Okay..."

Grayson put out a hand as though to ward Aaron off.

"Nevaeh, why are you here?"

Panic bounced down my spine with the force of a bowling ball.

"Because I want to be here... with you all."

"Do you, now? Since when?" Grayson crossed his arms over his chest and I had an overwhelming urge to fall to my knees and service him.

But there was so much more to be said.

"Since... the moment I left." I looked around the room, trying to connect with them all at once. "I'm so sorry I ran out on you the other day. I... behaved badly. I was scared, and overwhelmed, and I over-reacted."

Aaron walked closer; his aura softening for the first time. "What's there to be afraid of?"

I laughed, tears filling my eyes. "Are you kidding me? Everything. How I feel about you guys, what it will mean for my life. What I'll lose. What I'll gain. I'm terrified."

I laughed and hiccupped and wiped away the tears as they fell.

Fuck it. I'm all in.

"Look, ah... this is me. I'm a mess. I came here today to tell you I want to try to be what you want me to be. I'll move in, give you everything that I am, but you have to know... I'm not perfect. Nowhere near it. I'm totally broken... a mess... with a shit past. But if you still want me after all that." I spread my arms wide out in front of me. "Then I'm all yours."

Grayson stepped around me and called to Aaron.

"Sit. We're going to sort this out."

I felt awkward, but I stayed standing in front of them like I was giving a sermon.

Or a confession.

Or both.

"Ah..." How did I even start?

Grayson grunted. "Now, tell me what all this crap is about?"

I looked up at him, and sighed, the tension of the last few days getting to me. I was uncomfortable, nervous, scared and hopeful all wrapped up in one.

"I told you already."

"Yeah, you said you're a mess. Explain that to us."

God... where did I begin?

"Well, for starters, I can't cook. I grew up with nothing, so I have trailer park parents and an obsession for trinkets, so I collect everything. I'm a major hoarder. You may need to extend the house just for that issue alone." I took a shaky breath. "I'm a girl, so there will be makeup and bras and tampons all over the house and bathroom. I am not a neat person."

My chest heaved with the stress of revealing everything.

Brad and Aaron looked at each other but Grayson was staring at me.

"And? You think we'll be scared of your feminine products? Are you serious right now?"

He sounded offended, and that wasn't what I was hoping for at all.

"It's not just that. I'm bad news! Look what happened yesterday with the bears. That asshole came after me because I'm your mate and he deliberately baited you! If I wasn't around, he would never have hurt you guys."

Grayson held up a hand. "Hold up. What did you just say?"

"Um... Which part?"

"About the bears. Did they say something to you, about you being our mate?"

I nodded. Hadn't I told them this part yet? Probably not, because I hadn't seen them all together since we'd visited Brad at the hospital directly after Trevor ran off.

"Yeah. Sorry—I meant to tell you that part, but so much had happened. Anyway, Trevor told me that he didn't really want to date me all those years ago, but he could tell from the smell of me that I was a wolf shifter's mate. And the bears believe you guys are meant to die out... or something like that. So, they figured that if they kept me away from you, then your line would expire."

The room was so quiet you could have heard the proverbial pin drop.

Aaron sat forward on the couch. "Are you telling us that the bears can tell who our mates are, and are *deliberately* keeping them from us?"

They were horrified, that was clear.

I nodded. "Yes. That's what Trevor said."

Brad groaned. "Oh, that's fucked up. Here we are, like, dying of loneliness, and they're... what...."

The mood in the room had shifted. They were angry and upset, but it wasn't directed at me, and that gave me a nice break.

I took a breath while they discussed what they'd tell the pack.

I walked to the kitchen and grabbed a chair, dragging it into the living room so that I could sit across from them.

But as soon as I sat down, they swiveled around to look at me.

Aaron shifted on the couch seat.

"Nevaeh, you seem to have brought some of your... stuff. Why'd you do that? And how much did you bring?"

Now it sounded like he was interviewing me. Which, in a way, I suppose they were. A house-mate interview.

"I... brought everything I need. As to why..." I took a deep breath, "God, this is harder than I thought it would be."

"Nothing good is easy," Grayson said, his tone that of a man who could lead the masses. Strong and stable.

"True... okay." I pulled myself up to sit up straight. "I brought everything here, because I was hoping that your feelings about me hadn't changed. That you still want me to live with you. So... I brought everything I need to move in, if you'll have me?"

"If we still want you? Nothing's changed here. Why would it?" Grayson asked.

I threw up my hands.

"I don't know! Because you're mad at me and hardly speaking to me anymore? Because I ran away and you didn't follow. You didn't call, or anything. But then, when Trevor came to attack me, you knew... So, I don't really know what to think now."

Grayson continued to stare at me with those eyes that pierced my soul. "Well, we haven't changed our minds about how much we want you. If anything, after yesterday, a part of me wants to lock you in the bedroom so no one ever hurts you again."

I hiccupped out a laugh.

"I sort of understand that."

Because I felt the same way, especially about Brad. Maybe we could come to an arrangement where none of us would put anyone into a dangerous situation ever again.

Brad was grinning like a loon. "So, you're moving in. You're here to stay? You want to be our mate?"

I nodded. "I do. I can't promise I'll always totally get all this..." I gestured to the house and them. "But I'll try my best because I don't want to live without you."

They'd sacrificed themselves for me. They wanted me above all others. What more could I possibly want?

Grayson stood and I swallowed hard.

Decision time.

I looked up at him, not daring to blink in case I missed something.

"Nevaeh, we love you," Grayson said. "Our bond demands us to give you all that we are, and more. But you left us, rejected our lovemaking and all our gifts."

I nodded and hot tears slid down my cheeks, emotion clogging my throat.

I wanted to deny it, but it was time to grow up and be accountable for my outbursts and actions.

"Yes, I did. I was scared. And I am so sorry for hurting you all."

Grayson nodded, seemingly waiting for more.

My gaze dropped down his body.

Worshipping at the altar of Grayson was the best way forward. I knew that.

But to put myself out there, only to be rejected, would be my worst nightmare come true.

I fell to my knees.

These men had quite literally taken a bullet for me.

If they rejected me now, I could take it.

I could.

I dropped onto all fours and crawled over to him.

Yes, I *crawled*.

While I was unpacking, Claire had explained some things about the Alphas. They were truly dominant by nature.

Not assholes, but leaders, who needed the respect of their family and those who followed them.

The best way to show them that was to submit.

And Claire promised me that if I did that, truly did that, then my life would never be better.

"You showed me how amazing lovemaking could be. And I promise you, I'll never run from it again. No matter how scarily beautiful it is."

I rested on my heels when I reached his feet, and sat looking up, though my gaze kept catching on the bulge behind his zipper.

Grayson's arms fell to his sides and he stared down at me.

"What are you doing, little one?"

His tone had changed.

He wasn't angry anymore. He was aroused.

He swallowed, his throat working hard.

"I'm waiting for you to tell me I can suck your cock."

The words came out of my mouth as though I were a person standing on the ceiling looking down. I had no control over what I just said.

Shit.

"I don't need to give you permission," he said, a slow grin warming his expression. "After the other day, I think it would be better if you took what you wanted, Nevaeh. Actions speak louder than words, after all. So, I'll know you really want it."

Happiness swelled in my heart as I looked up at him and realized how much he loved me.

He was forgiving me for hurting him, and Aaron, and Brad.

And that's all I wanted.

To start over again.

I went up on my knees, and with trembling hands, reached for his jeans.

I undid the button and slowly pulled down the zipper, tooth by tooth.

Bushy hair was my surprise, no underwear to be found. I pulled the jeans apart and tugged them down until his cock bounced up at me, already thick, hard and wanting.

I hummed happily as I wrapped my hand around the impressive shaft and put the head into my mouth.

He was salty and hot and beautiful.

He grabbed my hair and held my head, thrusting his hips gently as gasps and moans filled the air.

I took as much of him as I could, saliva accumulating until I had to pull off.

He backed away and I cried out, "No."

The rejection kicked me in the guts.

He chuckled and landed on the couch with a thump.

"Oh, sweetheart, there will be more later, but I think Aaron deserves an apology too."

Aaron walked over and I looked up at him, keeping my face as sincere as possible so he knew I was serious.

"I'm sorry for hurting you the other day. I promise I won't do that again."

"You won't what? Fuck me and then leave me?" His tone was hurt and I nodded, realizing that before me were three very different men. And I would have to learn over time what each of them needed from me.

"No. Never again."

What else could I say?

"Then ask me," he said, and for the first time I was lost.

"Ah... Ask you what?"

He gestured down and I grinned. Oh, yes, definitely.

"Aaron... May I please suck your cock?"

He nodded but didn't move, and I attacked him more fiercely than I had with Grayson, maintaining eye contact the whole time as I took out his flesh and began stroking him.

He was still upset; I could feel it.

"Can I do anything else for you, Aaron? I really do want to stay with you... be here for you. Do you want me to quit my work for you guys?"

That was the last thing I wanted, but if that's what it took, I would consider it. I hoped that if they loved me, they wouldn't ask me to do that. But I would if that's what it took to make things right with these three men.

My mates.

"You'd do that for us?" he asked, stroking my cheek.

I nodded and pressed a kiss to the head of his cock, warm and pulsing in my hand.

"I'd do anything for you."

And I would. They deserved my loyalty and love.

"Thank you," he said and pushed my head down.

I slid his cock into my mouth, my mind spinning.

Did that mean he wanted me to stop working?

I pushed the fear down.

Did it really matter?

All I'd ever dreamed of was a house I could call my own, a home, and a partner to love me.

I'd gotten far more than that.

The rest was all superficial shit that I could let go of.

I could.

He tugged at my hair when I applied extra suction and staggered back too.

"Whoa... you're too good at that."

He was holding his cock tightly, like he was trying to stop an impending orgasm.

"Ah... thanks."

No one had ever told me that, and I glowed with the compliment.

I wanted to be good at it. I wanted to be good at everything. I never wanted them to want or crave for another woman.

"And just so you know," Aaron continued, "I'd never take your job away from you. It's handy having a nurse in the family." He grinned at me.

My heart broke and was remade in that instant.

I gave him my biggest smile and put all my love into the words as I said, "Thank you."

But I had one more to go.

I stood and walked over to the man who'd taken gunfire for me.

Brad was still sitting in his allocated spot on the couch. But as

I approached, he pushed his jeans down and opened his zipper for me.

"Can I suck your cock, Brad? Pretty please?"

He laughed and nodded. "Yeah, get down here."

With Brad, I knew it was more a token gesture than anything else. He had already forgiven me.

I moved to kneel on the couch so I could dive into his lap, when Grayson grabbed my shoulder. "Strip."

"But I..." *Needed to do Brad.*

"Yes. Strip, then get to Brad."

"Okay."

In the bright light of the lounge room? Sure. Why not?

I took off my tank and bra, letting my small boobs free of their confines.

Next was my pants.

I hated my legs. Too thin, some people said, yet all I could see were fatty lumps everywhere.

But this wasn't about me, it was about making them feel loved. So, I pushed through the incredible amount of discomfort I felt and heard the loud groan behind me.

"Fuck, woman. I almost came just from looking at you. You are too bloody hot."

That was Aaron, and as I looked over at Grayson, he growled and shook his head.

I glanced at Brad. "Is he okay?"

Brad laughed. "Oh, yeah. He's battling his shifter because his wolf wants you as much as his human half does. Come suck me, and he'll pull himself together."

I bit my lip and glanced back over at the Alpha.

I didn't understand.

Was he mad at me?

Brad squeezed my hand. "Hey, this is a massive compliment,

Nevaeh. Grayson is the most controlled Alpha in our whole pack, and you are his undoing."

He grinned and tugged at me.

When I looked over my shoulder at Grayson once more, he was stroking his cock and groaning, lust and need evident in his eyes.

Okay... I could do this.

The energy had changed in the room.

It was heavy and hot.

I knelt on the couch and put my lips around Brad's cock.

He put his hand on my head and I sucked on his flesh.

I moaned and tongued the saltiness, loving the feel of him in my mouth. Then suddenly, hands grabbed my thighs and a tongue thrust between my legs.

I released Brad's cock from my mouth at the shock. "Oh my God!" I screamed out as, I assumed it was Aaron, ran his tongue over all my aching parts.

Brad tugged on my head and I went down on him again, feeling his cock hard and large in my mouth.

Aaron slid his tongue inside me and I cried out, the sounds muffled by Brad's cock.

He moved to my clit, flicking it from side to side.

God, it felt amazing!

And then he was gone and my flesh throbbed. Needing, wanting.

No, come back!

Then Aaron was grabbing my hips and filling my pussy with his cock.

I moaned and came off Brad's cock to pant and cry out.

"That feels so good!"

I looked over my shoulder to confirm what I already knew.

From his hands, from his technique—it was Aaron—taking me hard and fast.

I couldn't concentrate, couldn't give to Brad.

I could only feel how incredible it was to have Aaron's cock back inside of me.

"I missed you... Oh... damn, I missed this... Oh... fuck."

I was going to come. My belly was too tight, my pleasure balancing on a precipice of feeling.

Aaron pounded into me, harder and harder, pushing me over the edge and making me scream out as the pleasure overtook me.

He came with me, his roar of completion making me close my eyes and soak up every second of this moment with him.

It went on and on, the stars of orgasmic pleasure bursting inside my mind as my body shivered and shook.

Aaron pulled out and I fell forward.

Brad caught me and arranged me over his lap.

His lips were on my face, in my hair, whispering to me.

"You are so beautiful. Tell me when you're ready to ride me, because I am dying to be inside you again."

As though his words had inspired the hunger, my belly squeezed and tightened in response.

I pushed back my hair and lifted myself up and threw my leg over his lap, over his cock.

Brad stared into my eyes, the depth of the brown irises making me ache inside my chest, where my heart was bursting with love.

He grabbed my hips and pulled me down.

His cock slid inside me, impaling me and splitting me in half.

I gasped as he captured my mouth in a kiss to end all kisses. It went on and on.

My beautiful, passionate Omega, Brad.

I threw myself right into him, the way I threw myself beneath a wave at the ocean. With vigor, passion, and abandon.

I rode him hard and fast, rolling my hips and taking him inside my body again and again.

I sucked on his tongue and clung to his neck until he pulled me down on him, hard, and the ripples of his orgasm pulsed inside me.

I opened my eyes and saw the pleasure flicker across his face. I kissed his lips over and over again, absorbing the love and acceptance, and beauty that I felt.

Brad smiled and sighed, letting his body relax into the bliss.

I'd had two of them and yet I knew there was more to come.

My skin tingled with need.

I looked around and found the Alpha waiting. Sitting on a chair with his jeans open and an intense look on his face I couldn't read.

I kissed Brad and stood up, careful not to hurt his leg any more than I already had.

I walked across the room slowly, the wetness between my thighs a reminder of everything I'd just done.

And that I would continue to do.

"You waited until last again. Why?" I had to know.

Grayson seemed to be the most selfless man, but was that really possible? For a man to be so wonderful?

He shrugged. "The pack's needs are more important than mine."

"Do you really believe that?"

He nodded, and for the first time in my life, I knew I'd met a true Alpha. A real leader. A man who would move mountains for his people, and it gave me an incredible amount of security and hope to know that I would benefit from that love and possessive streak.

"Am I part of your pack, Grayson?"

He nodded. "If you want to be."

"I do…very much. What do I have to do, to join?"

I couldn't believe I was having this conversation, fully naked, in the lounge room, the smell of sex thick in the air.

But Grayson needed this, the words.

I could tell.

His mouth flattened. "There are no strings attached, Nevaeh."

I knelt in front of him like I had before, showing my submission, trying to show with actions, and not just words, that I wanted to please him.

"I mean… What do you desire, Grayson? For me to be your perfect mate, tell me what I need to do."

He growled, a low, dangerous noise that made my pussy clench with want and my heart race to a new, invigorated beat.

"Tell me," I whispered again.

"Stand up," he said.

I did, shooting to my feet.

He stood also and dropped his jeans to the ground.

His cock wasn't fully erect yet, but it was thickening before my very eyes. Rising to point toward me.

It was hypnotic and I struggled not to stare.

"You'll be loyal," Grayson began.

"Yes." I nodded.

"You'll love us and be faithful to us."

"Yes." I nodded again. That was a given.

He began to walk forward and pushed me back until my spine hit the wall and he was staring down at me.

"Open your legs," he said, and I did, eagerly.

I was panting now, desperate to find out what he would do next.

I spread my legs as wide as I could while standing, and he slid his hand between my thighs.

His fingertips moved over my clit and around my opening, spreading the juices while I gasped and moaned.

"You will be honest with us, and scream at us, and fight with us, and moan at our touch, and fuck us, but you will not run away from us. Never again."

He thrust a long finger up inside my pussy and I screamed, the possessive presence inside my body making a statement.

I nodded again and again as he spoke, my eyelids too heavy to keep open as he worked my body with perfect precision.

His finger slid over my g-spot and pleasure swept through my belly. My knees buckled and he leaned against me to hold me up.

"Say it. Say you won't leave us again."

Tears gathered in my eyes, but I forced them to open.

"I won't leave again, I promise. If you promise you'll never leave me."

Grayson growled and removed his fingers.

I gasped at the loss, but as he grabbed my waist and lifted me, I knew I'd soon be full again.

Grayson pinned me to the wall with his huge body.

I was helpless and I loved it.

Because if I knew anything in this weird, crazy world, it was that this man loved me. And that he'd never hurt me.

He impaled me on his massive cock in one strong move.

I groaned and squeezed him tightly.

"Tell me, Grayson... please."

He reached under my ass and held me tight, moving in and out of me with measured thrusts.

"I'll never leave you. I'd die for you. I will tear apart that bear next time I see him."

I gasped and grabbed for his back, scratching at his skin as I ached to get closer.

Grayson set his lips to my ear and I wrapped my legs and arms around him, pulling him as close as I could.

"Will you give me babies, Nevaeh? Will you birth our child from this perfect body of yours?"

I nodded and squeezed my eyes shut as my love spilled over and the tears flowed down my face.

"Say it," he demanded and I nodded again.

He began to fuck me harder, faster, like he'd force the confession from my soul.

A baby... a true link.

Something I'd been terrified of my whole life—connecting myself so wholly to a person.

"Yes," I whispered.

The tears streamed down my face as my belly began to squeeze and tighten.

"Say it again," he demanded, grabbing my ass even tighter.

"Yes," I said, this time louder.

I held him to me, welcoming his cock into the deep recesses of my body, my soul, where I'd grow him a son.

Or a daughter.

Or both.

"Yes. I want your babies. I'll give you anything you want if you'll only love me forever."

His laugh mixed with his growl.

"Deal."

He fucked me into the wall, our bodies heaving against one another, straining until our orgasms mixed together. My body milked him of the seed that would grow the babies who would bind us together for life.

EPILOGUE

Nine months later
Grayson

I drove home from Little River, my car full of the thousands of things Nevaeh had requested for the babies. All the things she wanted in the house before they were born. Diapers and blankets, and a cot and a car seat.

Phew.

I pulled up behind the back of the house and sat for a while.

So much had changed in so little time.

I was stronger and more assertive than I'd ever been, and our family was flourishing.

I grabbed some bags from the passenger seat and went to open the door when I saw her.

My mate. Waddling over to Claire's house and knocking on her door. She leaned back over a hand pressed into her spine, her massive belly protruding forward.

Nevaeh had been a dream come true, in every sense of the word.

She was hardworking and tough, but super sweet and sexy as hell. She completed our pack, and I liked to think that we completed her, as well.

Nevaeh entered Claire's house and I got out of the car, carrying all the bags into our home and then coming back for the boxes.

So much stuff... and we didn't even know how many we were having.

Nevaeh had refused the ultrasound that Claire had offered. She was superstitious, and terrified that things would go wrong.

It had been such a strange nine months in that way. Nevaeh had turned from a beautiful young mate who barely had her footing in this world, to a terrified, and yet super-obstinate mama wolf.

Once I'd unpacked everything and Nevaeh still hadn't returned from Claire's, I decided to go visit my neighbors.

A slither of excitement coursed through my blood. It happened every single time I knew I was about to see my mate.

It was a great feeling.

And it still made me thank God every single night for the gift that was my Heaven.

I knocked on the door and waited.

Even after all this time, I liked to wait for Claire to open the door before barging in.

Dexter was still obsessed by her and their children, and he'd take my head off if I stepped out of line.

A smile lifted my lips. Or he'd try, anyway.

I was stronger and faster than I'd ever been, thanks to my mate's love and all the sex we had.

Though...thanks to Claire, Dex would be a close second in strength.

The door swung open and Claire was before me, a worried look on her face.

"What's wrong?" I asked.

"Um... your mate's in labor."

A grin stretched my lips. It was a few weeks early, but I believed that was still okay.

"Great. Where is she?"

"This way."

Claire directed me up the stairs to the bathroom, where Nevaeh was standing in the shower, naked and moaning softly, her eyes closed.

"Sweetheart, are you okay?"

She didn't look okay.

"Um... I don't know."

She began to groan louder, her head hanging forward as she leaned against the wall with her hands outstretched on the cold tiles.

I turned to Claire. "What's going on, Claire?"

"Nevaeh's in the late stages of labor. She's been having contractions all last night and today, but didn't tell anyone. She should go to the hospital, but she doesn't want to."

"No... I don't know... what... they'll be."

Claire ran her hand down Nevaeh's back. "Your babies will be like mine. Healthy and human, Nevaeh."

Nevaeh turned suddenly and grabbed Claire's hand, her huge, swollen belly rippling under the stream of hot water.

"No. I have you. That's all I need. Please, Claire... please... I..."

She broke off to groan and I turned away.

I needed to find Aaron and Brad.

"Sweetheart, shall I get the others?"

Nevaeh nodded but didn't seem able to speak.

I turned to Claire. "What do I do?"

She smiled. "I have everything we need. I brought it all here from the hospital when my babies were born. I'll stay here with Nevaeh, and you go get your pack."

"Okay."

I stepped into the shower and kissed Nevaeh quickly on the side of her face.

"I won't be long, beautiful."

I turned to leave, but Claire grabbed me. "Hurry. It won't be long now."

My heart jumped. I nodded and ran.

I found Brad at his parents' place, and Aaron at one of the clothing shops, buying something for Nevaeh.

I'd never been so grateful that the town was so small.

"Quick. We've gotta go."

They didn't question me, they just followed.

By the time we got back to Claire's house, Dex and the boys were camped in the lounge.

"Is she…"

There was moaning from upstairs and we bolted up to the second floor.

Nevaeh was still in the shower, but she was kneeling down on the tiles, some sort of thin padding beneath her.

"You're doing so well, Nevaeh. Just push, gently. Slowly."

Over the next twenty minutes, I watched a miracle occur.

My perfect, healthy mate gave birth to not one, not two, but three babies.

All girls.

All perfect.

I held one tiny babe, and my pack mates held the others.

I could have cried, if my heart wasn't so full of love and happiness.

Claire took them from us, one by one, and tied off their cords and wrapped them in blankets before handing our daughters back to us.

"Come on, Mom, bed's this way," Claire said.

She helped Nevaeh to her feet and dried her body.

Nevaeh was flushed and still sweaty, despite the shower.

She'd never looked more beautiful.

We all climbed onto the bed Claire told us to rest in, crowding around our mate and laying her babies on her body.

"You did it, beautiful."

She grinned up at us, her face alight with wonder. "I did. God, that was intense. Are you sure they're all okay?"

She looked from one to the other, their perfect little faces screwed up as they mewled like kittens.

"Yes. Claire said they're perfect," Aaron said. "And they are. Just like their mother."

Nevaeh rearranged one of the girls to take a nipple and the hungry little one latched on quickly.

"She's going to be trouble, I can tell already," Brad laughed.

"Three daughters?" I coughed. "I'm buying a shotgun."

We all laughed and I pressed a gentle kiss to my mate's lips.

Nevaeh was a miracle, as were our babies. And I now had more lives to protect and love. A perfect pack. My Alpha's calling.

Life had never been so perfect.

THE END of book 2.

SAVING THE PACK

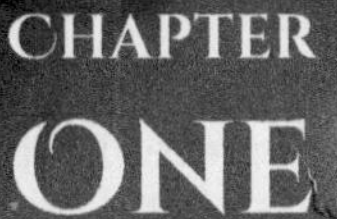

Celeste

I was going to be sick, and the toilet was too far away.

I ran as fast as I could, knocking my knee painfully against the bathroom door frame as I rushed into the tiny room. "Ow!"

The heat in my face rose and I grabbed for my hair, holding it out of the way as I launched my body forward.

"Bleh...."

The acidic bile rushed up my throat and into the toilet bowl, splashing against the sides and making me retch and choke even further. The smell burnt my nose and tears rolled down my cheeks, until finally, mercifully, it stopped.

I reached for the thin toilet paper beside me, pulling it from the roll and dabbing at my mouth.

I swallowed hard, though my mouth was too dry.

Yuck.

"Oh... dear God." That was terrible.

And it hadn't stopped yet.

Every day I'd been sick.

Every morning, to be precise. Until about lunchtime.

For two weeks.

I couldn't ignore the truth any longer.

"I'm in trouble here."

The front door to the apartment banged open and I jumped up off the floor and took a seat on the toilet, my head spinning with fatigue and low blood pressure.

"Celeste!"

I pushed the bathroom door quickly shut and pulled down my pants, so it looked like I was using the toilet for something more than vomiting.

In case he came in. Like he had done many times in the past.

There was no such thing as privacy if you were a member of the Little Rock bear's den.

I called out to him. "In the bathroom. I'll be out soon."

The bile rose again. *Oh, no.* My gut churned and tightened.

I closed my eyes and forced the vomit back down, swallowing hard against the automatic reflex to let it all out.

I couldn't let them know my secret.

I couldn't.

They'd never forgive me.

Loud footsteps walked up the hallway, then a fist pounded the door, hard.

I jumped, shivering with fear.

"Hurry up!" The voice was rough and loud. "The kitchen isn't going to clean itself, woman!"

I rolled my eyes, but only because he couldn't see me. If anyone in this place knew the kitchen needed cleaning, it was me.

"Um, one minute. Sorry. I'll be right out."

He grunted and walked away.

I relaxed against the commode as I heard his footsteps fade away, my whole body shaking with stress.

How long was I going to be able to hide this from the den?

And when they finally found out, which was inevitable, what would they do? Force me to get an abortion? Or something worse?

I exhaled in a long sigh. *Time to get moving before he came back and dragged me out.*

I opened the bathroom door and moved to the sink to splash some cold water onto my hot cheeks.

Uncle Dennis, my adoptive father's brother, was my "employer". He had set me up to work seven days a week in a job no one else would do—cleaning this run-down block of apartments.

The bears owned the apartment block. Some of the floors were rented out to outsiders, but the rest were occupied by members of the den, including me.

And the way I paid for my tiny bedroom in this apartment I shared with four others, was to clean every bathroom in the block.

All forty-six of them.

I took a deep breath and exhaled slowly, garnering whatever self-preserving courage I had.

Just one step at a time. You can do this.

I walked to the old kitchen and grabbed some saltine crackers from the cupboard, crunching on the only thing that seemed to keep the nausea at bay.

I took a moment to allow the food to reach my belly and settle the queasiness, and then I got to work.

Of course, it wasn't just my job to clean every bathroom in the block of apartments. It was also my *delight* to clean the kitchen and the entire apartment I slept in. Even though five of us lived here.

I had just finished wiping down the benches and cleaning out the kitchen sink, when my nose began to burn with a sudden foul smell. My throat convulsed. *Oh, no. The others were back.*

Then the front door flew open and three, burly, bear-shifting men walked in.

Great. My uncle was front and center, strolling in with two of the others who'd shunned me when they found out I was human.

The smell of them.... *Oh my God.*

I couldn't hold in the need to throw up, the second their musty stench hit my nostrils.

I rushed to the newly cleaned kitchen sink. My back heaved as my stomach emptied the meager contents I'd managed to keep down.

"What's going on with you? You sick again?" My uncle's voice was angry, annoyed. Like it always was whenever he spoke to me. Or at least, like it had been ever since I reached maturity and the bears had decided I was unworthy of a mate.

Not a single man from the den had wanted me.

Not that I'd wanted any of them, either. But it hurt. Despite all my hopes and dreams of a real family, I'd been rejected.

Wholeheartedly.

I nodded and rinsed out my mouth as quickly as I could. "Ah, yeah... sorry. I'll get back to cleaning."

I kept my head down, attempting to walk around the three man-mountains standing in the middle of the kitchen.

Each smelled as bad as the other.

"Stop."

The command in my uncle's voice made me freeze. Or as close as I could, considering I was shivering like a leaf in the Fall breeze.

"What...?" My uncle bent down and smelled me, sniffing loudly, before his lip curled up in a snarl. "You smell even worse than usual. Almost like a.... wolf."

My eyes closed and my stomach dropped to my feet.

They knew.

They must know, and they would punish me for my mistake.

Rough hands grabbed my chin and forced my head up.

"Open your eyes."

I did as commanded, and Uncle Dennis's eyes bored into mine.

"Tell me. Now."

"What... I mean... Tell you?" I was stammering, I was so scared.

My arms and legs shook. Goosebumps covered my skin.

I felt as if I would fall to the floor if he let go of my jaw.

"Lou, Davie, come here and smell her. Tell me if you smell what I do?"

Oh, God, no!

I kept my arms pinned to my sides and tried not to breathe.

This was the most humiliating thing about being part of this family. They all said I smelled weird.

Worse than weird. Bad. Disgusting.

Or that's what the bears said.

So, I scrubbed myself clean three times a day, even taking antiseptic into the shower some days to disinfect myself.

It hadn't changed anything.

They still hated me and said my smell made them sick.

"She's knocked up," Lou grunted.

"Yeah, but by who?" Uncle Dennis growled.

He shifted his grip to my throat and forced me backward until my spine touched the wall. I gasped for air, trying to control my growing panic.

No!

I grabbed for his hands and pulled on them, trying to loosen his grip, the pain making my head spin. He squeezed tighter, until I couldn't breathe at all.

Oh God... Am I going to choke to death, right here, at his hand?

"None of us wanted you, so it can't be a bear's baby. Who was it, you little slut?"

I couldn't lie. I had to tell them the truth. I'd been lonely and desperate, and the man I'd met made me feel more loved in a single hour than I'd ever experienced my whole life.

He released me enough that I could finally answer him.

"Just... a guy. In town. At a bar."

Uncle Dennis dropped me to the ground. I inhaled quickly, needing the air. I stayed where I was, on my hands and knees.

I wasn't getting back up just to be knocked down again. I'd learnt that lesson the hardest way, many times over.

As one of the only non-shifting women in the whole den, I was the weakest by far. I had the scars and the healed broken bones to prove it.

"It smells like a wolf," he growled above me.

I kept my head down. They weren't talking to me.

"We always knew she smelled like them," Uncle Dennis said.

"One of their human mates." Lou spat.

What?

I listened intently, though I tried not to show how interested I was.

A wolf's fated mate? How was that possible? I knew about the concept of fated mates, of course. I'd lived among the bear shifters for long enough. But... I was human. That seemed impossible, in my mind.

"You know the Alpha doesn't want the wolves getting any more of them," Lou growled and I heard Uncle Dennis's sigh.

Any more of them? Of what? Humans? Mates? What are they talking about?

"Let's take her to the Alpha and find out what he wants to do with her."

They hoisted me to my feet, and I went with them without complaint, even though the Alpha, Trevor, terrified me even more than Uncle Dennis. Being submissive to the bears had kept me alive and relatively well fed.

I relaxed as much as I could, calm descending over me. It was probably unnatural and unhealthy, this calmness, but I'd known this day would come, sooner or later.

They'd realize I wasn't suited for their den, and they'd either kick me out, or ship me off somewhere.

But now that the worst had finally arrived, my shakes and panic seemed to disappear. My mind worked faster than it ever had, focusing in on the one thought that mattered. There was more than me at stake now. My baby needed protection from the men who towered over us.

There was only one thing to do. As soon as I got the chance, I had to run.

And thanks to Lou inadvertently spilling the beans about my wolf-like smell, I now knew where to go for refuge.

Tayte, the Alpha wolf-shifter from the bar, had said something strange the night we met.

About a woman, a doctor, who was the first human mate they'd found in town.

I'd memorized that piece of information somehow through my alcohol-fogged brain.

My baby and I needed protection, and the daddy wolf who had made this baby with me was the only one who could give us the protection we needed.

~

DEATH!

They'd sentenced me to death!

The family that had taken me in as a baby, and raised me. The family I'd slaved for, all these years. Whom I'd tried to love to the best of my ability. I'd spent years caring for their children, their homes... and this was the result?

With a single word from the new Alpha, Trevor, they decided I needed to die.

I still couldn't believe it.

They'd all turned their backs on me.

I sat in my locked bedroom, still stunned at the turn of events. They had chosen to kill me in the morning, because tonight they were too busy with important bear pack stuff to bother with a little human like me.

They probably thought I'd never even consider escape. But they were wrong.

So wrong.

I placed my hands gently over my stomach. I had the incentive now, and I wouldn't sit around and wait to be killed, like they probably assumed I'd do.

Idiots. They hadn't even bothered to chain me up.

In the past I'd always meekly fallen in with their plans.

Not this time.

Not when my life, and that of my growing baby, was on the line.

As soon as the noise of the pack quietened down halfway through the night, indicating that most, if not all of them were finally asleep, I managed to pick the lock and break out of my bedroom. I'd done it before, when they'd left me alone, in case I ever needed to get away one day. Not that I thought I'd ever actually need the skill. But it wasn't difficult with the old locks, and a couple of hair pins bent in a particular way.

I crept through the apartment, avoiding the creaking wood panels I knew by heart, and ran. Through the exit door into the stairwell, down the many flights of stairs and out into the cold night air.

I didn't even stop to shiver in the tank top and thin jeans I wore. I just started running. Through the city, heading for the hospital. Toward the woman who might be able to help me.

A doctor, named Claire.

God... please.

The bear's apartment block was as far away from the inner city as they could get, almost on the outskirts of the city, in fact, but the streetlights lit my path, showing me the way to safety.

My heart galloped in my chest.

My throat burned as I gasped air in and out of my lungs.

And I didn't stop.

As soon as the bears realized I was gone, they would chase me, and I'd be done for. I had no protection, no weapon. The only things I had were my two legs and the will of a mother fighting for her child's life.

It had to be enough.

I kept running, city block after city block, though my tired body screamed at me to stop.

Adrenaline pumped harder through my system and I increased my pace, turning corners as quickly as I could.

The streets were deserted. It had to be past two a.m.

I didn't really know the exact time.

I kept going, pausing to breathe at an intersection to get my bearings, my chest heaving with exertion.

Which way?

They didn't let me out into the city very much and I wasn't familiar with the street signs, though I'd lived here all my life.

I looked and looked, then saw a sign I recognized.

Yes! The supermarket. It isn't far from the hospital.

Keep going.

I pushed off again, my legs screaming at me for those first few steps until I found my rhythm once more.

The hospital, safety, was about six blocks now, by my reckoning. My thigh muscles burned as I tripped on some uneven pavement, but I kept running.

The night was silent, except for my ragged breathing.

I could only imagine what would happen when the bears woke to find me gone. Growling and screams of rage would follow. I knew their tempers, their fighting and hunting abilities.

I'd watched them my whole life. And if I became the hunted, rather than the observer, then I was as good as dead.

Unless I could find her in time.

Claire. The doctor.

I turned one more corner and ground to a halt.

There it was.

A huge, white building with bright lights and doors that opened automatically.

I staggered the last hundred feet, my energy depleted and my body relaxing as my safe haven was finally in sight.

I stopped on the sidewalk, fear skittling through me.

The bears would be able to track me straight here if I went inside the hospital right now. They'd already tracked Claire there once.

I had to throw them off the scent, at least a little.

Damn it.

I staggered to the right, going another block down, though fear truly raced along my nerves now.

I ripped off my tank and dropped it onto a park bench.

I walked to the next bench and took off my jeans, leaving them beneath the seat.

"Oh my God." It was freaking freezing!

I jumped up and down, clad only in my old underwear, and then ran back to the hospital.

Hopefully that would help.

I ran straight into the Emergency Room and the bright lights enveloped me.

I was shaking, freezing, panting and half-naked. I felt as if I were about to drop to the floor in a faint.

Nurses rushed at me from everywhere, with blankets and juice, and nice words.

They admitted me straight away.

"What's happened dear, were you attacked? Shall we call the police?"

An old nurse was preparing a bag of fluid and as she came for me, needle ready to put in my arm. I stopped her.

"Can I please have a shower? I smell bad, and I'm so cold."

My scent would be greatly reduced after a shower. And thanks to the bears grabbing me early yesterday and then locking me up, I hadn't had one in over twenty-four hours.

"Of course, you can, after we've done a few tests."

I stood up. I couldn't let her win this one. "No please. It's important. I'm pregnant and I need to see Claire."

"Claire?" The nurse blinked and put down the needle. "She's not working tonight but I may have someone else who could help you."

I shuffled toward the shower room. "Please. I just need two minutes in the shower, then you can test me as much as you like."

The nurse nodded and I jumped into the shower, scrubbing my trembling body with the sterile-smelling soap and even washing my hair. Someone had left some shampoo in the stall and I couldn't resist. I didn't get that luxury much at home.

"Here you go." Someone stuck her arm into the cubicle and offered me a fresh white towel.

I turned off the water and reached for the towel. It was clean and fluffy. "Oh, that's heavenly! Thank you."

The person behind the door laughed.

"What's funny?" I asked, frowning her way, though she couldn't see me.

Surely the fact that a hospital towel was the cleanest piece of linen I'd seen in my whole life wasn't to be laughed at.

"I'll explain in a sec. I was told you came in with no clothes. I had some spare yoga pants and a sweater in my locker."

She placed the bag just inside the bathroom, then shut the door again.

Tears prickled in my eyes and I blinked them back.

"That's... ah ... so kind of you."

I quickly dried my body and wrapped my wet hair with the towel.

The yoga pants were the perfect size, though a little tight around my tummy, and the jumper was snuggly and warm, though way too big.

How tall was this woman?

I glanced at my reflection in the mirror. I was red and blotchy, but clean and safe.

I'd take it.

When I stepped out of the bathroom there was a young nurse sitting on the bed.

She grinned at me with a lazy confidence I'd only seen in the extremely powerful shifters in my den.

All men.

"Um... I'm Celeste," I said.

She grinned. "Nevaeh."

"Nevaeh..." I'd never heard that name before.

"That's why I laughed. You said, heavenly. My name is heaven spelled backwards."

I stared at her, wondering if she was joking.

She laughed. "It's true. Hippie parents. I used to hate it, but since meeting my guys, I don't stress anymore."

Had she just said "guys"? As in, more than one?

She didn't answer my question, though. Instead, she pulled her cell phone from her pocket.

"I know you wanted to see Claire, but she's at home. She's pregnant and working less hours. Why did you ask for her?" Nevaeh's tone was casual, but I had the strangest feeling she knew why I was here.

"Ah... that's great about her being pregnant."

Maybe I shouldn't have come here? I didn't know these people. How could I trust them?

This was a stupid idea.

I edged toward the door.

"Um... I think I'll get going."

Nevaeh stood up. "Hey, don't freak out. You're pregnant, too?"

I hesitated, then realized I'd told the first nurse the truth. So, I nodded.

Nevaeh moved around the room and gestured to the bed. "I'm not going to hurt you, I promise. Have a seat and I'll explain."

I had pretty good instincts when it came to evil intent, and as I reached out with those senses, I came up with nothing.

Hmmm... okay.

I walked back to the small bed, climbed onto the thin mattress and pulled the blanket over me. It was so nice to be warm.

Nevaeh stepped toward me, her movements slow and non-threatening. "Mind if I put the drip in now that you've showered?"

I nodded. "Sure."

Not for me, but for the baby.

I rolled up my sleeve and she walked the rest of the way across to me, sliding the needle into my hand effortlessly and then taping it down.

Wow. She was good at that.

"You need your fluids," she said, as though that explained everything, then sat again in the chair by the bed. "Look, Celeste, I'm willing to tell you everything about me and Claire, but you have to *show* me that you need to know. If you know what I mean?"

She smiled and waited. I got the drift and sighed.

What did I have to lose at this point?

"I've lived with the bear shifters just near the edge of town, for most of my life. But they found out yesterday that I'm pregnant and they decided to kill me. Me and my baby. So, I ran."

Nevaeh slid to the edge of her chair. "Holy shit."

"Yeah."

Then she snorted. "Sounds like my last month."

Sorry? "Ah... what?"

Nevaeh shrugged and met my gaze. "I'm not sure if you heard what happened with Trevor and his dad, but I'm the female that Trevor was stalking."

She was the girl? My gaze ran over the woman in front of me. Tall, thin and super-pretty. "You're the one who killed our Alpha."

I was shocked. I'd expected someone so much bigger, stronger, and more shifter-like.

Nevaeh nodded. "Unfortunately, yes that's me. He was trying to kill my mates."

She looked a bit regretful, but not overly sorry. And I didn't blame her, if what she said was true.

"Trevor's our Alpha now. I never much liked his father but Trevor's just as bad. Worse in some ways."

Then I slammed a hand over my mouth. I couldn't believe I'd actually said that!

Such a comment would have normally gotten me whipped, or my arms broken.

Nevaeh winced. "I wish I'd gotten him, too. *Bastard*." Then her gaze zeroed in on me.

"So, why are you here, Celeste? You obviously know about the shifting world. And you're running from the bears. How can Claire and I help you? And how did you know to come here for her, anyway?"

I licked my dry lips and Nevaeh handed me a bottle of water.

I smiled with gratitude.

She was being so nice to me. I needed to be honest with her. "I heard about Claire from Tayte, a guy I met in a bar a couple of months ago. He told me about his town, and how Claire was the first female mate they'd found in years."

Nevaeh's eyes opened even wider.

"Tayte told you about the pack? About Claire?"

She looked surprised, and a bit upset.

I jumped in to defend him. They probably weren't allowed to tell humans about their world. "Yeah. He could smell the bears on me, so he knew I lived with them. And he was pretty drunk... so was I. I'm not sure he meant to tell me so much, but don't worry, I never said anything to any of the bears about Claire. They knew anyway, somehow. That the wolves had found their first mate. That's why they tried to keep you away. Wait a minute."

All the pieces suddenly clicked into place. "You're a wolf mate, too!"

Her lips stretched up into a huge smile. "Yes, I am. But do you mean too, as in like Claire... or do you mean too... as in, like *you*?"

She raised her eyebrows and my hands flew to my still-flat stomach.

I didn't want to answer that, and if I were being honest, I

didn't really know the answer. I was going only on the word of the bears. What would they know about wolf fated mates?

"Is Tayte the father?" Nevaeh asked quietly.

I waited a heartbeat, then told the truth.

I nodded. "Yes, that's why I came here. To find Claire. To ask for her help in getting to the pack. I know I come with a whole lot of trouble at my back, but I need to find Tayte and see if he will be willing to protect me and the baby."

Nevaeh pulled her cell phone from a pocket and began pressing buttons.

"Who are you calling? It's probably three in the morning."

"Three thirty, actually." Nevaeh put the phone to her ear and gestured for me not to stress with a flutter of her hands. "Trust me, Grayson's gonna wanna hear this."

TWO

Tayte

I woke so abruptly from a sound sleep it was like someone had physically thrown me out of my warm bed. "What the...?"

Someone was banging on my front door, and they weren't stopping any time soon.

My eyes sprung open and I jumped out of bed.

"Tayte. What's going on?" My Beta, Sam, yelled from the back of the house as I jogged down the stairs.

"No idea," I called back up.

We never had this sort of drama in the middle of the night.

It was still dark out. Like, pitch black dark.

I turned on a light in the lounge and opened the door, my eyes blinking rapidly to adjust to the artificial brightness.

"Morning," Grayson said, stepping inside without an invitation.

Unusual for an Alpha.

We didn't invade each other's houses like this. It wasn't respectful.

"Still night," I mumbled, rubbing my eyes clear of sleep. "But come on in, Gray." Then I chuckled. "Oh, that's right, you're already in. What the hell is going on?"

Grayson grinned at me. "Put your coffee pot on, Tayte. You're gonna have a visitor soon. You and your pack need to wake up."

Despite my confusion, I stumbled to the kitchen and put the kettle on like he suggested.

Grayson was one of the few selfless Alphas in our larger pack of wolf shifters. If there was anyone I trusted beyond myself to care for my Beta and Omega, it was Gray.

"What's going on?" Sam asked as he practically fell down the stairs. He slept like the dead, that one.

Dane, my Omega, walked downstairs more slowly, already pulling a tank over his bare chest.

I only wore the trackies I slept in, and didn't see any need to dress further.

The Omegas were always more self-conscious than us Alphas.

"Hey, guys," Grayson greeted them, too cheery for this early in the morning.

"You going to tell us why you're here, Gray? Something wrong?"

Grayson had found his mate last month and gone through hell to get her away from a bear shifter.

His next-door neighbor, Dexter, had been the first to find a human mate in the pack.

I didn't know Dex's pack well, but to say I was jealous of their newfound happiness would be an understatement.

"Nothing's wrong. I got a call from Nevaeh at the hospital. Seems a woman staggered into Emergency last night, looking for Claire."

The hairs on my neck prickled up.

Ever since that night two months ago when I'd told a stranger about Claire, I'd been worried something like this might come up.

"Is Claire okay?"

"Yeah, she wasn't working tonight. So, Nevaeh looked after the girl, and she's bringing her home now."

Huh? Nevaeh was bringing another human female here, to the pack. Why? And why was it worth waking us in the middle of the night to communicate that odd piece of news?

Sam and Dane stared at me, clearly confused.

Then the pieces of the puzzle began to fall into place for me.

"This girl... blonde, blue eyes, about five feet tall?"

She had been tiny, and sweet, and very sexy, if my drunken brain hadn't exaggerated the details of that one-night-stand.

"Not sure. I haven't met her yet. But she asked for Claire by name at the hospital and she told Nevaeh that you were the one who told her about Claire."

Grayson gave me a hard look and if I'd been inclined to blush, I would have.

Instead, I thrust my hands into my track pant pockets and shrugged.

"Yeah, I did. And I'm sorry about that. I was drunk, and she already knew about the shifting world. It just kinda slipped out. Seemed natural to tell her, actually, in a weird way."

Sam looked from Gray to me. "So, what are you here to say? Is Tayte in trouble?"

Grayson turned to Sam. "Have you two met her? The girl Tayte slept with a couple of months ago?"

My eyebrows flew up, surprised by Grayson's swift change of topic.

Dane shook his head.

Sam said, "No. He mentioned it. But that night we were working late. Tayte went into town with another pack."

I frowned, trying to remember the details of the evening. I couldn't believe I'd had so much to drink. Why hadn't I waited for my own pack to join me for the trip? That was usually the way we did things.

"Oh, yeah, that's right," I said, as memories started to come back to me. "It wasn't even my night to go into town, but with the news of Claire, I wanted to get in there and at least start looking."

Grayson glanced at his cell phone. "Well, you may have met your destiny that night, Tayte. Looks like she's almost here."

Grayson stood up and went to move past me toward the front door.

I stopped him by grabbing his arm. "What do you mean? Are you telling me she's my fated mate? That's impossible."

There hadn't been any of the signs. No fainting, no intensely sweet smell— though I'd been drunk off my ass—not to mention the fact she smelled of bears.

"Grab a coffee, guys, and then make your way over to our place, all three of you."

Grayson shrugged out of my grasp, gave us a grin then headed out the door.

Dane turned to look at me. "Do you think it's possible, Tayte?"

"I... ah, don't really know."

And I didn't.

Sam crossed his arms over his chest. "And if she's your mate, does that mean she's ours as well? Like with Grayson and Dexter?"

I grabbed our travel mugs and Dane brushed me away, taking over the coffee preparations.

"Thanks."

He did coffee-making better than me.

"Well, we better get dressed, I suppose." I glanced down at my half-naked body. I wasn't sure how Nevaeh would feel if we turned up like this.

"Yep. See you back here in five." Sam jogged back up the stairs.

I was slower. My brain still hadn't quite woken up yet.

Gray hadn't waited for the sun to rise to share this information, which must mean he was excited by the news.

But why?

Was he so interested in building the pack that he was going to foster off a one-night-stand to me and my pack in lieu of the real thing?

A wave of sadness hit me.

I wanted so much more than that.

I craved my fated mate. A woman to complete our small pack. Someone to come home to. To love and cherish. I was old-fashioned that way.

And being born in this era, where there were no wolf-born women, was both frustrating and depressing.

I pulled on jeans, a long-sleeved shirt and some nice shoes.

May as well dress up a little for the meeting.

I trotted back downstairs and the guys were waiting by the front door, coffees in hand.

"Here," Dane said, handing mine over.

It was hot to the touch and warmed my hands nicely.

"What's wrong, Tayte?" Sam asked as we closed the door and began the walk toward Grayson's place.

His pack's house was on the other side of the central shops.

"Just worried I'm about to be disappointed."

There was a beat of silence around us as my words settled with my pack.

"What's she like? Do you remember?" Sam asked suddenly.

"Um..." What *did* I remember? I'd tried so hard to suppress any thoughts of women of late. It was too painful to be reminded of our loneliness all the time. "I remember feelings, more than anything else. She was sweet, and as drunk as I was." I shook my head. "I didn't want to leave her, but she took off straight after we had sex, and the other pack dragged me home. I remember feeling the need to go look for her but being talked out of it. Seriously... I don't have much."

I shook my head and swallowed my coffee, trying to settle the strange feelings shivering through me.

I was nervous and tense.

I stretched my neck from side to side and heard satisfying clicks and pops.

We walked up the street and stepped onto the sidewalk in front of Grayson's house.

The lights were on, the house lit up like a Christmas tree.

But there was darkness all around.

"Do you smell that?" Sam said, lifting his nose to the air.

I did. There was a faint... sweet...

"Oh. My. God."

It was her.

The three of us raced for the front door, opening it and barreling into the house like a bunch of eager puppies.

I righted myself quickly while Sam and Dane took their time, their reflexes not as sharp as mine.

Her smell hit me like a cloud of perfume. Instant, hot and perfect.

My gaze met hers and all the memories came flooding back.

Of her lips against mine.

The softness of her body beneath my hands.

The tiny gasp of pain as I took her for the first time.

"You were a virgin."

Her eyes widened even further. Oh damn...

"Fuck. Sorry—I didn't mean to say that aloud."

She had been, though. Looking back, I should have known before that point. Her reactions had been too innocent, her enthusiasm too real. The pain in that first thrust, too true.

There was an elbow in my side, as Dane and Sam waited to pounce.

"Oh, um... Dane and Sam, this is... Celeste."

Her name rolled off my tongue like it had always been there.

Great save, memory.

Celeste stood up and walked toward me, the oversized clothes not suiting her.

"It's you."

She reached up to touch my face like *I* was the dream, not her. I leaned into her caress, wanting to feel her skin against mine.

She was so tiny, I'd forgotten just how fragile and delicate her tiny frame had been. She cupped my jaw and I turned my face to kiss her smooth palm.

The gasp that ricocheted through the room deafened me.

She began to crumple. I swooped down to scoop her up before she hit the floor, and I began to shake as pleasure pulsed through every vein and muscle at the feel of her beautiful body in my arms.

I heard a female voice in the background, behind the rushing of blood in my ears. "Sam, Dane, touch her as well. Get it all over and done with in one go."

I didn't understand what the woman meant and bared my teeth to my pack as my Omega and Beta rushed forward to put their hands on my mate.

She cried out as if half-waking up, violently arching her back and shivering all over. Then she passed out fully again.

I glared at Dane, then Sam, fighting my wolf to stay down, and they backed away.

Grayson stepped closer and I snarled at the other Alpha.

He needed to stay away from my mate, or so help me God...

Then Nevaeh was there, pushing Gray back, away from me and my mate, and slowly stepping toward me.

"It's okay, Tayte. You've got her, she's safe now. I brought her home from the hospital for you. No one's going to take her away, now. It's all right."

Her words made sense. I knew that somehow, on a rational level, but I couldn't seem to interpret them properly.

My wolf was crawling up my back. Exploding through my humanity. Fighting to get out and take over.

Protect. I had to protect my mate.

Fuck... no!

I couldn't control the shift. Horror slammed into me. I was going to hurt Celeste because I couldn't contain my wolf.

I yelled at my Beta. "Take her, Sam. Quick."

He rushed over and even though I'd called him, demanded his help, a possessive growl erupted out of my throat.

Somehow I found the strength to release Celeste to Sam, and then I backed up to the front door and managed to wrench it open moments before my wolf ripped through me. Muscles transformed, fur sprouting through my skin as my clothes shredded and fell to the ground beside me.

I shook myself as the transformation completed. I looked around the room through my wolf eyes, everything in black and white and gray.

My mate was here, safe in Sam's arms. Safe with my pack.

Though Gray was still there, across the room.

My lip curled up as I glared at him. I didn't want to leave another Alpha alone with my mate. Not when Celeste and I were still unmated.

But I couldn't stay here. I had too much energy to burn off.

Grayson met my gaze calmly, nodding after a moment as

though he understood. "I'll come with you." He walked toward me, stripped off his shirt and jeans and his shifter emerged.

The silver wolf matched me in color and size.

An Alpha.

He nudged me in the shoulder with his head and we took off together, running through the woods. Running away from my destiny at this point. So that I could return, clear headed and stronger than ever, and accept whatever path my destiny led me down.

THREE

Sam

I stared down at the beautiful, tiny woman in my arms. My mate. And yet, Ihad no idea what to do with her. I certainly didn't want to put her down.

"You can lay her on our spare bed, if you want?" Nevaeh suggested, gesturing to the fourth bedroom in their house.

I shook my head, feeling stubborn. "Ah, no, I'd rather hold her for a minute."

Nevaeh smiled gently. "Sure, but how 'bout you guys sit down at least. I'll put some breakfast on."

Brad laughed and patted Nevaeh on the back. "She means, *I'll* put some breakfast on. The woman burns toast on a daily basis."

Nevaeh shrugged good-naturedly. "Told you when we mated that I couldn't cook."

Aaron, Nevaeh's other mate, stepped up and kissed her lips possessively, then pulled away with a grin. "Yep. We don't love you for your cooking."

Nevaeh blushed prettily and I began to relax.

She was right. We needed food and time to wait for our mate to wake up.

I found my way to an armchair and sat, pulling Celeste closer into my body and arranging her head on my chest.

I loved the sensations that ran through me, while I held her. While her scent rose up and tickled my nostrils. While tendrils of her hair fell across my bare arms.

"So, ah, what do we do about this, then?" I asked, and everyone else in the room laughed.

Everyone except Dane, that is.

He had his gaze firmly fixed on Celeste, and he pulled up a chair next to me, obviously not wanting to be too far away from the diminutive female.

Aaron and Nevaeh jumped onto the couch together and Brad went to the kitchen to make whatever he was going to make.

None of us liked to cook in our individual pack, so I was hopeful our mate had a little more skill than Nevaeh seemed to have in the kitchen.

But if she didn't—who cared, really? We'd managed okay so far, and take-out existed for a reason.

"No, like seriously. I have questions," I said, repeating my earlier query. "What do we do now? And how do we know if she's just Tayte's mate, or ours as well?"

I brushed her long blonde hair off her face and stared down at her. Even though her eyes were closed, she was beautiful. But she seemed very young.

"And how old is she?"

She barely looked legal. But surely Tayte wouldn't be stupid enough to have taken her if she were underage?

My stomach tightened at the thought.

Tayte had already had her. Been inside her.

My wolf growled and I tightened my hold on her.

"Relax," Aaron said from the couch. "I know you're feeling all sorts of weird, possessive, jealous crap, but it'll pass. Just, you know, focus on something else."

I glared at the other Beta. "You mean I should forget that my Alpha's already had her?"

Aaron nodded. "Yeah, definitely. Because when she wakes, you'll all have her, and she'll love all of you. Have faith in the system, my friend."

I grunted, not able to find the words to tell him to *get fucked* in an eloquent manner.

The anger in me began to rise. Soon it would reach boiling point.

I had to get a grip on myself. I took a few slow breaths, but it didn't help much.

Didn't they understand how frustrating this was?

"You might want to put her down now," Aaron said, and this time I heard the demand in his tone.

I forced myself to breathe deepeer, to think.

Aaron was right. I was only getting worse the longer I sat here with her draped across my lap.

Brad called from the kitchen. "Through that door, Sam. The bed's good to go."

I followed his directions and placed her down on the large bed in their spare room.

Dane was right behind me, staring down at her. "She looks like an angel."

I nodded. "Yeah, she does."

Her golden hair spread over the duvet and encircled her face like a halo.

I turned and walked away, unsettled by the way she made me feel. Angry, possessive, and worried.

When I got back to my seat, my wolf finally began to relax, to settle. I could breathe again. Though tension still held me in its grip, the anger dissipated.

"Told you," Aaron grunted and I nodded at him. Yeah, he'd been right.

"Thanks."

"No problem," he said. "Don't forget, we've been where you are, man."

Brad stepped into the room then, and placed food in front of us on the low coffee table.

Pancakes. Sliced fruit. Cream.

"Wow." The Omega had said he could cook. He clearly wasn't kidding.

"Eat as much as you want," Brad said as he put down a bunch of plates. We all served ourselves, the distraction of food helping with the strange mood that had gripped me.

I piled my plate up as Brad went back to the kitchen to make more.

I looked at Nevaeh, the one who'd brought us our mate.

"What happened tonight at the hospital?"

She picked up a strawberry, dipped it in the cream then ate it before she answered.

"It was a bit crazy, actually. I was just finishing my night shift and one of the nurses came in to say that there was a woman in the ER. She had stumbled in dressed only in her underwear, freezing cold and asking for Claire."

She had been... what?

I stared at Nevaeh. "What do you mean? She was running around town, in the middle of the night, in her underwear?"

Had Fate sent us some sort of cuckoo?

Nevaeh shrugged. "I went straight to her and she was already in the shower, scrubbing herself clean. That behavior, combined with the fact that she said she used to live with a pack of bear shifters, made me think she probably took off her clothes to knock them off the scent. She's young and pretty timid, but there's no doubting she's smart."

Pride blossomed in my heart at the same time as panic whistled through me.

"She was living with the bears? How is that possible?"

Nevaeh shrugged, seemingly unworried by this turn of events.

"I didn't ask her. But seeing as Trevor deliberately dated me, then stalked me for years to keep me from finding you guys, maybe they did the same thing with her? Maybe they smelled the wolf mate scent on her, the same way Trevor smelled it on me."

Dane gasped beside me. "And she somehow escaped them? A whole bear pack? And went straight for Claire. Pretty amazing for anyone to achieve that, let alone someone young and timid, like you say."

Nevaeh began picking at her pancake, eating small pieces of it with her fingers.

"I agree. Though, given she was drinking in the pub the night she met Tayte, its likely she'd be at least twenty-one, I think."

Well, that's comforting.

Dane sat forward on his chair. "And how do we know if she's our mate, too?"

Aaron answered that one. "Did she smell super-sweet to both of you? Like, intoxicating?"

I looked at Dane. "Yeah," we both answered in unison.

"She shook and gasped when you guys touched her, even after she'd touched the Alpha," Nevaeh said.

"Yeah. So?" I said.

Nevaeh grinned. "That's another sign she's your intended mate. It looks like you guys are very much designed to have one mate for your triad. Like us."

Stark relief, unlike anything I'd ever felt, raced through me. Tayte wouldn't leave us for Celeste, and she wouldn't leave us for him. Dane and I wouldn't be left alone, without an Alpha or a mate. "That's... great."

The front door banged open and I looked up.

The sky outside was decorated with red and orange hues now.

A perfect sunrise.

Grayson and Tayte paced back into the room, still in wolf form.

Grayson shook his pelt and stood up, rising from his silver wolf into his massive human form.

He grabbed his clothes from where he'd left them and pulled them back on.

I glanced across to Nevaeh and watched her devour him with her eyes.

Hopefully my mate would look at me like that someday.

When Grayson was dressed, he stared down at Tayte, who hadn't yet turned back.

"What's wrong?"

Tayte looked toward Nevaeh, then his clothes, which had been shredded by the force of his abrupt change.

"Oh, right. Yeah, hang on."

Grayson trotted up the stairs and came back a few minutes later with a pair of jeans and a sweater.

I almost laughed. Tayte was embarrassed to be naked in the room with Nevaeh, but earlier he'd shredded his clothes like a teenager, changing without even thinking about afterward.

"Here." Grayson laid the clothes on the back of the couch and Tayte raced over to the other Alpha, let go of his wolf, and stood up.

He was naked once again in the room.

I tried to distract Nevaeh as Gray's expression hardened and the tension in the room increased.

Alphas were territorial and this situation was uncomfortable for everyone.

"Um... anything else you want to tell us, Nevaeh? About our mate?"

Nevaeh grabbed another strawberry and bit into it.

"She's tough. I can tell you that. I saw a few scars on her, no doubt from injuries she's sustained over the years. Trevor is violent, and I'm guessing many of the other bears in that pack are, too. She may look fragile and innocent, but she'll have some strength to her."

Tayte, now dressed, walked over to where Dane and I sat, and stood behind us.

"That's good to hear," he said. "I hoped Fate wouldn't send us a mate who couldn't cope with our world."

"Oh, she can cope, all right. Those bears are rugged creatures." Nevaeh shuddered. "If she lived with them her whole life, as a human, then she's tougher than any of us realize."

I could feel that Nevaeh was leaving something out.

I stared at her, narrowing my eyes, and she glanced around the room as though avoiding my gaze.

"There's something else, isn't there, Nevaeh? Something you're not telling us."

She looked at Tayte and back to me and Dane, before nodding. "There is something else. But I can't tell you."

"Why not?"

She smiled gently. "Because Celeste will tell you."

There was movement behind Grayson, where he sat on the couch.

It was her... it was Celeste. She was up again!

Dane and I jumped to our feet, and Tayte released a low

rumble and crossed his arms over his chest. It seemed that none of us could still when Celeste was in the room.

She walked out into the lounge, her beautiful blue eyes shining at us with a mixture of fear and hope.

She didn't seem afraid of us, though. Whatever she was fearful of, it wasn't a bunch of wolf shifter possible mates.

She just came straight over to us, looking from Tayte, to me to Dane and back again.

"Did I pass out?" she asked, in a voice that sent ripples of awareness over my skin.

She was so beautiful, I couldn't believe it. Soft skin, shiny hair, big, blue eyes.

"Yes. Though your recovery was pretty quick compared to Nevaeh," Grayson answered.

Celeste put her hands into her pockets and glanced back at the other pack's Alpha.

"That's probably because I'd met Tayte before."

"God, you're beautiful," I said without thinking, and she turned her head and smiled brightly up at me.

"What's Nevaeh talking about, Celeste? Is there something we need to know?" Tayte asked.

She nodded. "There's lots of things. Like my background, the bears, everything. But I think..." She turned around to look at Nevaeh, "I think she meant one specific thing. It's the main reason I'm here."

We waited, the air around us completely still with expectation.

You would have heard the proverbial pin drop.

"And that is?" I prompted, dying of the suspense.

She lifted her gaze to meet Tayte's. "I'm pregnant."

Celeste

As soon as I said it—my secret, my truth—I heard the swift intake of breath from three shocked shifters.

I wanted to laugh at them.

Was it really so difficult to believe that after a one-night-stand there'd be consequences to our actions?

My hands went reflexively to my flat stomach, which wouldn't be flat for much longer.

I was over eight weeks along now, and Nevaeh had said that wolf shifter pregnancies were slightly different than normal human ones. I'd be bigger, and I'd likely show quicker.

My gaze was still connected with Tayte's, and because of that, I think, the other two men backed away.

To give us room, perhaps? I wasn't sure, but the further away they went, the more the tension in the room seemed to rise.

Tayte, on the other hand, stepped closer. "Are you certain?"

Are you certain it's mine? That was what he was really asking, and I glared up at him. The guy was a foot and a half taller than me, so I had to crane my neck.

"Considering you're the only man I've ever slept with and I'm eight weeks pregnant, vomiting and freaking out, then, yeah, I'm certain."

Part of me marveled at the way I was speaking to an Alpha, and the other part of me cringed a little, wondering if I would be punished for such forward, transgressive behavior.

Uncle Dennis would have back-handed me into the opposite wall if I'd ever tried to speak to him that way.

Tayte was so big and strong and clearly an Alpha leader. Usually, a man like that would terrify me. But even on the night we met, he'd been so sweet. So loving. And I hadn't been afraid at all. Instead, I'd just known, without a shadow of doubt, that he was different from all the others.

"That's... that's..."

He didn't seem to be able to find any words, so I jumped in to fill in the sentence for him. "What? Horrible? Terrible?"

"A miracle," he breathed, and pulled me into his embrace, holding me tight against his body.I closed my eyes, rested my head on his chest and sighed.

Sighed away the stress, the disbelief and the hurt.

I'd made it. I'd found him. The Alpha. My baby's daddy.

And it didn't seem like he planned to send me packing.

"Ah, Tayte." Nevaeh's Alpha, Grayson, cleared his throat. "How about you take your mate home? Get her some new clothes at the shop sometime today, and sort out your pack?"

When I pulled back from Tayte's warm embrace, I could sense storm clouds rolling in.

Not literally. These storm clouds were metaphorical ones. Centered firmly around the other two in Tayte's mini-pack, Sam and Dane.

Uh oh.

Nevaeh had said something about this being a triad of sorts.

"Um..." I wasn't quite sure what to say, but Tayte cut across my bumbling non-answer.

"Good idea, Gray," he said. "Thanks. And Nevaeh, thank you. We owe you. Like, big time."

Nevaeh laughed. "Yeah, yeah, just look after her."

"Goes without saying," Tayte said gruffly, before hustling me out of the house and onto the road. Sam and Dane followed quickly, as if they didn't want to be left behind, but their shoulders were rigid and neither of the other two were smiling.

I shivered with the cold of the early morning air, and everything I'd been through recently.

"So, where to now?" I asked, looking at the three men gathered around me.

"Ah... I think we need to go home and talk about everything," Tayte said, his gaze going to the other two men.

"Okay." That sounded sensible to me. "Where's that?"

I looked around at the clean streets and well-built homes.

The town was incredibly impressive. I hoped I would get the chance to stay here for a while and explore.

"This place is amazing." I sighed. "So fresh and well-maintained."

Though the grass was a little sparse and the town's main street clearly small and lacking in a range of amenities, I assumed that was due to the lack of females born to the pack in this generation.

It still kicked the ass off anything the bears had.

"This way." Tayte put a hand in the small of my back and I had to suppress a shiver of delight at his touch. We began walking along the street. There were more solidly built houses all the way along our route, and a group of shops were clustered in the center around what looked like a town square area.

The shops included clothing stores, a supermarket and a barber.

"I heard whispers about you guys from the bears."

"What did they say?" Tayte asked as the other two walked closely behind us.

Listening, probably, but not wanting to talk yet.

"Well, they said you couldn't have children anymore because there were no females born. Not for a whole generation."

Tayte nodded. "Yes, our mothers were some of the last females born to the pack. Wolf shifters, too. We thought that meant that we'd never have a fated mate, but it seems like the future of the pack lies with humans."

"Like me?" I asked, staring up at his handsome face.

He was so much better looking than I remembered.

My memory had not been kind enough to the strength of his jaw, his funky haircut or his caring eyes.

"Yes, like you." He squeezed my waist a little, then stopped suddenly.

"Grayson said to get you something to wear, but I don't think the shops open until nine-ish."

He looked toward the other two men, who shook their heads.

"Okay, then we'll head home and come back later for that."

"That would be great. Thank you. The last thing I thought about when I ran from the bears was bringing clothes with me."

And what I wore were some of the only decent ones, anyway, so it was no loss.

"You did an incredible thing, Celeste. Escaping them."

I could hear the admiration in Tayte's tone, but I shrugged. I didn't deserve that much praise.

"I didn't really have a choice. I had to protect my baby. And I had to find you."

He smiled at me with all the love I'd hoped for. "I'm glad you did."

We kept walking, and I began to feel strange. My stomach tightened and jumped around in excitement. Not a normal feeling for me.

Amazingly, I could sense no morning sickness or nausea this morning, which was unusual.

Whether it was due to the after-effects of adrenaline from my frantic overnight run, or the sickness had simply run its course and passed, I was unsure. Either way, I was grateful for the small respite.

"Which one is your house?" I asked as I pulled my hands into my sleeves and curled my fingers into fists to keep the warmth inside.

Assuming they had their own house? I wasn't sure how it all worked out here. Nothing about this place felt in any way similar to the life I'd led with the bears.

"Are you cold?" Tayte asked.

"Ah, a little. I'm not used to being outside very much. All my jobs kept me inside."

And I was always moving, scrubbing, cleaning, or running from someone yelling at me. I wasn't used to the fresh air, nor so little fear.

"No problem. We're not far now." He wrapped an arm around my shoulders and the gesture felt natural and comforting. We walked toward a large double-story house, similar to Nevaeh's home from the outside.

But this one seemed wider, and there was more brickwork visible to the eye.

"Is this it? It's beautiful." I stared up at the house that could very soon be my home. "It's like... a house out of a magazine."

I sometimes looked at the magazines in the stand at Walmart when I went shopping for the den.

Tayte opened the front door for me and gestured.

"Welcome."

Wow.

I looked back at Sam and Dane, who were watching me closely but still keeping their distance. I gave them both a small smile, then turned back to the house and took a step closer to the entrance. Tayte suddenly whisked me up into his arms.

I clung to his huge shoulders, pressing into his warmth. "What's happening? What are you doing?"

He chuckled and held me tight. "I'm carrying you across the threshold. Isn't that what you humans do when you mate?"

Heat flushed up my face as he carried me into the lovely home.

It was even bigger inside than it had looked, with twelve-foot high ceilings and huge, male-sized couches.

"Ah... well, I grew up with shifters, and we aren't mated yet..." I swallowed, waiting for the reproach for speaking out of turn, but nothing came.

So, after a few seconds, I continued. "But it's a beautiful gesture. Thank you."

My stomach gurgled loudly. I gasped, putting my hands to my belly.

Tayte grinned. "You're hungry. What can we get you?"

I swallowed hard as acid reflux made my mouth taste terrible.

"I have trouble keeping anything down at the moment. But if you have some water? Or plain crackers."

The smallest of the three men—Dane, I remembered him

being introduced as in Nevaeh's house before I fainted—marched over to the kitchen and pulled out a box.

He brought the packet back and handed it to me without saying a word.

"Thank you, Dane."

He was clearly annoyed, and although I wasn't sure exactly why, I knew I was the cause of it. And that upset me. Enough to make my stomach flip.

I took the cracker box. "I'm sorry. I seem to have done something wrong."

His face softened and his shoulders dropped, relaxing a little.

"It's not your fault. I know... I'm just..." He looked at Tayte and the other one. Sam, I remembered.

I felt drawn to touch Dane and I wasn't sure why. Perhaps an unconscious need to ease his obvious pain? But why?

"What is it?" I asked, my hand half-lifting.

Instead of touching Dane, my hand was grabbed by Tayte, who dragged me to the couch.

"Have a seat and we'll explain what's going on."

I sat where he told me, amazed to find the furniture so new. So clean. And it wasn't just the furniture. The whole house was spotless. Not a cigarette butt or a beer bottle in sight.

I crossed my legs and grabbed some crackers from the box, chomping on them and moaning softly when they settled the churning in my belly.

Maybe I'd been too hasty in assuming my morning sickness had disappeared?

"Okay. I'm ready," I said, staring at them all. The three men stood before me like lecturers. Large, medium and smaller-sized. Each incredibly handsome, but in completely different ways.

My stomach suddenly began to churn for a whole different

reason. I lowered my gaze to the floor, trying to control the heat that leached up from my neck into my cheeks.

"Ah..." Tayte stopped and Sam rolled his eyes.

No one was talking, so I decided I may as well help them.

They seemed lost.

"Nevaeh told me that in this wolf pack all the men have been put into male triad families."

"Yes." Tayte nodded. "An Alpha." He pointed to himself. "A Beta." He pointed to Sam, and then gestured at Dane. "And an Omega."

I grinned. "The perfect combination."

"The perfect family," Tayte said. "All we need is our fated mate to complete us."

"And that's me?" I asked.

None of this was surprising me. Quite the opposite. It was reinforcing what I'd already heard about the wolf shifters' fated mates, and what Nevaeh had said.

I wasn't scared of these guys. On the contrary, I already trusted them. My gut instinct told me they would never hurt me. And I was more than a little fascinated.

Tayte's eyebrows lifted up and down. "Well... yes. You don't seem phased by any of this."

I bit on another cracker and chewed. "I'm not."

"Ah, not that I'm complaining, but why not?" Tayte asked. "Most humans would freak out at pretty much every aspect of this situation."

I shrugged. "I already knew about the shifter world that exists alongside the human world. I've lived in it practically my whole life. And I knew that you guys were doing the male triad thing. I don't mind looking after you all. My job back at the den was to clean an entire apartment block. Forty-six apartments." I allowed a touch of pride to enter my voice. That was a lot of apartments. "And I can cook, too."

Three men would be easy to look after. I wasn't used to the sex side of things, but I could learn.

Surely, it couldn't be that hard.

Tayte's mouth kicked up at the corners. "You think we want a... housekeeper?"

I looked from Tayte to Sam and then to Dane, surprised by how happy and relaxed I felt in their presence. I wasn't sure I could trust this feeling. I didn't know them. They could be as violent and horrible as the bears if I gave them enough trust. But I kept going with my gut instinct, which told me this situation was nothing like what I had just fled.

To be honest, I didn't have much choice, not with the bears' edict for death, and my pregnancy. So, I was willing to give these three wolves everything I had, in the hopes it would be enough for them to keep me. And my baby.

At least it might be enough for us to be safe.

"Well, yes." Finally, I answered Tayte's query. "Isn't that the role? Housekeeper?"

Tayte began to laugh and so did the other two.

"She's too beautiful to be believed," Sam said, collapsing into a chair.

Well, that was a nice compliment. Maybe he wouldn't turn on me if I kept talking.

I looked at him. "Sam, why are you all laughing at me?"

He smiled broadly. "Because we thought we'd have to convince you to mate with all of us, and you seem ready to jump straight into the role."

He grinned again and my belly tightened. Not with nausea this time, but with an arousal I'd never felt outside that one night with Tayte.

Sam was gorgeous, too, and that smile of his was amazing.

So was Dane's, when I turned to study him, too.

Three sexy guys, all staring at me, waiting for my response to a question I wasn't sure I had gotten right.

"Well..." I didn't quite know how to process the fact that they all wanted me. At least, I think that's what he was saying.

After years of being rejected by every member of the den where I grew up, the idea of three men all wanting to mate with me was as confusing as it was flattering.

"I can't guarantee I can satisfy you all in the..." I swallowed hard. "I've only had, you know, the one time... with Tayte. But anyway." I put my hands to my burning cheeks, covering the evidence of how embarrassing I found this situation.

"I don't expect you guys to be faithful. The bears never were to their mates. But I'll do my best to satisfy you."

The mood in the room changed instantly.

One moment the guys were smiling and laughing, the next they fell silent.

I shivered at the sudden drop in temperature.

"Did I say something wrong?"

"Ah, yeah." Tayte stood up and began to pace. "Fuck, this is a mess." He stopped and sighed.

The disappointment coming off him hit me like a slap to the face.

I tucked my knees up against my chest and wrapped my arms around my legs.

Tears tingled my eyes. "I'm sorry. I didn't mean to upset you."

How had I made such a big mistake already?

Sam moved slowly over to my side.

I put my head on my knees and looked at him sideways.

"Celeste, you didn't upset us. And we didn't mean to upset you. Quite the opposite. So, let me explain a few things to you. As a pack, a family, we've been waiting for you, our fated mate, for years. When Dane and I touched you before, you responded to our touch in a way that means you're our fated mate too, just as much as you are Tayte's."

Tears slipped down my face and I wiped them against my jeans.

"Okay." I didn't know what else to say. I already knew that, so why were they upset? "I mean... that's good, isn't it?"

I still don't understand.

Sam went on. "And although we love the idea of you looking after our home for us—we're terrible at cooking and all those things—that's not why we want you. We know you already want Tayte. You've gone to bed with him... you're pregnant by him, but we..." Sam swallowed, and I could see the pain in his eyes.

Dane walked across the room and sat next to me too, sighing heavily. "Sam and I need you to want us, too. We don't want you to... you know, put up with us just because you have to."

I looked from one beautiful man to the other.

"You both want me?" I lifted my head so I could study them properly.

"Of course, we do."

"For... everything? You don't want to date other women?"

I couldn't believe that was possible. All the bear males cheated on their mates, all the time.

Dane laughed. "Are you kidding me? I never want another filthy one-night-stand ever again. I want a mate; we all do. But how can you really want us, after..."

He trailed off, glancing up at Tayte, whose massive frame towered over us all.

Were they worried I wouldn't care for them after I'd met their Alpha?

I bit my lip, wanting to reassure them, but not totally

understanding what their fears were. "Um... Tayte and I have barely even talked. We met in a bar, when I was blind drunk, depressed and seeking companionship to keep the loneliness at bay."

Dane's gaze dropped and I reached out to hold his hand. Tingles of awareness and attraction pulsed along his palm into mine. "What is that?"

He smiled softly, dimples pressing into his cheeks.

"I think it's something to do with us being fated mates," he said.

"That's awesome. It feels... good."

"It feels very good, beautiful."

I stroked his palm, running my finger along the lines bisecting the flesh.

"So, what do we do now, Dane?"

"What would you like to do, Celeste?"

"Um..." I looked from one man to the other.

I wanted to curl up in a ball and feel their protection all around me. But how could I be honest about that?

"Um..."

"You can tell us."

Could I really? There was only one way to find out.

I took a breath and gathered my courage.

"I want to cuddle. All together. Could we do that?"

Tayte chuckled and the other two grinned. "We can do anything you want, sweetheart, although I'm not sure these two are going to be able to stop themselves from ravishing you."

Oh my God, seriously?

I blushed, heat flooding my cheeks once again.

I still couldn't believe they all wanted me like *that*, instead of just as a housekeeper. After feeling ugly for so long, these three made me feel so sexy and wanted.

I was twenty-three years old and I'd had sex *once*. It was wrong. I wanted to remedy that, but how?

"I... don't mind if you want to. I... you know I've only had sex once. I wouldn't know where to even begin."

The men around me chuckled. "I would," Sam said from next to me. "Come with us, beautiful."

I let him drag me to my feet and tow me up the stairs.

My heart was in my throat, panic pulsing along my veins. The idea of being with three men at once made me want to vomit. Not from disgust, but from fear of disappointing them.

But I had to push the fear down and trust the fated mate link. Even though I had no idea what I was doing when it came to sex.

SAM TUGGED me into a huge bedroom.

"This is Tayte's room. It has the largest bed."

I glanced around. It was nice, but so male.

So plain, and blue.

I shivered as they drew me to the bed and began to undress themselves.

All three of them were about to be naked and I didn't know where I was supposed to look, or what I should do.

My stomach quivered and I wrapped my arms across my middle.

Tayte gently took one of my hands in his. "It's fine, sweetheart. Let's just lie down and we'll hold you. Don't worry, no one's going to seduce you today."

I looked around the group and expected sullen glares.

Instead, Sam smiled and Dane stared at me with nothing but hope in his expression.

The lack of censure over my obvious nerves made me want to try. For them. And for myself.

"I don't mind." My tone was shy, but hopefully they could hear the truth in my voice. "Like I said, I'll never reject any of you. If you really want me."

Tayte chuckled. "Come to bed, sweetheart, and explain all this to us."

In the end, the men kept their jeans on, climbing into the bed half-clothed instead of fully naked.

Even so, there was still plenty of naked flesh to feast my eyes on. I stared at them, blinded by the huge muscles and clear, tanned skin.

"You guys are so... perfect."

Dane chuckled and Sam grinned.

"What do you mean?" I asked.

"Come here, beautiful." Dane invited me with a gesture of his hand.

He was by far the smallest, and his belly was like slices of granite. Perfectly square and hard, though less intimidating than Sam or Tayte.

I went to him and lay on the bed next to Dane.

They moved around me and it felt like a warm cloud enveloping me.

I lay on top of Dane and the other two kept their hands on me.

My heart raced and I tried to settle it down by breathing deeply.

I waited for them to make their moves. To have sex with me.

But they didn't.

They just stroked me, held me, and sighed beneath me.

I couldn't believe it. Finally, I let myself relax, the tension in my muscles releasing into the room and somehow floating away.

"Tell us where this fear of acceptance and everything is coming from, Celeste. Tell us your story," Tayte said, kissing my shoulder and tucking a stray lock of hair away from my face.

So, I did.

I told them about me growing up thinking I belonged in the bear den, only to discover I was a human they'd found in the woods, years ago.

That none of them had wanted me, even the lowest of all the bear shifters. Of the disgust that the bears had shown toward me. Of all my years of servitude and struggle, and the anger and rage and moments of physical aggression that had led to broken bones and bruising.

I talked about how I'd finally had the chance to get out, and had gone to the bar that night to drown my sorrows.

That night, I'd found Tayte.

"And Tayte actually wanted me." I still couldn't believe it, and some of that disbelief must have been evident in my voice.

He laughed where he lay beside me, his leg thrown over mine. "Of course, I did. You were, and still are, beautiful, sweet, and quite obviously as lonely as I was."

I lifted my head off Dane's chest so I could look down at him.

"How come you guys thought I wouldn't want you?"

Dane ran his hand along my arm.

"Well, you've already been with our Alpha. I was worried we wouldn't be able to compete."

I smiled, hope filling me up like a waterfall into a tiny spring.

"And I assumed no man would ever want me. And that you three would have to *endure* me for the sake of the baby."

"Endure?" Sam's voice was a murmur.

Dane's hand slid down to cup my belly. My breath caught in my throat at the tender caress. It was the first time another person had recognized my pregnancy in a positive way.

He didn't say anything at that point, but I knew he wanted to talk about the coming baby. How did he and Sam feel about me having the Alpha's baby?

"Is it... I mean... Are you and Sam upset that I'm going to have a baby?" I turned my head to look at Tayte. "Are you upset about it, too?"

Tayte's exclamation echoed through the room. "Our baby is a miracle come true, Celeste!"

His sincerity shone in his eyes.

As much as I loved seeing that, his enthusiasm didn't mean the others felt the same way.

Tayte rubbed my thigh. "You know how we feel."

I glanced at Sam, who was being very quiet, then to Dane. "I know Tayte's okay with it, but what about you two? How does it work? Shall I have a baby with each of you, too?"

I didn't mind the idea. I wouldn't want anyone to feel left out.

Dane swallowed "We'd love that... but..."

He glanced at Sam, who finally said, "We want this baby to be ours, too. Not just Tayte's."

"Oh." That sounded amazing. "So, you want to adopt it, or something?"

Tayte chuckled. "We're a pack, sweetheart. Like Grayson and Dexter's pack. Claire's pregnant and they don't know whose babies she's carrying. They're simply the packs' babies. And they will all love them, equally."

Sam nodded. "We would have liked to be there too, the night this gorgeous baby was conceived, and next time you get pregnant, we're going to have to insist, I'm afraid." He grinned at me and I couldn't help but smile back. What a beautiful concept.

He continued. "But if you accept us as your mates, then we're going to say this baby is ours."

I looked at Dane. "Do you feel that way, too?"

He grinned, those sexy dimples coming out to play. "Of course. I'm not missing out on being called Daddy for another five years while I wait for my turn."

I looked from one man to the next.

"Are you serious? You all want to be my mate? And you all want to be my baby's daddy? Like... seriously?"

I'd definitely died, because this couldn't be real. Three hot, sexy and caring men who wanted to mate with me, and claim my baby as theirs?

After so many years of being alone, watching other people get married and have babies, and being shunned by a whole pack, I couldn't comprehend that this might be my new reality.

I could be happy here. Like, *really* happy.

No way could I have found my own version of heaven. Could I?

The chuckles around me rose and fell.

"Why are you all laughing?"

Tayte turned my face toward his with a tug of my chin. "Because, sweetheart, we're the ones who feel lucky to have found you. And it sounds like you feel the same way."

"Of course, I do!" I practically yelled at them. "The bears hated me. I knew it, even as a child. But I was a good worker, and strong for my size. It was the only reason they kept me."

"As a slave," Tayte said, his voice becoming dark and flat.

"Well... yes."

I almost added, *because what else is there?* But then I held back the words. Because, with these men, the possibility of knowing something bigger and better was right at the edge of my experience. I may not have ever known anything different, but perhaps it was possible to dream of something better in the future.

"Those days are gone, sweetheart," Tayte said. "In this home you will have equal say, equal rights, and more love, sex and attention than you'll know what to do with."

I glanced from one gorgeous face to another.

It sounded too good to be true. And yet...

"Sounds perfect."
Tayte turned my face toward him and drew me close for a kiss.

CHAPTER
FIVE

Dane

Tayte was already kissing her. Our mate. Sam stared at me like he was asking, "What the hell do we do?"

I shrugged. I had no idea.

I'd never had an orgy before, if this situation could even be labeled like that?

Should we take her separately? Together? I wasn't sure of the rules, and most of all, I didn't want to upset or hurt Celeste.

Sam looked away, a frown marring his face. Clearly, he wasn't coping with this either.

Then our mate, the beautiful girl, reached for me. Her little hand came back and found my arm, squeezing me.

I met Sam's gaze again, saw his eyes on Celeste's grip on me, and grinned at him.

Suddenly, I knew everything was going to be all right.

I lay down behind Celeste and began to kiss her neck. Her

scent rose up, so intoxicating that my whole body switched itself on.

She moaned and gasped, arching her neck as if she enjoyed my lips there, and this time reached over Tayte for Sam.

The energy in the room flipped like a switch.

It went from simmering to scalding in an instant.

Tayte slid off the bed and stood up. I glanced at him.

He said, "I think we should mate with her. All together. But as I've already been with Celeste, you two need to bond more strongly. I'll wait and watch for a bit."

I couldn't believe the Alpha was offering her to us, but I wasn't going to wait for him to change his mind.

I set my lips back on her neck and ran my hands around to her front, cupping her breasts and aching to strip her.

"That's so good, Dane," she moaned, then reached again for Sam who was now lying in front of her. "Sam, I want you, too."

I looked up and met his gaze over the top of her. He seemed torn, his brow furrowed down and his mouth a straight line.

"I..." He started to speak and then stopped. I knew what was in his mind, because part of me was worried about the same thing.

Celeste moaned again, softly. "You don't want to?"

Sam shook his head. "Of course, I do. But if *you* don't.... I can't..."

I whispered into Celeste's ear. "He's worried you're doing this out of obligation."

Celeste released a shocked little breath, then sat up and crawled closer to Sam. She touched his arm, traced her fingers over his chest, and I saw him shiver.

"You know I'm the virgin, right? Well, sort of," she whispered.

He nodded.

"Then you're going to have to teach me. I'm sorry, I have no idea how to show you that I want you, too. Or you, Dane." She glanced over her shoulder and smiled shyly my way, before turning back to Same. "Other than to say, please don't leave me. I couldn't handle the rejection. Not after everything."

Sam groaned loudly, and then crushed her to him, kissing her upturned lips and gripping her body tight, as if he never wanted to let her go.

I slid off the bed and walked around to the side where Sam held her.

I stripped off my jeans and knelt to pull her joggers off. But I couldn't get to her legs properly, not with the way she was draped all over Sam.

I tapped his leg. "Sam. Help me."

He pulled back and, when he saw what I was doing, helped Celeste to stand. Together, we removed her clothes until she was naked and shivering.

Wow.

She was damn beautiful. Thin, with the pregnancy not yet showing, but so feminine and soft.

"Am I... all right?" she asked, as she glanced down at her body.

I moaned as I stood up behind her and pressed my aching cock into the small of her back.

"You..." I grunted, cupping her perfect little breasts with my hands, "are fucking perfect." I thrust against her so she could feel how hard I was for her.

She leaned into me as Sam stripped.

I heard her gasp at seeing him and grinned as I kissed her back and shoulders.

I didn't know how we were going to take this slow enough for her, but we had to try.

"Lie down, beautiful. On the bed," I said.

She slid onto the sheets and lay there still for a moment, before covering her small breasts with her hands.

I looked at Sam, the Beta of my pack, waiting for his lead.

I didn't know what he liked to do, or not, in bed. We'd never actually discussed it. But I had a feeling the topic was going to become normal breakfast conversation from now on.

"You want top or bottom?"

"Bottom."

Hmm... I was surprised. I liked the bottom, too. For some reason I'd assumed he'd be the opposite to me.

I nodded and, being the Omega of the group, allowed him first choice as I crawled over to Celeste on the bed.

"Hello, beautiful. We're going to make love to you now, is that all right?"

She nodded, shivering where she lay, waiting for us. I ran my fingers over her curves, wanting to make sure her shivers were from arousal and not fear. She moaned and arched into my touch, her cheeks flushing with a delicate pink and goose bumps rising up on her flesh in the wake of my fingers.

"Oh, that feels so good, Dane. To be touched, with loving hands..."

Definitely arousal.

"You say stop, at any point, and we stop, okay?" I wanted her to understand that she had the power and control in this situation. "Time out."

She nodded again and I couldn't stop myself from kissing her, everywhere.

Kissing her upturned lips, her nose, her cheeks.

Every part of her exquisite face.

Bending further and taking one, then the other, of her beautiful nipples into my mouth and suckling. Then I released her beautiful breasts and raised my face to her again.

"Okay?" I repeated, so she knew. "We're serious. You ask us to stop, and we stop. No matter what. We're going to be together for a very long time, so we can wait. Forever, if that's what it takes."

Tears welled in her brilliant blue eyes, then slid down her cheeks.

"Can you kiss me again, please? *Ah...*"

Her eyes widened and her mouth fell open in a gasp.

I looked down her body.

Sam was lying on his belly between her thighs and looking up at her.

His finger was circling her clit. I groaned as more heat flooded my groin at seeing her perfect little pussy open like that for the first time, her legs wide and her mound lifting up as if to press harder into Sam's finger.

I swooped down to kiss her lips as Sam leaned in and began to eat her.

She gasped and groaned against my lips, arching her back in pleasure.

I took the opportunity and slid my tongue into her mouth.

Tasting her tongue in return. Loving her groans as they vibrated in my mouth and throat.

She grabbed for my back, digging her nails into my skin until I groaned myself.

I moved down her divine little body. Suckling her nipples again, until they turned into tight little pebbles and she threaded her fingers into my hair as if to hold me in place.

She was crying out, her belly shuddering with Sam's ministrations on her pussy.

I glanced down and jealousy swept through me.

I moved down and nudged him. "My turn."

He came up for air and licked his lips, wetness glistening on his face.

"Sure."

He crawled up beside her and dove down on her mouth, kissing her and squeezing her breasts.

I opened her legs wider to see all of her perfect pussy. She was wet, the petals of her sex open and swollen in arousal.

I ducked my head and set my lips around her clit, licking and suckling at her flesh until she was screaming out to me.

I slid a finger inside her pussy, her tight muscles gripping and squeezing me.

Fuck... I couldn't wait to feel those same muscles tighten around my cock.

I worked her from the inside, then added a second finger, stretching her for us. I thrust in and out of her wet channel until she was writhing beneath my hand, screaming for me.

"Fuck it."

I couldn't wait any longer. Her body needed me.

She needed me.

And I'd never needed a woman more.

I crawled up between her thighs and lay down on top of her.

Sam moved out of the way as I lifted her legs and positioned my cock at her entrance.

My balls ached and my belly tightened with need. I had to have her.

I grabbed the shaft and ran the head up and down over her swollen clit and around her entrance.

She lifted her legs higher, tilting her pelvis up to me in word-less invitation.

"Are you ready to take me, beautiful?"

She nodded.

I waited. "I need you to say it."

I never wanted my mate to regret this moment. And I needed

her to see that I was in full control of my lust, and could stop at any time. If she wanted me to.

It would kill me to do so, but I'd do anything to make her happy.

"Yes, please."

Those were the sweetest words I'd ever heard in my life.

I growled as I reset my cock at her entrance and gently thrust inside.

She gasped and moaned, her eyes going wide.

Then she arched up to me, making it almost impossible to move slowly.

"Oh, fuck." I gripped the sheets beneath her and forged inside. Into the tightest, sweetest, most perfect pussy I'd ever felt.

"Dane. Oh, Dane."

She was kissing my throat, my shoulders. Desperately. Lovingly.

I couldn't take much more of it. I was about to explode.

I allowed some of my weight to drop down onto her, loving the heat of her skin against mine. Her soft breasts pressed against my chest.

I began to move, thrusting in and out of her delicious body. The heat of her was indescribable, and the tightness... wow. It was like a hand-made glove, a perfect fit, squeezing me.

I wanted the sensation to go on forever, but I was never going to last.

She was too perfect, and I'd waited too long for her already.

I ducked my head, tasting her lips and using all my control to take her slowly, carefully.

But she was gripping me so tightly, so beautifully.

"I'm sorry, beautiful, but I'm never going to last. You're making me... come."

The heat flared up my back and through my belly.

I thrust a little harder and squeezed my muscles tight, trying to hold on.

But then she tilted her pelvis, taking me even deeper, and I was gone.

The hottest, most intense orgasm of my life was about to explode through my body and I had to let it out.

I began to ride her harder, thrusting into her and hearing her squeaks and moans of pleasure.

She wrapped her legs around my waist and whispered, "Please come for me."

I couldn't hold back after that. I thrust once more, deep into her belly.

The roar ripped through me as my seed pulsed into her in hot, long streams.

She gasped and dug her nails into my back, squeezing my cock with her channel walls and making the orgasm extend on and on.

I kissed her face, her neck, then relaxed onto her, trying to keep most of my weight up and off her.

But, fucking hell, it was amazing.

I hadn't realized I'd closed my eyes, but as I opened them and looked down on her, she smiled up at me. Beamed, actually.

"Are you okay?" I asked, my voice hoarse.

She nodded. "Oh, yeah. That was great."

Sam tapped me on the back. *Damn.* My time was at an end.

I kissed her lips once more.

A pathetic effort on my behalf, but luckily, I had back-up. "There's a lot more to come, beautiful."

I slid off her sweet body and rolled to the side.

Sam grabbed her legs and hauled her to the edge of the bed.

She squealed and laughed as he lifted her up and put pillows under her ass.

"Ready for me?" Sam asked her, his voice gravelly and dark. He was not going to last long either, it seemed. Not this first time, at least.

She smiled up at him, wiggling on the pillows as if eager for more.

She hadn't found release yet, but hopefully she would, soon.

Sam grabbed his cock, lined himself up, and thrust straight into her.

Celeste moaned and arched up.

Sam didn't go slowly.

He rode her fast, and hard, and deep.

The thwacking sounds as their flesh met made my gut tighten with renewed heat.

I knelt on the bed and caressed her hard nipples as she moaned and cried out.

Her face contorted and she began to gasp, as if she was right on the precipice of an orgasm.

Sam gave a strangled groan and then thrust forward once more, coming inside our mate just as fiercely as I had, judging by the shudders and moans coming from him.

Celeste was shuddering, too, clawing at the bed.

Sam pulled away, gasping for air.

And then Tayte stepped up.

Celeste blinked up at him, her skin flushed and her eyes brilliant with unsated desire. "Tayte... I need..."

"I know, sweetheart. Get on your knees. We're all here."

She rolled off the pillows, her soft skin shining with a thin film of sweat. Herlegs shook as she stood, then turned and knelt back on the bed for him.

Presenting her ass to the Alpha.

"I think she needs all three of us to make her come. Don't you sweetheart?"

Celeste bent down, pressing her face into the bedcovers, and said, "I don't know. I don't know…"

She was practically sobbing.

"Dane, Sam, touch her, push her to the highest limits."

Sam and I knelt either side of her and began to kiss her wherever we could reach.

Her neck, her back. Her beautiful shoulders. I pushed her hair to the side and nuzzled at her neck. Then I reached beneath her and cupped one of her breasts, the soft flesh filling my palm.

Sam cupped her other one, massaging it, then reached behind her and thrust the fingers of his other hand into her.

She cried out and gasped.

Tayte stood behind us, his eyes glittering with arousal. He was stroking himself, getting ready for her.

"My turn." His voice was a command.

Sam instantly withdrew his fingers and lay down beside our mate. I lay down on her other side, biting on her shoulder and licking her ear.

I heard the grunt and felt the thrust as Tayte filled her up.

"More. Please," Celeste begged.

He wasn't moving, I realized. Not at first.

But at Celeste's request, and another repeated beg, finally he began to fuck her.

Their bodies banged together until she screamed out to him. To Sam. And to me.

I reached beneath her and worked her swollen clit with my fingers, in circles.

Over and over.

Sam kissed her face and neck. Then she began to arch and gasp, her whole body bowing up as she began one long crescendo of sound.

And then it released like an arrow. Hard and fast and hitting center.

She shook and shuddered and cried out, grabbing hold of me and Sam, impaled by Tayte, and anchoring herself with all three of us surrounding her.

I looked over at Sam, who was holding her hand, too, then up at Tayte. That's when I felt the energy connection flowing between all four of us.

It was a moment that almost stopped my heart.

That made me feel whole.

Then it was Tayte's turn to tip over the edge.

Celeste cried out again, softer this time as Tayte roared and came inside her.

The three us had spilled our seed inside her, our genetics mixing together in her womb.

The way it should have been from the start.

The thought made me wonder if things would ever be equal between us. Would Celeste ever love me and Sam, or need us, as much as she did Tayte? The acknowledged father of her child.

The Alpha collapsed beside her, panting and gasping for breath.

I reached for her as she fell forward on the mattress, her eyes closed and her body obviously exhausted. She drifted into sleep as I watched.

I didn't really want to stay in Tayte's bed any longer.

I needed some space.

I loved being an Omega, a part of this family, but I wasn't sure how I was going to ever compete for an equal share of my mate's love with the Alpha around.

"I'm going to have a shower."

Sam stood up. "Me too." Possibly, he felt the same way.

Tayte scooped our mate up and held her against him. "I don't think she should be alone while she sleeps."

"Yeah, true. See you later, then."

Sam and I left, and Celeste slept on.

She didn't stir, obviously not noticing even on an unconscious level that we were gone, and I didn't blame her. Not really.

"So much for this being an equal relationship, huh?" Sam said as we headed to our end of the house.

"I'm gonna have a shower. You okay if I go first?"

I cringed a little as I asked the question. I was requesting permission to shower first, and yet I hadn't asked whether he cared if I made love to our mate first.

Seemed stupid somehow.

Sam shrugged and didn't look at me. "Whatever. Doesn't matter to me."

He went into his bedroom and shut the door.

A cold fist tightened inside my gut.

Damn it. How did this day turn from good to bad so quickly?

I went into the bathroom and had a long, hot shower, washing away the smell of my mate and of the sex we'd enjoyed together.

Hoping in a strange way that if I did that, I could wash away the feelings of imbalance and inadequacy as well.

After I was dry and dressed, I realized it was going to take a lot more than a shower to get rid of that feeling of rejection.

CHAPTER
SIX

Celeste

I woke up to cramping and pain.

"Oh, no." I grabbed for my stomach. "The baby."

Tayte, who'd been asleep beside me, jumped up out of bed and stared down at me with a shocked look on his face. "What's wrong?"

Panic gripped my heart as my belly tightened once again. "I think it's the baby."

I couldn't be miscarrying! No! Not after everything I had risked to keep it safe.

"Fuck! What do we do?"

Tayte was already pulling on jeans.

I didn't know. What should we do?

"Um... do you have a doctor here?"

I checked between my legs. There was a lot of wetness.

But I wasn't bleeding. Not yet.

"Claire! Let's get you to Claire." Tayte grabbed for my clothes and helped me dress, then scooped me up into his arms and ran down the stairs.

I clung to him, but my grief sat on top of me like a cloud.

He called to the others, "Sam! Dane! We gotta go."

Dane came running at the sound of Tayte's voice. "What's wrong?"

I sobbed when I saw him and reached out for my sweet Omega.

"Dane..."

Worry shadowed his expression and he grabbed my hands.

"She's cramping," Tayte said. "There's something wrong with the baby."

Sam walked into the room as Tayte spoke and I saw his face pale when he heard the words.

The cramps hit again, the tightness and pain making me cry out. "Ow!" And another sob left my throat. "Oh, no. I'm going to lose it, aren't I?"

Tayte dropped a kiss on top of my head.

Sam ran to the front door and wrenched it open. "Let's go."

They ran with me through the town and I clung to Tayte, burying my face in the crook of his neck and breathing in the comforting scent of him.

What had I done wrong?

Was it because I'd run away last night?

Or because I'd let all three of them make love to me at once?

Or was this always going to happen because I was a weak little female who couldn't handle a strong baby like Tayte's?

They rushed me inside a house I hadn't seen before.

"Claire! Help!" Tayte's voice was urgent, and a nice-looking woman came rushing forward to greet us. This must be the doctor, Claire, that I'd heard so much about. She looked a little older than me.

She frowned when she saw me in Tayte's arms and quickly showed us into a small bedroom off the lounge area.

"Put her down on the bed, please, Tayte. Now, what's happened?" she asked.

All three men started talking at once and Claire stopped them with a wave of her hand. "You three go out and cool off. I'll help your mate, okay?"

She literally shoved them out the door and I called out, suddenly too worried to be left alone with a stranger.

Human or not.

"No! Please. Can Dane stay?"

I didn't know why I called only for Dane, but his calm strength was what I wanted in this moment.

He'd been the first to make love to me today.

The first one to kiss me.

The first one to look into my eyes and make me feel incredibly loved.

Dane looked at his pack mates, unspoken words passing between them. Then he nodded and rushed back to sit by my side and hold my hand.

I clung to him and turned so I could put my head on his lap.

He stroked my hair and I finally felt safe again.

Claire pulled up a chair and sat next to us, studying me.

"Ah... this isn't the exact introduction I was expecting for the newest mate of the pack, but I'm Claire. I'm a doctor at the hospital where Nevaeh works, and I'm pretty sure you're the one who went looking for me last night."

I stared at her from my place in Dane's lap. "Yes, I did. I'm Celeste."

"Hello, Celeste. How can I help you today?"

She was so calm. Her manner was lovely and soothing. I knew

she would help me if she could, but if this pregnancy wasn't meant to be, then physician or not, she couldn't save it.

"I... I think I'm losing my baby."

My throat tightened and I swallowed the cry that threatened to rise up.

"How far along are you?"

"Um... about eight weeks." I hadn't seen a doctor of course, but my period was a month late.

"Okay. Are you bleeding?"

"No, not yet. I don't think so."

Claire stood up. "So, why do you think you're losing the baby?"

I gathered my strength and sat up, wiping away the tears that fell down my cheeks.

"I'm..." Another wave of pain hit. "Cramping."

I put a hand on my belly.

"Like you're getting your period?"

I shook my head. "No, worse. It's like a deep soreness."

Dane reached for my hand again and held it tight.

Claire looked between us. "Have you been having sex this morning?"

Dane leaned forward. "Yes. Why? Could that have done something? Is it our fault?"

Claire smiled gently. "No. But from what Nevaeh said, Celeste is very inexperienced, yes?"

She looked at me and despite all the fear in my heart, I found myself smiling. She seemed so kind and trustworthy.

"Ah... yes. Tayte was my first and that was two months ago."

Claire grinned. "And let me guess, all three of them doted on you and made you orgasm this morning, probably for the first time."

Now this conversation was getting embarrassing. I had to

remember, she was a doctor. It was all right to discuss these things with your doctor, surely?

"Um, yes."

Dane blinked at me. "You didn't come the first time with Tayte?"

I shook my head. "No, of course not."

Dane looked up at Claire, his mouth open a little.

Claire looked as if she was biting back a smile when she said, "Almost impossible for a virgin. You three did well today, it seems, Dane."

He looked away. "It wasn't me. Or Sam. It was Tayte."

Claire reached over and touched his hand and I turned toward him, too. Was Dane feeling bad about the incredible morning we'd had? How was that possible?

Claire said, "Dane, you don't know much about the mating triad yet, but you'll soon learn that we human, fated mates need all three of our men. All of you, equally. We don't do well without all of you."

I slid my head back into Dane's lap and turned my cheek so I could kiss his leg. "This morning was perfect. You were perfect. You all were. Equally."

There was silence in the air until Dane finally slid his fingers through my hair once again. He seemed more relaxed, suddenly.

"So, Doc, what do we do?" he said. "Does this mean the baby is going to be okay? It's just Celeste's body getting used to the aftermath of an orgasm?"

Claire shrugged. "Look, I'll be honest with you. If Celeste is going to miscarry, there's nothing I can do. Miscarriage is very common, especially in first pregnancies, and it doesn't mean anything is wrong with the woman. It's just... sometimes how things go, sadly. But most women go on to have very normal, healthy second pregnancies."

I pressed my head against my Omega, my heart aching and tears filling my eyes once again. "Maybe it's for the best. I know you and Sam don't like the idea that I'm having just Tayte's baby. I..."

I lost my words again and stopped talking, my throat squeezing shut with tears and pain.

"Oh no, sweetheart, don't say that." Dane pulled me up into his arms and held me as I cried.

It hurt so much.

I'd wanted a family, a baby, for so long, and now it was possible I was going to lose it.

Claire left us alone then, and I kept crying.

Sam came into the room and sat down on the bed with us, stroking my back and putting an arm around me.

Tayte hadn't returned, and I didn't mind too much, at least for a little while.

Sam and Dane provided more than enough love and support.

When my tears dried up, Claire returned to the room and got my attention again.

"I think you three have a bit to talk about, but from a medical perspective, Celeste, I'll tell you this. Rest today. See how things go. If nature decides to take its course, I can advise you then. But if this is what I think it is, which is lots of sex and orgasms in someone not used to it, then you'll be better by tomorrow and have no bleeding. So, watch for blood, and if you're still concerned, I can take you into the hospital tomorrow and do an ultrasound."

I clung to Dane and nodded. "Okay, thank you, Doctor."

Claire waved her hand at me.

"Stay here for a few hours. I have to do a little shopping, and my boys are all out at work, so you'll have the house to yourself."

"Um, is Tayte all right?" I had to ask, given he hadn't yet returned.

"He's fine. I advised him to go make himself useful somewhere else so the three of you can bond for a little while. The triad thing can be hard when there's so many people wanting love and acceptance, but I can already tell that you four will be just fine."

She left and closed the door and I sagged into my men.

"I should probably check if I'm bleeding."

I moved to stand up and Dane grabbed my hand. "Um, before you do, I have to say something."

"Okay."

He looked at Sam and they both seemed so sad.

"What's wrong?"

Sam coughed and cleared his throat.

"We're both... um, struggling with this. That you and Tayte seem so much closer than we could ever hope to be."

A wave of sadness washed over me, dragging me into the darkness.

"So, you're glad I'm going to lose this baby." I nodded my head, the cramps in my belly continuing, though strangely, they were no longer as sharp.

They were more like the pains of muscle strain now. "Yeah... I suppose..." I wiped at new tears. "We can make more babies."

Dane grunted as if in shock. "Is that what you think?"

Before I could say anything in response, Sam grabbed my hand and pulled me over to him.

"Sit, sweetheart."

I sat on his lap and looped my arms around his neck, putting my head on his chest so I could be as close as possible.

The world was so cold and dark now, when only a few hours ago it had been filled with possibilities and hope.

"Celeste, we do *not* want you to lose your baby."

I pulled away so I could look up at him, his brown eyes intense.

I wiped at the tears that would not stop falling.

"You don't?"

"Of course not. We were excited about being a family so soon."

That part I understood.

"But you... you don't like that you weren't there. And if this baby... goes away, then we can make one together."

I was trying, I was really trying to see the silver lining of this day.

They shared a look that I couldn't read, and horror struck my heart.

"Unless... if you're only keeping me around because I was pregnant, does that mean you'll send me away now, if I lose the baby?"

My arms dropped away from Sam's neck and I began to fall. Fall into the abyss that swirled around me.

I didn't know how I was going to pull myself out of this one.

Where would I even go if these men rejected me?

Sam grabbed for my shoulders and held me to him again, while Dane slid closer and cupped my face.

"Celeste, stop and look at us, okay? We know you've been hurt and betrayed in the past, and been unloved for far too long. But that isn't the case now. Not with us. That will never happen again."

I didn't believe them, but I nodded anyway.

"Okay."

"Listen, and listen closely. We *love* you... do you understand that? We love you. We don't want you to ever leave us. And whether we have one baby, or fifteen, we will love them all. Because they will be a part of you, and us. Our pack."

A sob built in my throat and escaped this time.

"But how…"

"It's the fated mate bond. You are our heaven, our perfection, and we will love you with every breath, every minute of every day. No matter what."

I looked from to Dane to Sam and saw the same stoic strength. The same heart that beat in them both.

"But… you left me this morning; I felt it. You didn't want to stay in the bed with me and Tayte, and I know this baby is unwanted."

Sam growled a little, his chest vibrating with his breath. "Your baby is not unwanted. He or she brought you to us. Without the pregnancy, we may never have found you."

That was probably true, but I still didn't quite believe them.

They were just trying to make me feel better, which said a lot about the strength of their characters and the beauty of their hearts.

"Thank you for saying that."

Sam growled again.

"We aren't just *saying* it—"

Dane burst in with, "We felt rejected, like we were third wheels in the situation. Unwanted add-ons to your relationship with Tayte."

Silence descended as their words sunk in.

Then I began to laugh.

I sounded hysterical, and I probably was.

"Um… you felt… you guys…." I couldn't stop laughing. *They* had felt rejected? By *me*?

I had to get up.

I staggered to my feet, then fell into the chair Claire had placed by the bed.

Dane and Sam stared at me like I'd gone nuts.

"Oh, come on... You two..." I took some deep breaths, forcing myself to breathe, to calm the racing of my heart.

This was a little too hilarious.

"What's funny, Celeste?" Sam asked, his tone bordering on annoyed.

I forced myself to sober quickly. They were beginning to look offended again.

I reached over and held each of their hands.

"You two are super-hot, powerful shifters. I'm just a little, ugly human. Do you know how blessed I feel to have you both? To know that you want me, even a fraction of how much I want you?"

It still seemed totally impossible to me that these men desired me.

Professed to love me.

And would protect me against all enemies.

Sam grinned and Dane's smile was so beautiful, I took a mental picture to capture for all time.

"So... I'm going to the bathroom to see if these cramps mean what I think they mean, and then can you please take me home?"

The men nodded, their concerned faces making my heart sing.

This baby may have been the only reason I escaped the bears, so maybe it was fated on more than one level?

SEVEN

Celeste

In the end, the cramps subsided and an ultrasound proved the baby was healthy and strong.

Just one little baby was inside me.

Claire was adamant that it was all the sex and the massive orgasm that had caused the cramping.

So, the men didn't touch me.

For weeks.

Until I practically pounced on them and they *had* to make love to me.

But, boy, were they gentle!

Too gentle.

The weeks wore on and I grew bigger and bigger.

My one baby made my appetite skyrocket, and my belly protruded through all the new clothes the boys had bought for me.

But despite the early fear of miscarriage, and the fact that they were all too nervous to touch me in a sexual way, we fell into a beautiful rhythm of sleeping together all night, then I'd wake to one of them bringing me breakfast before they headed off to work.

I'd clean the house, if I felt up to it, and bake for them.

They'd come home at lunchtime to check on me, and Claire and Nevaeh were frequent visitors.

I'd never had female friends before, and it was a lovely addition to my life.

Especially all the mothers-in-law.

Three of them.

All pleased as punch to have a grandchild on the way.

And the best part of all?

We hadn't heard a thing from the bears.

They hadn't found me. I was finally beginning to feel safe.

Or at least, I wanted to think I now felt safe, but when the door opened one lunchtime and my heart leapt with stress, as it always did, I realized I had a way to go in that regard. Too many years of watching and waiting for a flying fist still had me jumpy.

As Tayte walked into the house, full of smiles and laughter, I let the anxiety go down a notch.

It was taking longer than I thought it would, to feel safe and "normal".

According to Claire, my version of normal—a Cinderella-type slaving away under a whole bunch of abusive bears—was *not* normal.

A part of me just *knew* that this beautiful dream I was currently living in would shatter sooner or later.

That these lovely, kind wolves would come to their senses and realize I wasn't worth loving, or keeping.

But for now...

"How's my beautiful sweetheart?" Tayte asked as he picked me up and gently twirled me around.

When he put me down, his hand cupped my belly and stroked our baby with a possessive air.

"Have you eaten lunch?"

I shook my head. "No, I've been waiting for you. There's tuna pasta in the oven if you're hungry, or I can just make some sandwiches?"

"If you've cooked a hot lunch already, that would be great."

Sam and Dane came through the front door as I was serving Tayte the pasta.

I got kisses and cuddles from both of them, and the love surrounded me.

I so wanted to accept that this new reality was one that would last.

My men sat at the table and ate, talking about their work and the food I'd made for them.

"This is so good, sweetheart," Tayte said as he finished his second bowl. "Thank you."

I sat and picked at my food.

"You okay, beautiful?" Sam asked.

"Yes. It's funny, I just... you know, no one ever said thank you to me for cooking for them, before. And you guys thank me all the time. I can't quite get my head around it."

Dane jumped up from the table and moved behind me to put his arms around my waist, or what was left of it.

"Oh, beautiful, you deserve compliments for everything you do. The house looks amazing, the food's brilliant, but it's you we come home for. You know the pizza place delivers, right?"

I laughed as he rubbed my belly in soothing circles and my pussy pulsed in response.

I swallowed down the moan.

I'd been holding on to my desires for months.

And I wasn't sure I could keep being the quiet little girl they'd been wrapping in cotton wool, for too much longer.

"Are you going back to work, or...."

Tayte was a builder and both Dane and Sam were bricklayers. That explained the solid house and the incredible facade of our home.

Tayte stood up and cleared the table, then arranged everything in the new dishwasher they'd installed for me. Such luxuries.

I was too spoilt already.

Tayte replied with, "We could go either way. Back to work, or not. Do you need us to do something for you?"

I licked my lips.

I most certainly did.

But could I convince them to stop treating me like I was made of glass?

Since the miscarriage scare, they'd all been too nice to me.

I needed to be *taken*.

I wanted to feel the desire that had built on that first day with the three of them.

The passion, and lust, and need.

Claire, who was even more pregnant than I was, reassured me that it was completely safe for them to—how had she phrased it? —*bang me into next week.*

Heat crept up my neck and into my cheeks. I wasn't sure I could use that phrase here in front of the boys.

Sam grinned at me. "What'cha thinking, gorgeous? You look like you're blushing."

I took a breath and forced myself to get it over and done with.

Surely, they wouldn't reject me?

"I'd like to go to bed, please."

"Bed, as in you're tired? Would you like me to carry you up?" Sam asked, standing quickly.

I almost laughed. Almost. But then frustration took over.

Did I have to strip naked and do a dance to get them to notice my other needs?

How were they so blind?

"No... um, I want you all to make love to me."

Tayte growled with the sexy Alpha noise that was uniquely his, and scooped me up into his arms.

"Well, that we can do."

I clung to his neck as he trotted up the stairs, carrying my weight easily.

I giggled, unable to conceptualize just how crazy this was.

That I was going to have to tell them what I craved.

Tayte set me on my feet in our bedroom and the three men began to undress.

The heat in the room became charged, sizzling with energy.

I pushed my leggings down and pulled my top off. Though they loved to undress me, I wanted to show them how desperate I was.

"Whoa... hang on," Tayte said as I reached for my bra.

But I ignored him and tossed my bra to the ground and pushed my knickers down my legs.

I'd put on weight everywhere in the past three months. My boobs were huge, and my ass had never been so big.

But as the masculine groans sounded around me, I was once again assured that my size didn't seem to turn them off.

Quite the opposite.

Tayte rubbed my back. "Lie down, sweetheart."

I didn't move, though the submissive side of me was anxious to do what the Alpha commanded. I'd been working on denying Tayte. Every day, just one little thing at a time.

It was one of Nevaeh's tips.

For un-programming the things the bears had made me believe and feel about myself, and the world around me.

Asserting myself, and saying no sometimes, was a huge step in that process.

"I'd rather start another way, please."

I dropped to my knees and crawled over to where Tayte stood, already partly aroused in preparation for our session.

"What are you...?"

I wrapped my hand around Tayte's cock and looked up at him.

I wanted to suck him, so much. To feel his hot flesh in my mouth and give him pleasure as much as me. But how did one do that? This was where my inexperience was definitely not my best friend.

Tayte pulled out of my grasp and my fantasy slipped away.

He grabbed my elbows and hauled me to my feet.

"Sweetheart, you don't have to do that."

His face was too kind, too soft. Too understanding.

I didn't want that.

I pulled away.

"Stop it. All of you. I'm not breakable! This baby..." I cupped my belly, "is strong and healthy, and I want you to stop treating me like a *fucking China doll!*"

I'd never spoken to anyone in such a way, let alone three large and muscled men who could beat me to a pulp if they chose to.

My heart pounded and my stomach was tight with fear, but in that moment, I'd never felt so alive.

Tayte's face changed, his eyes hardening, darkening. But there was no censure in his expression. Far from it. The look in his eyes sent desire spiraling right to my core.

"Then what do you want, sweetheart? Tell us."

I want... I want...

I stepped back, needing to look at all three of them. I'd had so many fantasies, detailing loving all three of these men in the strongest, hottest and fiercest of ways.

"I want you all to take me... every way, as much as you want. I want you to hold nothing back."

Tayte, Sam and Dane looked at each other with wide, scared eyes.

They were going to say no, I just knew it!

"Please. I need to feel wanted, desired, lusted after. Please don't make me feel like I'm second class—not good enough. Please."

I began to cry, *damn it*. I dashed away the tears.

"Stupid hormones. Ignore them. Please."

Dane crept forward first. "Tell me what you want, beautiful."

I swallowed.

Oh my God, I never thought I'd have to say this.

But there was only one way to do this, and that was with complete openness and honesty.

"I want to suck your cocks."

Dane was the first to react, his mouth dropping open.

The joke was just sitting there for me to make, and I couldn't resist. I reached up and briefly touched my finger to his lips. "Yes... like that."

He choked on a laugh.

"Um, okay. Where do you want us?"

I glanced at the bed. "Standing against the edge of the bed, please. All three of you."

Dane rushed over to where I pointed, with Sam and Tayte moving more slowly. Then they lined up for me.

Three men.

Three cocks.

I pressed my hand to my mouth, the beauty of the smorgasbord before me overwhelming in the extreme.

And the best part? They were all mine.

I dropped to the floor and crawled over to where they stood, going for Dane's reasonably sized cock first since it was slightly less intimidating than the other two. Only slightly, though.

I knelt before him and stared at it, absurdly feeling like Goldilocks at a feast of a very different kind.

I glanced across at the three men, all at varying degrees of arousal, their large heads and long shafts getting bigger with each man. Dane, then Sam, then finally the largest, Tayte.

I exhaled, my courage deserting me even though I'd been given what I wanted. Served up on a platter.

But I wasn't backing out now. If I gave up, they'd never give me the chance again.

I leaned forward and put my lips around Dane's cock.

He thrust forward, straight into my mouth, and I moaned.

He pulled back, the hard flesh slipping from my lips, and I frowned up at him, not understanding why he'd withdrawn.

"Fuck. I'm sorry, Celeste. Your mouth was way too hot."

I blinked at him. He was apologizing?

"Don't be sorry. Do it again. Teach me what to do."

Dane glanced at Sam and Tayte.

I waited, my heart pounding against my ribs in equal measures of fear and desire—fear of not doing it right, and yet the need building within me at the sensuality of the situation.

"Come on, Dane."

Then he stepped forward and put his hand around the back of my skull, cupping my head.

"Open your mouth."

I did.

And he fed his cock back between my lips.

"Now, suck it, lick it, do whatever you want to it."

His words made my cheeks burn with heat. But I did what he said and explored his rigid flesh.

I came off the end and nibbled down the side, loving his groans as I licked around the bulbous head.

Such an amazing and interesting piece of equipment.

Dane backed away and I shuffled on my knees over to Sam, who was standing, arms by his side and hands clenched into fists.

"Are you okay?" I asked as I knelt before him, looking up at my big man.

His cock seemed ready. It was red and swollen and looked about to explode.

He nodded his head and I bobbed forward, running my tongue up and down the slit and tasting the saltiness of his seed.

I licked my lips, savouring the unusual flavor, before sucking the rest of the head into my mouth.

Sam didn't grab my head, nor did he move. But he trembled beneath my touch and the power of his deliberate submission flooded through me.

He was enjoying this, but I knew he was fighting it for some reason.

I reached up and touched his balls, the soft skin wrinkling and moving up as I caressed him.

He groaned loudly and flexed his hips forward. I swallowed more of the shaft and used my tongue to taste him.

Eventually Sam pulled away, gasping for air.

"Oh, God. That was too good. I can't take any more without coming."

He moved away, as though he couldn't be tempted to even be close to me.

I turned toward Tayte.

Tayte was hard but not yet fully erect, his long cock standing at half-mast, as if he was waiting his turn for arousal.

"Hmmm...." I crawled closer and put my hand around his length, pulling him up to my lips for my treat.

"You don't need to do this, beautiful," he said as he threaded his fingers into my hair.

I could hear it in his words, the warning, the desire to tell me I didn't *have* to go down this path. Not if I didn't want to.

But I wanted this, with everything in me.

I put my mouth over the large head and began to suck.

His grip on my skull tightened as he began to thrust his hips gently.

I moved on him, using his groan and the growing flesh in my mouth as a guide to what he seemed to want. I pulled my hand up and down the shaft and concentrated on the huge head with my lips and tongue.

He moaned as his cock thickened in my hands, the silky skin stretching over the hard flesh beneath it.

Then, he, too, was pulling away, gripping his cock and pushing it down and away from me.

Why?

To stop himself from coming? If that was the reason, then I'd done a good job.

I got to my feet, my pussy aching and needing them.

I'd never been so aroused in my life, and they hadn't even touched me yet.

"I want all three of you at once. Can you do that?" I looked at Tayte, knowing he'd understand what I was asking.

His face went completely blank for a moment, probably from shock, then a smile began to stretch across his face.

"You really want this, Celeste? To feel all of us inside you?"

I nodded quickly. "Yes, please. I want to know what it feels like to be at the center of the triad, loved by all of you."

Sam let loose a low growl I'd never heard before and Dane came over and hoisted me to my feet. "I need to prepare you first. Lie on the bed."

I considered saying no. After all, I wanted this to be different from every other time.

But I couldn't. Dane's eyes were wild, flames of desire licking at his irises.

And as he pushed me toward the bed and pulled my legs out from under me, I realized he wasn't asking.

I lifted my knees as he knelt on the floor and dove down to place his mouth over my already swollen sex.

"Oh... fu...uck."

I grabbed for his head as he ate my flesh with a ferocity I'd never experienced.

He licked and sucked and flicked my clit until I was gasping for air.

"Enough," Tayte commanded and the pleasure stopped.

I grabbed for Dane's head, needing him back there, working on me. But he was gone.

Then Tayte lay on the bed next to me, obviously close to the edge, judging by the strained look on his face.

"Get on top of me, Celeste."

The Alpha had his legs hanging over the end of the bed and he looked like he'd topple off if he wasn't careful. He was that close to the side edge.

But I did as I was told, trusting my Alpha and what he had in store for me.

He held his cock upright with one hand, the head sticking up, pointing like an arrow at the sky.

I threw my leg over his thighs and settled over him.

I smiled down at Tayte as he looked up at me. What an incredible position to be in.

I tilted my pelvis back until I felt the smooth, hot flesh of him sliding into my core. Then I slowly lowered myself down onto him, feeling him forging deep into me.

I pressed further down, breathing hard as I was filled with the most incredible pleasure. Both physical and emotional.

They all wanted me.

They really did.

I could feel it in the air around me. In the heat of the room. In the barely controlled way the men breathed and panted.

Not to mention the hard cock beneath me, impaling my body.

"That's a girl. Now lean forward."

I put my hands on the bed and leaned as far forward as I could, with my belly resting against Tayte's.

He grinned at me.

"Hello, sweetheart."

"Hello, my love."

I wanted to kiss him, but I couldn't lean forward that far.

Then I felt hands on my back, moving down and opening my ass.

"What...?" I glanced around and there was Sam, slicking up his cock with the lube we used sometimes.

"You wanted to know what it was like to have us all at once? Well, this is it."

I swallowed the lump in my throat as fear of the unknown began to ride me.

Sam pressed his cock to my back package and gently slid in.

Pain pierced me and I moaned, both from the unexpected entry and the pleasure of such a naughty, intense experience.

"Breathe. Focus on me," Tayte said as he tweaked my nipples with his fingers and thrust up into my pussy.

Sam slid in and out gently, going a little deeper each time.

My belly was beginning to tighten, the pleasure over-riding the pain.

I was going to come.

No. Not yet.

"Dane. I need you, too."

My Omega was by the side of the bed, standing next to my head.

Ah... that's why Tayte has us so close to the edge.

"Here you go beautiful. Suck this."

I pulled his cock into my mouth and mere seconds later, my orgasm hit. Being loved by all three of my men at the same time was beyond anything I could ever have imagined.

I moaned around his flesh as my pussy and back passage rippled around the cocks inside me.

Tayte and Sam groaned and gasped as I began to shiver.

My eyes rolled shut and I moaned loudly.

"Oh, damn... Tayte, I'm never going to last," Sam said from behind me.

I came off Dane's cock long enough to say, "Good. Don't last too long, please. This is too much."

I was so full, the feelings of possession and submission so intense.

"Should we stop?" Tayte asked and I wanted to scream at him.

No, this was what I wanted. What I'd asked for. What I craved!

But the reality was far more than I'd expected and my body wasn't going to be able to cope with the pressure much longer.

"Don't you dare! I want you to all come inside me." The crescendo was building again. I couldn't stop the waves of desire rushing up again.

Fuck.

My belly tightened and pushed me over that incredible cliff of pleasure into spasms that fel like they would never end.

Tayte and Sam began to move faster. Tayte thrust up into my pussy, making my clit tingle and throb, while Sam fucked my ass.

I screamed as the next wave of orgasms hit.

I couldn't stop shaking and clenching. I could barely see for the stars exploding in front of my eyes.

I grabbed Dane's cock and pumped it with my hand.

I looked up at him, meeting his gaze. "You too, please. Come with them at the same time."

He nodded, desperate need in his gaze, and guided my head back to his cock.

I sucked on his flesh as deeply as I could, while breathing hard through my nose.

I couldn't handle much more of this.

They were filling me in every way they could. I could feel their love, their desire, their cocks. Their everything.

I came off Dane's flesh to beg. "Please... please..."

Sam began to cry out. "I'm gonna blow."

Oh, thank God for that.

Tayte grabbed my hips and began to fuck me hard.

Fast.

Frantically.

Giving me everything I'd ever wanted.

My eyes closed as my head fell back.

I was surrounded by them, their need, their desire for me.

I pumped Dane's cock with my hand as Sam grabbed my hair, crying out as he came. "Fuuucckkkk!"

He filled me with his hot seed, which set off yet another orgasm, this one even more intense than the previous ones.

I screamed and shook, my whole body milking my men's cocks as they gave me their all.

Tayte went next, growling beneath me and pumping his seed into my pussy. Dane was the last to release and, as I squeezed his shaft with my hand, hard, his cock splashed cum across my breasts in hot, long spurts.

I couldn't see.

I couldn't think.

I could only feel the rolling intensity of giving everything to my triad and receiving all they had in return.

Sam pulled out of my ass and I gasped with the loss of the strange pleasure/pain that he'd inflicted on me.

Dane jumped on the bed and reached for me. I went with him and we all piled onto the pillows, a tangle of arms and legs.

And sperm. Everywhere.

No one spoke.

Instead, the room was filled with frantic, uneven breathing and pounding heartbeats.

I stared up at my men, who looked intensely happy.

Shocked, but happy.

"Next time," I said, and they all looked to me, "can you all swap around so I get to feel you all in different places?"

Dane grinned and Tayte growled.

Sam dropped a kiss on my lips as they all began to laugh. "Oh, yeah, sweetheart," he said. "Anything you want."

CHAPTER

EIGHT

Tayte

The weeks went by and our beautiful mate grew bigger and bigger.

Claire said the baby would arrive in a few short weeks, and although we were excited, we were on tenterhooks waiting for the arrival.

Every day one of us would stay home from work, and if we had no choice but to be away, one of our moms would stay with our waddling, grumpy girl.

She was "done" according to her.

Done with being pregnant, and with being "fat".

We loved her being so big, but only being a hair over five feet tall, it was obvious how uncomfortable she was.

There was a knock at the door. I left Sam with Celeste to answer it.

"Oh, hey, Gray. How are you doing?"

Another great thing about us finding our human mate was the closeness we'd developed between our pack and Grayson's.

Dexter's pack, too.

Having our women had brought us all together.

"I'm good, we're all good. Hey, Celeste. How are you doing?" He waved from the front door and Celeste waved back.

"I'm okay, Grayson. Looking forward to getting this baby out."

He chuckled. "Yeah, Claire is, too."

Grayson dropped his voice. "Can you come outside? I need to fill you in on something."

Sounded serious.

"Yeah, of course." I stepped outside and shut the door. "What's up?"

"The bears are on the hunt. We've had sightings and their scent is everywhere."

The hairs on the back of my neck stood up. They were looking for Celeste.

"Are you sure?"

"Yes. I've gone out myself to check. They've surrounded the pack. The smell of them is everywhere."

I suppressed my shudder. My mate. My baby.

"Do you think this is because of Celeste? Do you think they've seen her? Tracked her here?"

Grayson shrugged. "Don't know, and it doesn't really matter. They've been coming for us since the moment Claire was found." Grayson's jaw clenched and tightened. "And they hid Nevaeh from us for years."

I nodded. "I told the elders what Celeste had told me when she first came to the pack. That the bears believe we're meant to die off. And that Fate wants us to be the last of the wolf shifters."

Which was totally fucked, but what could we do about it?

Grayson crossed his arms over his chest.

"Yeah, we've been talking about that. So, would the bears attack again to grab our women? Even though they knew the humans were our fated mates? Will they try to grab them now they're pregnant? Or will they attack the whole town?"

Tension tightened in my shoulders and I rolled my neck.

"If that happened, a lot of people would die. They've got an extra generation of female shifters, not to mention more numbers in total. We have our mothers, who would want to fight, of course."

I grimaced.

Grayson continued, "There would be chaos. Our fathers would be split between protecting their mates and fighting for the pack. It would be a complete and utter cluster fuck."

I ran my hand through my hair. "We can't let that happen, Gray."

"I know... I know... but what do we do?"

I crossed my arms over my chest.

I had an idea, but how the hell did we mediate it?

"If we could put together a meeting, Alpha to Alpha, between the bears and us, maybe we could establish some rules, a fair fight, something...?"

Grayson nodded. "Yeah, that's an option. Otherwise, we're going to have to go on the offensive and take a hunting party to their den. We can't just sit here and wait for them to attack. We're too vulnerable. The way we have the town set up, it's beautiful, but a whole pack or two could go down, and the rest of the pack at large wouldn't even know."

Fuck.

He was right.

I'd have to ask Celeste for help with this plan.

"I agree. Maybe I can.... Shit, I didn't want to have to do this."

Grayson knew what I was going to say. "Maybe you can ask

your mate for some help? She'd know the layout of their den, maybe ask them about the structure of their day? Weaknesses? Anything that could help us?"

I groaned.

Deep down I'd known it would come to this. After the bears had attacked Dexter's pack, then Grayson's. They wouldn't stop until one of our shifter families was dead.

And it wasn't going to be us.

"I'll ask her. I didn't want to put Celeste under this sort of pressure, feeling like she has to betray her own family. But I will."

I'd known we'd need Celeste's help, but I hadn't wanted to ask her. After everything she'd been through, this was additional stress she just didn't need, especially at this time during her pregnancy.

"I'll speak to her and get back to you."

I patted Gray on the shoulder and walked back inside my home.

Celeste was up and making some dinner for us all.

"Can we help you, sweetheart?" I asked, glaring at Sam. He knew she was meant to be resting.

My Beta glared right back. "Don't look at me like that. I tried."

Celeste grunted.

Yep, *grunted*, from the kitchen. "I'm not helpless, Tayte. I know I look like a beached whale, but I've got four weeks to go, so I've gotta keep moving or I'll go crazy. So... spaghetti for dinner?"

She didn't sound like she was asking, and an annoyed vibe was radiating from her now.

"Um, sure, sweetheart. Do you mind if I ask you a few questions while you're doing that?"

She looked toward me while she pulled out the pasta and put some water on to boil.

"Yeah, of course. Sit. Is this something to do with what Grayson came over to discuss with you?"

She wasn't slow, this one.

"Yes. The pack has noticed the scent of bear shifters around town, and we were hoping you could tell us more about the den where you lived."

I kept my voice as soft as possible, but I saw the way my once steady girl began to shake.

"It's okay, sweetheart. You're safe here, with us. I promise."

She dried her hands with a towel. "Yes of course. I know that. It's just... well, the thought of them so near. Even if they were just passing by, or maybe scouting around for info." She shuddered. "What do you want to know?"

"Things like numbers within the den, how many do you think would fight if they all attacked at once?"

I knew it was a hard question to start with, but it was what I most needed to know. What gave us the most concern.

Celeste bit her lip and leaned against the island bench.

"Okay... let me think. Forty-five apartments, times five, at least."

I didn't know what she was calculating but I trusted what she was doing in her head.

She caught my eye and continued. "There's at least two-hundred-and-fifty bear shifters in that den."

"Ah... say what?"

I couldn't believe it. That was twice as many as we had anticipated.

"Not all of them would fight if they attacked here. There're children and lots of elderly, too. But I'd say at least a hundred of strong, fighting age. All shifters. Male and female."

"Whoa."

Now I was surprised they hadn't attacked already.

Celeste smiled at me. "You're wondering why they haven't wiped you guys out already, aren't you?"

I nodded. "Was I that obvious?"

She began to move around the kitchen, getting things out to make a tomato-based pasta sauce.

She grinned like she already knew the answer. "It's because they're lazy, and unorganized, not to mention unfit. To get all of them to attack at one time would be way above their capabilities."

"So, we have the advantage, then?"

She nodded thoughtfully. "Yes. But what for? You're not thinking of attacking first, are you?"

"I honestly don't know, sweetheart, but we can't wait. We're sitting ducks."

We had to improve the security, set up an alarm system.

Something.

We were under attack, or would soon be.

Celeste came around the bench and slid her hands around my neck. "Please be careful, Tayte. You know you're the anchor of this family. We'd all die without you."

I chuckled as I ran my hand over the swollen belly that housed my child.

"Sweetheart, I have more to live for now, than I have ever had in my life."

But I also had more to protect. More to lose than I'd ever had before.

I kissed Celeste and excused myself.

I needed to talk to Dex or one of the elders. I had to give them the information I had, and perhaps set up a meeting for them to talk more with Celeste.

They'd have more questions, and I was sure she could answer them.

I was stepping out the front door when suddenly Dexter arrived, dragging a bleeding Omega with him.

"Dex! Speak of the devil, I was just coming to find you. Who have you got here?"

I didn't like to step into another man's pack and tell him how to do his job, but this Omega needed some protection, obviously. But it wasn't Dexter's Omega, so whose was he?

"We found out who the mole was." Dex spat as he threw the Omega at my feet.

I helped the guy up, but he could only stand on one leg. His left eye was swollen shut and his shoulder looked oddly-shaped. It had clearly been dislocated. The man must be in enormous pain.

"What do you mean?" I asked Dex.

Mole? We had a mole in our pack?

Dex nodded at the bleeding guy. "I mean... we knew there was someone feeding information to the bears. It was the only thing that made sense. How else could they have attacked within a day of us bringing Claire home? Now we know they've been scouting for more information."

I turned on the Omega, who'd obviously been beaten to reveal the information.

"Is this true?"

He ducked his head. "Yes, Alpha."

"But why? Why would you betray us?"

He lifted his gaze and deep in the darkness of his eyes, I saw true hatred. Hatred for us. For his own kind. It disgusted me.

"Because I could. Because they paid me. Why wouldn't I?"

He stuck his chin out in defiance I'd never seen in a pack member, particularly an Omega.

I was tempted to punch him right in the face. To wipe that look off his mouth.

But he'd taken as much beating as he could, and I not the kind of Alpha to beat an Omega half to death.

"What the hell do you mean? You betrayed us! You could have gotten Claire, or any of the others, killed."

He shrugged and looked away. "What do I care? I'll never have a mate like you guys have. I don't even have a triad pack."

He tossed his hair and glared at me with his one remaining good eye. "And thanks to me, you guys probably never will, either. Once they get here."

I grabbed his bad arm and he cried out in pain.

I didn't let go.

"Tell me their plan. Now."

There was movement behind me as my pack surrounded us, but I didn't take my eyes off the Omega.

"Tell me."

I squeezed his arm a little harder. What was a little pain compared to what the bears would bring our way?

"They're going to... ah...."

He swallowed hard, his eyes closing, probably from the pain.

"Tayte. You're hurting him." Celeste drew close to me and the Omega looked at her, his one good eye bulging when he saw how pregnant she was.

I took advantage of that moment. "Is that what you want, Omega? To have Celeste captured? Killed? Because you know that's what's going to happen when the bears arrive."

"The bears? They're coming? I thought they were just, I don't know, scouting around a bit." Celeste gasped and shrunk back.

I couldn't look at my mate to reassure her, because my wolf teeth were bared and I couldn't retract them. I didn't want to scare her even more.

"Omega, you're going to call the bears and set up a meeting

with them. I want to work out what the fuck is going on, and you're going to help me."

The Omega, bless his courageous heart, actually threatened me.

"Or what?"

I laughed and gripped tighter to his shoulder. He wanted to know what I'd do to protect my pack?

I pulled his dislocated arm down and twisted until he was kneeling on the dirt screaming at me to stop.

I let go, a little.

"Or I'll rip you apart, piece by piece, I swear it. On the life of my unborn child, Omega. You have no idea what I'd do to keep them both safe."

The Omega nodded and I let him go.

"Okay... I'll call them."

And he did.

The meeting was set.

We just had to work out what they wanted more than our extinction, and figure out how to give it to them.

I CONVINCED my pack to go to bed, to stay safe, while Gray, Dex and I went into the forest to talk to the Alpha of the bear's den.

We didn't have much of a plan, other than to broker a truce.

Somehow.

"If Trevor actually turns up, guys, I swear I'll kill him," Grayson said as we walked up the road and into the clearing where we'd organized to meet.

Not too far from the pack, if we needed back-up.

"You keep your feelings to yourself, Gray," Dex threatened. "We need this to be as impersonal as possible."

Grayson snorted.

I had to laugh. "Impersonal, Dex? Then you should have sent some of the elders to this meeting. It doesn't get much more personal than this for me, you and Gray."

The others grunted in agreement.

Dex nodded. "So, we stick to the plan, and hope to God they haven't brought an army with them."

Grayson said. "If they have, we shift and run. We won't stand a chance of winning out here against a hundred bear shifters."

Dex said, "My pack's on standby, and so is the rest of the town."

We trudged forward and I glanced behind me again.

I had the strangest feeling we were being followed, but every time I looked behind us, I saw nothing.

My heart, which was already beating too hard, began to bang against my ribs.

"Do you smell that?"

The scent of bear was on the breeze, and it suddenly became too strong to stand. A stench.

Why did they never bathe or clean themselves? Disgusting creatures.

I forced myself not to cover my nose, so they didn't see my revulsion if they were around.

And then they were there, in front of us.

Five of them, all big brutes. But at least they were in human form—for now.

I'd half-expected them to bring bodyguards in the shape of their bear shifter forms.

"I see you brought back-up," Dex called out.

The agreement had been for three only.

"Well, you can never trust a wolf to keep his word," the big guy in the middle said, then laughed at his own joke.

I heard Grayson's low growl and stepped closer to him, but didn't say anything.

I didn't know if everyone could keep their cool at this meeting, but doing so was the best chance we had to avoid outright war.

"We kept our word, Trevor. There's three of us. And we're here. How about we get down to business?"

Trevor narrowed his gaze at me. "And what business is that, wolf?"

"I'm Tayte. I'm…"

"I know who you are. You're the guy who knocked up Celeste."

The bears around Trevor growled all of a sudden, the mood within the group changing. The anger ramped up a notch and my wolf threatened to rise up in response.

I took a slow, deep breath.

I needed to play this carefully. Cards close to my chest.

They couldn't know how important Celeste was to me, or we'd all be lost.

Brains over heart, in this case.

"Yeah… that's me. How'd you know?"

"I can smell her on you, even now. That stench we all had to put up with for years. Ugh." He shuddered as though my mate repulsed him and the wolf inside of me howled.

But I pushed him down.

I needed to show Grayson and Dexter how to stay calm, even when the bears baited us.

"Back to the business at hand, Trevor. We know you guys have some sort of plan to attack the pack, and we need to come to an agreement before that happens."

There was a beat of silence.

Yes, that confirmed it.

"Why would I want to do that?" Trevor asked.

I could see his point, but no matter how they played their attack, they'd lose numbers on their side, too.

"Because there's no fight between us. We've done nothing to you, you've done nothing to us. There's no reason we need to fight at all."

And as far as I knew, that was true.

Even the elders couldn't understand why the bears wanted a war with us.

Trevor grunted. "My father believed that you wolf shifters were meant to die out. Become extinct."

I'd heard this from Celeste and was ready for this argument.

"But Fate found a way around it and sent us human mates. Doesn't that say something? That we're not meant to die off?"

Trevor grimaced and I saw a small amount of reasoning come to life in his eyes.

"There are a lot of people who believe what my father believed. That you all should be left to rot. And after Celeste betrayed us, then ran off, my den wants revenge. They want to attack."

I paused. He didn't want this. Nevaeh had told me once that Trevor's father had forced him to date her. Surely, he'd want to just walk away?

And I could work with that.

I smiled calmly. "But if you don't want to risk your den by attacking us, surely you, as the Alpha, must be followed."

Trevor was nodding and I could almost hear the cogs in his brain clicking around. "I may be able to hold them off until a treaty can be organised, but you need to give us something in return."

Anything.

"What do you want? Supplies? Cash?"

"We want Celeste back."

Cold dread skittled down my spine. I had expected that, but hearing it out loud made the threat against my mate seem more real. "Why?"

I already knew. They wanted to kill her. Punish her. I could tell.

Trevor looked amongst his den mates, puffing up his chest like a dickhead.

"She was sentenced to death by me, and the sentence must be carried out. It'll be the only way to appease my den, maintain order. A sacrifice for the greater good. Surely you'd do that."

I didn't move, or speak, I couldn't.

And the Alphas alongside me weren't helping.

They knew my struggle and would never sacrifice their own mates for the good of the overall pack.

"You want me to send her back to you so you can kill her?" I had to repeat his words back to him, just so I was one-hundred percent sure what he was saying.

And I had to hold my temper.

Dexter and Grayson and I had sworn to each other not to show our cards.

Not to declare the importance of our fated mates in our lives, as Celeste had confirmed that the bears didn't have such mates.

And he showed me she'd been correct when he said, "You can get another mate. Women are interchangeable."

I nodded and cleared my throat, working out what to say. I had to buy us some time to work out a new plan. Because I was never giving her up. I would die first.

"I agree... women are interchangeable."

The lie tasted like ash on my tongue.

Dexter turned to me and shook his head in the smallest of gestures, but I focused on Trevor, a plan forming in my mind.

"You know our pack is childless, woman-less."

"Yes." He grinned and exchanged satisfied looks with his den mates.

I wanted to squash their arrogance with my fist. But I pushed down my anger.

"Then give me four more weeks. After that, I'll hand Celeste over to you and you can do with her as you will."

There was the faintest gasp, a whisper on the wind that tugged at my attention, but I couldn't focus on it.

This was too important. I had to buy us time, so I could save our pack.

"What will four weeks change?" Trevor asked.

"I told you, our pack is childless, and she's pregnant with my baby. Let me get my kid from her first. It's only a few short weeks away, then you can have her."

Oh my God, my heart actually hurt to say the words.

Never!

"You'll surrender her to me?"

Like hell I will.

"Of course, once I've got my baby you can have the human."

My wolf screamed inside my mind. Howled like a crazy at the moon. But I wasn't stopping this line of argument. Not now that I'd started along this path.

It gave us time, and it showed the pack how crazy the bears truly were.

"Okay, then we can talk about a treaty. My father is gone, and honestly, I just want to get on with our lives. Though... I've seen your houses and I want one like that. We don't have what you do."

That's because you're fucking lazy!

"We're all tradesmen; we can help you with everything. Let me go back to the elders to work out a deal."

Like hell we'll work for free for these guys.

"Fine, wolf. You get your four weeks. Then we're coming for the little slut."

I nodded as if I agreed with his statement, though I wanted to reach out and close my hand around his neck. Squeeze hard until the life left him and he fell to the ground at my feet.

How dare the bastard threaten my mate? My true love?

I swallowed rage, and then we retreated.

We had to get back to the pack.

The smell on the breeze as we turned away from the bears was strangely familiar.

What was it...?

"What the fuck was that?" Dex spat at me, finally speaking.

My wolf was practically bursting through my skin.

"Calm your farm, Dex."

I began to strip and so did the other two, the energy between us burning angry and bright. No way could I stay in human form with this much adrenaline rushing through me.

"I bought us time. Nothing else. Those bears are gonna die."

My wolf ripped through my body, my human side unable to stay in control with the rage that filled me boiling through my blood.

We ran back to the pack as quickly as we could, around the forest that protected our families.

There didn't seem like a way around this war now. We'd have to fight.

Because there was no way they were *ever* getting my mate.

Celeste

Bile rose in my throat and I choked on it. Tayte wanted to hand me over to the bears?

I couldn't let them hear me; I couldn't.

So, I swallowed the acid, and the tears.

I had to get out of here.

I crept away and began to run, stumbling over tree roots, long grass and thick shrubs. My belly was so cumbersome, but I carried myself the best I could as I cut across the forest. Away from the bears, and more importantly, away from the pack I had thought was my family.

They were going to kill me!

The bears for honor, and the pack to save their own hides.

What had I done to deserve all this?

Be born human.

The tears ran down uncontrollably down my face as my baby

rolled and kicked within my womb. It was as if the child sensed its mother's anguish.

I had to get away from here.

Those wolves were not going to take my baby from me.

And they were certainly not going to send me back to the den for my *punishment*.

Anger pushed me harder. I ran, tripping and stumbling, through the forest.

But I didn't stop, though the cold ate at my skin and the pain in my heart made me want to cry.

I have no idea how long I ran. My legs trembled and my whole body shivered with fear and the pain of rejection.

I turned back my head to look over my shoulder. Had any of them heard me, when I inadvertently let out that gasp? What if they'd heard me?

I face the front again, and took another step forward, and then I was falling, slipping down a hill I hadn't noticed.

And the world went black.

SAM

I woke to a cold hand on my shoulder, shaking me awake. It was Tayte, and by the look of him, he'd only just returned from a run.

"Hey, where's Celeste?" Tayte said. There was an urgency to his voice that had me sitting up.

I glanced to the other side of the bed, where I'd left her.

She was always surrounded by pillows these days, and didn't like us getting too close in sleep. She got too hot and her back hurt, so we had temporarily given her some space.

But the place that should have housed my mate was empty.

"I don't know. Where's Dane? Maybe she's with him?" But as I said the words, cold fear spread through my gut. That tone of Tayte's had not been conducive to low stress. "What's wrong?"

"She's gone. I can't find her. Dane's getting dressed. Get up, get some clothes on."

I pulled on some jeans and a sweatshirt as quickly as I could, though it was pointless. I could feel my wolf stir and Tayte's speech was a little garbled as he struggled to talk through his shifter teeth.

Our clothes would be shredded soon if the mood continued like this.

"What's going on, Tayte?"

I followed him down the stairs and Dane met us in the living room.

"Where's Celeste?" Dane asked.

My brain was empty, free of all thoughts, as my shock rammed into me. "She's eight months pregnant; where the hell could she have gone?"

The front door opened and Dexter walked in. "She's not at my place and Claire hasn't seen her."

Tayte's fingers tightened into fists. "Fuck! I knew it. I felt her —I even caught her beautiful scent—but I thought I was imagining it. This is all my fault."

I grabbed my Alpha's arm and shook him. "What the hell are you talking about?"

He sighed heavily, running his hands through his hair.

"I... ah, I think Celeste followed me into the woods tonight."

"Why would she do that?"

Tayte shrugged. "Maybe she was worried about us? Maybe she wanted to help? I have no idea, but I heard a few noises as we walked into the forest and thought we may have been followed. But I dismissed the idea, because who would be that stupid?"

Good point, but dear God, she could be anywhere.

I groaned. "Okay... fine. Where is she? We need to find her."

Tayte grimaced. "We do. But you need to know something before we go. If she heard what I said to the bears, then she'll be running away from us."

"But... why would she do that?" I grabbed him by the shirt. "What did you say?"

I could barely talk now.

My teeth were shifting, and my eyes had flashed to wolf's night vision.

I could only see in black and white, though a red haze was covering me.

Tayte sighed, not looking at me. "I told the bears they could have her once the baby was born."

I pulled back my arm and punched my Alpha as hard as I could.

Pain cracked through my wrist as Tayte reeled back, blood dripping from his nose.

"If something's happened to her or that baby, Tayte..." I panted and began to strip.

She was in danger. I could feel it. And it was all *his* fault.

I let my wolf tear through me. My black Beta wolf that was almost as big as my Alpha. Today, I would take him down if I needed to.

I ran straight out the door and put my nose into the air.

Blood. My mate's blood.

Oh, fuck, no.

I began to run, the other wolves behind me.

They were on my tail, but I ran faster.

How could he do this to us?

To her?

After everything she'd been through.

I pushed down my anger, the feelings consuming me and making me want to turn around and fight my own pack.

But my mate needed me. That was more important now.

I'd deal with the guilt later.

The scent of her sweetness, her blood, made me turn off the road and into the forest.

She'd come this way. I could smell her. Frightened and bleeding.

I skittered all the way to the edge of a cliff and looked down.

All my nightmares came true in that one moment when I stared down to the bottom of the cliff.

Celeste's broken body lay in a tangle of brush. Her blonde hair was strewn over a fallen tree branch.

I threw back my head and howled, alerting my brothers to the pain I was in and letting loose the raging feelings bottling up in my head.

Then I ran, making my way down the cliff as fast as I could, slipping and sliding on the loose dirt, the rocks cutting my paws.

Oh my God, she's dead.

She's dead.

The baby... please no.

I hit the ground and put my nose against my mate, my heart pounding in my chest as I checked to see if she was alive.

If I felt her dead, cold skin against my nose I didn't know what I'd do.

Kill Tayte would likely be first on the list.

But she moved. She moaned.

She rolled her head and I let go of my wolf so fast, my human skin hurt as it stretched back to fit me.

"Ah... fuck..."

My head spun with the speed of my shift, but I put my fingers to her neck, feeling a pulse.

I looked up, where my pack and Dexter's wolves stood on top of the cliff.

I called out to them. "She's alive! You need to get Claire! And an ambulance!"

Dexter and his pack took off and Tayte howled.

I knew he wanted to come down also, but I didn't want to deal with the Alpha at this moment.

"Find a safe way down for Claire."

I squatted next to my mate, wishing for blankets and towels and an air lift.

I cradled her face gently, careful not to disturb her neck.

She could have broken anything.

Or everything.

Then her eyes opened, slowly, and she began to cry.

"Sam.... the baby, the baby's coming. I'm bleeding."

I looked down and realized there was blood over her jeans.

A lot of it.

That's what I'd smelt.

That's how I'd found her.

How horrific.

I'd tracked my mate, because she was bleeding out.

I cupped her face. "Just hold on, Celeste. Hold on. Help's coming."

She tried to sit up, but I pushed her shoulders gently. "No. Please, don't get up, beautiful."

"Tayte... he's going to send me away. The baby..."

I let loose a growl I'd never made. "He will never send you away. Do you understand me? I'll kill that bastard first. You will live with us, and give us more babies forever, do you understand me?"

I was crying now, and I couldn't stop.

"Celeste! Celeste!"

She closed her eyes and she wasn't waking up this time.

Oh my God, what do I do?

There was noise above and around me.

I wanted to drag my mate close and hold her.

But I was too scared to damage her, and knew that I couldn't do anything.

I just stood next to her almost-lifeless body, doing nothing. Feeling useless.

"Help me! Please!"

Claire was suddenly there next to me, with a bag and blankets.

"Move out of the way, Sam. The paramedics are on the way."

Claire checked Celeste's pulse and the baby's heartbeat with a stethoscope.

"They're both alive."

"But... the blood." I gestured to the blood staining Celeste's thighs. "Surely the baby can't survive this."

"Cover her up. Quick. Keep her warm."

I followed Claire's orders.

"Claire, tell me. What are her chances of surviving this?"

Claire's face was grim, her lips twisted as she considered how to answer me.

"I don't know what her injuries are. If she's fractured her spine, or has massive internal bleeding, she'll be in for a big struggle."

"And the baby?"

"The bleeding is probably an indication of a placental abruption, so the baby is still alive. But we need to get her to the hospital for a C-section as soon as possible."

"How long do they have?" I asked.

Claire shook her head. "I don't know, Sam. I honestly don't know. But we need to get her to hospital. Now."

I could hear sirens.

I didn't know how much time had passed but Celeste was getting paler by the minute.

Claire glanced behind her. "Oh, thank God, they're here. Tayte's gonna bring them down, but we may need to help them through the brush. This isn't an easy spot to get to."

I growled, loudly. "You get Tayte away from her, or I'll kill him. This is all his fault."

"Sam..."

"Claire, I'm serious."

"Fine. I'll go get the paramedics."

Claire disappeared and someone called out to me.

I looked up and Dane was throwing down a pair of rolled up jeans. They snagged on a tree, then fell down in the dirt.

I hadn't even considered my own nakedness. I grabbed them and pulled them on.

That would have been fun to explain to the humans, why I was naked and in the middle of the forest with an unconscious woman.

It was going to be hard enough as it was.

"Here she is."

Two men with a stretcher hurried over and Claire pulled me out of the way.

"She's thirty-six weeks pregnant and bleeding. We'll need to prep the OR for an emergency C-section as soon as we get back."

The men tied Celeste to the white stretcher and carried her off to an ambulance.

"I'll ride with her," Claire said to me. "Get your car and drive to the hospital. I'll meet you there."

I nodded.

I didn't want to let Claire take her, but there was nothing more I could do. And there was no extra room in the back of that tiny ambulance with her. I could see that.

So, I trusted Dexter's mate to take care of Celeste.

I had to. Because my own pack had sure as shit let her down.

As the ambulance drove off, I was left with a sinking, horrible feeling. One of pure grief and despair.

I'd never recover from this if Celeste and her baby died.

Tayte was suddenly next to me and I was no longer alone with my feelings. Instead, my need to hurt him was pure and nasty, and bigger than me.

I looked at him and spat. "If she dies, you're dead."

Tayte nodded. "I know. Because I won't be able to live without her."

His grief came at me in a wave. I couldn't handle it. What he carried was too much for me now.

Grief *and* regret.

"No."

I let go of my human self and shifted back to my wolf, and I started running home.

I needed my clothes. I needed my car and I needed my mate.

Our baby's life hung in the balance, and my family was in tatters.

What the hell could go wrong next?

Celeste

Waking up was harder than it had ever been.

What was wrong with my eyes?

My arms?

My body?

I licked my lips and swallowed the cotton wool feeling in my mouth.

"Celeste? Hello?"

I knew that voice.

It was Dane, I was sure of it.

I blinked, and blinked, and blinked, until my eyes finally opened.

Bright lights shone down on me.

"Where am I?"

Dane was there, gripping my hand. "You're at the hospital."

Hospital? Why would I be at the hospital?

I reached for my belly with my free hand and the baby swelling was gone.

My eyes popped open and I looked down on my now flat-ish stomach. "The baby... my baby?" My voice rose, almost hysterical. "Where is it?"

Dane cupped my face and forced me to look at him.

"She's out and she's doing well. A little premature, and on oxygen in the ICU for a few more days, but she's strong. Just like her mama."

Tears pricked my eyes and I struggled to sit up.

Dane picked up a control and pushed a button. The bed lifted me up until I was almost sitting.

I winced as pain shot through my ribs and I let my head rest back against the pillows.

"She? I had a girl."

I'd always wanted a girl.

Of course, I would have been happy with a boy, with twins. A puppy, even. But a baby girl was the true fantasy.

"Yes, you did, my love. And she's beautiful. Sam's watching over her as we speak."

"What happened?" I didn't remember much at all. "Why am I here?"

Dane pulled up a chair and sat next to me, gripping my hand like he'd never let go.

"You ran away, into the forest, and fell down a cliff embankment. We thought we were going to lose you both, but you were very lucky. You've got a cracked rib or two and some cuts and bruising, but considering how far you fell, we're all thanking our lucky stars that you got away from it so unscathed."

Cracked ribs? I looked down at my hand where a drip was inserted, probably with some very good painkillers too.

"Why would I run away from you all?"

Then the memories came flooding back and I gasped, pulling my hand from Dane's grip.

"You're going to give me to the bears! You don't even want me."

I began to scream. "Help! Somebody! Help me!"

Dane grabbed for my hands again.

I pushed at him, my heart pounding against my ribs. "No! Get away from me! I want my baby! Give me my baby!"

Two nurses and Claire came rushing in. "Celeste, calm down. Please."

I grabbed for Claire's arm and held her tight. "They're going to send me back to the bears; you need to protect me, please. My baby, I need my baby. They're going to steal her from me."

Claire grabbed my hands and squeezed hard.

"Celeste, listen to me. Okay? Listen. No one is taking your baby away. She's in a crib, in the NICU. I can bring her to you, but you can't hold her yet, okay?"

I nodded but couldn't stop shaking.

Claire tried to move away but I grabbed her arm tighter.

"Claire, you can't leave. Tayte said he was going to hand me over to the bears once the baby came. If she's here, then he'll throw me away."

My throat closed up as the betrayal truly hit home.

After giving myself entirely over to them, they were going to get rid of me. After I'd finally let down my guard, let myself believe that they loved me.

A sob rose and I couldn't hold it in.

Claire grabbed for me again. "I'm not going anywhere until we figure all this out, okay? Nurse Myers, could you bring Celeste's baby to us, please?"

I watched the woman go and relaxed a fraction. But I wasn't letting Claire's hand go. No way.

Dane was still in the room, and I shot him a glare before looking back at the doctor.

"They're going to kill me."

I'd known it was all too good to be true.

The wolves had been waiting for me to grow them a baby, and then they were done with me.

The nurse came back into the room, wheeling a clear-sided box with a baby inside.

She was barely dressed and so beautiful my heart broke in half, only to fill up with a love I'd never known existed.

"Oh my God." I let go of Claire's hands and reached for the box. "She'll be cold like that, won't she?"

The baby turned toward my voice and blinked up at me with huge blue eyes.

Oh my God. She's here.

"Hello, baby, I'm your mama. I can't believe I missed your birth." I looked at Claire. "How many days has it been?"

Claire came close and smiled. "She's not cold, don't worry. These humidicribs are kept at a constant ninety-seven degrees, so she's nice and warm. And she was born only twenty-four hours ago. You haven't missed much at all, Mama."

Claire glanced at the door, but I didn't want to take my eyes off my baby.

"Now, you can touch her through these special little sleeves," Claire opened up an access point for me.

I placed my hand inside and reached for my baby. I touched her soft skin on her arm and her tiny little hand.

Her fingers wrapped around my finger and I began to cry, tears slipping down my cheeks.

"How long will she need to stay in here, Claire?"

I'd been four weeks from my due date. How dangerous was that for my baby girl?

"Just a few more days, I think, Celeste. We'll reassess her each day. Now, I'm going to leave her here with you and I'm going to deal with something in the corridor. Just yell if you need me."

"Okay."

I was never going to need anything else, ever again.

I had my little angel.

She'd survived that horrible fall.

We both had.

And now I had to work out a way to survive the next fifty years of my life, because there was no way I was letting the wolves use me as a sacrifice now.

CHAPTER
ELEVEN

Tayte

It was four o'clock in the morning when Celeste woke up. A single day had passed since that nightmare of her falling down the cliff.

Sam still wouldn't talk to me and Dane moped around like a puppy with a broken tail.

Our family was falling apart, and somehow, I knew it was all my fault.

Then the door to her hospital room flew open and an angry doctor came at us.

"What the hell is she talking about?" Claire hissed at us.

Oh, fuck.

My fears had come true and poor Celeste had remembered immediately why she'd run from us.

I sighed. "It's my fault, Claire. Ask Dexter about it, he was there. He'll explain everything."

Claire narrowed her eyes and poked me in the chest with her pointed finger.

"You are going to tell me right now what the hell is going on. What was that girl doing at the bottom of a cliff in the middle of the night?"

Claire was practically panting, she was so angry.

I let my shoulders drop, the weight of my guilt too heavy to bear.

"When Grayson, Dexter and I met with the bears, they told us an attack was imminent, and from what Celeste had told me about their numbers, I knew that much of our town would die if it came to war. So, I asked them for a treaty, a way to buy us some time to work out a full solution."

Claire put her hands on her hips. "Okay. So, what did you offer them?"

I glanced over at Dane, who met my look and then grimaced.

I turned back to the doctor who'd saved my child's life.

"They wanted Celeste, so they could carry out the death sentence they'd imposed on her six months ago."

Her mouth dropped open. "You didn't say yes?"

I ran a hand through my hair and tugged at my shirt.

"I had no choice. It was the only thing I could say to put them off attacking. I told them to give me a month, until the baby was born, and then I'd send her back to them."

Claire glared at me with the fury of a thousand suns. "Tell me you're joking."

Why didn't anyone understand that I'd been lying through my teeth? As if I'd *ever* give up my mate. The one person who completed me.

"I would never have done it, ever. You weren't there, ask Dexter. I was in an impossible situation, so I lied. It was just to buy us some time, so we could come up with a plan."

Claire rolled her eyes in a dramatic fashion.

"Oh. My. God. Please tell me she didn't *hear* you lying to the bears."

Dane nodded. "She did, we think. Because she snuck out in the middle of the night and ran off. Nothing else makes sense."

Claire sighed. "She definitely heard you because she was just telling me that you're going to send her back to the bears. Jeezuus... That poor girl."

Claire slapped her palm against her forehead. "What a mess."

My chest cracked open, pain pouring into my wounds like salt.

"I know. What do I do, Claire? How do I explain to her that I was never going to go through with it? That I was saying it to save the pack and give us time to come up with an alternative?"

I clenched my teeth against the wave of nausea that rolled through me.

I'd been sick to my stomach every single moment since this had happened.

Not only did I have to find a way to save my pack and the lives of those in our town, but my mate was hurt and no longer trusted me.

More than that, she thought I was actively involved in wanting to have her killed.

The walls were tumbling down around me and I didn't know what to do.

"What should I do, Claire?"

"You need to explain, apologize and beg forgiveness."

"I know. And I will. But I don't want to upset her any further."

Claire nodded, her phone beeping.

She pulled her cell out of her pocket then sighed. "I'm going to make a phone call, then come back. You three wait out here and I'll be back in a few minutes."

Claire walked off and began talking on her cell.

Sam and Dane sat in the plastic chairs in the hallway and I loitered around, doing laps on the linoleum.

When Claire came back, she had a grim look of determination on her face.

"Okay. Let's go. Tayte, you're with me."

I followed Claire into the hospital room where my mate was talking to our baby through a little incubator box.

I hung by the doorway, ready for the attack.

Claire moved over to her patient. "Celeste, I just spoke to Dex about the other night to confirm what Tayte said about his conversation with the bears."

Celeste pulled her arm out of the incubator and turned to me.

I inhaled sharply when I saw her face. Her anger sliced through my heart like claws through flesh.

"Get him out of here."

I looked toward Claire, who took over.

"Celeste, you need to hear him out. Your whole future, and that of all the packs in the Woodlands depends on it."

That seemed to give Celeste pause, because she drooped, her shoulders sagging as she crossed her arms over her chest.

"Fine. Talk."

"I know you heard what I said to the bears about giving you up after the baby was born. But I would never do that."

She glared at me, her face not changing a single bit.

"I don't believe you."

I laughed sadly. "Well, that's ironic, because I was lying to them, not you. How could you think, after all the love we've shared over the past six months, that I'd ever abandon you?"

She looked away, but I could see the pain in her face.

I went down on my knees to beg.

"Sweetheart, look at me, please. I lied that night. Lied my ass off. You heard me tell them that you weren't my mate, and you know that's a lie. I had to buy us more time. You told me that they outnumber us two to one. My whole town will die if the bears attack as one force. I had to tell them something to give us enough time to mount a proper defence. I will never, ever give you up. Even if you and Sam and Dane vote to kick me out forever, I'll sleep on the doorstep for the rest of my life. To make sure the three of you remain safe. The three of you... and the baby."

She looked at me this time, her blue eyes as dark as granite.

"I know you want the baby... you don't want me."

I shook my head. "You're right about one thing, and horribly wrong about the other. Of course, I want the baby. She's ours, she's yours. But I want *you* even more. How can I prove it to you?"

I stayed on my knees, hoping she'd see how truly sorry I was.

She sighed, but her arms didn't uncross.

"I don't think I'll ever forgive you for what you said that night. I'll never be able to let my guard down with you again. I'll never believe you again when you say that you love me. It's all just... broken. We can't go back."

Hot tears were in my eyes, then on my cheeks.

I dashed them away and looked at the floor.

"Um... okay. I understand."

I got to my feet and backed up to the door.

"I'll move my things out of the house, and you can come home with Sam and Dane. Neither of them forgives me either, so it's probably best that you three stay together."

I moved to walk away, and Celeste called out. "What did you mean, the pack was in danger?"

I turned back to face her. "The bears want blood. Mine, yours, they don't care. They want our pack extinct, gone. So, we either need to change their minds, or we need to fight them."

"Oh, so I was going to be a sacrifice for peace. How noble of you."

Her tone was hard, unforgiving, and the darkness of my guilt consumed me.

"You have it all wrong, sweetheart, as Dexter and Grayson can attest. I lied to the bears to give us a few weeks to plan. Nothing more. I'd rather die than ever see you hurt."

She didn't answer me, only turned back to face her baby once again.

There was only one way forward and that was to eliminate the bears once and for all.

"I love you, Celeste. With all my heart."

She didn't look my way again, but it didn't matter. I was able to say the only words I wanted her to hear. Then I left.

I left the hospital, and I left my pack.

The bears wanted blood, so I'd give it to them.

CHAPTER

TWELVE

Sam

I watched my Alpha walk out of the hospital and for some reason, I had the most horrible suspicion I'd never see him again.

"I think we need to go speak to Celeste now."

I stood up and walked into the hospital room with Dane.

Then I stopped.

My heart filled.

I couldn't believe how beautiful she was, sitting there with our baby within arm's reach.

"Celeste." I went straight to her hospital bed and tried to gather her into my arms. "You're awake. Please, never leave us again. We love you too much to go through that fear again."

She laughed as she put her head on my chest. "Put you through it? What about me? I missed out on my daughter's birth and seemed to have toppled off a cliff."

I kissed her upturned face. Her button nose. Her forehead. Her pale pink lips.

"You did. And you survived it all. My perfect, brave, strong girl."

I cuddled her close and sighed. "This feels so good. I didn't realize how much I'd miss you until I didn't have you for a day."

She laughed again and pulled away. "So, you weren't part of the plan to toss me away as soon as the baby was born?"

I frowned at her. "Of course not. There's never been such a plan, and there never will be. You're our fated mate, and no one's taking you away from us."

Celeste screwed up her face. "That's not what I heard the other night."

I grimaced. "Yeah, I know. I still can't believe how stupid Tayte was to try and bullshit his way through that meeting."

Celeste blinked up at me. "So, he really was lying?"

"Of course, he was! Are you serious right now?"

Celeste chewed on her bottom lip.

"Tayte said he's going to move out. I'm not sure where he'd go but..."

I gaped at our mate. "He what?"

Celeste's eyebrows rose on her forehead. "I don't think it's a bad idea, actually. We don't need him and I can't forgive him for what he did. He betrayed me."

I reeled backwards, feeling like Celeste had smacked me with an open palm. "Don't need him? Don't *need* him? He's our Alpha. He's the one who holds our family together. Who will save our pack if it comes to a fight?"

Celeste's gaze dropped away and she began playing with her hair, twirling it around her finger and staring at the strands. "Well, you can do that, too."

Now I wanted to shake her.

Sure, Tayte had been stupid and we all wanted to punish him for the consequences of his actions, but she didn't get it.

"I can, but you're not understanding the difference between an Alpha and a Beta."

Celeste shrugged and I began to panic. Tayte looked after us. Guarded us. Would die for us. He was the glue that kept this family together.

"Look. I know what he said was dumb and foolish, and resulted in us almost losing you and our baby. I haven't spoken to him since that night and I was planning on punishing him for a while yet. But breaking up our family... that's a different thing altogether."

I didn't want to lose our pack. It wouldn't function without him.

"I need to find him. He can do his penance another way."

I ran out of the room and along the corridor.

He couldn't have gotten far.

I made my way outside and sniffed the air. Nope. Nothing.

I jogged over to the car park and went up to level three where we'd parked the car.

The truck was still there, and next to it was Tayte's car.

He hadn't taken it, so where was he?

I jogged back down the stairs and went to the cafeteria.

It was five in the morning and no one was around, but I'd been hoping Tayte had come to get a stale coffee, or some food from one of the vending machines.

But there was nothing.

No sign of him.

I walked back to Celeste's hospital room slowly, sniffing the air as I went and not coming up with anything from my Alpha.

When I arrived back at the room, I took a big, careful breath, then informed my Omega and our mate that he was gone.

Dane gaped at me. "What do you mean, he's gone? Gone where?"

Celeste sighed. "What does it matter? Won't he be fine, wherever he is?"

I turned on her and growled. "You don't understand. Tayte has lost his pack, his mate and his baby, or so he thinks. And he has a bear den who wants your blood. How do you think he's going to solve that problem?"

Celeste's eyes began to widen and then her mouth dropped open.

"He wouldn't..." She licked her lips, "He wouldn't do anything stupid, would he?"

My heart was pounding like a runaway train.

"He's going to sacrifice himself to the bears, I just know it," I said.

"But how... why?"

I growled at her again and she paled. "Celeste, you aren't getting it. Tayte is an Alpha. He lives only for his pack. If he believes it will keep you safe, keep all of us safe, he'd sacrifice himself a hundred times over. If those bears want someone's head, then he'll go serve it up on a silver platter."

Oh fuck.

What had I done?

I'd been angry with Tayte... so angry that he'd put Celeste's life in danger. But I never wanted this.

"But he can't... I mean..." She swallowed hard, her eyes turning glossy from unshed tears.

I groaned, feeling frustrated and impotent. Just like I had last night when Celeste's life was fading away before me.

Now it was Tayte whose life could end soon.

"I know you're still mad at him and you can't forgive him for lying about such an important thing, but you need to think. What if it was you? What would you do for someone you truly loved? Our daughter. What level would you stoop to? What lie would you tell? Would you die for her?"

Silvery tears slipped down Celeste's cheeks. "I'd do anything to keep her safe."

I nodded once, feeling the strange calm of an impending battle descend over me. "Then you have your answer as to why Tayte did what he did, and now why he's gone to sacrifice himself."

Celeste let out a sob and I turned away.

"I need to leave. I'm not losing Tayte. Not today."

Celeste grabbed for my hand as I tried to walk away. "What can I do?"

I squeezed her hand. "You can keep our baby safe and get better. Because you are the only thing that matters to us."

"I..." Celeste swallowed, "I didn't realize he would..."

I cupped her face, willing some courage into her.

"None of us did. But you need to remember that we grew up knowing about the fated mate bond and you didn't. You don't understand it the way we do. It is love at first sight, in every way for us. We would die for you. And our daughter."

She sobbed loudly this time, more tears flowing down her cheeks. "I'd rather you lived for us."

I pressed a kiss to her lips. "I'll bring him back."

"Dane, let's go."

We started running and I got on the horn to Dexter and the elders.

It was an hour's drive from the pack to town. Forty-five minutes if they broke every speed limit along the way.

I prayed to God that wouldn't be too late.

We needed to save our Alpha from doing something we were all going to regret.

THIRTEEN

Tayte

Finding the bear's headquarters was easy enough. I just followed the stench and the information that I'd accumulated from Celeste about them.

She'd told me that they were on the furthest outskirts of town, in a ramshackle apartment block that looked like it was barely holding itself together.

I stared up at the building I'd found in my walking quest.

Celeste had lived here her whole life?

How had she survived?

There were beer cans and cigarette butts littering the grass and not much else around.

It was still early, maybe seven o'clock in the morning.

The humans in the surrounding neighborhood had stirred. Some were on their way to work, school, or whatever else they did.

But the bears didn't seem to have woken yet.

I walked forward, up the path to the apartment block.

Surely, they'd wake up for this? An Alpha wolf coming to surrender?

I lifted my hand and knocked on the door. I waited for a while, then did it again.

What time did these creatures rise? Or more rightly, what time did they go to bed?

Eventually the door opened. A sleepy-looking woman in her twenties or thirties blinked up at me.

"I'm here to see your Alpha."

She yawned at me. "He won't be awake for a while."

Geez, you'd think this sort of thing happened every day.

"It's important. I'll wait."

"Suit yourself."

She showed me inside to a living area, where there was a rundown snooker table and a leather couch with a great big hole in it.

"You may be waiting a while."

So much for charging to my death.

"No problem."

I sat on the couch, avoiding the hole and feeling a strange buzz in my veins. A weird desire to chuckle and laugh aloud overtook me. There was no anger or regret, only warm feelings I couldn't identify.

I'd once read that some people experienced a sort of euphoria before they died. This was what they must have meant.

I chuckled to myself, realizing how ridiculous I sounded even inside my own head.

I waited what felt like hours, but it probably wasn't that long until a young kid stumbled into the room.

He saw me and stopped short. "Who are you?"

He smelled like the wrong end of a horse, and unfortunately my wolf-like senses made me cringe.

"I'm Tayte. Can you get the Alpha for me?"

"Hmm. Okay."

And he wandered off.

Oh my God. Why was I so worried about an attack from these people?

They were unclean, unorganized and slept all day.

But then I heard it.

The rumble of the bears.

The hairs on the back of my neck tingled as a dozen men stepped into the room.

Trevor, their Alpha, was in the center of a the large group.

Celeste was right about their physicality. They were soft bodied and unshaven, and on the surface looked unfit. But they were big, and like the bears they shifted into, I knew they would be fast and strong and mean.

"What the hell are you doing here? I thought you said a month?"

Oh, so they'd partied and relaxed, had they? Thinking they had time before they had to do anything with us.

Maybe I should have come back with a hunting party. Every Alpha and Beta in our pack could have taken these guys down.

But my pack didn't want me. My Beta wouldn't even look at me and my mate had rejected me.

Why would I risk the lives of anyone else, when a simple sacrifice was all these bears wanted?

I squared my shoulders and said what I'd come to say. "I've come to take her place."

Trevor blinked, then glanced to the men at his side, who seemed equally confused.

"What do you mean?"

"I mean exactly what I said. You want Celeste here, so you can carry out your sentence. I'm here to take her place. A peace offering to stop all the fighting."

The men gaped at me.

"But... but... you're an Alpha. You can't do that," Trevor said.

One of the beefy old guys at his side, said, "This is a trap. I'm sure of it."

I wanted to laugh. Why was this so hard for them to believe? Celeste was my *mate*. Of course, I would do anything to save her. Did they not know that?

"Look, this is a simple trade, with one condition. That you swear off attacking the wolf pack and worrying about if they have their mates or not. That was your father's agenda, wasn't it, Trevor?"

The bear shifter lifted his chin in the air. "Yeah. So what?"

"So, you had to date Nevaeh for how long because of all that crap? You lost years when you should have just been here, in your den, with your woman."

Woman? Women?

I didn't know the terminology. And although I'd love to smash Trevor's face in for what he'd done to Nevaeh in the years he'd been with her, this was a negotiation. I had to keep my cool.

"We can't do that," one of the younger guys said.

Trevor looked torn, so I kept talking, hoping to sway him.

"Hey, look. I'm handing myself over to you. If you want to show the den how strong you are, just destroy me. I won't fight you. That'll be enough. And you can leave the rest of the pack alone."

My brain searched for another argument. I hadn't really thought the bears would need convincing, but then it came to me.

"Leave them to their human mates. The wolves will never be

as strong as you when the next generation comes through. Those kids might not even be able to shift!"

I had no idea if my daughter would be able to shift or not, but I didn't care. She was perfect and beautiful.

But I was betting the bears would care.

There was a rumble of ascent.

Trevor began to laugh. "That would be an even greater victory, wouldn't it? To see that pack turned into a group of humans!"

He practically rolled on the ground he was laughing so hard.

And I let him.

Whatever he needed to believe to keep my mate safe.

"So, we're agreed?"

"Yes. We're agreed."

That was great. But how was I going to make sure Trevor followed through with his deal?

"Does anyone have a phone, so I can let my elders know the deal's done? Then I'm all yours."

One of the younger kids was pushed forward and he timidly offered me a cell.

Again, strangest scene, ever.

I punched in the numbers for Sam's cell. He never answered his phone.

His voicemail kicked in and I cleared my throat, now strangely tight.

"Sam, it's Tayte. The bears have agreed to my terms and will take me in exchange for Celeste. They've also agreed to leave the pack alone, and everyone is to get on with their lives."

I hesitated to say more while the bears still listened.

"So, you take care. Thanks."

I hung up and my heart dropped, aching and bare.

Trevor clapped a hand over my shoulder.

"I have to say, wolf, you've got balls. I'll give you that."

They herded me out of the room, and I went willingly.

"Well, you know. Anything for the family, right?" I looked at him, Alpha to Alpha and expected to see some sort of camaraderie.

But instead, he looked away, then pushed me out the back door.

Into a fenced-in backyard filled with men and women and children.

"Welcome to your execution, wolf."

FOURTEEN

Sam

"That fucking idiot!"

I trembled with rage as Dane and I awaited the arrival of the cavalry. Dexter and Grayson and every other Alpha and Beta wolf in the pack were on their way.

We needed help taking down these bears and rescuing our Alpha.

We couldn't do it on our own.

And so I trembled with fear, a block away from the bear's apartment block.

"What now?" Dane demanded, pacing the sidewalk and cussing as he went back and forth.

I hung up the phone after I listened to the voice mail.

"Tayte. He's..." I swallowed. I knew he'd done it.

Before I'd gotten the confirmation, I knew he'd gone to the bears and offered himself up. But to hear it on my cell was a whole other level of grief.

I cleared my throat. "He's made a deal with the bears. His life for Celeste's, and peace between the two packs."

"He fucking what?" Dane glared at me.

I glared back. "What the hell are you looking at me like that for?"

"This is your fault! You blamed him for what happened to Celeste."

"So did you!" We all had, Claire included.

"I didn't want him to fucking die, though!" Dane's voice cut out halfway through his words.

I swallowed the lump in my throat as I struggled to hold back a wave of grief.

"I know... I know. Neither did I. I was just angry."

Angry that Fate had dealt us such an ugly hand. At Tayte, for being stupid enough to lie about the most important thing in our lives. And Celeste, for believing what she'd heard and not coming to us to find out if it was true.

I groaned as the realization hit.

I was angry at Celeste.

But I hadn't been able to feel that part of it. After what had happened to her that night, I'd pushed the anger down.

But part of me felt betrayed.

Betrayed that she'd snuck out to follow Tayte like he was doing something wrong. Betrayed that she'd run from us the first chance she got. Betrayed that she'd believed such an obvious and stupid lie.

After everything we'd said and done for her, that one lie was what she'd believed? So much so, that she'd endangered her own life and that of our daughter. And now, her disbelief had endangered Tayte's life, too.

I focused back on Dane as the screech and rumble of the pack's trucks pulled up and caught my attention.

"First thing's first. We have to save our Alpha before he becomes bear meat."

The procession of cars and trucks filled up the whole street.

The pack was here.

Dex jogged straight to me. "What's the situation?"

"Tayte's offered himself in exchange for Celeste and to stop any future attacks against the pack, so the bears have him and intend to kill him. They may have already done so."

I didn't think they'd be so quick about it, but what did I know about the execution strategies of bear shifters?

Dexter groaned. "This was not meant to happen. Tayte only said that stuff about Celeste to buy us some time to work out a better strategy than all-out war."

I glanced behind me, where dozens of young, healthy men were piling out of their cars.

"Well, it looks like the war is on."

Dexter nodded and went over to the rest of the pack members to explain what was going on.

"We need to go. Now." Dane nodded at a bunch of kids who'd spotted us.

They looked like bears, somehow, and when they began to run, we went after them.

We didn't want them alerting the adults to our presence.

"Dex! Gray!"

We ran, following the kids to a huge apartment block and straight through the front door of the place.

We could hear a ruckus in the backyard and charged down the corridor to where a horror story was unfolding before me.

Tayte was chained up against the fence, and it looked like they were taking turns beating him up. He was naked, bleeding and sliced.

"No!"

The shift came on me faster than it ever had.

I ran straight at the man with the knife, who was poised to stick it straight into Tayte's belly.

I clamped onto his wrist and ripped flesh from bone. Blood spurted through my teeth and I growled as I tore harder.

That's when the screaming began.

Women began to run, grabbing children, as my pack charged for the men.

Bear shifters began to shift and charge the wolves. The fight was on.

Whether we meant to begin a war or not, it seemed we were in one.

I stood in front of Tayte, growling and snapping at anyone who attempted to approach.

Then Dane's small, brown wolf bounded past me and shifted back to human.

"Oh, damn it, Tayte. What have you gone and done now?" Dane complained as he pulled at the bonds, managing to get Tayte off the fence.

I glanced at my Alpha. His arm was hanging at a weird angle. His gut was partially sliced open and as he fell forward and grabbed his belly, I almost vomited.

They'd actually gutted him, or tried to.

Part of his belly was spilling through his fingers.

I whirled around at the sound of vicious growling behind me.

A huge, black bear was down on all fours, charging me.

It was Trevor.

He was dead.

I ran straight at the bear, using the momentum to jump over him before twirling back and biting at his ears. His claws swung at my head.

I rolled and ducked and went for his hind legs.

Then there was another black wolf, flashing into my vision, coming to help me, and two huge silver wolves beside him.

It was us against them.

Two Alpha and two Beta wolves, taking down an Alpha bear.

I tore at his neck, sinking my teeth in and drawing blood.

This wasn't a fight where we'd just walk away after our point was made.

No. One side had to lose. Permanently.

And it couldn't be us.

Dexter's wolf tore at Trevor's eyes and face.

The other bears began to back away, not stepping up to support their Alpha but instead, running for their lives.

Some of our other wolves went after the bears that ran but I stayed and shifted back, my heart pounding in my chest as my human eyes took in the state of my Alpha.

He was on his knees with Dane beside him.

Oh, God.

They'd burnt his face and gashed his ear, too.

"We need to get you to the hospital. Let's go."

Dane and I put our arms around Tayte and he groaned in agony.

"My shoulder's... broken."

I tried to avoid touching his injuries, but it was almost impossible with the amount of wounds and blood on him.

"Your belly's more of a worry at the moment, Tayte. Let's go," I said.

I dragged my Alpha to our car and we rushed him to emergency.

At this rate we were going to need to build a hospital in our own town.

CHAPTER

FIFTEEN

Dane

My Alpha was in surgery, my mate was recovering from falling down a cliff and my daughter was in a humidicrib because she'd been born prematurely and by emergency C-section.

I put my head in my hands and closed my eyes.

"Things can't possibly get any worse," I muttered to Sam, as we sat in the horribly uncomfortable white chairs that lined the hospital waiting room. My stomach was in knots.

"I hope everyone else from the pack is okay."

Sam patted me on the shoulder. "Our pack is alive. Let's hold onto that. We'll find out about everyone else soon, I'm sure."

I stood up and stretched my back. "I'm going to see Celeste and the baby."

Sam nodded and ran his hand through his hair. "I'm gonna stay here and wait for the surgeons to come out and tell me about Tayte."

"Okay. Thanks, Sam."

I walked away from my Beta, my whole body feeling like it had been put on a torture rack and stretched.

What a day.

I pushed open the door to stop dead at the sight before me.

"She's out!" I said.

Celeste was breastfeeding our daughter, her beautiful flesh pressed against our daughter's bare skin.

Celeste looked up and beamed at me. "They said she's doing way better than they expected, and I finally got to hold her. To nurse her! Look how strong she is."

I walked up next to the bed and watched as the baby suckled strongly.

I kissed my mate's forehead, the warmth in the room making Celeste feel hot to the touch, even in the light gown she barely wore.

"You're amazing, she's amazing. Hey, have you thought of a name yet?"

She looked up at me, her blue eyes big and wide.

"I have, but I wanted to ask Tayte before I told anyone else. Where is he? Is he okay?"

Not really.

I grabbed a chair that leaned against the wall and pulled it over to sit closer to my mate.

I couldn't resist reaching out and stroking the baby's soft head. "She has blonde hair."

Celeste grabbed my wrist. "Dane, how's Tayte?"

I ran my hand through my hair. "He's um...."

"He's not dead. Tell me he's not dead." Her voice sounded panicked and I rushed to reassure her.

"He's not dead."

That was all I could tell her, though.

"Then where is he?"

"He's in surgery."

She swallowed, hard, her already pale skin going even more pale. "Why? I mean, what's the surgery for?"

I didn't really want to recall all the injuries my Alpha had sustained.

"Ah... dislocated shoulder, knife wound to the belly, burned face, cut off ear..."

Tears sprouted and slid down Celeste's face.

"Burned face... knife... oh my God."

I grabbed her hand and squeezed it.

"I suppose we have to be grateful the bears were taking their time killing him, or we may have arrived too late."

"I don't know what to say. Is he going to be okay?"

"I don't know."

She began to cry as she rocked the baby.

"Dane, I didn't want this to happen. Not like this. I mean, I was so angry at him, but now..."

I stroked her head and kissed her hair. "I know. It puts it all in perspective, doesn't it?"

She nodded. "Yes, it does."

The baby came off Celeste's nipple, her eyes closed and her mouth still open.

Milk dribbled down the side of her face.

"Do you want to hold her?"

I glanced down at her.

"I'd love to, but I'm not very clean."

I gestured down to my clothes that were some of the spares we kept in the car in case of emergencies.

"The doctors asked why Tayte was naked when we brought him in, but we didn't have much of an explanation."

Celeste put the baby over her shoulder and gently rubbed her back.

"So, what's going to happen? Do you know?"

I shook my head. "I have no idea. Wolf shifters have abnormal healing powers, which probably is one of the reasons the baby is doing better than they all expected. We're strong and fit and healthy, but Tayte's injuries were... extensive."

I swallowed hard against the lump in my throat.

"We can only wait, I suppose. Sam's sitting in the waiting room now."

Celeste nodded, then sobbed softly.

"I can't believe this all happened. Actually, I can. I always knew my baggage would haunt us, follow me. But I never thought... I hoped it would all be okay."

I could see the tide had turned and Celeste was going to start to blame herself now.

"Sweetheart, this isn't your fault. It's no one's fault, really. It's some, fucked-up twist of Fate. A lesson we needed to learn, a fire we had to walk through. I don't know. But the only thing I need to know is if you'll still love us when this is all settled?"

I stared at her, hoping, praying that these past few days hadn't changed her mind about us.

She gasped for air as though she'd been holding her breath.

"Of course, I still love you! Loving you all has never been a problem, but after I heard Tayte say what he said, I felt so betrayed! So hurt. I couldn't believe that after everything we'd been through..."

She stopped, gasping for air again and that's when I grabbed her hands and made her look at me.

"That's exactly where you should have stopped, turned around, and demanded an answer from Tayte. And if not from him, then me or Sam. You can't just run away at the first hurdle,

Celeste. That's not what this relationship is about. There's three of us to check on, and you can't run because one of us pisses you off. That's not fair to anyone."

Celeste nodded and gulped.

I grabbed a glass of water and handed it to her.

"Yes. I know," she said, once she'd taken a few sips from the glass.

"Good. Because we adore you. Every single, tiny part of you."

She nodded and swallowed some more water.

I sighed, utterly exhausted.

I hadn't slept properly in two days, and I couldn't even reach out to my daughter because there was blood on my hands.

Quite literally.

"Excuse me while I go wash up a bit in your bathroom."

I opened the door and ran water into the sink, wiping at my face, my hands, my arms.

"What happened with the bears? You didn't tell me."

I ducked my face under the water and washed away the grime of the morning.

Then I patted myself dry with one of those small, white hospital towels, then threw it on the floor, in the corner.

Sorry to the staff member who had to launder that one.

"Um…" I walked back into the room to watch Celeste swaddling up the baby, then holding her while she slept. "I don't know, completely. We were winning when I left. But I needed to get Tayte to the hospital, so we'll have to wait to find out from one of the other Alphas. Hopefully there weren't many casualties on our side."

She nodded, then put the baby into the crib beside her bed.

"Okay, but will they still be after us? Is Trevor…"

"Oh, no." I kept forgetting she wasn't there. "We killed Trevor. He's gone. And a lot of the male bear shifters, too."

Celeste's eyes widened again and her skin turned even more pale.

"Well, that's... great. I suppose."

"Are you okay?"

I understood that she'd be feeling a combination of happiness and sorrow. After all, they had been her family for a very long time.

"Yes, I just... never thought I'd be happy that someone was dead."

I almost laughed. But thought I might get slapped if I did.

Instead, I sat next to my mate and held her hand.

"I get that."

"So, what do we do now?"

"We wait."

Tayte

Damn, my head hurt.

I forced my eyes to open, though they didn't want to. There was Sam, by my side. In a stark white room I had to assume was the hospital.

"Hey." I swallowed, trying to make my mouth work properly. I was as dry as the desert.

"Hey, yourself," Sam said, standing up. "How are you feeling?"

"Like I got pulled through a hedge—backwards."

Everything hurt. My head, my chest, my belly, my legs.

"Yeah, well you did a pretty good job of almost dying, but we weren't gonna let you."

"How? Oh…"

The memories of this morning came back to me in a flash of pain and knives and cruel laughter. "The bears."

"Yes, the bears. What were you thinking, giving yourself over to them?"

He sounded angry at me, which was strange. After everything that had happened with Celeste, I'd thought Sam would be relieved to get rid of me.

"I was fixing all our problems in one go. The bears would leave the pack alone, and you three could be happy without me."

That got me a soft punch in the arm.

"Ow."

My head spun from the pain and he shoved a handle into my palm.

"Push this button. It's morphine."

I glanced down at the green button and pressed it. Anything to help with the throb in my brain.

"Thanks."

I lay my head back and tried to swallow again. It was like the desert in my mouth.

"Is there any water?"

Sam handed me a cup and I swallowed some down, the brief wetness enough to get my tongue to unstick from the roof of my mouth.

I closed my eyes, the pain dragging on me.

"How's Celeste? Is she okay?"

There was silence in response to my question and then the whoosh of a curtain.

"How 'bout you ask her yourself?"

I lifted my head and opened my eyes.

There was my beautiful mate, standing in the doorway. Her hair fell around her like a halo, and she held our baby in her arms.

Tears filled her eyes as she stared at me.

I tried to smile, unsure of the response I'd get from her. I was pretty sure last time we'd spoken, she'd broken up with me. "Hey, beautiful."

Celeste sobbed as she threw herself down on to the bed with

me. I suppressed my groan of pain as she placed her head on my chest, the baby cradled between us.

"Tayte... oh my God. You're okay."

She lifted her face to me, her eyes shiny with the unshed tears.

She'd forgiven me?

I tentatively reached down with my good hand and cupped her face.

"Of course, I'm okay. How are you?"

She sobbed again and pushed herself up so that she could kiss my lips, the saltiness of her tears on my tongue.

When she pulled back, my heart ached. I'd missed her love so much.

She sniffed and wiped at her face. "I was so worried about you. I am so sorry about what happened the other night. I should never have even been there, let alone believed the lies you told the bears. I should have known better, and I am so, so, sorry for everything."

Tears fell down her face and I looked to Sam for guidance.

He just sat in the chair, watching and waiting.

I rubbed her back with my good arm, then pulled it back in close to me, the pain too great to move far.

"Stop crying, Celeste, it's okay. I totally understand why you wanted me to move out. It's your right to reject any one of us, if you have cause. And you did. But I couldn't stand by while my pack and the whole town was in danger. I saw a way out, for all of us. So I took it."

Celeste hoisted up the baby and placed her on my chest on her stomach.

She was the most perfect little thing. Rosebud lips and pale, soft skin.

I would have missed all of this.

Celeste shook her head. "No. You should have stayed and

fought to remain in our family. This little girl needs her daddy, and I don't want you to ever, no matter what, think of leaving us again. I promise you, it will be the same for me. No more running away."

I looked at my mate, and then back to my daughter, my eyes burning with the strangest feeling.

I swallowed hard. Did this mean that everything was okay? That they still wanted me?

"What have you called her?"

Celeste smiled and stroked the baby's head.

"I haven't named her anything yet. I wanted your approval."

I raised my good arm to touch my baby's soft hair.

"All right. What would you like to call her?"

Celeste met my gaze and I saw a lot of love and uncertainty there. "Destiny. After all, it was Destiny that brought us together."

I smiled as the sound of our daughter's name rolled around the room.

"Sounds perfect to me. Contingent on the rest of the family's approval, of course."

I glanced at my Beta and Omega, both of whom nodded happily.

"We're happy with anything you choose."

"Destiny, then."

I lifted my daughter up higher on my chest and kissed the top of her head.

Celeste leaned close and rested her cheek against my shoulder.

I had to ask—my head was whirling with all the uncertainties left.

"So, we're okay? After I get better, I can come home?"

I never thought I'd have to ask my pack such a thing, and Sam's eyes were shadowed as he stared at me.

"It's only a home with you in it, Tayte. You're the foundation of everything in our family."

I blinked away the tears that gathered in my eyes once again and put it down to all the drugs in my system.

I let my body relax into the pillows and looked at my family.

They weren't going anywhere, and thanks to a stroke of luck, now… neither was I.

EPILOGUE

I looked down at the white stick and smiled as my stomach flipped over.

Two pink lines. Clear and visible.

I was pregnant.

Again.

"Oh."

We'd celebrated Destiny's first birthday only yesterday, and I'd been feeling a little queasy all day.

I'd had my suspicions, of course, but I'd wanted to wait until after the party to do an official test.

Unlike that day, all those months ago when I found out I was pregnant the first time, this day would be cause for celebration, not despair.

What a difference a year and a half made.

I slid the cap back on the test stick and placed it into my back pocket. The men were out, but they'd be home for lunch soon.

"How you going, baby girl? You ready to get changed?"

Destiny was sitting in her highchair, having inhaled a banana, a sandwich and some berries.

She ate more than I did.

I glanced at the clock and counted. I had about ten minutes before my triad arrived home.

"Let's go, beautiful girl."

I picked up my daughter and carried her to the nursery, cleaning the crumbs and berry smudges off her angelic face.

I squealed a little as I opened the new t-shirt and changed her into the outfit that I'd ordered online. It had arrived last week and was a perfect fit for my daughter.

I stood her up and she teetered a little.

Her t-shirt read, "*I'm going to be a big sister.*"

"Perfect."

Destiny toddled over to the corner of her room and began to play.

What a year it had been!

Tayte had spent months recovering from his injuries and surgeries. The wolf genes helped his healing tremendously, but it still took a long time before everything was well again.

Both with him, and with us.

But every day we'd worked on rebuilding the trust again.

Every day I loved them all that little bit more.

So much so, that now, if I heard them tell anyone I wasn't their fated mate, or they'd get rid of me to save the pack, I'd laugh in their face.

My men lived and breathed our family.

They loved me and my daughter, and since the moment I put Destiny on Tayte's chest, I hadn't looked back.

Not at that night I thought they wanted to get rid of me. Not to my horrible childhood or the months before I met Tayte.

My life was blessed.

I was Cinderella in my fairy tale, and I had three Prince Charmings to love, and who loved me back. Every single day.

"Celeste!"

My heart leapt as they entered the house—loudly—as they always did.

"Daddy!" Destiny called out as she stumbled, trying to run past me. She got a few more steps into the living room before she fell to the floor and cried as she always did.

Tayte laughed as he scooped her up and showered her with kisses.

"How's my perfect girl? Have you been good for Mommy?"

Sam came for me first, which was nice, and gave me a swift kiss. "Are you okay? You looked a little pale this morning."

I nodded. "I'm great. How was work?"

"Busy."

Dane came in and shut the door, grabbing for Destiny and whirling her around.

"Something smells good. What's for lunch?" he asked.

None of them had noticed Destiny's top yet and my stomach was in knots, waiting for them to discover the surprise.

Of course, I assumed they'd be happy about the new pregnancy. After all, they put in daily efforts to make sure I was constantly filled with their desire for me.

But it didn't stop the anxiety that rattled through me.

"Um... lamb curry. I wanted to try a new recipe."

"Great. I'm starving."

The men all piled into the kitchen and I started serving them, putting lots of rice in every bowl as I knew how many calories they burned through in a day.

"Hey, Celeste?" There was a strange note in Dane's voice.

"Yeah?" I asked as I put each bowl down in front of my men.

Dane was looking at me with a huge smile on his face. "What does this mean?"

He pointed to Destiny's top, where she stood on his thigh and clung to his neck.

He turned her around and showed the other two men, who went silent.

My heart leapt in my chest and I swallowed quickly, my hand trembling as I pulled out the stick from my back pocket.

"Well... I'm pregnant."

The three men looked at one another for a single second, then jumped to their feet, whooping loudly.

"That's brilliant!"

Sam grabbed me and kissed me, then Tayte picked me up and twirled me around.

"How are you feeling?"

I put my hand out to steady myself. "A little woozy, but happy. Are you three happy, too?"

Dane kissed me soundly, still holding Destiny, then wrapped his arm around my shoulders.

"We couldn't be happier. More babies for our family, and a baby brother or sister for our perfect girl."

He nuzzled his nose against Destiny's face, who cackled and wriggled to get down.

Dane put her on the ground and she toddled off to her room.

My triad surrounded me, holding me in that long, intense way they had, that always made me feel loved.

"I love you. All of you," I said. "Thank you for my new life."

Tayte swung me into his arms and carried me up the stairs.

"Lunch can wait. I think we need to celebrate now."

Dane stayed with Destiny and Sam followed us into our main

bedroom. They'd swap after a while, and if I passed out from exhaustion, one of them would call into work and tell them they were taking the afternoon off.

My life truly was perfect.

I had my men, my child and a village of people who loved and supported us.

It seriously couldn't get any better than this.

THE END